THE LONG EDGE OF NIGHT

Broken Galaxy Book Three

Phil Huddleston

CONTENTS

ISBN eBook: 978-1-7351396-6-1
ISBN Paperback: 978-1-7351396-7-8
ISBN Hardcover: 979-8-5091463-2-9

Cover by MM Rainey Creative Art
mmrainey.creative@gmail.com

NOTE TO READERS

Always remember: the madness of love is the greatest of heaven's blessings.

Plato

FROM BOOKS ONE AND TWO

Broken Galaxy - The name used to describe the current state of affairs in the Orion Arm of the Milky Way. The ancient Golden Empire lasted for twenty thousand years; but two thousand years ago it collapsed, throwing the Galaxy into a Dark Age. Much knowledge and technology disappeared, including the advanced drives and weapons of the lost Empire warship *Dragon*.

Earth Defense Force (EDF) - the starship fleet of Admiral Rita Page. Originally a rag-tag lend-lease fleet on loan to Rita by High Councilor Garatella of the Nidarian Empire. Garatella intended the loan of the fleet as a test, to see if humans were intelligent and aggressive enough to defend their planet against the Singheko invaders. After the Battle of Jupiter, which narrowly pushed the invading Singheko fleet out of the Solar System, Rita kept the fleet and renamed it the Earth Defense Force. Supplemented by captured Singheko ships from the battle, it now consists of 19 warships, including two battlecruisers.

Jim Carter - Retired U.S. Marine turned mercenary pilot turned airshow performer turned semi-retired hermit turned space pilot. Fought the starship *Jade* at the Battle of Dutch Harbor. Fought the Singheko invasion at the Battle of Saturn and the Battle of Jupiter. Recently promoted to Commander Attack Group (CAG) on the battlecruiser *Merkkessa*. Forced to decide between two lovers - Bonnie and Rita - he chose Rita, leaving Bonnie bitter but accepting.

Bonnie Page - Ex-Air Force fighter pilot and former lover of both Jim Carter and Rita Page. After the massive Battle of Dutch Harbor involving *Jade*, *Corresse*, Russia, America, and Canada, Bonnie hitched a ride on the *Corresse* to ask the Nidarian Empire for help in saving Earth from the brutal Singheko. Bonnie was blackmailed by Nidarian High Councilor Garatella to find the ancient and highly advanced starship *Dragon* - a relic of the former Golden Empire. In time, she located the long-lost warship - but disobeyed Garatella and kept it for Earth. Assigned as Captain of the *Dragon* by Admiral Rita Page, her former lover.

Rita Page, Admiral of the Black - Clone created by the renegade starship *Jade* with the dual memories, knowledge and feelings of both Jim Carter and Bonnie Page. As a result of her dual consciousness, she was in love with both Jim and Bonnie. Took Bonnie's last name since she didn't have one of her own. Fought *Jade* at the Battle of Dutch Harbor. Went to Nidaria with Bonnie. Came back with a rag-tag Nidarian lend-lease fleet to fight the Singheko invasion. Against all odds, drove the Singheko away from Earth, but not before the Singheko imprisoned more than 96,000 human slaves and carried them away in large, pentagon shaped slave ships.

Tatiana - A young half-English, half-Ukrainian woman arrested by the Russian police for drug smuggling. She was handed over to the Singheko as they were filling their slave ships with human prisoners. Currently imprisoned in a large wire cage on a slave ship enroute to Singheko, along with 12,000 other human prisoners.

Dragon - an advanced destroyer of the ancient Golden Empire, lost for two thousand years in a canyon on Mars. Re-discovered and repaired by Bonnie Page and the EDF.

Technology obtained from *Dragon* is being retrofitted to the remainder of the EDF Fleet in preparation for a counterattack on the Singheko. Plans for the *Dragon*'s advanced stardrive were also sent to High Councilor Garatella of the Nidarian Empire in partial fulfillment of the bargain to help Earth; but plans for the advanced weapon of the *Dragon* - the gamma lance - were held back by Rita Page as a bargaining chip for further Nidarian assistance.

Jade - a sentient scout ship which crashed into the Canadian Northwest Territory in 1947 and lay undiscovered for more than a century. Found by Jim Carter and brought back to life. Falsely claimed to be Nidarian but was actually Singheko. Intent on escaping Earth and returning to Singheko to effect the enslavement of humanity, Jade created the clone Rita to assist in her repairs and take back as a specimen of humanity. Destroyed by Jim, Bonnie, and Rita at the Battle of Dutch Harbor.

Arteveld - Captain of the Nidarian corvette *Corresse.* After the Battle of Jupiter, Rita sent the *Corresse* back to Nidaria to inform Garatella and the Nidarian government that Earth would not release *Dragon*'s high-tech weapon to them until a mutual defense treaty was in place between Nidaria and Earth. Has not yet returned and is overdue.

Florissian (Flo) - Ship's doctor of the *Corresse*, wife of Captain Arteveld. Assisted Bonnie Page in the destruction of *Jade* and became friends with both Bonnie and Rita.

Captain Bekerose - Flag Captain of the battlecruiser *Merkkessa*, the flagship of the Earth Defense Force. A Nidarian.

Captain Tarraine - Flag Aide to Admiral Rita Page; her most trusted adviser next to her husband, Jim Carter. A Nidarian.

Mark Rodgers - Former U.S. Army General specializing in Intelligence and Weapons Research. Captured Jim Carter and tortured him to reveal *Jade*'s whereabouts but was unsuccessful. Later, upon the advice of Jim's sister Gillian, let Jim escape. Saved Jim's life at the Battle of Dutch Harbor. Fell in love with Gillian and married her.

Gillian Hassell - Former Assistant Director in the CIA Weapons Directorate. Sister of Jim Carter. Shanghaied by Mark Rodgers to help with her brother, fell in love with Mark and married him.

The Bear - A big male grizzly that attacked Jim Carter in the Canadian Northwest Territories, leading him to discover *Jade* in his attempt to escape. Now a large bearskin in the Flag Cabin of the battlecruiser *Merkkessa*.

PROLOGUE (FROM BOOK TWO)

On the Singheko Slave Ship

Inside the cage, Tatiana had learned how to squat in the corner, one wall of wire on each side. Now she could manage a somewhat comfortable position to watch the rest of the women surrounding her; a boring drama of fear, anger, discomfort, and stench.

Their Singheko captors fed them once a day - some kind of glop that flowed into a trough on the back wall of the cage. It oozed along like porridge - with strange, undefined lumps in it.

The first time it happened, there was a mad rush to the back of the cage, everyone fighting for the food.

Tatiana stayed out of the melee, too shocked by events to move from her corner.

But by the second evening, she was too hungry to let it pass. She stood, watching, as a half-dozen women fought and shoved to get to the food while the rest of the cage stood by.

How stupid! The food is the same for everybody! And there's enough for all!

Then she realized it wasn't about the food.

It was about primacy of place. They were establishing the pecking order.

Even in a cage of slaves, someone had to be on top.

A big woman, one Tatiana hadn't noticed before, seemed to win the second battle, pushing and shoving others aside, leaving one with a bloody nose.

When the more aggressive ones were done, Tatiana and the rest of the women got their food. They had to scoop it from the trough with their hands, eat it with their fingers.

Afterward, Tatiana washed off at one of the two water faucets mounted on the wall.

The next morning a half-dozen of the big Singheko guards came into the hallway between the cages with what looked like a fire hose.

Sure enough, they opened the valve and hosed down the cages, washing away the bodily wastes into a recessed drain at the back of the cage, spraying the women indiscriminately, the force of the water knocking many of them to the floor where they slid to the back.

Tatiana, in her secure spot at the rear corner, was able to huddle down and get clean without getting knocked over.

Thus their day and night cycles were defined.

Evening was the glop oozing out of the wall into the trough, the hierarchy of the strong taking their turn, followed by the rest of the women, with the weak or sick at the last.

Morning was defined by the hosing down of the cage, washing away the stinking mess of the previous day, knocking down any who were unprepared.

It was on the third day out from Earth that the big woman came to Tatiana in her corner. It was after the evening feeding; the group was settling in for the night, their schedule now adjusted to a cycle dictated by their masters.

The big woman stared down at her. Tatiana looked up, uncertain of her intent.

"I'll take your corner, bitch," said the woman in Ukrainian.

Tatiana shrugged, got up, and walked away. She had seen the big woman fight. A corner wasn't worth the beating.

But she hadn't taken two steps before the woman had her in a choke hold, dragging her backward into the corner.

"And I'll take you too, bitch," growled the woman. She twisted, throwing Tatiana back down into the corner.

Tatiana bounced off the wire mesh of the cage wall, and back onto the woman's feet.

It was pure luck; but when she bounced back, she somehow took the big woman down to her knees.

It wasn't good luck. It was bad luck.

Now the woman thought Tatiana had done it intentionally. She piled into Tatiana, all fists, elbows, knees, gouging and scratching, cursing a blue streak in Ukrainian, slamming her up against the wire mesh of the cage over and over.

Tatiana folded up, rolling into a ball on the floor, trying to protect herself. After a few minutes, the big woman finally stopped hitting her and stood up, breathing hard.

"Get your ass in that corner and lie down, bitch."

Tatiana crawled into the corner. The big woman lay down on her and started having her way with her, roughly, punishing her, hurting her.

It wasn't sex; it was a lesson. A humiliation.

Tatiana let her mind go far away, trying to remember the happy times before her life went to shit.

Before she had thought it a lark to smuggle some drugs into their hotel in Krasnodar.

Before her boyfriend had abandoned her at the first sound of boots on the stairwell, flying out the window and gone, leaving her holding the bag as the police burst into the room.

Back when she had been the privileged daughter of a high-ranking Naval officer, a commander in the British Royal Navy. A man who had fallen in love with her Ukrainian mother, married, had a daughter, given them a kind and loving home - even if he was away for months at a time on sea duty.

Until her mother died when she was seventeen.

Until she and her father were left bereft.

Until one fell into a pattern, dropping out of college, trekking around Europe with various boyfriends, a pattern of drugs and drink and parties and sex.

And the other one, using sea duty as a soporific from the pain, sending a monthly check while turning a blind eye to the long downhill slide of his daughter.

The big Ukrainian grew tired of abusing her. The woman shoved her away, settling down into the corner, showing everyone she was now queen of the cage.

Tatiana crawled away, as far as she could get, all the way to the other corner of the cage.

Finding a spot next to an older woman, Tatiana sat, not crying, not angry, not anything. All her emotions had gone away, somewhere else.

She sat for a long time, unable to move, unable to think. Frozen, a statue of loss and pain.

The woman next to her slid closer, put an arm around her, leaned her head on her shoulder.

"It'll be alright, dear," she said.

Then the tears came. They came suddenly, without warning. All that she had lost, all the mistakes, everything flooded out of her. She cried, as quietly as she could, until she had no more tears to cry.

Then she slumped into the other woman, a stranger, whose name she did not know, and they held each other for a while.

Finally, they slept.

Portsmouth, England

The pub was nearly empty. Just the bartender, a couple arguing in a back booth, a bored waitress; the usual Saturday night drunk slumped over the jukebox looking for songs that weren't there...

And Luke, sitting alone at the bar, nursing his third pint.

So, he knew something was up as soon as the woman slid into the seat beside him.

There were a half-dozen empty chairs on either side. She could have chosen any of them.

But she didn't. She sat right beside him.

Bloody hell, a damn hooker, he thought.

He stared into the long mirror running behind the bar,

expecting to see a worn-out bimbo in a slinky dress, with too much makeup and a desperate look on her face.

What he saw took his breath away.

One of the most beautiful women Luke had seen in his life sat beside him, meeting his eyes in the mirror. Perfect, symmetrical face. An elegant nose, not too small, not too big. Subdued makeup, exactly right. Perfectly coiffed blond hair cut in a bob, falling evenly above her collar, tastefully highlighted.

And green eyes that seemed to go on forever, drawing him in like a man sinking into an infinitely deep ocean - and one any man would willingly sink into - if that's what it took to be with this woman.

Then the uniform registered on his brain...a strange uniform, deep navy blue, sleeve rings like a Royal Navy captain, epaulets on the shoulders - but a cut and fit not from the Royal Navy.

"And just what the hell do you want, Captain?" he growled. "Another inch of skin off my backside?"

Bonnie Page smiled wryly at the mirror, still meeting his eyes.

"Much more than that, Commander. I'd like to give you a job."

Luke shook his head, threw back his pint, and drained it. He stood up, threw a couple of tenners on the bar, and turned to go.

"Not a Commander anymore, as I'm sure you know quite well, Captain. And I don't need any job that comes with a uniform."

He took a step toward the door, stuffing his wallet back in his pocket.

"Even if it meant you could kill Singheko?" came a voice from behind him.

Luke stopped.

Kill Singheko.

He turned back to the woman.

The memory of his daughter Tatiana came to him, a picture

in his mind unbidden, her face as bright and beautiful as the last time he saw her.

Before the Russians threw her into prison.

Before the Russians sent her to the Singheko slave ship.

"Kill Singheko?" he muttered again, staring at the woman. "How many can I kill?"

Bonnie smiled at the man.

"As many as you want, Commander. As far as I'm concerned, you can kill them all. But first, you'd have a job to do, and you'd have to do it my way."

Former Royal Navy Commander Luke Powell stepped back to his chair, stared at the woman for a second, and sat down.

"And what is your way, Captain?"

Bonnie gestured to the bartender, pointed to the empty pint in front of Luke, and held up two fingers. The bartender nodded and started drawing two more pints.

Bonnie turned back to Luke.

"No more wild and crazy schemes. No more jumping off into the wild blue without full support and planning. My way."

Suddenly, Luke recognized her.

"You're Bonnie Page," he said. "Captain of the Dragon."

Bonnie nodded. The bartender placed two pints in front of them.

"I am," she said.

"So, what do you want from me?"

Bonnie took a long draught of her pint, laid the glass down, and wiped foam off her perfect lips. She turned back to Luke.

"Before you decided to go off and take on the entire Russian army by yourself to get your daughter back, you had a reputation as one of the best and brightest ship commanders in the Royal Navy. That's exactly what I need right now. A ship commander with the smarts to be my XO on the Dragon."

Luke was stunned.

"But...the Dragon's a starship! I'm a wet navy puke! How the hell could I do that job?"

Bonnie grinned.

"I don't need an expert on starships, Commander. I have plenty of those already, and the rest of it we can train. What I need is an expert on running a crew. Logistics. Training. Selection of personnel. Maintaining discipline and order. The remainder you can learn on the job like the rest of us are doing."

Luke shook his head.

"Why me? Why a cashiered officer stupid enough to think he could rescue his daughter from the Russians?"

Bonnie looked at him carefully.

"Because you did try to rescue your daughter. Because you were willing to put your life and your career on the line to try. Because you had the leadership skills to put together a team that almost pulled it off. And because maybe I think you got a bum deal from the Royal Navy."

"But I failed," Luke said. "I failed her."

His voice reflected an agony of pain he had not let out for months. It was all he could do to hold back tears.

Bonnie, overwhelmed by the moment, reached out a hand to him and placed it on his shoulder.

"Commander. You did not fail. Humanity failed. We failed to protect our people. But now we have a second chance. A chance to take the fight to the enemy. And maybe, along the way, find our lost people and help them, or even rescue them. I can't say that with certainty. But it's a possibility."

Luke turned away, overcome with emotion. He took the pint, lifted it halfway, looked at it, then gently placed the glass back on the bar.

Quietly, he spoke.

"You should know I've been drinking quite a bit lately," he said.

Bonnie also spoke softly.

"Can you manage it?"

Luke nodded. "Yeah. I can manage it."

"OK. What else?"

Luke knew what she meant.

What else prevents you from leaving Earth and going off to kill Singheko?

"Not a bloody thing," he muttered. "Not a bloody damn thing."

1 - IN THE CAGE

In the wee hours of the morning, Tatiana awoke.

Her mind was clear. She had made a decision while she slept.

Maybe her subconscious mind had made it earlier, and it was only just now bubbling up.

Or maybe in her dream state, it had come to her.

But she had decided.

The big woman will come back for me again. She has to have a victim, someone to abuse, to show the others who's boss.

I will not be a victim.

She remembered something her father had told her once in a letter.

Be happy in your life. Live for the joy in the day. But also be prepared for the worst, the unexpected, the danger. By being prepared, you can be without fear, without worry. Prepare for the unexpected - but never let the preparation lead you from joy.

Now Tatiana let those words resonate in her mind.

I will not be a victim here.

She looked carefully at every inch of the cage. Was there anything she could use to her advantage? Anything she could use to defend herself?

Turning, she examined the wire mesh of the cage behind her. She pulled it, pushed it, looking for any weakness.

As she did so, she noticed one of the cage wires had a tiny crack in it, right where it crossed over another.

Pushing on the wire, she saw it move a little. Working it, she thought she saw the crack widen. She continued to work the wire, until an hour later, she managed to break off a small piece of it.

It was not long - maybe four inches in length. By the time she curled it up in her hand to use as a weapon, she had only one inch sticking out.

It will have to be enough. I know she'll attack me again.

Sure enough, after the guards came through and hosed them down next morning, the big woman stood up, shaking off the water.

"Hey! Brytanskyy!" she shouted. "Let's party some more. Come over here and lick me clean!"

Tatiana stood up but didn't move. She just waited.

She knew it wouldn't take long.

And it didn't. When she didn't move to the woman, the big Ukrainian started toward her.

"Hey, bitch! When I call you, get your ass over here!" she shouted.

Around her, women scattered as they realized another fight was starting.

Tatiana waited. The wire was curled up in her right hand. Now she turned slightly, hiding her right side, and slowly moved the wire out until an inch of it was exposed, sticking out of her fist.

The big woman was nearly to her, and reached out, intending to grab her by the neck and choke her out again.

Tatiana ducked under the arm and swung her fist, stabbing the wire directly at the woman's right eye. The point of the wire missed the eye directly and hit above it in the forehead. Tatiana pulled it down as hard as she could. The wire cut a raw chasm down her attacker's face from her forehead to her cheek. Blood spattered and the woman fell away, screaming.

"I'm blind!" she screamed. "I'm blind!"

Tatiana stared at her, ready for another assault if necessary.

"Only in one eye, you stupid bitch. Come at me again and I'll take the other one."

Then Tatiana moved her gaze slowly around the room, at the hundred-odd women crammed into the wire cage, all staring at her.

Something happened in her at that moment. Something strange.

Something welled up in her she had never felt before.

We cannot be victims.

She knew instinctively her chance would come only once, and she intended to take it.

"All of you - listen to me. We are being stupid. Fighting among ourselves! Forming up into gangs! This plays right into their hands!"

She pointed at the hallway outside the cage.

"From now on, we don't fight each other! We fight those bastards out there! In here, we help each other. We protect each other. And when we get to wherever - whatever - we fight those assholes with everything we've got!"

Tatiana walked around the cage. People made space for her as she moved. They leaned in, listening.

"Anyone can roll over and die. Anyone can start victimizing the weak, ignoring the threat outside. But we're not going to do that. We're going to form a resistance movement right here - right inside this cage! We're going to organize, plan. When they let us off this ship - regardless of what they do, regardless of where we are - we're going to find a way to take the fight to them. Got it?"

There was a jumbled murmur of agreement from some of the women around her.

"Got it?" she shouted again.

A small cheer went up.

"Got it?" she yelled again.

"Yes!" came a loud, resounding answer.

***

The big Ukrainian woman had been huddled on the floor for twenty minutes, blood dripping down her face. Periodically she would roll from side to side and moan, or whimper "I'm blind, I'm blind!"

Tatiana walked to her and crouched down.

"I don't think you're blind. I think your eye's just full of blood."

The woman raised her head slightly, looked at Tatiana with her good eye, holding her hand over the other. Blood oozed out between her fingers and dripped off her face.

"Go fuck yourself."

"If I could, I would," grinned Tatiana. "But I don't have the right equipment. What's your name?"

There was no response. The woman lay silent, ignoring her.

"Listen. I have an idea to organize us to fight the Singheko."

"Go to hell."

"No. Let's send the Singheko to hell instead."

There was a silence as the big woman slowly stopped moaning and began to think again.

"Bullshit. What can we do?"

"What can we do if we don't try? And isn't it better than sitting here waiting to die? What's your name?"

After a long silence, the big woman responded.

"Marta," she grunted.

Closing her eye and slumping back down on the floor, Marta turned away.

Tatiana thought she'd lost her chance to get through to the big woman. She sighed and stood up to walk away.

Then she heard Marta.

"And what would I do?" asked the Ukrainian, still facing away from her on the floor.

Tatiana crouched beside her again, talking to her back.

"I'm not sure. But I know you're the strongest person in this cage. If the two of us work together, we can put together some kind of organization. I can help with the brains, at least."

"How come you'd be the brains?" growled Marta.

Tatiana smiled.

"Who's lying on the floor bleeding?"

After a silence, Marta grunted.

"Point taken."

Then Marta spoke again.

“It doesn’t matter. You won’t survive another week in this cage.”

“What do you mean?”

“Look across the room.”

Tatiana turned on her heels, gazed around the cage.

In the corner that she had once occupied, and which Marta had taken away from her, another big woman had already taken up residency.

“Her name is Sonja,” Marta grunted. “As soon as she gets it in her head, she’ll kill you.”

“But why?” asked Tatiana.

“Because compared to her, I’m Jesus Christ. She’s not as strong as me. But twice as mean.”

Tatiana turned back to Marta.

“So again. We organize, we fight these alien bastards. If we have to fight Sonja, we do that too. Why not join forces? You help me, I help you.”

Marta grunted, but at least she rose, moved herself to a sitting position. She turned to look at Tatiana, her hand still covering her face, dripping blood.

“I should kill you for what you did.”

“Maybe. But that gains you nothing. Joining forces with me gains you brains and something to do - kill Singheko.”

Marta thought about that for a bit. Slowly, a wry little smile started on her face.

“I would surely like to kill some of those bastards.”

“Then get on your feet, go over to the water, and clean yourself up.”

“And then?” asked Marta.

“I heard someone say you were an officer in the army. What were you?”

“Captain,” grunted Marta.

“Then you know military organization. That’s perfect. Find out anyone else who was in the military, or who knows things that would help. Organize them into a Headquarters unit. Divide the rest into squads and platoons. Get us organized.”

Marta nodded slowly.

"You're fucking crazy, you know that, right?"

Tatiana grinned.

"Of course. No sane person would think this is possible."

Slowly, Marta started to get to her feet.

Tatiana stood, reached out a hand, and helped her up.

Marta glared at her for a long moment, and Tatiana wasn't sure if she was going to go clean herself or start another fight.

"I really should kill you, you know," Marta added. "There's a half-dozen women in this cage I'll have to fight to keep you alive."

Then a grin broke out on Marta's face.

"But you just might have the balls to pull it off, you crazy bitch," said Marta.

"Tatiana. Tatiana Powell."

"Ah, right. You're a Brytanskyy - an Englander."

"Yeah. My father was English."

"OK," said Marta, still holding one hand over her damaged face. "I'll help you for now. Until you screw up and I get to kill you."

"Until I screw up," grinned Tatiana.

Marta shook her head.

"I don't think that'll take long," she said, as she turned and headed for the water faucet at the back of the cage.

2 - DRAGON

Admiral Zukra Akribi slammed the ball hard.

It went up and across the playing court, bouncing off the wall three meters above his head.

The ball's momentum carried it; and with a slight thump, it went through the narrow circular goal, just barely passing through the hole.

Victory!

Growling in his excitement, Zukra raised his arms as the crowd went wild. He took a victory lap around the court, shaking his fists. Thousands of spectators shot to their feet, joining in with their own growls and chants.

Finally, after two laps around the court, he stopped near his opponent, who sank to the ground near one end of the playing court.

His opponent was not Singheko; he was a member of a species known as the Taegu. His fate was sealed, and he knew it. He had no place to go.

Five attendants came out. Four of them gathered around the defeated opponent, placed a large wooden block on the ground, and tied the creature's arms behind his back, followed by his feet.

The fifth attendant handed Zukra a broadsword. With a flourish, he swung the sword, testing the heft of it, and then held it up to the crowd. A fresh roar of approval came out of the stands, mixed with whistles and growls of approval.

Zukra walked all the way around the court, holding the sword up in front of him, basking in the adulation. Eventually he came back to his starting point, and stared down at the

Taegu, now bound and tied and bent over the block.

Zukra pointed to him, playing to the crowd.

"There! The natural position of the Taegu!"

The crowd went wild. Zukra waved the sword, making it glint in the bright sun of the Singheko home world, Ridendo.

He thought about taking another lap around the playing court, but finally decided against it.

He had a meeting to get to.

With a last flourish, he turned to the defeated slave at his feet, positioned himself, and raised the sword over his head. Waiting for the roar of the crowd to swell to a peak, he brought the sword down smartly, lopping off the head of the Taegu with a crunch that could be heard fifty meters away. The head rolled out across the playing field, leaving a trail of red in the sandy ground. Blood sprayed from the body, pooling in front of Zukra.

Zukra raised the broadsword again as the crowd went wild. Now he did walk around the court again, close to the stands, allowing the crowd a good look at the bloody blade.

Finally he reached the end of the court, and with a final wave of the sword to the crowd, he handed it to an attendant and took a towel to wipe his face. His aide, Captain Orma, waited patiently until Zukra had finished, then spoke gently.

"Admiral, we have only an hour to get to the Admiralty for your meeting."

"I'm well aware of that, Orma," spat Zukra.

Orma smiled, holding his tongue. He had worked for Zukra long enough to know it was a no-win situation. If he failed to remind him, Zukra would berate him. And if he reminded him, Zukra would still berate him. So he had learned to choose the lesser of two evils.

"Meet me outside the showers, Orma," the Admiral growled and stalked away into the locker room.

Orma had expected it. He went to the exit from the locker room and stood easy, a position of loose parade rest that befitted an Admiral's Aide - even if Zukra was the lowest rank of Admiral in the Singheko Navy, a Libaax. A Libaax did not sit at a desk in the Admiralty. No, indeed. A Libaax sat on the Flag bridge of a warship, leading a fleet - a fighting Admiral, one who would take their place on the front lines during a conflict.

And Zukra was the Libaax of the Singheko Home Fleet - the fleet guarding the home planet, Ridendo.

Not that it had ever been needed. In the entire modern history of the Singheko, no enemy had ever appeared to challenge them. They were the undisputed masters of their area of space.

Except for the damn Nidarians, thought Orma. *They are the only ones who have ever fought us to a draw.*

But they never entered this system. No enemy has entered this system since the fall of the Golden Empire two thousand years ago. And they never will.

Twenty minutes later Zukra come out of the locker room in his dress uniform and strode powerfully toward the stadium exit. Orma fell in beside him, quickly adjusting his pace to the admiral's.

"A good match today, sir. You dispatched the slave with exceptional flair."

"Bah," growled Zukra. "Those Taegu are no challenge at all. He never even got close to a goal!"

"True, sir," responded Orma. "But he played with spirit!"

Zukra scoffed. "Spirit I don't need. I need opponents who give me a challenge!"

"Perhaps these new slaves coming in a couple of months, sir. From that species called 'Humans'. They may give you a run for your money."

"I doubt it," Zukra said, shaking his head. "I've seen pictures of them. They are small, puny, almost as weak as the Taegu. I doubt they'll pose much of a challenge in the ball court."

"Ah, yes, sir. I expect you're right. But at least, giving the audience some new type of heads to lop off will be entertaining."

Zukra muttered an assent, his mind already moving on to

something else.

His meeting with his boss, Rabaax Admiral Ligar.

His request to transfer to an expeditionary fleet. For a chance at real combat.

Reaching his ground car, he climbed in the back as Orma held the door. Soon they were racing through the streets of Mosalia, Ridendo's capital city. In a dozen minutes, they were at the Admiralty.

Leaving his car, Zukra ran up the steps.

He was anxious to get to this meeting. He had a lot riding on it.

As he entered the building, he noted his reflection in the glass door - an impeccably dressed Admiral, seven feet tall. His medallions and ribbons were shined to perfection, his cap in place. His mane was perfectly prepared, fluffed and radiant.

Who could resist me? I am the epitome of Singheko military perfection!

Waving his badge at the guard, he entered the elevator and rode swiftly to the top floor. The office of Admiral Ligar was at the end of the hall. Inside, he paused in front of the receptionist, but she quickly waved him on.

"He's waiting for you, Admiral," she said.

Nodding, Zukra entered and presented himself at attention in front of Ligar.

The old admiral was going gray now, after thirty years in the Navy. But his eyes were still sharp and his brain as well.

"Relax, Zukra. Have a seat," said Ligar.

"Thank you, sir."

Ligar leaned back and smiled at Zukra.

"So we're going to go through this again, I see."

"Well, sir, I feel I've earned it. I've been the Home Fleet commander for three years now. I watch the other fleets go out to fight. I watch them come back with new territories to add to our Empire, with slaves and resources. Yet here I sit, guarding the home system. So, yes, sir, I am once again requesting an expeditionary command."

Ligar grimaced.

"And yet you go out to fight in the arena. It's disgraceful. An admiral in our navy, fighting in the court like a common gladiator."

Zukra shrugged.

"I crave combat, sir. I need to fight. And there is nothing to fight in our system."

"But we must have the best protection possible for the home system, Zukra. At the moment, we have three assault expeditions deployed - the Taegu, the Bagrami and those new ones - I forget what they're called..."

"Humans," interposed Zukra.

"Right, Humans. No challenge there, they don't even have stardrives. But still. We are spread thin here in the home system. If any of our ancient enemies decided to strike at us - the Nidarians, for example - your fleet would be the only thing standing between Singheko and disaster - at least until one of the expeditionary fleets is back."

"Paagh!" snorted Zukra. "The Nidarians? They are the least of our concerns. They are like seaweed floating on the current. I could take their planet with the Home Fleet in two days."

Ligar shook his head.

"I think you underestimate the Nidarians. And possibly some of the others too. For example, the Taegu."

Ligar leaned forward, tapping an electronic tablet on his desk.

"I received a courier package today. We've taken the Taegu home system and shipped back a dozen slave ships. But we still haven't found the bulk of their fleet. They're in hiding somewhere. More than a dozen warships, including two battlecruisers. Enough to ruin your day if they come blasting into this system and catch you off guard."

"That will never happen, sir. My fleet is constantly on guard, and ready for anything."

"Just don't let confidence turn into arrogance, Zukra. Sometimes reality bites. Suppose the Taegu managed to put together an alliance with the Nidarians...you could wake up one morning and find a dozen battlecruisers coming at you. Would you be ready for that?"

Zukra smiled, shaking his head.

"The Nidarians won't do that, sir. They know the retribution that would come back to them if they formed such an alliance. It would be the end of them."

"I hope you're right, Zukra. I surely hope you are right. But..."

Ligar shook his head sadly.

"I can't transfer you. I have too many expeditions out, we're spread too thin at home. I'm sorry, Zukra."

"I understand, sir," smiled Zukra. Sensing the meeting was over, he rose to his feet. "Thank you, sir."

"Good to see you again, Zukra. Carry on," said Ligar in dismissal.

Zukra left the office, deep in thought.

I expected this. So - the die is cast. No more waiting. If Ligar won't give me what I want...then I'll take it myself.

Operation Broadsword is a go...

***

Commander Luke Powell stood on the tarmac at RAF Lakenheath, just outside the wastelands of former London.

The shuttle in front of him was flat black, a blended wing like the long-retired Dream Catcher spaceplane.

Luke Powell stared at it.

What the hell am I doing? Once I get on that thing, I go to space. I've never been in space before.

What if I spend my entire first week puking? What if they have to send me back down as unfit for space duty?

Suck it up, mate. Suck it up.

Ducking his head, he entered the small hatch of the shuttle. Inside, he found an interior that looked like most military transports. Rails on the floor secured two pallets of cargo. In front of the cargo, sling seats lining both sides of the ship were mostly empty, although there were two officers sitting next to each other on the far side.

They stopped chatting and looked up as he entered.

"Good morning," he offered up. Both leaped to their feet and saluted.

Luke raised a hand in a perfunctory salute, then smiled.

"Reporting to the *Dragon*?" he asked.

"Yes, sir," said the female, bobbing her head. "I'm Lieutenant Gibson."

"Lieutenant Worley," said the other one, the male.

Luke positioned his bag and smiled at them again.

"Good," said Luke. "I'm looking forward to working with both of you."

The female spoke again.

"Sir, aren't you Commander Lucas Powell?"

Luke nodded. "Yes, I am, Lieutenant Gibson."

There was a long silence.

He could almost hear their thoughts.

Luke Powell. The madman who put together a snatch team of former SAS operators. The madman who attacked the women's penal colony at Krasnodar, Russia to free his daughter before she could be sent to the Singheko slave ship.

The madman who failed, because she had already been sent and the slave ship launched earlier than expected.

The madman who stole a Russian patrol boat to escape and made it all the way to Istanbul before the Turkish Navy captured him.

And the madman the Turks returned to the British, to be drummed out of the Royal Navy in disgrace for precipitating an international incident.

A shadow darkened the hatch and another officer came on board, an American. At least, Luke assumed he was American - he was wearing the uniform of an American Marine. A major.

The Marine looked around and assessed everyone, then took the empty seat to Luke's right. He nodded at Luke, who reached out a hand.

"Commander Luke Powell. How are you?"

The man returned the handshake.

"Major Oliver Coston. Most folks call me Ollie," he said.

"Well, pleased to meet you, Ollie. I expect you'll be the CO of the Marine contingent?"

"Right, sir. If you can call it a contingent. Thirteen of us total, I'm told. Just one squad."

"Ah. Well, you never know when you'll need a squad of Marines. Glad to have you on board. I take it you haven't had time to get a new uniform?"

"No, sir. Been on a plane all night from the States. I didn't know anything about this until yesterday. My CO called me in and said I'd been seconded to the *Dragon*, and to get my butt to Lakenheath by..."

Major Coston looked at his watch and grinned.

"...by now. I just made it."

Luke smiled back at him.

A Chief came on board and sat by the cockpit, followed by a group of ratings who sat beside him. Luke heard the engines start to spool up. An announcement came over the PA.

"Everybody buckle up and stand by for departure. Oh, and make sure you have a sick sack handy. Do NOT mess up my shuttle."

Oh, great.

***

Thirty minutes later, the shuttle pulled up next to the *Dragon* in orbit and inched its way to a docking port, until with a light "clunk" it was connected to the destroyer.

Luke glanced around the cabin and noted there were only four people who hadn't puked - himself, Major Coston beside him, Lieutenant Gibson across from him, and the Chief Petty Officer by the cockpit.

Lieutenant Worley looked especially pale, his eyes closed and his head tilted back, sweat beaded on his brow.

Luke decided to try a distraction.

"Lieutenant Worley. How much do you know about the stardrive on the *Dragon*? What do they call it? The tDrive?" he asked.

Worley pulled his head down, wiped his hand across his brow, and tried to speak.

"Uh. Not much, sir. Uh. It's fast. Faster than the older Nidarian drives by a factor of ten. Thirty-three light years per standard Earth day."

"Excellent. Then how long will it take us to get to Singheko?"

Worley looked marginally better, his mind now working the math.

"Uh. Let's see. 550 light years...16.5 days, if we run full bore all the way, sir."

"And for an old wet-navy type who doesn't know a damn thing about starships - how do we get artificial gravity? I really don't understand that."

"Well, uh. The same process that the system engine uses to generate a push against the vacuum - well, the same effect can generate a push toward the floor of the compartment. At least, that's what the Nidarians say. We don't have any physicists who understand the effect yet, but from an engineering point of view, it's pretty straightforward. You fire up the reactor, you turn some switches and dials, and you've got gravity."

"And if something breaks?"

Worley smiled at last.

"We replace it, sir. We may not understand the underlying physics, but we know how to replace parts. We'll keep it going for you."

The hatch in the side of the shuttle opened and a young rating stepped in. He surveyed the cabin, shook his head at the many sick-sacks displayed, and stepped to one side.

"Everyone watch your step as you disembark, please," he intoned. "And drop your sick sacks in the bin as you go out."

Luke unbuckled and stood up, took his case, and went to the hatch. He ducked, stepped through...

And found himself on the deck of a starship for the first time in his life.

There was a non-skid floor and a young ensign standing behind a desk, electronic tablet in hand.

On the left bulkhead was a flag, painted on the surface. Luke saluted the flag, turned to the young ensign, and asked, "Permission to come aboard?"

"Permission granted, sir," said the Ensign, saluting.

Luke returned his salute and gave his newly issued ID card to the ensign, who checked his name off the tablet and returned the ID. Luke noted the ensign's nametag - Goodwin.

"Welcome aboard, sir. Do you need a guide to your quarters?"

"No, I know the way, Ensign Goodwin," said Luke.

He had spent more than two hours going over every inch of the ship's layout on the diagram Bonnie had sent him. He knew exactly where he was going.

Now Luke set off into the innards of the ship, soon finding himself at a ladder leading up to the next deck. Going up, he came out on E-deck, one level below the bridge.

To his right was the wardroom - the Officer's Mess. To his left was his cabin.

Entering, he surveyed his new home.

It was small. The entire cabin was the size of his bedroom in Portsmouth. There was a small bed, a locker for his clothes, a desk, a tiny bathroom with shower, and a miniature refrigerator in the corner.

Home, sweet starship. I've seen worse.

He threw his bag on the bed and started to go back outside the cabin. As he neared the hatch, a voice came from an overhead speaker.

<Commander Powell, please set a door code before exiting, six numbers are required>

The AI of the ship, he realized. *The first time I've encountered one of those.*

"Oh, OK," Luke said. He thought for a second. "1-7-2-6-1-7, please."

<Door code set> said the voice. <You may address me as

Dragon when needed>

"Got it," replied Luke. "*Dragon.*"

Strange talking to a ship like a person. We don't have that *in the wet navy.*

Luke exited and heard the door lock behind him. He went up the ladder to the next level, to the bridge entrance.

No time like the present to check it out.

He tried the hatch, but it was locked.

<Commander Powell, you may use your door code for now. You will be required to select a new bridge code at your duty console>

Luke looked to the side and saw a keypad for the hatch. He keyed his door code and the hatch clicked open.

Entering, Luke looked around his new duty station. The bridge was somewhat rectangular with rounded corners, with a large, curved screen stretching from wall to wall in the front.

In the middle was a large holotank, the first he had seen in real life. It floated above the floor, about eight feet in diameter, with a slight orange tint to it.

In the holo he could see the *Dragon* at the center of the display, the shuttle still attached.

Below was the Earth, blue and white and brown and achingly beautiful. Stretching off into the orbital distance were other ships of the EDF - ships once called Nidarian, but now taken over by Admiral Rita Page for the defense of Earth.

Well in front of them, a hundred klicks away, Luke could see the *Merkkessa* - the flagship battlecruiser of the EDF.

Close to her Luke could see her permanent escort - two destroyers - flanking her sides.

In the front vision screen, which simulated an actual window into space, he could barely make out the running lights of the coal-black ships.

But in the holotank, their images were clear, distinct, marked with icons showing their position, speed, and projected vectors.

"What do you think of her so far?"

Luke turned to see Captain Bonnie Page come through the hatch. As he was reporting for the first time on the ship, he braced up, saluted.

"Commander Luke Powell reporting for duty, mum," he said.

His newly issued book of EDF Naval Protocol - so new, it was just a couple of dozen printed pages stapled together - had given him the proper terms of address for his Captain.

Bonnie returned the salute, then shook his hand.

"Well?"

"She's beautiful, Captain. There's something about a ship - wet navy or starship - you know?"

Bonnie smiled at her new XO.

"I know exactly what you mean."

3 - LONDON

"Rita, it can't be done with less."

The flat statement from Jim Carter really pissed Rita off. For several reasons - but the first one that came to mind was his disregard for protocol in front of others.

"Commander. You forget where you are."

Bekerose and Tarraine looked at each other. A tiny smile lifted the corner of Tarraine's lips, but he quickly suppressed it.

At the far end of the briefing table, Jim Carter nodded.

"Apologies, Admiral. But my statement still stands. I cannot protect this fleet and still press an attack against the enemy with less than six squadrons of Merlins."

Rita stared at him, unhappy.

"And where do we stand now?"

"We have three squadrons - forty-eight birds. We just received number forty-eight - it's waiting in the hanger for an acceptance flight. AirBoeing is producing three Merlins per week. So another sixteen weeks to bring us to full strength."

Rita looked off to one side, staring at a picture on the wall. It was a habit she had when she was mad or upset.

"I will not sit here on my ass for another sixteen weeks."

Captain Tarraine interjected.

"We still have two squadrons of the Devastators."

Jim shook his head.

"Too old, too slow. We'll be up against a numerically superior enemy with top-of-the-line equipment. In the Battle of Saturn, our Longswords were cut to pieces trying to get close to the Singheko capital ships. The Devastators are twice as good as the Longswords, but they're still not good enough.

They'll be decimated."

"We don't actually know we'll be outnumbered," said Tarraine. "We won't know anything about the disposition of their home world fleet until the *Dragon* sends intel back to us."

Rita stood and started pacing.

Another sign she was not happy.

"And the *Dragon* hasn't even launched yet," she said bitterly. "She's still fighting logistical and personnel problems."

It was quiet at the table as Rita paced around in the space between the conference table and her desk at the back of the briefing room.

Finally she turned, came back to the table, and sat down.

"Commander Carter, you will find a way to increase Merlin production and get us ready for departure in no more than six weeks. I don't care what you have to do. Pull the AirBoeing management kicking and screaming out of their offices in Toulouse and drag them down the cobblestone streets. I don't care. Just get it done."

Jim looked like he had swallowed a lemon. He shook his head.

"It's impossible, Admiral," he said.

Rita glared at him and she was very much not happy.

"You want to try that again, Commander?"

Jim nodded in surrender.

"Aye, milady. Six weeks."

Rita turned to Bekerose.

"Captain Bekerose, you will adjust the schedule for all ships to depart in six weeks."

"Aye, milady."

"Captain Tarraine, get with Bonnie and see what she has to do to get things expedited for her departure. I want *Dragon* out of here and on her way to scout the enemy in no more than two days."

"Aye, milady."

Rita stood, and this time everyone else around the table stood with her. Clearly, they were being dismissed.

"Thank you all. I know everyone is working hard to get us ready. But let's kick it a little harder, alright?"

Rita turned and walked away, past her desk and into her private quarters behind the briefing room of her Flag Cabin.

Bekerose and Tarraine gathered their electronic tablets and moved toward the door.

As they passed Jim, standing at the end of the table, they gave him a look of sympathy. He returned a wan smile to them as they passed.

Sure. Just have AirBoeing quadruple production of the Merlin fighters. No problem.

In frustration, Jim turned and followed the others out of the room. But when they turned left to go to their stations, he turned right to the flight deck.

I need to burn off some energy. And some frustration.

***

Thirty minutes later, Commander Jim Carter stepped into the launch bay of the *Merkkessa* dressed in his pressure suit and carrying his helmet. He walked to a new Merlin fighter, fresh off the assembly line from the AirBoeing factory at Toulouse, France and ready for the final acceptance flight by the EDF. The black wedge-shaped fighter was a thing of beauty. At least to Jim.

And Jim, as CAG - Commander Attack Group - intended to check this one out personally.

Climbing the ladder, he settled into the slightly larger seat of the Merlin. The original Devastators received from the Nidarian Empire had been a bit cramped for a big man like Jim Carter. At six feet one inch and 200 pounds, Jim had felt shoehorned into the old Devastator cockpits.

But this. This is much, much better, he thought, settling into the seat. *This one was built for humans.*

Plugged in by the support crew, he received a tap on the helmet and saluted them goodbye. He powered up the craft; as the electronics came online and the displays settled down, he closed the canopy.

"Merlin Charlie-Sixteen, redesignate yourself as *Angel*," Jim said out loud.

<Roger, I am redesignated as *Angel*> responded the AI in Jim's comm.

"*Angel*, prepare to launch."

<Roger, *Angel* to sortie deck now>

With a lurch, the autolauncher cradle began moving the Merlin into the sortie deck. In seconds, Jim was locked into position. Behind him, a pressure door slammed shut with a loud thunk. A high-pitched scream began as turbopumps removed the air from the sortie deck.

Another slight clunk told him the cradle beneath had retracted out of the way. A klaxon went off briefly in his comm and the outer door of the sortie deck slammed open.

A quick countdown started in his comm.

"Five. Four. Three. Two. One. Launch."

The force of the electromagnetic catapult pushed him back into the seat at four times the force of gravity as the Merlin was ejected out of the battlecruiser. The force was so strong pilots had to be taught not to touch the controls during launch, to prevent accidental control movements - or an erroneous response due to induced vertigo from the g-forces.

Waiting a few seconds for his inner ear to settle down and the Merlin's AI to navigate them a safe distance from the *Merkkessa*, Jim reached for the controls.

"My bird," he said out loud.

<Your bird> responded *Angel.* There was a *chirp chirp* as the autopilot turned off.

Now I'm a pilot again. Just me, a fighter, and the solar system.

For the next thirty minutes, Jim Carter had fighter pilot's playtime. He put the new fighter through every maneuver he could think of - everything he had learned in a bit more than ten years of flying combat aircraft in Earth's atmosphere and three battles against the Singheko in space.

Making a mock attack against the *Merkkessa*, he found the Merlin far more effective at hiding from the big battlecruiser than the older Devastators. With his stealth systems tuned to maximum and at best attack speed and acceleration, the Merlin could approach to near-missile range before the warship detected it. In fact, in two mock attacks, he got within thirty seconds of the huge ship before he was detected.

That was four times better than the Devastators, which were lucky to get within two minutes of a warship before detection.

Finally, Jim was satisfied.

It's a good design. It'll serve us well. But we need a lot more of them. We can't go to battle with less than six full squadrons. We need another three squadrons of these.

Jim sighed. He knew Rita would never wait for that many Merlins to be delivered. She was dead set on attacking the Singheko home world long before that.

And he knew there was nothing he, nor anyone else, could do to sway her.

Well, she's the boss.

And my wife.

Which makes her the boss...

Jim chuckled out loud at his joke.

Turning away from his last mock attack, Jim cleared out of *Merkkessa*'s control zone and took a course into the Black. He wasn't going anywhere in particular; he just wanted to fly for a while. He accelerated to 300g and let the Merlin run, on a course to nowhere.

Then he let his mind wander.

Lately, it seemed to be wandering to Bonnie Page.

The woman he had left for Rita. The woman he had not chosen.

Damn it.

Why can't you stop thinking about Bonnie?

Jim sighed, staring at the vast empty Black in front of him. Even that wasn't enough to push Bonnie out of his mind.

He pulled a piece of paper out of his pocket. A piece of paper he shouldn't be holding on to after all these months.

A piece of paper he needed to throw away but couldn't.

Unfolding it, in the dim light of the cockpit as the Merlin flashed through space faster and faster, he read the words.

Dear Jim

I told you in Antarctica you would have to choose between us - that we couldn't make the choice for you.

Now I see that you have chosen. You just don't know it yet.

I see it when you look at Imogen, and then at Rita, with a laugh in your eyes and your heart. I see it when she hands you the baby and touches you on the arm. I see it when you kiss Imogen and then smile at Rita.

So there it is. I'll go off to scout the Singheko in Dragon. *By the time the fleet arrives, you and Rita will have things sorted. So that's good.*

I won't hold on to you or drag things out. I'm not that person. I'll move on. Just take care of Rita and Imogen. Be safe and be happy.

I will leave you with one thing, though. Just so you know how I really felt about you, and how I'll feel about you someplace in my heart forever, even long after you and Rita are gone from me and I'm with someone else.

Even then, there will be this one little place in my heart - maybe a tiny spot, hard to find - but it'll be there. And in that place, I'll have you.

Jim folded up the letter. He held it in his lap for a few minutes. He looked over at the moon, now approaching quickly.

She's right. I love Rita. I love being with her, being with my baby.

He drew even with the moon, moving now at more than 3 million kilometers per hour.

Well, hoss, you've never been one to lie to yourself. Don't start now.

You still love Bonnie too.

It felt like he was having an argument with himself. And he

was losing.

You're an idiot.

Stop thinking about it.

I can't.

You made the choice. You chose Rita.

But was it just because she had your child?

No. It's real. You love Rita. You know it every time you hold her.

And yet you still love Bonnie.

Jim passed his gaze across the Black, the starry display outside as wondrous as anything he had ever seen.

He could see the Milky Way, a river of stars crossing the heavens, taking his breath away.

The universe seems to be most beautiful when you can't see any humans, he thought.

Jim re-focused. He was a long way from the *Merkkessa*. He started his decel and made his routine equipment checks, ensuring that his power, engine, environmental and navigation equipment was functioning correctly. He decelerated and got the Merlin headed back toward Earth.

Then he let his mind wander again.

Hanging on to the past is a waste of time and energy. You've got to let Bonnie go.

Like Caroline.

Let her go.

The thought of Caroline Bisset hurt Jim's heart.

She had left Mars on one of the last shuttles out. She had just arrived home when the bombs hit.

Because he told her to get out. Because he told her the Singheko were coming, and Mars was too dangerous, she had gone back to her home in London.

She had died there. Because he told her to.

Jim glanced at the planet coming up quickly now. England was in daylight, on his side of the planet.

I really shouldn't, he thought. *I'll get yelled at by both of my bosses...*

Then with a shrug, Jim adjusted his course. He reduced

his decel slightly and let the Merlin overshoot the orbit of the *Merkkessa*, entering the Earth's atmosphere over the North Atlantic.

Slowing to atmospheric entry speed, Jim headed for London. Bringing up the UK air traffic control system on his comm, he called ahead for clearance.

Surprisingly, it was granted.

I guess they don't mind an EDF fighter taking a tour over the ruins...

Slowing to normal airline speeds of 500 knots, Jim approached London - or what was left of it.

The 50-megaton bomb of the Singheko had left a crater a kilometer in width, and 400 meters deep.

Almost every building had been wiped off the face of the Earth for 20 kilometers from the center of the city.

For another 25 kilometers beyond that inner circle, ruins could be seen. But most of them were burnt-out buildings, uninhabitable even if the radiation didn't kill you first.

And for another 15 kilometers beyond that, even though some buildings survived, the thermal pulse had killed almost everyone. Even most of the trees and plants.

A great, blackened circle 120 kilometers in diameter, where nothing moved, surrounded the place that used to be London.

Jim bowed his head. Tears formed in his eyes, but he fought them off.

The last thing Caroline would want is for me to cry more tears for her. She'd laugh her ass off. That woman was hell on wheels.

Jim forced his thoughts elsewhere.

Give it up. Focus on today.

Jim lifted his head, looked around at the desolation around him. Despite his resolution, tears blurred his vision.

He set his teeth and pulled on the stick, taking a vector that would put him back in orbit - and back to the *Merkkessa*.

As he departed the planet, he let the speed build up in atmosphere until the external overheat alarm went off in the Merlin.

He slowed down until the alarm stopped.

That was for you, Caroline.

***

Marta and Tatiana sat on the floor at the back of the cage, next to each other, facing the front. A small circle of a dozen women surrounded them.

In front of that group, women milled about aimlessly, looking for all the world like a herd of restless animals, randomly pacing in the front of the cage.

But effectively screening the small group in the back of the cage from the corridor in front.

"OK. We have our basic organization," Tatiana continued. "But we need a lot more people than this. We need to recruit other cages down the corridor. So we start a communication chain. We talk to the next cage; they talk to the one after that. And so on."

A woman leaned forward.

"How about the men? Do we recruit them?"

"Of course. We can't do this without them. Your name was Norali, right?"

"Yes. Norali. I was in military intelligence."

"Good. Excellent. Well, we must have the men. It's all for one, one for all."

"But they'll try to take over."

"Yes - they'll try. If they can prove themselves smarter and more capable, then fine, I don't care. But until they prove that, we are our own organization. We don't take orders from them. That's the way we play it."

Marta growled. "Good luck with that."

Tatiana smiled.

"Yeah. But that's the way we play it. We are our own independent underground unit, unless they prove they can lead better than we can."

Norali shook her head. "They'll ignore us, then."

Tatiana smiled again.

"I think you're forgetting something."

"What?" asked Norali.

"We have what they want."

Marta laughed out loud.

"Oh, yeah," she grinned.

Tatiana continued, smiling.

"As long as we get fully organized, and all of us stay together, they can't do anything to us we don't want them to. That means they'll listen to us if nothing else. And that's half the battle."

Norali nodded slowly. "I'm not sure that'll work, but we can try."

"We have plenty of time to make this come together," Tatiana spoke. "Weeks before we arrive. By that time, I want us to have at least three cages of women fully organized into an effective combat unit. If the men want to join us, fine. If not, they can go to hell."

Suddenly there was an interruption toward the front of the cage. A loud voice. Then several loud voices.

The big woman called Sonja pushed through the circle of women and stood in front of Tatiana and Marta.

"Enough of this!" she shouted. "All you are going to do is get us in trouble! I'm taking over this cage...now!"

Marta jumped to her feet. Her damaged face still showed a raw, black wound, like a partially burnt steak. But it was healing. Her eye had not been permanently damaged; her vision had come back slowly.

And she was going to need that eye right now. Marta and Tatiana knew this was a cusp in time - a critical moment in their budding resistance movement. If Sonja had her way, it was all over. There would be no resistance, no underground movement of slaves seeking their freedom.

There would be only Sonja, forming a gang, sucking up to their captors for any advantage she could get. Selling out the weak and the sick, building her own little empire on the bodies of her comrades.

Marta and Tatiana had talked about it. Knew it was coming.

Knew the consequences of losing this fight.

Behind Sonja, a dozen of her gang stood with her. Tatiana felt the movement as her own team gathered beside her, forming up for battle.

God, why does it have to come to this? Why is there always someone who wants to use violence to get power over the rest of us?

Sonja's gang had planned it well. Sonja charged. Avoiding Marta, she charged at Tatiana. At the same time, three of her gang charged at Marta, to entangle her and keep her from helping Tatiana.

It was a good plan.

But it was a plan that Tatiana had foreseen. Behind Marta, four of Tatiana's crew stepped out, blocking the path to Marta. Marta side-stepped to put herself directly in front of Tatiana.

And the battle was on. Fists flew, bodies crashed together, cries and groans filled the cage.

And Marta, with a hard thrust, put her knuckles into Sonja's neck, the blow so strong it spun Sonja sideways.

Sonja dropped like a poleaxed steer, grabbing for her throat.

On her knees, gasping for breath, Sonja gave a glare of hatred at Marta, then collapsed forward and lay still.

Suddenly there was utter silence, utter stillness. Everyone was frozen. Women from both sides lay injured on the floor.

Marta looked at Tatiana.

With a huge sigh, Tatiana stepped forward to Sonja's unconscious body. She raised her head and surveyed the dozens of women nearby and with another sigh, shook her head.

"This was so unnecessary," she said loudly, so that all could hear.

"There is no need of violence against each other. Don't you understand? Don't you understand our enemy is outside this wire…?"

Tatiana pointed toward the front of the wire cage.

"When we fight each other, we play into their hands! That's exactly what they expect us to do! This is stupid!"

Now Tatiana began to pace around the room.

"We ARE going to organize. We ARE going to create a resistance movement. I'm not saying that all of you must participate - if you don't want to be part of it, that's fine! None of us will hold it against you - as long as you don't work against us!"

Tatiana stopped, put her hands on her hips and glared at the assembled women.

"But - make no mistake about it!"

"If you fight us - you will pay the price! I will not have it! You can be part of this movement. Or you can ignore it and stay away from us. But you cannot be against us. Is that clear to everyone?"

There was a low mumble from the women.

Tatiana made a slow circle, turning to face every part of the cage as she did so.

"Am I clear?"

There was a slightly louder response this time, and from the back of the cage Marta and the rest of Tatiana's team added a loud shout of assent.

Tatiana stood silently for a moment. Then she walked to the back of the cage and stared down at Sonja.

"Someone help her," she said.

A couple of the women moved to Sonja. They picked her up and carried her to the back of the cage, near the water faucets. Turning on a faucet, they began to splash her with water, trying to rouse her.

Tatiana glanced at Marta.

"You didn't kill her, did you?"

"No, but I wanted to."

"No. No killing, not unless it's a last resort. We'll give her one more chance to come around."

Marta smiled.

"Fine. But she's not going to be talking for about a week."

"OK. Round up her gang over in the far corner and have a long talk with them. The first one that opens their mouth to the Singheko about anything we do in here will find themselves suddenly dead. Make sure they understand.

"It's not something I want to do, but all of our lives are at stake. If we must make an example of one of them, we will."

Marta grinned.

"Nothing I'd like better..."

4 - DEPARTURE

Dragon's wardroom doubled as the briefing room. Bonnie entered the compartment and sat down at the head of the table, gazing around at her command staff.

"I know some of you have already met, but introductions are still in order, I think. Let's keep it short, please, we have business to attend to. Commander Powell, would you begin?"

Luke looked around the table.

"Luke Powell, XO. Started my career on HMS *London* a long, long time ago, just before she was laid up, if any of you remember that far back. Intel Officer on the *Invincible* during the First Africa Crisis, later seconded to the Aussies on the *Australia* as Operations Officer. Returned to the RN as XO of the *King William* two years ago."

Luke stopped.

I'll leave the rest to rumor and innuendo, I think.

Across the table from Luke, the next officer was an attractive, slender woman with black hair. She cleared her throat and glanced around at the assembled staff.

"Commander Sarah North, Chief Engineer. I've spent the last twenty-five years in the wet navy, keeping the lights on and making sure the ship can move. I'll get you there, the rest is up to you," she smiled. A titter of laughter spread across the room.

The curiosity of the humans around the table was readily apparent as the next officer began to speak - a Nidarian.

Many of them had never seen a Nidarian in the flesh before. Lirrassa was like a human in many ways, but short - only five feet tall. Her nose was nearly non-existent, just a small bump on her face. And she had a head that was somehow more squarish than a human's, although it was hard to put your finger on what exactly made it look that way.

"Commander Lirrassa, Tactical. Admiral Page asked me to transfer over from the *Merkkessa*. As technically the *Dragon* still belongs to the Nidarian Navy and is only on loan to you Humans, my main job is to make sure none of you screw up this ship."

Another titter of laughter went around the table. Even Bonnie couldn't resist a small laugh.

"We'll do our best, Lirrassa," Bonnie interjected. She looked down the table at the next officer.

"Lieutenant Commander Stephanie Warner, Medical Officer. I'll be the one stitching you up after you screw up, so try not to screw up," said an attractive young female officer with a distinctive Boston accent.

Bonnie leaned back in her chair as the introductions continued around the table.

They're establishing the tone of the ship right from the get-go, and I think I like it. Some ships are too serious, some ships are too frivolous. I think this is about right - a layer of humor covering a solid competence beneath. A good tone for a warship heading into harm's way.

I hope we can still laugh six months from now.

"Lieutenant Commander Naditta, Operations," said the next officer at the table, the male Nidarian in the room. "My last posting was also on the *Merkkessa*, as ATO - Assistant Tactical Officer. My focus on this deployment will be bringing the human crew up to speed on the *Dragon*'s systems and developing standard operational procedures. I also want to apologize for my accent, my English is still developing, but I'm getting better."

Bonnie leaned in to reassure him.

"Your English is fine, Naditta. I can understand you better than some of the Irish and Scots we've got aboard."

Everyone laughed, especially after the next officer down the table leaned forward and spoke with a strong Scottish accent.

"Lieutenant Commander Harry McMaster, Weapons. My job is to learn all about these new weapons on board and how to use them effectively. I'm just coming off a deployment with HMS *York*, where I was also Weapons Officer. While I can't be sure, I suspect my posting here is because I have a degree in Physics. And to be sure, the rest of you are the ones with a strange accent."

Everyone laughed. Down the table, the next human female in the room took her turn.

"I'm Lieutenant Rachel Gibson, Assistant Tactical Officer. Just coming off a deployment with the *King Charles*, where I was Assistant Operations Officer. Glad to be here."

"Lieutenant Dan Worley, Assistant Engineer." The young Lieutenant stopped talking abruptly, a bit intimidated by the senior officers around him. Finally, he managed to stammer out, "Also coming from the HMS *York* - I was Third Engineer there."

At the corners of the table, two young ensigns sat. Now they looked across the table at each other, not sure if they should join in the introductions or not. Then they looked at Bonnie, uncertain.

Bonnie nodded.

"Please," she said, gesturing to them.

"Ensign Emma Gibbs, assigned to Weapons," said the first one, jumping into the fray. "U.S. Naval Academy, just seconded to the EDF."

"And will also act as Assistant Logistics Officer," added Naditta.

"Ensign Gary Goodwin, assigned to Operations and Navigation," said the second young ensign. "Also from the U.S. Naval Academy."

Now Bonnie took up the thread of the conversation.

"Thank you all," said Bonnie. "Also, Major Oliver Coston can't be here right now, he's loading weapons for his Marine squad and getting the Armory squared away. You'll meet him later."

Bonnie leaned back in her chair and surveyed the group.

***

"You probably have a lot of questions. I'll try to run down the more obvious ones first - then everybody can dive in and ask the ones I miss."

"First - why a crew so biased toward the Royal Navy? Let me give you the concept. Admiral Page and her staff discussed how to integrate the EDF as rapidly as possible across all the relevant governments of Earth."

"So - each ship is being re-staffed with a mixture of personnel to serve as a breeding ground for the future. Once your initial tour is over, you'll be mixed - spread out across all the ships of the EDF fleet. After we've done this a few times, the fleet will be a good cross-section of all the major countries of Earth."

"For this first deployment, we'll keep each ship at least in the same language family. And for that reason, Admiral Page is restaffing the *Merkkessa* with as many qualified American, Canadian and Australian personnel as she can find."

"She is restaffing the newly repaired battlecruiser *Asiana* - the one we captured from the Singheko - with as many Chinese, Japanese, Korean and Mongolian crew as possible, with a requirement that every one of the crew members speak at least one of the other languages. Captain Sato will be on that ship, as third in command after Rita and Bekerose."

"The other two captured Singheko cruisers are being staffed similarly. For example, the *Moscow* will have Russian, German, Austrian, Polish, and so forth. You get the idea."

"Of course, every ship will have a complement of Nidarian officers and crew, as they are the most familiar with the systems and weapons. The Nidarians will be training us for this deployment. After the first year, most of them will rotate back to the Nidarian Empire and we'll be on our own."

"So - having said that, the *Dragon* was selected to be predominantly United Kingdom, with some Americans,

Australians and Canadians thrown in to start the mixing process. You can expect to be together for about eighteen months if all goes according to plan. After that, you can expect to be reassigned to a different ship as part of this distribution process."

Bonnie couldn't help a stray thought.

If we're alive in eighteen months...

She suppressed the grim thought and continued.

"Any questions on that aspect of things?"

Everyone shook their heads. Most of this they had heard before, and Bonnie was just confirming the concept for them.

"Next - where are we going and why? Well, we're going to Singheko on a scouting mission. And no, we are not going to go in guns blazing, killing as many Singheko as possible."

Bonnie looked rather pointedly at Luke.

"We'll be doing that later for sure. But not yet. For now, our job is to sneak in, get the lay of the land, classify their fleet, try to locate the human slaves, and do all this without getting caught."

"Without getting caught, folks. Let me be sure you understand that. We will not engage the enemy. We will not rescue the slaves, not on this mission. If anything unexpected happens, we will cut and run just as fast as *Dragon* can carry our butts out of there. Any questions on that?"

Again, everyone shook their heads. Bonnie's discussion matched the scuttlebutt they had already heard.

"Finally, your secondary mission is to learn the systems of this ship as rapidly and thoroughly as possible. Regardless of how carefully we plan and how carefully we sneak into the Singheko home system, there is always the chance we are detected and must fight our way out. Be prepared for that. Know every aspect of your systems, your weapons, your crew, and their capabilities, and be ready to fight at a moment's notice."

The table was quiet. Bonnie let the silence sit for a while.

"One more housekeeping item. Anyone who hasn't already

gotten their comm implant, go to sick bay and have them implanted. Don't be afraid of them, I've had mine for nearly two years now. There's nothing to it. You lie in a medpod for a half-hour and when you come out, you'll be able to comm on the command channel directly from your brain."

"Any questions before we break?"

Around the table, people looked at each other, then turned back to Bonnie. No one had any questions.

"Then let's be about it, folks," she said.

The group rose and began filing out of the room. Luke remained, as did Sarah North. When everyone else had left, Bonnie looked at Sarah.

"Cheng, how do we stand on prep for departure?"

"We'll be fully ready for departure in six hours, mum," said Sarah.

"Good. Luke, how about supplies and weapons loading?"

"Four hours and we'll be done," Luke replied. "We have a few more pallets of supplies to bring onboard. All crew have reported aboard. We have twelve officers, counting Major Coston, and seventy-six ratings. We are fully staffed."

"How many Nidarians?"

"Eighteen. The two officers, Lirrassa and Naditta, two Chiefs, and fourteen ratings."

"Can we do this with only those few?"

"Yes, we'll be fine. The Nidarians have committed to training us as rapidly as possible. We'll train on the way, with a focus on Engineering and Weapons. We'll be ready."

"OK," responded Bonnie. "I'm going to slow us down a bit on the trip out. Instead of going full speed, we'll go three-quarter speed. That'll stretch the trip out to twenty-three days. Gives us a bit more time for shakedown and training."

"Good idea."

Bonnie stood up. She looked at the two officers.

"Thank you both."

"Aye, mum," they responded, departing the briefing room.

***

At last *Dragon* was ready for departure. Bonnie called Admiral Page on the comm.

"We're ready, Rita."

"Good. Go find out what we're up against. Don't get caught, don't get killed. Got it?"

"Got it. There's one thing we haven't talked about, though."

"I know. Do I have to say it?"

"I think it would be better if you did, just so it's on the record."

Bonnie heard a sigh from Rita.

"Captain Page, if the *Dragon* is in imminent danger of capture by the Singheko, you will destroy that ship, regardless of circumstances. You cannot allow it to fall into the hands of the enemy."

"Now, was that so hard?" smiled Bonnie. "Now we've got it on the record, and there won't be any ambiguity."

"Good hunting, Bonnie. And one more time - try not to get yourself killed."

Bonnie laughed as she signed off.

I'll try not to, baby. I know what you're trying to say. It's a bit much to say 'I love you' over a recorded command channel.

An hour later - after the inevitable last-minute delays and surprises - the *Dragon* was fully ready to go. Bonnie took her seat on the bridge and watched as the crew brought the engines online. When all was ready, she nodded at Luke.

Luke paused. He had always savored this moment - the first movement of a new mission. The first command to take a ship into harm's way.

"Take us out, please, Mr. Goodwin."

At the Navigation console, a very distracted Ensign Goodwin looked helplessly at Naditta, sitting at his elbow. Naditta whispered into Goodwin's ear and pointed to the display, training him for the Navigation role.

Of course, the actual movement was controlled by *Dragon*'s AI. All Goodwin had to do was authorize the command sequence and monitor in case of a malfunction.

Something he didn't know how to do yet.

Naditta whispered to him again, Goodwin pushed the console screen, and the *Dragon* started to move. Luke looked over at Bonnie and shook his head.

"We'll get there," Bonnie whispered to him. "Give them time."

Luke nodded, turning back to the holotank.

Below, the Earth was visible, a blue, white, and brown ball two feet wide in the holo. Below them the *Merkkessa* and her two escort destroyers slowly fell away as the *Dragon* left orbit.

<Message from *Merkkessa*> called the AI over the bridge channel. <Good mission and good hunting>

"Reply to *Merkkessa*: thank you and see you soon," spoke Bonnie.

<Message sent. Message acknowledged>

The Earth fell away in the holotank as they cleared the near-Earth speed limits and could accelerate. Soon they were making 300g, increasing their speed by 2,942 meters per second every second. Within nine minutes they passed the Moon's orbit, traveling at more than 5.6 million kilometers per hour on a course that would slightly bypass Saturn.

"ETA to the mass limit?" asked Luke.

"7.6 hours, sir," called Goodwin, peering at his screen.

"Excellent," said Luke. "*Dragon*, secure from planetary operations."

<ALL HANDS. SECURE FROM PLANETARY OPERATIONS. SECURE FROM PLANETARY OPERATIONS>

The announcement was repeated in Nidarian.

Bonnie grinned at Luke.

"Some of the new crew will be scratching their heads wondering what that means."

"Yes. But it sure is nice to have an AI around. Makes life much simpler."

"You bet. It won't be long before you'll be wondering how you ever got along without one."

Bonnie rose and stretched a little.

"OK, Luke, we're on our way. Too late to go back home now."

"Aye, mum," answered Luke, a big smile on his face.

"Commander, come into my lair and help me think through a couple of problems."

Luke rose and followed Bonnie into her day cabin. She sat at her desk and pointed to an old-fashioned yellow pad on the table in front of her.

"Sometimes it helps me to use the old way of doing things - writing it down."

***

"We have to integrate a crew that comes from a dozen different backgrounds," Bonnie began. "We've got Brits, Americans, Canadians, some merchant marine, Nidarians, a couple of Aussies - and there are a few I'm not sure if their mothers know where they came from."

Luke laughed.

"Yep. That's a fact."

"And the EDF is so new, we have no policies or procedures for managing these people. So..."

Bonnie tapped a pencil against her desk. "We need to develop some additional rules for *Dragon*. And right at the top of the list is fraternization. You know what I mean."

Luke nodded.

"Indeed I do. When there are boys and girls together, sparks will fly."

"Yep, exactly. So... We can forbid it and punish those who get caught - that's what the Americans and the RN do - or we can allow it, within limitations - as the Nidarians do. What do you think?"

Luke put his head down in thought, then lifted it again.

"If we take the strict approach, then how do we handle the Nidarians? It's their culture. So do we punish the Nidarians for living their culture? And if we don't, how can we punish the humans for the same offense? So I'd like us to at least consider the Nidarian approach."

Bonnie nodded.

"I tend to agree with you. But at the same time, we can't let it get out of hand. We have to set some limits."

"What do the Nidarians do?"

"It's not the same thing. Their culture doesn't have the same envy and jealousy reactions that humans do, primarily because they have their mated groups. So what works for them, wouldn't necessarily work for us."

"Geez, I forgot about that," said Luke. "I saw something about that on TV, but it slipped my mind."

"Yes. Nidarians have six-way marriages. Three males and three females form a mated group. It's a contract type of marriage - the marriage can be for any period, from one year up to twenty years. But they don't mate for life, and to the best of my knowledge, they never contract for more than twenty years at a time."

"Wow," exclaimed Luke. "That's different."

Bonnie leaned back and grinned. "Isn't it."

Luke thought some more.

"OK, how about this. You can't fraternize with a direct report, or with your direct subordinate. Otherwise you're good to go."

"But what if they're married?" asked Bonnie.

Luke was shocked. "Do we have any married couples on board?"

"No human ones. But we have at least two Nidarian mated groups on board. So again, how can I prohibit humans from marrying if the Nidarians are?"

Luke grinned.

"Crap. Can we just kick all the Nidarians off the ship?"

Bonnie looked at the moving map display on her wall, showing the *Dragon* now about 21 million kilometers from Earth, traveling at 29.1 million kph.

"Probably too late to do that."

They laughed together.

"OK," said Bonnie. "Here's what we're going to do, I think. See what you think about this. We ignore fraternization if it happens off duty, and not with a direct report or anyone in your own department. Married partners cannot be in the same department - and that goes for the Nidarians too. How's that?"

Luke thought it through.

"I like it, but it may be hard to do in practice. *Dragon's* a small ship - with only seventy-six ratings, it's going to be hard to implement. But I think it's the best we can do."

"OK. Item one is settled," said Bonnie, marking off the first line on her yellow pad.

5 - SINGHEKO

"Did you see the intel we received this morning about the Nidarians?" asked Zukra's aide, Orma.

"I did."

"What do you make of that, sir?"

"Not a bad idea on Garatella's part. Giving a fleet to the Humans. He claims in his public statement that they got only old, worn out ships. And he put a Human Admiral in charge. So if they manage to damage one of our ships, and we make a fuss about it, he can always claim the Humans did it, not Nidaria. Pretty smart move on his part."

"Do you think they'll have any impact on the Earth expedition?"

"No, nothing serious. But I've been looking at these Humans' history. They're incredibly violent and aggressive. Nothing like the other species we've run across. If they got their hands on enough modern weapons and had enough time, they could be a real thorn in our side. I'd much prefer if Garatella hadn't given them that damn battlecruiser."

"The *Merkkessa*."

"Yes. It's an old ship, true. But it was overhauled and refitted only four years ago. I think Garatella is playing both ends against the middle here."

"Should we put together a contingency plan for it?"

"Yes, as crazy as it sounds, do that. I'm positive the Humans would take the fleet straight to Earth to try and fight off our expeditionary force there. But still…it won't hurt to put together a plan for the other case, where they come here."

"That would be suicide on their part."

"Yes. But even a suicidal attack could hurt us, could damage ships and cause casualties. So yes, put together a contingency plan for that scenario - the *Merkkessa* charging into our system with the rest of those Nidarian relics, hell-bent on doing as much damage as they can."

"Aye, sir," responded Orma.

"Oh, and Orma..."

"Yes, sir?"

"Double our drone coverage in areas where a small ship could hide. It's not beyond comprehension they might send in a small scout ship to get the lay of the land. If they do, I want to know it right away."

As Orma departed, Zukra leaned back in his chair, relaxing.

And I have one more contingency plan, Zukra thought with a smile. *One that even Orma doesn't know about.*

Then I won't have to wait for Ligar or anyone else to give me what I want.

***

Onboard *Dragon*, COB - Chief of the Boat - Michael Nash was not happy. As sometimes happened when he was pissed off, his Dublin accent came to the fore.

"Candridge! You call this squared away?"

"Yes, Chief!"

The response from Candridge was acceptable - but it didn't go at all with the smarmy smile from the missile technician.

"How the hell did you ever make E-4, you sorry excuse for a real sailor?" yelled Nash. "Look at that feed rail! Can't you see it's mis-aligned?"

Candridge lost his smile. Glancing down at the feed rail to the Number Four missile launcher, he realized Nash was right.

"Yes, Chief!"

Nash looked around the gun deck at the other members of the Number Four missile crew.

"I'll be back in one hour. And God help you if that missile feed tube is not ready to go!"

Spinning on his heels, Chief Nash stalked away to the next

location on his surprise inspection. A parade of junior Chiefs and Petty Officers followed in his footsteps, their tablets in hand to take notes.

Candridge waited until the Chief was out of sight, then shook his head.

"Asshole!" he muttered.

"Shut up, Ross," said his assistant, David Gray. "Don't get us crosswise of Nash!"

"I'm not afraid of that asshole," replied Candridge. "He's just throwing his weight around."

"Well, he's got the weight to throw around. If he lands on you, watch your ass!"

Muttering, Candridge turned to the missile feed tube and started adjusting it.

Walking to the next compartment, Michael Nash was not happy.

We've got a good crew for the most part. But there's always one bad apple in every barrel. That Candridge is gonna be trouble. How that idiot got on this ship I'll never know.

***

At the other end of *Dragon*, Lt. Dan Worley was literally up to his elbows. The big pyramid in the middle of *Dragon*'s tDrive engine room was silver, streaked with black at seams that ran around it every twelve inches. At the base of it, Dan's hands and arms were down in a hole in the floor, pulling at something.

He grunted and pulled harder. There was a loud click.

Pulling his arms out of the opening, he looked up at Commander Sarah North standing on the deck at the base of the pyramid. He wiped sweat off his brow.

"Well?" she asked.

"Don't we have some ratings to do this? Or bots?" Dan asked woefully.

"Of course," replied Sarah. "But in the middle of a battle, anything can happen. You need to know how to reset the reactor on your own, if it comes to that."

"Well, it's reset now," he responded. "And I hope I never have to do that during a battle."

"If you have to do that during a battle, you'll be the only one left in Engineering, I suspect," said Sarah. "So let's hope for all our sakes that never happens."

Dan pushed the floor tile back over the hole. He reached for his tablet nearby and checked off another item.

"OK, that's done. Next it says, flush the HE-4 filters."

Sarah grinned.

"Oh, now comes the fun part." She pointed to a floor puller lying beside Dan.

"Pull up a half-dozen tiles here..."

Sarah pointed to another spot a dozen feet from Dan.

"...and you'll find large gray boxes underneath. Each of them needs to be sealed off from the HE-4 flow, removed, cleaned, new filters installed and then the boxes re-installed in the reverse order. Shouldn't take you more than about, oh, say four hours."

Groaning, Dan picked up the floor puller.

Five hours later, Dan stepped into the wardroom, dog-tired. Slumping into a chair, he was too tired to even get a cup of coffee from the pot.

Staring blankly at the wall, he felt someone come in behind him and get coffee. Then Lt. Rachel Gibson appeared, coffee in hand.

"How are things in Engineering?" she asked, taking the seat across from him.

"Ugh. Commander North has me checking and re-checking everything on the annual maintenance checklist. Right down to the spit shine on the light bulbs."

"Maintenance checklist? Where in heck did we get a maintenance checklist for a two-thousand-year-old starship?"

Dan sighed heavily.

"Evidently the AI had it all tucked away in its little memory, just waiting for us humans to come along."

"Well, we're going to be a long way from home. And in enemy territory. I guess it's good everything is being double checked."

"Yeah. I get it."

Footsteps sounded behind them, and Rachel looked up, then stood rapidly to attention. Dan started to rise but felt a hand on his shoulder.

"At ease, folks. No need to snap to in the wardroom, OK?"

Dan recognized the voice of Luke Powell, the XO. Rachel sank back down into her chair, so Dan did likewise. Luke got coffee and came around to join them at the table, sitting beside Rachel.

"So Sarah's working you pretty hard in Engineering, I take it," he smiled at Dan.

"Yes, sir, I guess."

Dan turned to Rachel.

"How's your ATO training going?"

"Great, sir. Commander Lirrassa really knows her stuff. She's got me working two hours a day in the simulator and then of course standing my watch at the actual Tac console while she looks over my shoulder."

Luke nodded, commiserating with her.

"I know it's a tough schedule, folks. But we don't have much time to get acclimated to this beast. We're not going full speed on the way to Singheko so we can have more training time, but even so it'll be a quick trip. So we have to use every hour we can cobble together."

"Oh, we understand," answered Rachel, glancing at Dan. "We don't mind."

"Good," said Luke. "Glad to hear it. Well, I'll be on my way. I have my own training agenda. And the Skipper runs a tough syllabus. See you tomorrow."

Despite Luke's earlier dispensation, both Rachel and Dan rose to their feet as he left the room. Then Dan shook his head.

"I'm going to hit the rack," he said. "See you tomorrow."

Rachel watched Dan depart.

He's kinda cute, she thought. *A bit shy, but kinda cute. I think he's completely clueless about women. It's gonna be a long mission.*

Maybe I should go for that...

***

The third planet of the Singheko system was the home world. Like Earth, it was a temperate planet, with oceans, deserts, jungles, steppes.

Here a creature much like a lion had evolved, a predator that ranged the plains of a southern continent for millions of years.

And here, somehow, the spark of intelligence had arisen in the creature. An evolutionary jump that brought the creature into a feedback loop which moved it progressively closer to an upright stance - as its brain continued to increase in size and complexity.

Until it became a seven-foot-tall tawny beast with vestigial claws and fangs - but as intelligent as any Human or Nidarian.

The Singheko.

But that evolutionary feedback loop had never been able to remove the predator from the beast.

Captain Orma watched in silence as his boss, Admiral Zukra, crept through the jungle two dozen yards in front of them.

Zukra had given strict orders to stay behind him - even though Orma carried the rifle that would serve as the last-ditch survival tool if Zukra got into trouble.

And Zukra was in trouble. He froze, unmoving, as a three-hundred-pound male *zeltid* stood at the edge of the little clearing, flicking its tail, sniffing the wind with its nose, aware that something was amiss.

A three-hundred pound killing machine, needing only a little more information from its senses to detect the anomaly and charge.

A killing machine that could charge at 65 kilometers per hour...

A killing machine that had four-inch claws to rip and tear apart the flesh of any other animal...

...including a Singheko.

Slowly, carefully, Zukra tried to move his spear down a bit to a better position to meet the charge that was coming.

Orma shuddered, fear trickling down his back and pooling at the base of his spine. The upright ears on his head flicked back and forth in dismay.

If Zukra failed to stop the *zeltid*...

...it would come straight for him next.

Beside him, the native beater was also frozen in fear. The *zeltid* had appeared out of nowhere, well before they were prepared for it.

Zukra had a grin on his face a mile wide.

"How does he do it?" thought Orma. "Facing almost certain death if he misses by even the slightest..."

With a roar that curled the hair on the tips of Orma's ears, the *zeltid* found his target and charged.

Within two bounds he was at full speed as he charged Zukra, roaring again and baring his fangs.

Zukra planted the butt of the spear in the ground and waited, grinning, as the beast approached. As the *zeltid* leaped, Zukra made a tiny adjustment of the spear. Holding it for all he was worth, Zukra was still pushed back as the *zeltid* impacted, knocking him to the ground two meters back.

The spear drove deep into the *zeltid*'s chest, pivoting him to one side. The huge tawny creature fell to the ground, groaning and coughing as his lifeblood ran out.

Zukra climbed to his feet, dusting himself off. He turned to Orma.

"Did you see it? Did you see it, Orma?"

"Aye, sir, I saw. You planted the spear perfectly."

"Damn right, Orma. If I had not, I would not be here now."

The zeltid coughed again and with a glare of hate at Zukra, fell back and died. Zukra walked over to it and stood, one foot on the dead *zeltid,* and turned to Orma.

"Pictures, Orma! Pictures!"

6 - SONJA

In the night, one of the older, sicker women died. Tatiana had the others move the body to the front of the cage, right by the door.

The Singheko guards' reaction next morning was anti-climactic. The guards came to wash down the cage and saw the body.

They used the fire hose to drive the women back from the cage door, then opened it and removed the body. Then they simply locked the door, finished washing the cage, and dragged the body away.

"It means nothing to them," observed Tatiana. "They could care less."

Marta nodded.

"Yep. We're just animals to them. Pigs in a pigsty."

Tatiana glanced at the rest of her core team, sitting around her in a circle.

"Have we established communications with the men yet?"

Norali answered.

"Yeah. We've been able to establish contact with them. The next two cages past ours are women, like us. Then there is an opening for one of the exit ramps. After that, the men start. So we are evidently near the end of the female cages."

"If each cage holds a hundred people like this one, that means there are 200 women to our right, followed by 6,000 men. Then the rest of the women as you wrap around the ship."

"Good," mused Tatiana. "That's pretty much what I expected, because as we were boarding, I saw only men to our right on the next ramp."

"Yes. In a way, we're lucky, because we only have to pass messages through two cages of women to talk to the men."

"And so far? Any interest on their side in forming a resistance?"

"I would say yes. They were cautious at first - they didn't believe females could come up with such an idea - but I think I've convinced them, at least the first cage. Some guy named Mikhail. It'll be up to them to pass the message on and get it to the next cages."

"Fantastic," said Tatiana. "OK. Keep the messages moving. But I want to limit this first effort to only a half-dozen cages - 600 people. I think any more than that, we run too much risk of the Singheko finding out. Did you make that clear to them?"

"Yes, absolutely."

"OK. Good. So six cages. Three of men, three of women. We want a Cage Leader for every cage until all six cages are accounted for. Tell them how we're organizing, what our goals are, and to keep us informed."

"And to keep an eye out for Sonja types - traitors and collaborators," growled Marta.

"Yes. Absolutely," agreed Tatiana. "Norali. You are in charge of Intelligence. Make sure you warn every cage to keep an eye out for the Sonja types."

"Got it," answered Norali. "We'll watch for them."

***

Two cages away, Mikhail closed his eyes. Leaning back against the wire, he shook his head in frustration.

Lord, help me deal with these idiots.

Finally, he opened his eyes.

"Look. The women down the way have gotten themselves organized. We need to do the same. We need to put together an underground resistance to fight these bastards."

The two men sitting with him laughed.

"Women! You expect us to join with women to fight these fuckers?"

Mikhail leaned forward, idly tapping his fingers on the floor as he talked.

"You're underestimating what women can do. Think about it. The bastards won't expect the women to do anything. They'll be watching us men like hawks. We won't be able to make a move without them knowing. But they won't be paying nearly as much attention to the women."

The two men in front of Mikhail looked at each other, as if they hadn't thought about that.

Which they hadn't. Their names were Leo and Denys. Leo was the smarter of the two, but not by much.

Leo looked back at Mikhail.

"OK. Suppose for the sake of argument you're right. What do you want us to do?"

"Both of you have military experience. The word from down the hall is that every cage should form a resistance cell. A Cage Leader, with a headquarters staff consisting of communications, intelligence, operations, logistics, and so forth. So we recruit officers for those roles first. Then we'll divide the rest of the men into squads and platoons. Then we copy that organization on to the next cage, until we've got three cages of men organized - ours and the next two past us."

Leo grunted. "And I suppose you'll be in charge?"

Mikhail shook his head.

"Leo. I don't care. If someone is better qualified than me, then they can have it. That's fine. I just want to get things moving."

"But you were a colonel in the army, right?"

"I was. But I'm not hung up on being in charge."

Denys spoke at last.

"All the more reason you should be in charge. The best leaders are the ones who don't want power."

Beside him, Leo nodded in agreement.

"So," Mikhail continued. "The women have already gotten their side organized. Some woman named Tatiana is in charge. She's close, just two cages away. That makes communication easier. Let's get ourselves organized and start putting together a joint plan with them."

Leo and Denys thought about it for a while, then looked at each other and nodded agreement.

"OK. We're in," said Leo. "For now."

***

Dragon came out of six-space with a whine, 200 AU from the Singheko home system.

Every pair of eyes on the bridge stared at the holo, checking for any enemy ship nearby.

Computing quickly in her head, Bonnie realized the light speed delay to the Singheko home planet was almost twenty-seven hours. Anything they could see would be twenty-seven hours out of date.

Good enough. I just want to see what I can see.

"Luke, can you make out anything?"

Luke Powell was hunched over his XO console, trying to tune the holotank to show anything available to the passive sensors from such a long distance.

"Not much, Skipper. We can see their home planet, but not much else. Too far to make out any ships."

"OK. But you don't see anything in our immediate area that would present a risk?"

"No, mum," answered Luke. "It looks severe clear."

"Very good," said Bonnie. She turned her attention to Chief Blocker at the Nav console.

"Chief, plot us a course to Point Baker-Two."

"Course plotted and laid in, mum," Blocker answered quickly. During the two weeks of their voyage, he had been well trained by Naditta.

"Execute."

With another high-pitched whine, the ship sank back into six-space. A few minutes later, they translated back into normal space on the other side of the star system, now only 100 AU away from the enemy home planet Ridendo - with a bit more than thirteen hours of light-speed delay.

Luke bent over his console, tuning the passive sensors. After a while, he shook his head.

"Nothing that I can see between us and the Kuiper belt, mum. Farther in, I just don't have enough resolution to make out anything."

"That's good. That means they most likely won't have the resolution to see us, either."

Bonnie rose from her chair and stretched. They had been at General Quarters for the last hour, and it was draining for both her and her crew.

"Let's not get impatient at this point. We'll sit here for fourteen hours, just to make sure we have updated information on everything in-system. We can stand down from General Quarters, I think."

"Aye, mum." Luke pushed his screen and the announcement went out over the ship's speakers as well as their internal comms.

<SECURE FROM GENERAL QUARTERS. SECURE FROM GENERAL QUARTERS>

"Commander Powell, will you join me in my day cabin, please?"

"Aye, mum," said Luke. He followed Bonnie. In her cabin, Bonnie sat at her desk and faced Luke as he came in. He sat in front of her, wondering what this was all about.

Bonnie leaned forward as she spoke.

"I want to make sure we're clear about something, Luke. We're poking our head into the lion's den. I need to make sure I don't make any mistakes. So I'm counting on you for good advice and counsel as we go through this. If you see me about to screw something up, you tell me, and you tell me quick. Got it?"

Luke grinned. "Got it, mum."

"And in private, please just call me Bonnie, if you're OK with that."

"Bonnie it is."

"Now. How should we proceed?"

Luke rubbed his forehead, thinking.

"I would move into their Kuiper belt, and sit there for a couple of days to see if anything looks funny."

"My thought exactly. Then what? Assuming we don't see anything suspicious..."

"There's that Neptune -size planet - planet seven - with all the debris around it, sort of like a combination of our Saturn and Uranus. It looks like a failed ring system, or one that is disintegrating. I'd advance into that debris field and try to look like a rock for a couple of days, see what else we can find out."

"Good. So far, we're thinking exactly alike. That makes me feel better."

Bonnie rose from her desk, started pacing back and forth behind it.

"It's what comes next that brings us to the area of real risk. They'll have regular patrols around their home planet, commercial shipping moving in and out of the system, all sorts of activity close in - tugs, excursion boats, you name it. Once we get inside the seventh planet's orbit, we're vulnerable to being spotted by all of that."

"Yes. We'll need to be careful."

Bonnie sat back down at her chair.

"What else?"

"Nothing from my side."

There was a silence. Bonnie looked at him, just a bit too long.

"Luke," she began, then stopped.

"Yes?"

Bonnie had a strange look on her face. But suddenly it passed, like a cloud leaving the sun.

"Never mind."

"I'm your XO, Bonnie. I'm here to ensure your wishes are carried out for the safety of the ship and the completion of the mission. So anything at all is fair game. Lay it on me."

Bonnie shook her head.

"No, I'm sorry, Luke. Never mind."

"Ah."

Luke rose to leave.

Bonnie looked up at him.

Luke felt he was falling into those blazing green eyes again. Eyes that would take any man to his knees to make the woman behind them happy.

Finally he managed to speak again, his voice hoarse from the tension.

"If you need anything, Bonnie..."

Bonnie nodded slightly.

"I know where to find you..."

Luke turned and departed, leaving Bonnie alone.

She sat, her mind whirling with forbidden thoughts.

What am I thinking? It's stupid, it's crazy. Stop thinking it, woman! He's your XO! It can never happen!

You don't need a man. You don't need Jim, you don't need Luke.

You don't need anyone!

***

Tatiana wasn't sleeping when Norali came, but she was trying.

"Message from the men down the hall," Norali said.

Tatiana roused, sat up, and rubbed her eyes.

"Yes?"

"We've gotten final agreement from the men. They're in. They've elected some guy named Mikhail to be their Big Y."

"Big Y?"

Norali grinned hugely.

"Yeah. They think we should use code words for our leadership. They're afraid the Singheko will catch on and torture someone. So they're assigning code words. They assigned their leader the code word "Big Y".

"Whatever for? Where did they come up with that?"

"Think about it. Men don't have two X chromosomes; they have a Y chromosome instead. So Big Y."

"Oh," mused Tatiana. "I guess someone was a biologist. Well, OK. Whatever they want."

"Oh, it gets even better," said Norali. "They assigned you a code word too. Big X."

"Big X. And why am I Big X?"

Norali grinned from ear to ear.

"Because women have two X chromosomes. So Big X."

Tatiana was tired. Her head hurt. Day after day of boredom was taking its toll.

"God, I'm too tired to think through shit like that," complained Tatiana. "Whatever."

"Oh, and more news," added Norali. "One of the cages farther out has picked up a bit of the guards' lingo. Evidently they've got someone who's getting rather good at understanding them."

"So?"

"So they heard the guards talking. We're fifteen days out."

"Good," Tatiana said dully. "That's about what we estimated."

"Fifteen days to prepare."

"Plus a week before we attack," said Tatiana. "We give ourselves a week after arrival to get the lay of the land, find out their weaknesses, figure out where we can go, and then we move."

"So twenty-two days."

Tatiana nodded.

"Twenty-two days and we kick these bastards to hell and gone."

***

Two days later, the *Dragon* lurked inside the debris field of the seventh planet. Her engines were off and her systems at minimal power, idling.

Trying to look like just another rock in the disintegrating ring system of the big blue gas giant.

"Anything new?" Bonnie asked as she came onto the bridge, a few minutes before changeover from Third Watch to First Watch.

"No, mum," reported Commander Lirrassa. She rose quickly

to vacate the Captain's chair for Bonnie, her duties now over as OOD - Officer of the Deck.

"It's been a quiet night. Nothing new to report. We've got good readings on ship patterns for all ships leaving or entering the system. It seems they tend to avoid this area, probably because of all the debris around here."

"Excellent. Then we picked the right place to hide."

"Aye, mum."

Lt. Gibson came into the bridge. She walked to the Tactical console and stated, "Mr. Goodwin, you are relieved."

"I stand relieved," murmured Goodwin, giving up his chair.

Rachel Gibson had rapidly become one of Bonnie's favorite officers, especially at the Tac position. Only Commander Larissa could do a better job in the Tactical role. So Bonnie had ensured that Rachel was always on duty for First Watch, when Larissa was off watch.

As Lirrassa and Goodwin left the bridge, Lt. Commander Naditta entered, followed closely by Luke. Naditta took his seat at the Ops console, while Luke took his seat beside Bonnie in the XO chair.

Over the next minute, the remainder of First Watch came onto the bridge, and the rest of Third Watch departed.

When they were fully ready, Bonnie stood from her chair to address the bridge crew.

"Girls and boys, today we're going to advance farther into the system. This is the most dangerous part of our mission. I want everyone to remember our three highest priorities."

"One - don't get caught."

"Two - don't get caught."

"Three - don't get caught."

There was a titter of laughter across the bridge. Bonnie smiled.

"Seriously, however. Our priority is don't get caught. Our true second priority is to find out everything possible about the Singheko fleet and their home system. Let's try to accomplish both of those objectives and then pass our information on to the fleet safely."

There were nods and acknowledgments around the bridge.

"Lt. Gibson, can you plot the shipping lanes and military patrol patterns for me on the holo?"

"Aye, mum."

Bonnie sat back down and examined the holo. On the display, long streaks of light showed where the Singheko commercial shipping patterns and warship patrols had been plotted over the last few days.

"Luke, see that one spot well above the ecliptic…"

Bonnie pointed with a laser pointer that highlighted her target in the holo.

"…right there? I don't see any ships going near that point."

"I agree, mum. I think that's our best bet."

"Gibson? What do you think?"

"I agree, mum."

"Very good. Then advance us to that spot, please, Luke. Very quietly, very slowly, very carefully."

"Aye, mum."

Luke moved over to the Nav console where Chief Blocker was working. He watched over Blocker's shoulder, speaking quietly as they worked out a course. Finally, he clapped the Chief on the shoulder.

"Excellent," he said quietly. He turned to Bonnie.

"We're ready, Skipper."

Bonnie nodded.

"Execute."

Over the next several hours, the *Dragon* advanced slowly into the inner system of the Singheko. They started by moving almost straight up, to get well out of the ecliptic. Given their black-as-coal exterior and their stealth systems, they felt reasonably confident they would not be detected in their initial move.

It took most of the day to get to the position they wanted, but nobody left the bridge. It was a moment of high tension. After they had reached a position above the ecliptic, they moved diagonally toward the Singheko home planet, still rising above the line of the planets.

If the Singheko possessed better sensors than expected, this was the time they would find out. And they might have to run for their lives at any moment.

Finally, ten hours later, they reached the point selected. So far, there was no indication the Singheko had detected them.

Bonnie directed the engines to standby and all systems idled. Only passive sensors remained powered up.

And now, from this closer vantage point, they could clearly see warships in their parking orbits around the home planet and its two moons.

There was a lot of traffic. Their Nidarian database - copied from the *Merkkessa* - showed the Singheko had six star systems in their budding Empire at this point, scattered across a sphere three hundred light years in diameter.

That was a lot of commerce moving back and forth.

And a lot of warships to keep it under control.

***

It was just minutes before dawn, ship time.

Tatiana had convinced the women to develop a kind of normalcy in their lives. When the lights came on in the morning, they called it dawn.

"We're not going to become animals," she told them. "That's exactly what they want. They want us to forget everything about our civilized lives and become rank animals, following them like a camel on a string."

"Well, we're not doing it. We'll keep a schedule. We'll exercise, to keep our bodies fit. We'll have classes, to teach those that need teaching. If we must do it naked and afraid, then that's what we'll do. But we don't give in."

And that was exactly what they had done. The process had spread to other cages; now thousands of people woke up each morning and started calisthenics and yoga.

They started classes for the less educated, teaching verbally.

They performed a type of medical clinic - those who were

sick were treated by those with medical training. Word would be passed from cage to cage regarding the symptoms, and then word would come back from the few trained medical personnel in some distant cage regarding a recommended course of action.

They didn't have medications, of course. But they could do other things. They learned to isolate those with anything that seemed contagious to one corner of the cage and allow only a few designated caregivers to approach them. And they tried other things, such as massage for those who were in pain, using their hands and fingers to distract them and re-focus them on getting well.

It was primitive. But it was something.

Thus the time had passed.

Sonja had been quiet for days, recovering from her rough handling by Marta. She avoided Tatiana and Marta and the rest of the command team, staying as far away from them as possible. Several of her gang had abandoned her after Marta had given them warning of the dire consequences of fighting Tatiana's plans.

But Sonja had not given up. She had recruited new gang members, quietly, out of sight and hearing of Tatiana's team.

And it was just minutes before dawn, ship time, when Sonja made her second attack.

Tatiana was sleeping in her usual place in the corner of the cage. Marta and Norali were next to her, and the rest of the team was spread out around her in a group. They had developed the habit of sleeping together, in case of another attack.

And Tatiana had taken one other precaution, hidden from Sonja and the rest of the women in the cage.

She gave the short piece of wire to Marta every night when they lay down to sleep. Their only real weapon.

She still carried it during the day, curled in one hand or the other, like a badge of office.

But at night, she secretly slipped the small weapon to Marta as they went to sleep. They were both sure that Sonja would try once more to take control of the cage.

And logically, Sonja would go for the wire - the only weapon in the cage.

Tatiana came half-awake as she heard a rustling in the cage, a noise, something unexpected.

Then a rush of women struck, all at once. At least three of them ran over the bodies of others directly to Tatiana.

Suddenly she was pressed down by the weight of them, one on each side sprawled across her hands, digging for the wire, while the other sat on her chest.

Sonja.

And then Sonja had her fingers around Tatiana's neck, choking her. Sonja's voice snarled, her fingers locked around Tatiana's throat.

"Not so tough now, are you bitch? Not so tough when you don't have your bitch Marta to back you up..."

Tatiana could hear a terrific commotion going on around her, and guessed that at least five women were on Marta, holding her down and trying to control her long enough for Sonja to get the wire.

"Give me the wire, bitch, or I'll choke you to death."

Tatiana could feel the two women on each side of her digging at her fists, trying to open them to get to the wire they thought she had.

She kept her fists closed, hoping they would continue to think she had it.

But Sonja was choking her out. In a few more seconds, she'd be unconscious.

She tried to talk, but she couldn't get enough air to say anything. She could see bright lights in her eyes, lights that shouldn't be there.

She needed oxygen or she was going to die.

Suddenly she heard a scream close by, and then another.

"Marta's got the damn wire!" shouted one of Sonja's companions. "Look out!"

Then another scream.

Tatiana felt Sonja turn, try to look behind her in the darkness. Sonja's hands relaxed a bit on Tatiana's throat. Tatiana was able to gasp in a breath.

Then she bucked for all she was worth, to throw Sonja off her. It partially worked; Sonja fell to one side, not completely off, but giving Tatiana a bit of leeway - a little bit of room to work.

Tatiana bucked again, twisting, and knocked Sonja's arms away, then pushed her to one side.

Grabbing blindly in the dark where she guessed Sonja's head was, she found it. Twisting as hard as she could, she wrenched Sonja's head hard, causing a loud scream.

Then she slid her hands down to Sonja's neck and got her arm around it from the back.

Now the tables were turned. She was behind Sonja, her arm wrapped around the bigger woman's neck. Tatiana squeezed as hard as she could. The bigger woman slapped at her, pounded her with a fist, twisted and turned trying to get away.

Tatiana held on for dear life. There was a tremendous commotion going on around her as the battle raged. She could hear screams, thumps, slaps, cursing. The occasional body would slam against the cage wall or fall to the floor.

"Tat! Where are you?" she heard Marta from nearby.

"Right here," yelled Tatiana. "I've got Sonja. Help me!"

She felt a hand touch her back, then move quickly up to her shoulder. The hand tapped her twice.

"Is that you?"

"That's me," grunted Tatiana, Sonja flopping around in her arms like a fish on a line.

Sonja was gradually weakening as Tatiana squeezed.

"I think I've got her under control. Just keep the rest of them off me," Tatiana grunted.

"You got it," said Marta.

Tatiana felt Marta turn, press her back against Tatiana's in the dark. They were back to back now. Thumps and bumps told her Marta was still fending off attacks, but they seemed to be weakening.

Tatiana felt Sonja go limp at last. Unconscious.

"She's out," she said to Marta over her shoulder. "Sonja's out."

Marta yelled loudly.

"Give it up! We've got Sonja choked out. Most of your gang is down now. You can't win!"

It got suddenly quiet.

And the lights came on.

Tatiana found herself with Sonja still in her arm, the woman limp, her eyes closed. She let go, letting Sonja's unconscious body slump to one side.

Standing up, Tatiana looked around.

Bodies lay everywhere, some unconscious, some moaning. Blood was all over the floor - the evidence of Marta's use of the wire.

With a groan, Marta stood up beside Tatiana. Tatiana looked at her.

"You OK?"

Marta grinned. Blood oozed down her face from a scalp wound. Scratches were evident all over her face and arms. She was bruised all over her body and covered in blood.

Not much of it was her own.

"Never better," Marta replied, smiling.

Tatiana noticed that Norali was also standing now. She also had bruises all over her. One of her eyes was blackening, but she was otherwise intact.

"Norali. Can you get a triage station going?

Norali nodded and called to several of their cohort nearby who looked functional. They started dragging unconscious females to a point in the back of the cage near the water fountains.

Those who could still walk got up and slowly moved back to the same point. Other women started to take care of them, washing off the blood, resetting broken fingers, doing the best they could under the conditions.

Tatiana stared down at Sonja. She felt Marta come up beside her.

"You know what we have to do, don't you, boss?" asked Marta.

Tatiana sighed.

"I know. But I don't have to like it."

7 - DERIKO

"I've changed my mind about Imogen."

"What? What do you mean?"

"It's getting real now. We'll be launching for Singheko tomorrow. Jim..."

Rita looked up at him, tears in her eyes.

"...I can't take her into harm's way. We have to leave her with Gillian when we go."

Jim sat down beside her and placed a hand on her back, giving her a slight rub.

"I know you're right. I know it's the best thing for her. But - I'll miss her so much."

"Not as much as I will. But I've realized, I just can't take her into a campaign. It makes no sense."

Jim nodded glumly.

"I've known all along that you'd come to this decision. So I'm not surprised. But I'm going to miss the little bug."

"Will you take her down to Gillian tomorrow morning? Before I change my mind again?"

Jim leaned over, wrapped her in his arms.

"Admiral Rita Page, did I ever tell you what a wonderful mother you are?"

Rita folded into him.

"I'm so tired, Jim. So tired. There's so much to do."

"Just rest, darling. Just lay down, rest, let the Fleet take care of itself for a while."

Jim held her for minutes until she closed her eyes and slept. Watching her sleep, he realized that all doubts had left his mind.

This is the woman I love. There will never be another.

Carefully, he disengaged from her and went to the hatch, turned out the light, and left.

***

"The court will come to order."

Tatiana stood at the back of the cage, surrounded by her command team.

In front of her was a small space. Beyond the space, six women held Sonja locked in their grip.

With three on each side, they kept Sonja's arms pinned up behind her, holding her immovable. Occasionally she would struggle, but even with her strength she couldn't break free from that many women.

In front of the somber scene playing out in the back of the cage, the rest of the women moved randomly back and forth, screening the back of the cage from the view of the front corridor.

The next cage beside theirs was also watching, hanging on every word. A low mutter could be heard from the far side of it as communicators reported everything down the line to other cages.

"Sonja Gorlukovich, you have been found guilty by this court of treason and sentenced to death. Do you have any last words?"

"Go fuck yourself, bitch!" snarled Sonja.

"Very well. Sentence will be carried out."

Tatiana looked at a woman standing beside her, named Anna. Anna and her daughter had been badly injured in the fight. Her daughter was still unconscious in a corner of the room, suffering from a severe concussion. It was not assured she would recover.

They had thought to draw lots for the execution duties. But Anna had insisted it was hers to do - for what Sonja had done to her daughter.

Now Anna rose to her feet and stalked to Sonja. She moved in behind Sonja, out of her sight, and waited, looking at

Tatiana.

Tatiana stood up and raised her voice slightly, so that it could be heard by everyone in the cage.

"I never wanted it to come to this. I'm heartbroken that it has. I value life above all else - except freedom."

"But make no mistake about it, people - freedom is at stake here."

Tatiana paced, restless, trying to think how she could get through to those who had not yet come over to her movement.

"If Sonja had won - if she had taken over - then have no doubt in your mind. She would have collaborated with the Singheko, for whatever she could gain. She already said as much to members of her gang. They were planning to tell the enemy about our plans, in return for becoming tyrants over us."

Tatiana stopped pacing. She gazed around the room.

"Ask yourself. What is most likely in front of us?"

There was a mutter around the room.

"Most likely, death. These Singheko look at us as animals. They'll treat us as animals. They'll work us 'til we die. There is no doubt in my mind of that fact."

"So. If death is inevitable, why not fight for life? There is no chance whatsoever if we don't fight. They'll work us 'til we die.

"But if we fight - we have a chance. It's a small one, I grant you. But any small chance is better than no chance at all."

Tatiana turned and looked at Sonja.

"Sonja elected to fight us. She was given a warning weeks ago, but she ignored it. She knew the penalty. She chose to attack us again. And she intended to turn us in to the Singheko for her own advantage."

Tatiana turned back to the women in the cage.

"The penalty for treason is death."

Tatiana looked back at Anna and nodded.

Anna reached to Sonja's neck and put her arm around it, then squeezed, shutting off Sonja's air.

Sonja twisted, fighting, grunting, trying with all her power to break free. The women surrounding her managed to hold her.

It was an ugly death. It took a couple of minutes for Sonja to finally go limp. When she did, the other women let her sink to the floor. Still Anna held on, keeping her air shut off for another five minutes to be sure she was dead.

Finally, a woman checking Sonja's pulse nodded, and Anna let go.

One of the other women stepped up to Anna and led her away. Anna moved back to her unconscious daughter and sank down beside her, crying.

Marta waved to two of the team, who took Sonja's body and dragged it to the front of the cage, by the door.

Now Marta turned to another group of women, huddled in the other corner, guarded by a group from Tatiana's team. Marta stalked to them and glared at them.

"You have one and only one choice, folks. Give up your idea of taking over - or follow Sonja's path. Remember what you saw today when you make your choice."

Marta nodded to the women guarding the prisoners.

"Let them go."

The guards stepped back, allowing the bruised and battered remnants of Sonja's gang to flow back into the general population.

Marta returned to Tatiana, who had moved to the water fountains in the back of the cage and was splashing water on her face.

Marta could see she was crying.

***

Five days later, the *Merkkessa* plowed through six-space, already 167 light years from Earth on her way to Singheko. Rita came into her briefing room, electronic tablet in hand.

Waiting at her briefing table were Captain Bekerose and her newly promoted Flag Aide, Captain Dallitta.

And Jim.

"At ease, folks," said Rita. She sat, and everyone followed

suit.

"Captain Bekerose. How are you this fine morning?" asked Rita.

"I am excellent as always, Admiral," Bekerose answered. "Except for one thing."

"And that would be the fact the *Corresse* did not return before our departure, and is overdue by forty-four days now, correct?"

Bekerose sighed, a very human sound.

"Sometimes I wonder why I even bother, milady. All I ever do is tell you things you already know."

Rita smiled.

"Bekerose, you are my right hand. Don't ever think otherwise."

"Thank you, milady. But I still hope to someday bring you news you haven't already heard."

"Be careful what you wish for, Captain. So what do you think? Why didn't the *Corresse* return on time?"

"It can only be bad news, milady. Either she ran into technical difficulties - which I doubt - or Garatella prevented her return - which is my feeling."

"Yes," nodded Rita. "Mine as well. Garatella has always had some hidden agenda with us humans. Despite giving us this fleet, I believe he is still playing us for his own ends. Now he has the designs for the fast stardrive, and the *Corresse* to use as a model. What do you think he'll do next?"

"Whatever it is, milady, it will be good for Garatella, but not necessarily good for Earth."

"Do you think he would go so far as to throw us to the wolves? Sit on the sidelines and let the Singheko come in and take us?"

"He very well might do that, milady, if he thought it was to his advantage. I cannot be sure, though. I wish we could contact Arteveld."

"Could we send a corvette - say, the *Banjala* - and have them sneak into the system, find out what's going on?"

"Not a chance, milady. Garatella will have the Nidarian system buttoned up tight. He knows the Singheko are constantly sneaking around, trying to find any weakness in his defenses there. And he'd also expect you to try something like that. So...no. I don't think there's any point in that."

"How about sending a corvette in to a position just short of the system and trying to work a fighter in without detection?"

"I would argue against it, milady. I think you would just end up losing both the fighter and the corvette. If Garatella is up to something, he'll be prepared for all those scenarios."

Rita sighed.

"Very well. We'll continue to Singheko and fight that battle first. If nothing else, perhaps that will force Garatella to come out in the open."

"Yes, milady."

Rita sat for a moment, deep in thought.

If Garatella is playing us false...if he decides to come in on the side of the Singheko...

Surely not...

Surely Garatella would recognize the danger of the Singheko in the long run...

Coming out of her reverie, she looked around the table.

"What else, folks?"

Bekerose glanced at his tablet. "We're due to receive *Dragon*'s intel via *Kaimina* at point M-275 in 6 days. Assuming *Dragon* makes her rendezvous, we'll have enough to make a preliminary plan of attack."

Rita nodded slowly.

"Then let's hope *Dragon* makes her date."

***

High above the planet Deriko in the Singheko system, Bonnie Page stepped on to the bridge.

"What's the count now?" she asked. It was the beginning of the fifteenth day.

"We've got four battlecruisers, eight cruisers, fourteen destroyers, eight corvettes and a dozen other small boys."

Bonnie sighed heavily.

"And that doesn't count what may be off on other missions or in other systems elsewhere."

"Aye, mum. They are definitely building up their fleet for a major expansion."

"Well, that fits with what Garatella told us back at Sanctuary. He said they wanted to create an empire in the Arm, and it certainly looks like they're well on their way."

Luke waved a hand at the holo, where all the Singheko ships were red icons surrounding the planets and moons of their anchorage.

"There's no way we can take on a fleet that size in the near term."

"Agreed. But we found out what we need to know. Let's head for our rendezvous point and get this intel back to Admiral Page."

"Aye, mum. Are you ready to depart?"

"Yes, I think so. We've collected ELINT for weeks and mapped every warship in the system. I don't see that there's anything left for us to do here, do you?"

"No, I agree. Time to go."

"Very good. Plot us a course to get out of here and let's go meet the *Kaimina*."

Bonnie rose to go to her day cabin.

"We have a new type of ship entering the system, mum!" called Rachel. "One of those big slave ships!"

Quickly, Bonnie sat back in her chair.

"Where?"

Rachel highlighted in the holo with a laser pointer.

"Just entering the system, mum. Well below the ecliptic, on a course for the fourth planet."

Bonnie looked at Luke. She could see the stress and tension in Luke's face. She spoke quietly, so that only he could hear.

"I'm sorry, Luke. I forgot what day it was."

"That's OK, Skipper. No worries."

"No. I should have remembered. Today is the estimated time

of arrival for the first batch of slave ships that left Earth."

Bonnie wheeled back to the holo, watching the vector shown by the AI. Even as she watched, another of the big pentagon-shaped slave ships entered the system.

"Commander, there's no way to know which ship is hers. These could be any of the eight that left Earth before we smashed their fleet."

Luke managed a wan smile.

"I know, Skipper."

"And if that is Tatiana, we'll find her and rescue her. But not now. First, we work our plan. Then we have to kick some Singheko butt."

Bonnie looked over at Luke. The pain on his face was all too evident.

"Then we'll go get Tatiana."

Luke nodded, unable to speak. His face worked.

Bonnie looked back at the holo.

"Still, I want to stay here and see where that ship goes. We'll watch it and see what they do. Let's take a chance. Rachel, send a drone to shadow that first ship so we can get a closer look."

***

The planet was a lot like Mars.

If Mars was quite a bit larger, with an oxygen/nitrogen atmosphere that was thin but breathable by human standards.

If Mars had vast steppes covered in tall grass, with small rivers coursing out of the mountains onto the plains.

If Mars was home to nearly half a million slaves.

The Singheko called the planet Deriko.

The slaves there called it Hell, in whatever version of Hell existed in their respective language. There were many species present on the planet. The Singheko, of course - huge seven-foot-tall slavemasters, looking like evolved, upright lions, armed to the teeth with stun guns, shock sticks, clubs, whips, rifles, pistols, and anything else they felt useful in managing their different species of slave labor.

The Taegu - a species not too different from the Nidarians.

Smaller than humans, but much like them, with almost no visible nose. They were clearly a sister race to the Nidarians at some point in their evolution. But the Taegu were not protected by the cease-fire agreement in place between Singheko and Nidaria - so the Singheko had attacked them and taken thousands of slaves away from their home planet.

The Bagrami - a species descended from something that, to a human, would have looked like a bear. And they still looked a bit like bears. Evolution had taken away their claws and fangs, reduced the size of their muzzles, taken away most of the hair from their bodies. And left them a bit slow-moving, compared to the Taegu.

And now the Humans.

Tatiana felt a slight bump and knew they were down on the planet. It was not a surprise; from overhearing the guards talk, they were well aware of the scheduled landing.

The huge slave ship landed beside a large complex. The guards came out and set down ramps leading to large holding pens.

Then it was unloading time.

They unloaded the women first. Tatiana had expected it; she knew they would want the women locked away safely before they dealt with the men.

As it happened, they started on her end of the cage row. She heard a clang and saw bright light pouring in on the other side of the two cages next to theirs, as the guards opened a hatch to the outside. A breath of cold air hit them as the freezing atmosphere of Deriko poured into the ship.

Tatiana watched as the women were marched out of the second cage down the hall from her, the one nearest the exit hatch. The guards rousted the women out, using their shock sticks on any that were slow, ill, or injured.

Then the next cage went, shuffling toward the band of light streaming in through the open hatch, leading to an unknown fate.

Then it was their turn. The door to the cage clanged open

and Tatiana led them out, now only 92 strong.

Eight women from their cage had died during the trip.

Tatiana marched boldly forward, leading the rest of them toward the bright light of day pouring in through the hatch.

It didn't matter what was outside; getting out of this ship of the damned was all she cared about now.

Exiting the hatch, the light was too bright for her eyes. She had to slap her hand over, blocking out the light, making a tiny crack between her fingers so she could see to continue down the ramp.

In front, she saw women fall to the ground, too weak or sick to continue. The Singheko guards used shock sticks to get them up and moving again.

Tatiana stopped to help one, an older woman, and got her to her feet, helping her down the ramp. Together they stepped off the ramp into the holding pen at the bottom.

At the other end of the holding pen, there were two exits. A sturdy pipe fence marked out lanes leading to different destinations.

The left lane led to the huge building, which Tatiana could guess was the processing facility for incoming slave labor.

The other path - on the right side - appeared to lead around the corner of the building, out of sight.

Watching, she noted the guards separated out the sick or injured into the second path. They were forced through the right exit, down the lane and around the corner of the building.

She knew what was happening. The sick and weak would disappear, never to be seen again. The Singheko didn't need them.

Holding the ill woman next to her tightly, she whispered into her ear.

"I'll help you to the exit. When we get there, make sure you stand straight and look strong. Go for the left exit. Don't let them send you to the right."

The woman nodded. They moved slowly, shuffling along, as

the guards processed them.

It was bone-chilling cold. Tatiana guessed it was around 40 degrees Fahrenheit - about 5 degrees Celsius. They were still naked, as they had been for the entire trip. Everyone was shivering uncontrollably.

Finally they reached the exits. Tatiana supported the woman beside her until the last moment. As they came up to the sorting point, she whispered to her one last time.

"Remember! Look strong! Look confident!"

Then Tatiana let her go. The woman straightened up, squared her shoulders. The Singheko guards glanced at her, and waved her to the left, as they did for Tatiana.

As soon as they were past the sorting point, Marta and the rest of Tatiana's cadre fell in close behind, blocking the view of the guards. The woman collapsed back into Tatiana's arms. Tatiana felt Marta come up behind her and take the woman from her.

Marta was muttering under her breath.

"I don't know why you take these risks. There'll be dozens of women like this, maybe hundreds. You can't save them all," Marta complained.

"I can save one," said Tatiana.

***

Dragon stayed in place for another day. From their drone feed, they watched as thousands of humans were unloaded from the ship and moved into a large complex on the surface of the planet.

"That building isn't big enough to hold all of them," remarked Luke. "There must be an underground facility there."

"I wonder...," mused Bonnie. "What do you think they're doing under there?"

"Keeping something well hidden," replied Luke.

"But why? Why build an underground complex? Why not just build it on the surface? There's enough atmosphere."

"Who knows? Probably because it's easier to control the

slaves. Keeping that many slaves on the surface would be a nightmare for control. But underground - where can they go?"

Bonnie grimaced.

"Mum!" called Rachel. "Part of that fleet at Ridendo is moving out!"

Bonnie and Luke spun to look at the holotank. Bonnie exercised a control on her seat console, and the holotank magnified its view to zoom in on the third planet.

The enemy ships were so far away it was hard to see the actual movement. But the AI painted arrow-shaped vectors in front of them, showing their projected tracks, and faint trails behind them showing their wake.

Clearly, a significant part of the fleet was moving out.

"We'll stay here until we see where they're going," said Bonnie.

"Aye, mum," agreed Luke.

They watched the large fleet's movement until it reached the mass limit and sank out, disappearing from view.

"Final count of the departing fleet - two battlecruisers, four cruisers, eight destroyers, four corvettes and two supply ships. That right?" asked Bonnie.

"Aye, mum," agreed Rachel.

"And we've got a clear recording of their outbound vector?"

"Aye, mum, it's all recorded."

"How many warships left behind in the system now?"

"Two battlecruisers, four cruisers, six destroyers, four corvettes, mum. That'll be the Home Fleet - Admiral Zukra."

Luke looked at Bonnie.

"That certainly evens the odds a bit," he said.

"Doesn't it…OK, XO, let's blow this joint."

Luke managed a smile; the first Bonnie had seen since the slave ship entered the system. He turned to Chief Blocker at the Nav console.

"Chief, lay in a course for our rendezvous with the *Kaimina*, and get us the hell out of Dodge. We've got places to go and people to see."

***

Hours later, Bonnie tried to sleep.

Their journey to meet the *Kaimina* for intel exchange would take 24 hours. She was way overdue for a sleep cycle.

But sleep wouldn't come. Jim was haunting her thoughts again.

She remembered.

She remembered the sound of his voice.

His skin on hers. The heat of his body.

The touch of his hands...

She shuddered as the delicious memories overtook her, driving her farther and farther away from sleep.

I must stop doing this. I must stop thinking about him. He's gone. He made his choice.

Or did I make it for him? When I sent him that letter, did I push him to Rita?

Well, even if I did...it was for the best.

Let it go, Bonnie girl. Let him go. You did what was right.

Lying in her bunk, Bonnie opened her eyes and stared at the darkness.

But God, I miss him.

Rising from the bunk, she went to her desk and opened the bottom drawer.

Taking out a bottle, she poured herself a stiff drink. Knocking it down, she poured another and started that one more slowly.

Leaning back in her chair, she stared through the darkness at the dim glow of LED lights on the various displays and monitors in her cabin.

I need a distraction.

And with that, the thought of Luke came to her mind before she could stop it.

No, no, no! Don't even go there!

But it was too late. Her mind was off to the races.

She thought about his long, lean body. His chiseled face, his flashing blue eyes.

...the smell of him when he was close to her.

Stop it! He's your XO!

But the thoughts wouldn't stop coming. And as the whiskey began to take effect, her resistance faded away.

I'm only human.

If I only think about it, but don't do it...that doesn't break the rules, does it?

And as the whiskey in the glass got lower and lower, Captain Bonnie Page grew closer and closer to human as she let herself think about exactly what she would do with the long, lean body of her XO.

8 - FACTORY

The Singheko forced them through the processing center. Their heads were roughly shaved by creatures that - to Tatiana - looked like the Nidarians she had seen on Earth videos.

"Nidarian?" she whispered to the one cutting her hair, hoping he might understand the word.

The creature shook his head.

"Taegu," he whispered back, glancing around to make sure no Singheko were nearby.

Interesting, thought Tatiana. *They look like Nidarians. But not.*

Then they were pushed along, into a long hallway where they were issued clothing - a rough tunic, coarse trousers, plastic shoes that reminded her of something a child of Earth would wear.

The Singheko kept them moving. As they neared the end of the building, a long ramp led downward.

They were going underground.

It was a long march. Tatiana started counting her steps. She wanted to start mapping out the facility in her mind.

After the first 500 meters, the route split into multiple tunnels, splayed out in every direction, like starfish arms. They were directed to a tunnel leading to the far right.

Then they passed row after row of cages, identical to the ones on the ship. The first several hundred cages were empty.

After another kilometer, they were stopped and pushed into cages, one hundred per cage.

Tatiana immediately gathered her cadre around her in the back of the cage and started planning.

"The first thing we do is re-establish communications," Tatiana reminded them. "Get in touch with the other cages. Map out where everybody ended up. Then I want to relocate so we are next to Big Y."

"Relocate?" asked one of the women. "How do we do that?"

Marta grinned.

"Hell, these idiots can't tell us apart. We just go out of this cage in the morning and go back into a different cage in the evening. They'll never know the difference."

***

At 0600 hours next morning, the guards rousted them out. They were marched to a large auditorium of sorts, although there were no chairs. There were about two thousand of them, Tatiana estimated, a mixture of men and women. She had no idea where the rest of the humans were.

She wondered if Mikhail was in this group. She looked around, but of course she had never met him. She had no way of recognizing him.

A Taegu, like the one who had cut her hair, stood on a stage at the front.

He spoke in broken but understandable Ukrainian.

"You work. You build. This is factory. You build well. If you no do well, you die. If you fight, you die. If you get sick, you die. If you no work, you die. No questions. Now go work."

The Taegu turned and departed the stage. Their Singheko guards then pushed them out of the auditorium and down a long corridor into a factory. Assembly lines stretched into the distance for what looked like forever.

Tatiana was shoved roughly into a position on the assembly line. She had managed to bring the woman she had saved yesterday - Alina - with her, keeping her safe. Now Alina was directly across from her, on the other side of a suspended conveyor that hung above them. On Tatiana's left was Marta, and to her right the rest of her command team.

A horde of Taegu entered the building, spreading out and taking positions behind them. There was one Taegu for every two to three humans. They lined up behind the humans and waited.

The overhead conveyor clanked and started moving. Far in the distance, Tatiana could see activity beginning. Something appeared on the conveyor, moving toward them.

The Taegu behind her came closer, between her and Marta.

"You take this..." He pointed to a hose and nozzle hanging from an overhead hook.

"...you put in warhead, there..."

He pointed down the line. Now Tatiana could see a long line of bullet-shaped objects approaching, suspended from the overhead conveyor.

Missile warheads.

She glanced over at Marta.

Marta shook her head in dismay.

"Pouring explosives into missile warheads. This can't be good," she grunted.

"No talk!" yelled the Taegu. "You talk, Singheko come, you die! Put in warhead! No mistakes! You mistake, we all die!"

Tatiana nodded at the creature, reached up, pulled down the dispenser nozzle, and waited. The warheads moved down the assembly line toward them. Tatiana saw many Taegu to her left moving up to the assembly line, showing the humans what to do.

Then the first empty warhead arrived in front of Marta. Their own personal Taegu came up beside Marta and showed her how to insert the nozzle, filling the warhead to a marked line.

Then the Taegu pushed the warhead away.

When it was pushed, it automatically moved to the other side of the overhead conveyor, where another woman stood. Another Taegu coached the other woman to insert a dummy safety plug into the nose of the warhead and use a wrench to tighten it.

Another warhead came down the line, arriving in front of Tatiana. The Taegu moved to Tatiana and repeated the lesson, showing her how to insert the nozzle, fill the warhead, and push it to the other side of the conveyor, where Alina was coached to put in the safety plug.

Then Tatiana's Taegu coach stepped back. More of the warheads came down the line at them. Then both Marta and Tatiana had warheads in front of them, the gaping holes in the noses waiting for the liquid explosive.

Tatiana inserted her nozzle and filled the warhead to the line. She pushed, and the warhead moved to the other side of the conveyor, to Alina.

Alina inserted the plug and tightened it. The warhead moved on.

And then another warhead was in front of Tatiana, and she had to rush to fill it.

And then another, and another. It became a grind, a race to survive. The warheads came faster and faster as the day wore on.

She and Marta were a bit faster than some of the others, but not by much. They both knew the slightest mistake would screw up the assembly line.

And they were right. A woman a dozen paces down from them made a mistake, dropping her nozzle on the floor, letting liquid explosive leak out on the concrete.

The sound of the nozzle hitting the floor caused a collective gasp that ran through the entire area, an exhalation of breath from the humans - and the Taegu, still standing behind them, watching.

There was a loud pop.

The head of the woman who had dropped the nozzle exploded, disappearing from her body. One second it was there. Then it wasn't.

Her body collapsed to the floor, blood spurting from her neck in a gush of horror.

On the catwalks overlooking the factory floor, a trail of smoke curled from the rifle barrel of one of the Singheko guards.

Two of the bear-like creatures called Bagrami appeared from a side corridor, grabbed the body, and dragged it away.

Quickly, one of the Taegu stepped up and took the empty spot where, seconds before, a human female had been working.

And the assembly line moved on.

***

After another day in the factory, Tatiana and her organization relocated themselves to the cage at the end of the women's section, next to the men.

It was as Marta had predicted. The Singheko - and for that matter, the Taegu - couldn't really tell them apart.

So in the morning, they left their cage for the factory as usual.

At the end of the day, as they were taken down the hall to return, they casually exchanged places with a group of women from the other cage.

And that was it. Now they were next to the men, separated only by a short corridor leading to an equipment room.

Mikhail and his unit had also relocated, so he was next to Tatiana's cage.

They stared at each other from eight feet away, separated only by the two layers of wire between them.

"Hello, Big Y," said Tatiana.

"Hello yourself, Big X," grinned Mikhail.

***

"We've got a problem," said Mikhail.

He and Tatiana had learned they were the only people in the two cages who could speak French.

Not good French, maybe, but enough to communicate. It allowed them to speak without using so much code. There were always Taegu collaborators walking by, or the occasional Bagrami maintenance workers. Sometimes there were Singheko guards, patrolling the corridors in the evenings. They didn't know how much the enemy could understand, so they had developed codes to use for communication.

But when Tatiana and Mikhail spoke French, they didn't feel the need to use the codes.

"Only one problem?" quipped Tatiana quietly.

It was late, after lights out. She lay on the floor against the wire, as close to Mikhail as she could get. He was in a similar position in his cage, eight feet away. They spoke just loudly enough for the other to hear.

"Yeah, well, only one big one. I've got a breakaway group forming up, just like yours with Sonja. They say we're moving too slow. They want to attack immediately."

"To what end?" asked Tatiana. "What are they going to do, steal a slave ship and slowly ascend into the sky, while a fleet of Singheko warships pounds them into parts and pieces?"

"No; they want to take over the processing center. They think they can hold the building long enough to free the rest of the slaves. They think the Taegu and the Bagrami will come in with them. Then they can negotiate with the Singheko for safe passage off the planet."

"God, they are stupid," said Tatiana. "First of all, the Taegu won't come in with them, they're scared shitless of the Singheko. Neither will the Bagrami. And secondly, they won't be able to free more than a few thousand before the Singheko are all over them. And third, the Singheko won't negotiate with them. They'll just kill them and go to lunch. It's stupid."

"I know. I've told them until I'm blue in the face. But they won't listen."

"Well, there's nothing we can do about it. Nothing that I can see. Let them take their best shot. At least we'll learn something about the Singheko response."

"God, I hate it. So many will die."

"I know. Why don't you make one more attempt to talk them off the ledge?"

"I will. I'll let you know how it goes."

There was a short silence. But Tatiana wasn't yet sleepy.

"What did you do…you know, before?" she asked.

"I was a colonel in the air force," Mikhail replied.

"How on Earth did a colonel end up in prison?"

Tatiana heard a short laugh from across the corridor.

"Got crosswise of the wrong politician. You?"

"Got crosswise of the wrong boyfriend."

Mikhail laughed again, softly in the darkness.

"I heard your father was a big shot in the Royal Navy."

There was a long silence.

Mikhail realized he had hit a nerve.

"Sorry, Big X. Forget I said that."

"No, it's OK. It just hit me hard for a second. I wonder where he is now, you know? Probably on some ship, sailing around the world, wondering where I am."

"Sorry I brought it up. I know it hurts to think about home."

"Did you have anyone...back there?"

"No. My wife died a few years ago. Car wreck. I threw myself into my work after that."

"Yeah. Wish I'd done that when my mother died. But I threw myself into drugs and parties instead. That was a mistake."

"Well..."

Another silence.

"...you have a new life now. Make the best of it."

Tatiana was quiet for a long time. Finally, she spoke.

"We can't win, you know," she said softly.

"I know," came the reply from the darkness. "Does it matter?"

Tatiana shook her head, even though she knew he couldn't see it.

"No. We'll kill as many as we can, then they'll kill us. But it's what I have to do."

***

Thirty-four light years from the Singheko home system, the corvette *Kaimina* waited patiently. Captain Pojjayan's orders were clear.

Go to the first rendezvous point and wait for the Dragon. *Collect the intel. Return it to the second rendezvous point and meet the* Merkkessa *to transfer the intel.*

He had been waiting patiently for five days now. The rendezvous was scheduled for this morning - ship time - but he had arrived early in case the *Dragon* needed assistance.

Sitting in his command chair on the bridge, Pojjayan rubbed his forehead.

He enjoyed commanding the *Kaimina*, but he had to admit corvette duty could be boring at times.

Go here. Collect that. Go there. Bring that.

On the other hand, nobody was shooting at him.

That's a plus, he thought.

The Tactical Officer made a call.

"Contact! Blind call from the *Dragon*, codes match!"

Pojjayan lifted a hand, spoke.

"Very good. Respond with our code. Maintain battle stations until we're positive of ID."

"Aye, sir."

A few seconds later, the Comm officer spoke again.

"IFF signal, 400 k-klicks, shows as the *Dragon*!"

"Good. Bring up our IFF, drop our stealth."

"Aye, sir."

The *Dragon* became visible in the holo as both ships dropped their stealth and turned on their identification beacons.

"Damn, her stealth is good," exclaimed the Tactical Officer. "She was right in front of us and I never saw her."

"They knew what they were doing when that ship was built. It's hard to accept - but here we are two thousand years later, and we still can't build them that well," mused Pojjayan.

"Yes, sir," said Tac. "I guess that's why she got the scouting mission."

"Yes," agreed Pojjayan absent-mindedly. "Bring us alongside and let's prepare to go over."

Moving next to *Dragon*, Pojjayan and his XO boarded a shuttle and went across to the larger ship. Once on board, they were guided to Bonnie's wardroom. Bonnie stood at the head of the table as they entered.

"Welcome, gentlemen," she spoke in Nidarian, giving them

the Nidarian hand-touch as they came in and sat at the table. "Glad to see you. It's been a bit lonely out here."

Pojjayan smiled.

"I'm sure. Were there a lot of Singheko in the system?"

"Lots of them," answered Bonnie. "But not so many now. Let me show you."

She turned on a holo over the table and pointed out the shipping lanes and military patrol patterns to them.

Then she showed them the large fleet that had departed the system. And the vector they took out of the system.

"Captain Pojjayan, where do you think they're headed?"

Pojjayan squinted at the vector on the holo.

"Dekanna, I think," he replied.

Bonnie nodded in agreement.

"That's our thought as well. We've looked at the data, and we think that's the most logical explanation of what we see. That's an expeditionary attack fleet for sure. And the intel we loaded from *Merkkessa* shows no other potential targets along that vector except Dekanna."

"Those bloody bastards!" exclaimed Pojjayan. "They have a peace treaty with Dekanna, and they're going to launch a surprise attack on them!"

"That's our take on it," said Luke. "So...it's only 450 lights to Dekanna. They're still operating with the slow drives. That means we have about nineteen weeks. Not a lot of time. Our orders are to return to Singheko and continue to monitor the system. So get that intel back to Rita and see what she wants to do."

Bonnie tapped her pencil on the tabletop, a nervous habit - especially in a time when pencils were no longer used.

"I wish we had some way to get the warning to Rita sooner. By the time you meet her at the rendezvous, and she dispatches a ship to warn Dekanna, another five days will have passed. And they'll need every day possible to prepare for the invasion."

Suddenly they were interrupted by the voice of *Dragon*'s AI -

the artificial intelligence that ran the ship.

<Pardon me for intruding, Captain, but may I speak?>

Bonnie answered immediately.

“Of course, *Dragon*. You may speak anytime you have something important to tell us.”

<Why not use the ansible to transmit the intel to the *Merkkessa* immediately?>

There was a long silence.

“We don’t have an ansible, *Dragon,*” said Bonnie at last, looking at the others with puzzlement on her face.

<Of course we have an ansible, Captain. It’s built into my stardrive>

Bonnie sat stunned while Luke asked the next question.

“What’s an ansible?”

Bonnie looked at the puzzled faces around her at the table. It appeared no one else recognized the word except her.

“An ansible is a transmitting device that can send data instantaneously across light years. Faster than light,” she said.

The group sat in shock.

Bonnie was the first to recover.

“*Dragon*, let me get this straight. I want to be sure I understand you. You are saying your stardrive has the functionality to serve as an ansible?”

<Yes. It’s built into the system>

“Does this mean that the ships in the fleet which we’ve converted to the new design also have an ansible built in?”

“Yes. I can send a message to any of the ships in the fleet which are equipped with the new drives>

“Why are you just now telling us this, *Dragon*?”

<You have never asked me. And we had no need to use the ansible until now>

Bonnie shook her head in total exasperation.

“*Dragon*, are there any more hidden functions in your design we should know about?”

<There are not>

“I don’t know whether to be overjoyed or disappointed that

you have no more tricks up your sleeve," said Bonnie. She turned to face Luke.

"Dig into this with *Dragon*, figure out how to format and transmit the data, and how to get their attention on the other end to recognize our transmission when it arrives."

"Aye, mum," grinned Luke, jumping up from the table. "This is a mind-bender."

Pojjayan jumped into the conversation.

"Mum! Admiral Page sent the *Corresse* to Nidaria with messages. And she has the new drives!"

"*Dragon*!" snapped Bonnie. "Are you able to detect the *Corresse* at Nidaria? Can you send a message to her?"

<I cannot detect the *Corresse*. Either she is powered down, or someone has put a block on her ansible>

"Damn!" swore Bonnie. She turned to Pojjayan, handing him a data pack.

"Well, Captain. I think the best thing for you is to head out for the M-275 rendezvous as originally planned. If by chance this ansible trick doesn't work, you still need to deliver the scouting report to Admiral Page. And if it works, we'll be able to divert you to the M-550 rendezvous to meet the fleet."

"Aye, milady," answered Pojjayan. Clutching the data pack in his hand, he and his XO headed for the door.

***

On the bridge, Luke had recruited Rachel to help him.

"*Dragon*. You say you can detect all ships which have been converted to the new drives?"

<That is correct, Commander>

"And you can detect the *Merkkessa*, right?"

<Yes. I can detect the *Merkkessa*. She is 241.4 light years from us, enroute to Singheko>

"So what happens if we send a message to the *Merkkessa* on the ansible?"

<The data will arrive instantaneously. A light will start blinking on the Comm console of the *Merkkessa* letting them know a message has arrived, and a notice will go out over

the Command channel that a high-priority message has been received>

Luke looked up at the ceiling, raising his hands in frustration and shaking his head in disbelief.

"And we had this functionality for the entire trip and you never told us?"

<I made an incorrect assumption that you already knew about it>

"*Dragon*, try to remember - we found you after two thousand years of a Dark Age. We knew almost nothing about your technical capabilities when we found you. You have to lead us by the hand."

<I have no hands>

Luke looked at Rachel, rolling his eyes.

"That means you have to tell us the small details of any technical function, if you think we don't know them already."

<I understand>

"OK. We've got a formatted data pack ready to send. Can you send it?"

<Now?>

"Yes, now!"

<Data pack sent to the *Merkkessa*. *Merkkessa* has acknowledged. Transmission complete>

"Well, I'll be screwed," said Luke before he could stop himself.

Rachel nodded with him involuntarily.

Luke smiled at her; a bit embarrassed by his outburst.

"Sorry, Lieutenant. That just slipped out. Let's get back on station. Set us a course back to the Singheko system."

"Aye, sir."

As the *Dragon* departed back to Singheko, the *Kaimina* waited for two hours, ostensibly to check systems before departing.

Then the *Kaimina* also sank out. But it failed to take a vector toward the oncoming EDF fleet as planned.

Following *Dragon*, *Kaimina* approached the Singheko

system and fired a tiny message drone toward Ridendo.

It was addressed to Admiral Zukra.

9 - ANSIBLE

It was 5 AM ship time. Rita was awakened by her command channel implant.

<Priority One message received from *Dragon* via ansible>

Drowsily, she lifted her head. For a moment, she thought she was dreaming. But beside her, Jim also stirred, then sat bolt upright in bed.

"Did you hear that?" he asked.

Rita realized it wasn't a dream.

"I think so. Something about a Priority One message. But I thought it said from the *Dragon*...that can't be..."

Jim wiped his hand over his forehead and rubbed his eyes.

"*Merkkessa*, repeat last notice."

<Priority One message received from *Dragon* via ansible>

"What the hell's an ansible?" asked Jim.

"Instantaneous transmission across light years," answered Rita. "Science fiction."

<Not science fiction, Admiral> responded *Merkkessa*. <Very much real>

The next hour was a hectic mess of questions, disbelief, an impromptu staff meeting in Rita's briefing room, review of the data received from *Dragon*, and more disbelief.

Finally Rita called a halt.

"Everyone, it's early, we're tired. Let's take a breakfast break, get cleaned up, and come back to revisit this at 1000 hours."

A mumble of appreciation went around the room. Rita waved Dallitta and Bekerose away and went back to her bedroom, Jim following.

"Can you believe this?" he asked.

"I guess we have to. *Merkkessa* said the function is built into all the ships with the new stardrive design we copied from *Dragon*. We just didn't know about it."

"The limitations of AI. A human would have recognized the criticality of that little bit of knowledge right away."

***

At 1000 hours, the team assembled in the briefing room again.

"Who are the Dekanna?" asked Rita.

Bekerose smiled.

"Actually, their planet is called Dekanna, but the species is called the Dariama. And of all the species known to us, the Dariama are the closest to humans in appearance. They look remarkably like you. But in temperament, they are not nearly as aggressive. They keep to themselves. They have little trade with others and rarely venture far from their home star. And they're extremely paranoid. They don't like visitors."

Rita looked at Bekerose suspiciously.

"Why have we not heard about them before?"

Bekerose shrugged. "I guess it just never came up."

"So. The Singheko have sent an invasion fleet to them. Why? What do they have that the Singheko want?"

Bekerose looked at Dallitta. She shrugged. He looked back at Rita.

"If I had to guess, I'd say their proximity to Nidaria. The Singheko know they can't take over the Arm without going through Nidaria. By taking the Dekanna system, they'll have a base much closer to Nidaria. Plus a base of slaves in place to build more warships and weapons for a Nidarian invasion."

"And do the Dariama have a fleet? Can they defend themselves?"

Bekerose shook his head. "I doubt it. Because of their paranoia, they have a good-sized fleet. Probably equal to our EDF fleet. But their temperament isn't suited to warfare. I suspect they'll fold like a pack of cards as soon as the shooting starts."

Rita looked down the table at Jim. She lifted an eyebrow.

"Commander Carter, you seem to be deep in thought. What are you thinking?"

"Well," Jim started. "We should at least warn them, if nothing else."

"I agree. Anything else?"

"Well, if they have a good-size fleet, but are lacking the leadership to win…"

Jim hesitated.

"Spit it out, Commander."

"We could offer to give them a commander who could help them out."

Rita looked at Bekerose.

"Any chance they'd go for that?"

Bekerose shook his head.

"It'd be a hard sell. They're so paranoid, they'd probably view that as an attempt to take over their fleet. I think they'd shoot the messenger."

Rita thought about it for a while. Visibly, she came to a decision, sitting up straighter in her chair and looking at Dallitta.

"Captain Dallitta, send a corvette to Dekanna with a warning. I'll prepare a message for them to take. We'll also send our most suitable candidate to help them tactically - if they'll accept our help. I'll word the message as purely an offer of tactical advice, and we'll hope for the best. Bekerose, who do you recommend we send?"

"Actually, Admiral, if I could make a suggestion…I'd recommend Commander Carter send his best squadron leader, with a couple of Merlins. The Dariama are known for their fighters, and their fleet is heavily oriented toward fighter warfare. A fighter pilot might be the best candidate to have some rapport with them without appearing to be a threat. And sending them a couple of advanced fighters would be the best way to impress them."

"Done," said Rita. She focused on Jim at the end of the table.

"Commander Carter, can you mount a couple of Merlins on a corvette for the trip?"

"Yes, we learned how to do that at Jupiter. No problem."

"And you have someone in mind to take the mission?"

"Lieutenant Commander Winston. She's my best. I hate to lose her, though. And she'll be pissed to miss this campaign."

"Tell her I'm sorry. But duty calls. Get your crew in gear and get the mission ready to launch. I'll have the message ready for you in an hour."

"Aye, milady. I'll need to send a second pilot with the other Merlin."

Rita nodded. "Get it done, Commander."

Rita stood, indicating the meeting was over. Jim, Dallitta and Bekerose likewise rose. Dallitta and Bekerose turned to leave, giving Jim a sympathetic look as they departed.

It was always slightly embarrassing to Jim. Protocol demanded that, as the senior officer, Rita leave the room first.

Which she did, going through the door to their private quarters.

Which required Jim to stand, silent, until she had passed through the door.

Then Jim could leave to pass through the same door, exchanging his role as CAG for his role as husband.

A smile quirked his lips as he stepped toward the door.

Now CAG...he thought as he approached.

Now husband...he thought as he passed through.

Rita was waiting when Jim came through the door.

The look on her face told him there was a problem.

"What's the matter, babe?" he asked.

Rita sat on the bed.

"Am I a robot, Jim?"

For a moment, Jim was speechless. Finally, he sat beside her, put an arm around her waist, and pulled her in. She came to him, but stiffly. The tension in her body was evident.

"You're not a robot, Rita."

"I'm a clone. So I don't have a soul. That makes me a robot, I think."

Jim, stunned by her statement, shook his head in wonderment.

"Rita. That's not true. You're as human as me or anyone."

"That's not what the crazies on Earth say. I'm not blind to what they say about me, Jim. They say I don't have a soul."

"Rita. There's absolutely no evidence that anyone has a soul. So you're no different than anyone else. C'mon, you know those pseudo-religious nuts on the fringe. They make up stuff in their heads and then claim it came from God. You can't let that throw you."

"But I was cloned, Jim. I wasn't born!"

Jim released her waist, sat back, and moved a bit so he could look her in the eye. As always, he was stunned by her beauty. It was hard for him to concentrate on the discussion when he looked at her like this.

"She has the face of a queen," he thought. *"Perfect, glowing, intelligence written all over it. And yet she doubts herself. I don't understand how she can do that."*

"Rita. How did Jade clone you? Did she create you as an adult, from scratch?"

Rita looked at him, not quite a glare but clearly a bit pissed.

"You know how Jade cloned me."

"So say it. Humor me."

Rita stared at him.

"She took DNA from the packing cases you and Bonnie were loading."

"And what did she do with that DNA?"

"She created an embryo with it."

"So she didn't create you as an adult. She cloned you into an egg and then let the egg develop normally."

"Not normally. She accelerated the growth. She brought me to adult status in three months."

"But you grew from an egg. Just as I did. Just as Bonnie did. Just as every other human."

Rita shook her head.

"I don't know, Jim. I don't feel like I have a soul."

Now Jim reached for her, laid her down on the bed, then lay beside her, holding her.

"Rita. You're not a robot. You have as much soul as any human. It's a matter of faith. Pretty much all the religions agree on that one thing - you either have faith, or you don't. So...please. Have a little faith. Stop thinking about this and move on with your life."

There was a long silence. Slowly Jim felt her body relax, some of the tension leave it.

"What about the Nidarians, then?" she asked. "Do they have souls? Or what about the Singheko?"

Jim thought about it for a few seconds.

"I don't think the Creator would allow souls to be the unique possession of humanity. So yes, as much as humans have souls, then so do the Nidarians."

"And the Singheko, then," Rita stated quietly.

"Yes."

"And we're going to kill a lot of them," Rita added, her voice even more subdued.

"Yes."

"Do you think the Creator will forgive me for that?"

"I think the Creator allows us to defend ourselves. We're saving our planet from a vicious enemy who attacked us first. As long as we don't set out to destroy out of greed or cruelty, or attack without cause, then I believe the Creator will understand. And forgive.

"And don't forget, you're not doing this alone. The thousands of people in this fleet are here because they volunteered to defend Earth. Every one of them has a job to do, and so do you. You're not going out to kill Singheko by yourself. Your fulfilling the role you're best suited for, just like everyone else in this fleet."

Another long silence ensued. Jim felt Rita relax even more, her body slowly returning to normal.

"So...we'll be entering their system in a week. What have I

forgotten, Jim?" she finally asked.

Jim smiled. Silently, he pulled her to him.

A Commander's work was never done.

***

Luke had never lied to himself. It was one of his failings.

Even when it was in his best interest to lie to himself - he couldn't do it.

It did two things for him.

It made him one of the best officers in the EDF.

It also put him through agony when he couldn't shut it off.

And right now, he couldn't shut it off.

They were on their way back to Singheko after the meeting with *Kaimina.*

Back to the place where his daughter Tatiana was a slave on the fourth planet, Deriko.

Back to the place where she might be alive or dead - and he had no way of knowing.

Oh baby girl, I failed you completely. When your mother died, I ran to the sea to hide myself. And left you all alone…

I wasn't there for you when you needed me. I know that.

Where are you now? Are you OK?

Lying in his bunk, Luke threw an arm over his face, trying to block out the faint light in his cabin - and the memories.

It didn't help.

Tat, if there is a way. If there is a way I can find you, I will. I promise you, this time I will be there when you need me.

Luke swore and turned over in the bunk, staring at the wall.

You need sleep. Think about something else.

Oh, shit. Not that. Don't think about her.

But he couldn't control it. His mind was beyond all reason - he couldn't stop it. The image of Bonnie's green eyes blazed through his mind.

O Captain, my Captain, I'm in trouble.

He shook his head, pissed at himself.

I can't believe I let this happen to me.

I'm in love with her.

***

"Dammit! No! Don't make me do this, Commander!"

Lieutenant Commander Michelle "Winnie" Winston glared at Jim Carter, the anger in her eyes evident.

Jim sighed.

"I'm sorry, Michelle. Believe me, I know how you feel. I'd go myself if I could. But you're tagged. You're the best qualified to advise them on tactics and on the Merlin."

"Dammit, Commander! We're days away from starting the most important campaign in the history of humanity! I've trained my entire career for this! You can't do this to me!"

"Winnie," Jim said, reverting to her call sign in an attempt to calm her down. "Look. Chances are they'll refuse your help, and you'll be back here before the campaign's over. And if they accept your help, you'll likely be fighting the Singheko there at Dekanna. So either way, you'll have your chance."

Winnie closed her eyes, stiffening her arms and shuddering in frustration.

"If I don't get to fight in this war, Commander, I'll come back here and cut your balls off," she said quietly.

"Fair enough," Jim smiled. "Who do you want for your second pilot?"

Winnie thought for a second.

"Roberto. He's great tactically, smart, knows the Merlin backward and forward. I think he'd be the best choice."

"OK, you got it. Go tell him, then the two of you get your gear together and load up. You can have the last two Merlins we received - they've got all the latest bells and whistles. I'll get the crew in the launch bay busy mounting them to the *Banjala* while you pack. You've got about four hours, I think. And don't forget final pre-packing SOP."

Winnie looked at him, using her pissed-off face.

"Yes, Commander. We'll be sure to record final messages for the loved ones before we go."

***

Leo was screaming at Mikhail.

"Mikhail, you are being stupid!" he said. "We can't go on like this! We lose a couple of dozen people every day!"

"We're not ready, Leo," Mikhail answered. "We need another two weeks. We're scouting the factory, the tunnels, learning where everything is. Give us more time, please!"

"Bullshit!" said Denys. "We've waited long enough. We go tomorrow morning!"

They were talking through the cage wire. Leo and Denys had ended up in the next cage, the one beside Mikhail's. They were close enough to talk to each other directly.

"All you're going to succeed in doing is screw things up for everybody else," Mikhail said. "You're going to get a lot of people killed and maybe bring down the whole organization."

"You've been talking to that woman Tatiana too long," said Denys with a sneer. "You're turning into a woman yourself."

Mikhail shook his head sadly.

"Denys, try to understand. Tatiana knows what she's doing. She's a good planner, and a good general. She's putting together something that will work. But you going off half-cocked is going to set us back by days, maybe weeks."

"I don't care," said Leo. "I've had enough. We've all had enough. We're going tomorrow morning."

Mikhail sighed.

"OK. I can't stop you. I wish you luck. But count me and my team out. We're going to stick with Tatiana's plan."

***

At 0600 next morning, Leo and Denys launched their attack. As the Singheko guards marched them to their factory, a group of fifty men rushed the guards, fighting them for their weapons.

Mikhail made sure his own cage fell back, staying out of the battle.

The attack was initially successful; Leo's people managed to capture two dozen pistols, and then they swept forward, overpowering more Singheko guards, taking more weapons, killing every Singheko they found, their ranks swelling as more people realized an uprising was in progress.

In the end, they made it all the way to the processing building, maybe a thousand strong by the time they arrived there.

Bursting out of the ramp on to the surface level, they met a battalion of Singheko, waiting for them with heavy weapons mounted on tripods.

Then another battalion of Singheko came in behind them, catching them in the jaws of a trap.

It took a while. There were so many of them, the Singheko couldn't kill all of them at once. It took them nearly thirty minutes, cutting down the ranks in front and back, trapping the rest of them in the middle, then slowly advancing through, killing the rest of them methodically, ensuring there were no survivors.

When it was over, the Bagrami were sent in to clean up. The slow-moving bear-like creatures dragged the bodies away for disposal, then started cleaning the floor.

It wasn't the first time they had done it.

***

Admiral Zukra was ecstatic - so happy, he was tempted to jump to his feet and dance around his desk.

"You're sure?" he asked again.

"Yes, sir. Definite contact with a foreign ship at Eta. It was hiding in the rings, trying to be a rock. We didn't detect it immediately; it was really stealthy when at idle. But then it took off up above the ecliptic. Our drone there barely caught it as it departed."

"And we have a vector?"

"A partial one. We lost it soon after it departed. We sent additional drones to the target area, but it wasn't there. But we know it was up there somewhere above the ecliptic, looking down at us."

"Hot damn!" said Zukra. "Some action at last. What was the signature?"

"Something new, sir. Not anything we've seen before. But if

I had to make a guess, I'd guess Nidarian."

"Nidarian. Well, that sucks. I can't blow a Nidarian out of the Black without warning. We have a cease-fire in effect with them."

"But it's not likely to be Nidarian, sir..." Orma continued. "Given that it is skulking around our system, it has to be the Humans."

Zukra grinned hugely.

"Then we can blow it to hell!"

"Yes, sir," commented Orma. "I set Intelligence to signature analysis. That's their first priority. They're comparing the signature to every ship in our database."

"Excellent. And Recon's first priority is to find it."

"Yes, sir, they're on the job. We'll find it."

Zukra smiled at Orma, a rare occurrence.

"Orma, you've made my day!"

"Yes, sir," smiled his aide.

Zukra waited until Orma had departed, then called another officer.

An officer who worked for Zukra alone.

An officer who had processed a message drone sent by Captain Pojjayan of the corvette *Kaimina*.

"Damra? Did you get everything decoded?"

"Aye, sir," came the reply from the other end. "Garatella came through for us. We start retrofit on the first cruiser tomorrow."

10 - REBELLION

"Kill them all," said Tatiana.

Marta nodded.

"You got it."

Tatiana's plan was not totally different from the failed plan of Denys and Leo. But it had three major differences.

One - it was designed to start at night, as they were being driven back to their cages for the evening. The cover of darkness allowed the other aspects of her plan to succeed.

Two - she had learned where the barracks of the local Singheko garrison was located. She would take it out at the beginning of her attack. She intended to leave no local Singheko troops to interfere with the rest of her plan.

Three - her objective was not to negotiate with the Singheko, but to kill them. As many as possible. And then escape to the mountains, conduct guerrilla warfare for as long as possible.

Tatiana knew they couldn't win, not in the long run. Hers was not a plan for escape. Hers was a plan for a brutal, grinding war against a relentless enemy, until all her troops were dead.

As she knew they would be - eventually, all of them. She was taking on an Empire.

But she would do it anyway.

Now, the day had arrived. They had waited for a week after the failed revolt of Leo and Denys. The Singheko had slowly gone back to their normal routine. Everything was quiet.

Glancing over at Marta one last time, Tatiana nodded. Their shift in the factory was ending.

"Every one of them in the barracks."

Marta nodded again.

Marta had the barracks attack. It was the most critical part of the plan. Everything else had a bit of leeway, a little slack in the plan that could be taken up if things went wrong.

But the barracks attack had to go perfectly. They had to cover their backside. If the barracks attack failed, the two battalions of Singheko they had so carefully identified and scouted would come swarming into them, killing them all before they even got started.

The whistle blew, and the assembly line stopped. The next shift would arrive in an hour. The Singheko required the time to perform maintenance on the assembly line, clean up broken parts or pieces that had accumulated during the day, and perform their own shift change of the guards high overhead on the catwalks.

Tatiana had noticed the Singheko guards were always eager to leave, eager to get to their evening meal. When the whistle blew, they were off like a shot, trotting down the catwalk to the stairs at the far end, closest to their barracks and mess hall.

They never even looked back at the slaves being escorted out of the factory by other guards, who didn't carry rifles - only shock-sticks, whips, and pistols.

As Tatiana and her cohort left the factory and marched along the corridor, they came to one of the starfish junctions. There were five corridors leading off in separate directions.

The one to the far right led to their area. They shuffled into it, preparing themselves.

Just past the junction, there was a short stretch of corridor with no cages. The hum of machinery could be heard coming through the concrete walls. It was far enough down the corridor that the junction was out of sight.

As they entered the area, Tatiana shouted one word.

"Now!"

Four hundred men and women turned on the guards, moving so fast that not a single guard managed to get a shot off from their pistols.

It was over in seconds. Forty Singheko guards lay on the floor, dead or dying, most of them bleeding out from the homemade knives the prisoners had so carefully made from scraps and pieces in the factory, ever so carefully ferried back to their cage in the evenings, sharpened on the concrete floor and walls at night, secreted back in their clothes for this day.

Norali walked around, supervising her intelligence team as they collected weapons from the Singheko bodies, dispatching the odd few who weren't already dead.

And getting the keys to the cages.

Tatiana gathered Marta and her team around her.

"OK. We're all in now. There's no going back. Go get it done."

Marta nodded.

Norali's team came up and passed out the weapons to Marta and her team, keeping only a few.

Marta waved her team forward and they disappeared back in the direction of the factory.

Tatiana and the rest of her team resumed their march back to their own area. Arriving, they quickly began unlocking cages, working their way down the line, letting people out who wanted to join the fight.

Many did not; Tatiana estimated that sixty percent of the prisoners refused to come out of their cages, afraid of the consequences.

Those they locked back in the cages. There was no use cluttering up the corridors with them.

***

Moving as quietly as possible, Marta and her team moved back to the factory.

They had learned where the Singheko barracks was. It was just on the other side of the factory, down a long corridor and through a set of blast doors. This they had learned by simple means. In the confusion of two thousand people leaving the factory floor at the end of a shift, members of Norali's intelligence team would slip into one of the cleaning closets. There they would wait until two or three A.M. Then they would scout the area while everyone slept. In the morning, as two thousand Humans returned to the factory to start the morning shift, they would merge back into the mass of people and return to the assembly line.

Now, entering the factory quietly, Marta and her team crouched down, scanning the huge floor for danger.

All was quiet. All the Singheko guards up on the catwalk were gone.

The Taegu had completed their maintenance checks on the assembly line and had left for their dinner.

There were a dozen of the slow-moving Bagrami scattered around the floor, pushing their brooms and mops around.

Waving her team forward, Marta worked her way around the edge of the factory floor to the metal stairs leading up to the catwalk.

The Bagrami hardly looked at them. A couple of them glanced toward the Humans, then resumed their cleaning.

Ascending the stairs, Marta and her team ran to the other end of the factory. It was nearly two kilometers.

"Quiet!" Marta hissed, as someone stumbled on the metal catwalk and made a loud clang.

They froze, looking down at the factory floor below them.

All they could see were the Bagrami, cleaning the floor.

Resuming their run, they continued until they reached the other end of the factory.

Here the finished warheads were packed up for shipping. Hundreds of them sat in their crates, some already sealed.

The humans were never allowed in this area. Only the Singheko or the Taegu could come here.

Marta and her team of thirty ran down the stairs to the factory floor. Grabbing an open crate of warheads, they dragged it to the door at the end of the room. Opening the door, they dragged it through to the other side and quietly closed the door behind them.

They were in a dimly lit maintenance tunnel. Working in teams of two, the women began transferring the heavy warheads down the tunnel.

At the other end of the tunnel, there was another door. A door which came out in a sub-basement storage area.

Directly beneath the Singheko barracks.

In their secret midnight scouting expeditions, Norali's intelligence team had found the door normally unlocked.

But now it was locked.

They tried it for several minutes, unbelieving. Their entire plan depended on getting through this door quickly. And they couldn't do it.

Suddenly there was a sound at the other end of the tunnel. They dropped, aiming their guns at the crack of light there.

Something was coming through the door. Something big.

"Hold your fire, hold your fire," hissed Marta. Something about the shape caught her attention.

It wasn't Singheko.

The big Bagrami shuffled down the corridor toward them, holding a mop in one hand.

Arriving in front of the women lying on the ground, the bear-like figure held out something.

"You might need this," he said in perfect English.

It was a key.

***

Marta stared at the Bagrami in astonishment. But her wits came back to her quickly. She grabbed the key and passed it behind to her Number Two. She heard the team get up and the door open. She looked around at them as they started moving the warheads through the door.

Then she looked back at the Bagrami, still in shock.

"You speak English?" she asked.

The Bagrami smiled - if it could be called a smile, with a face that still showed the hint of a muzzle not yet fully erased by evolution.

"We speak many languages, Marta. And we know far more than we let on. Good luck to you. I must get back to my mopping."

"Wait!" exclaimed Marta. "Will you join us? You and your people?"

The Bagrami smiled again.

"If you succeed in your plan, we may join you. We haven't decided yet. First you must take out the barracks. Then we'll see."

And with that, the Bagrami shuffled away with his mop, back toward the door into the factory.

Marta turned to see the last of her team disappearing through the door. She quickly followed, closing the door behind her.

Inside the sub-basement, they went to work.

There were eight support columns in the sub-basement. They set four of the warheads against each support column. They pulled out the safety plugs in the nose of each warhead. In the dark hole that was left, they could see the raw explosive inside.

Now they pulled out homemade fuses. They had made them from their clothing, soaked them in cleaning fluid from the janitor closets, and woven them into their clothes.

When all the explosives were set and fused, Marta waved her team back through the door. She set the master fuse alight and they departed quickly, trotting down the corridor to the other end. Cracking the door open, they peeked through.

Far off, they could see a few Taegu supervisors coming in, their dinner finished.

In a few more minutes, the Singheko guards would come back to the catwalks.

They began their run for the other end of the factory.

***

The explosion was quite satisfying.

Tatiana was crouched in the corridor, just outside the factory.

Far behind her, Norali and her team continued to open cages. They had freed upwards of four thousand Humans from their cages, and at least a thousand Taegu and Bagrami.

Yet many were too terrified to come out of their cages. They would rather face the known of slavery than the unknown of rebellion.

But Norali kept moving, opening more and more cages, collecting more and more people, sending them to follow members of her team who assembled them in the corridor.

Everything paused when the explosion went off.

The walls shook, vibrating like tuning forks. Dirt came off the ceiling into their hair and eyes, nearly blinding them. Some people fell to the floor, terrified.

Poised just outside the chamber leading to the factory, Tatiana and Mikhail grinned at each other.

Marta had done it.

If all had gone as planned, Marta had blown up the barracks housing nearly two thousand Singheko soldiers and guards, at evening meal, when nearly all of them would be in the mess hall on the ground floor.

Directly over the explosives.

With a battle cry, Tatiana launched forward, Mikhail right beside her.

Behind them came thousands who had elected to throw in their lot with the resistance.

11 - AMPATO

It was midnight, ship time. Zukra was having his way with one of his female slaves when the call came in from Admiral Ligar.

Cursing, he shoved the female aside and moved to the screen at his desk, pulling on his pants. He ran his fingers through his mane and checked his appearance in a hand mirror, then activated the screen.

"Zukra! Are you sleeping on the job again?"

Ligar's pissed about something...

"No, sir, of course not. How can I help you, Admiral?"

"You can start taking care of your damn responsibilities, Zukra! What kind of a slipshod operation are you running on Deriko?"

Zukra was puzzled.

"Sir, I don't understand - what about Deriko?'

"The slaves, man! The slaves have rebelled! They took out an entire processing center and a missile factory! Are you not reading your dispatches?"

"I'm sorry, sir. I'm a little behind. I've been searching for this Human destroyer for several days now."

"Well, these damn Humans are turning out to be a real pain in the ass. Evidently it was a bunch of them that took over the slave complex at Alpha-16 and wrecked it. Casualties are high, Zukra. I'm catching a lot of heat from higher up. Do something about it!"

And with that, Admiral Ligar slammed his fist down on the desk and broke the connection.

Zukra sat at his screen in amazement and shame.

A slave rebellion? On Deriko?

The Taegu would never rebel. Neither would the Bagrami.

So it must be those new Humans that came in from Earth.

Zukra swore.

Dammit! What is up with these Humans? Are they trying to make my life miserable? First they put a spy ship in our system, then they start a slave rebellion?

"Orma!" shouted Zukra. In a few seconds, the hatch opened, and his aide stepped through.

"Yes, sir?"

"Get me General Arzem!"

***

High in the mountains, a good thirty kilometers from the Singheko complex they had destroyed, Tatiana sat on the rocks with her team.

Below her, stretched out in a long line, 7,200 creatures - Human, Bagrami, Taegu - made their way slowly in a long column up the trail into the rocky center of the mountains.

They had left behind more than 7,000 who were too fearful of the Singheko to join them.

That was OK. Tatiana understood.

Fighting in a lost cause wasn't for everybody.

After Marta blew up the barracks, there weren't enough Singheko left to put up a good battle. A few hundred resisted.

Those they killed.

The rest they turned out into the desert to the west and told them to start walking.

They had collected roughly three thousand weapons - a couple of thousand rifles, a thousand pistols, and hundreds of knives and other things they might find useful.

They had emptied the explosive from a hundred warheads and brought that along.

They had found fifty-odd heavy weapons on tripods and brought all of those.

And they had enough charge magazines to reload every weapon at least ten times over.

Tatiana sat on the rock and watched the sun go down in the west. Mikhail sat on her right, and past him Marta.

Sitting on her left, the big Bagrami who had given the key to Marta in the tunnel also watched quietly. Norali sat just past him, and beyond her was the leader of the Taegu who had joined them - Woderas.

"You certainly had us fooled," said Tatiana to the Bagrami.

"Call me Baysig," the Bagrami said. "It translates to "Big B" in your language. Or something close to that."

"Baysig. Big B. I like that," smiled Tatiana.

"And yes, we have played the fool for a long time with the Singheko. They are too stupid to notice."

"But the Taegu know?"

"Yes, the Taegu know. They've known about us for a while. But they keep our secret. The Taegu are also in this fight with us. They just take a different approach."

Tatiana looked down at the column winding its way up the trail to the pass. There were roughly a thousand Taegu in there, she remembered. They had come at the last minute, a contingent willing to sacrifice their lives with the Humans for a chance to strike back at the Singheko.

Those, along with the five-hundred-odd Bagrami who had joined, were a surprise to Tatiana, but a welcome one. She welcomed any who were willing to fight the Singheko - but especially those with knowledge of the enemy.

After they turned out the few Singheko survivors and collected the weapons and food they would need for their escape, they had left the camp, walking into the cold desert to the East. They walked all night and all day, putting as much distance behind them as they could before Singheko reinforcements came at them.

Which they would. It was just a matter of time.

Tatiana's only goal now was to get to a defensible position, where she could put up a good fight.

She had no illusions about long term survival.

"The sunset is beautiful," she said quietly.

Baysig grunted an answer.

"Yes. Creatures are so foolish to fight and kill when there is so much beauty to be found in the universe."

It had been six and a half months since Tatiana had seen a sunset.

Baysig leaned forward, turning to look at Tatiana with his pushed in bear-like face.

"I have an idea, if you're interested."

Tatiana looked at him.

"Sure. What do you have in mind?"

"There is another concentration camp just forty-five kilometers east of here."

A gleam came into Tatiana's eye.

"You don't say..."

***

"Don't shoot!"

Marta hesitated. She was lying on a large flat rock. She had her sights aligned perfectly on the Singheko standing at the foot of the trail, three hundred meters below them. It was an easy shot. And Marta was no slouch when it came to using her newly liberated Singheko rifle.

The Singheko blood on it bothered her not a bit. And here was a chance to kill another of the hated enemy.

But she held her fire. Turning, she looked over her shoulder.

Baysig and Norali were standing behind her. The voice had come from Baysig. He had his perpetual gentle smile in place, but his voice was somehow commanding. Full of strength.

"That's not a Singheko," he growled.

Marta glared at him.

"Bullshit. I know a Singheko when I see one."

"No, you don't. That's an Ampato. Indigenous to the planet. They hate the Singheko worse than you do."

Marta grunted, rose on one shoulder, and twisted around to face Baysig.

"You have got to be shittin' me," she said. "There's a species native to this planet? And they look just like Singheko?"

"Yes, they are native to Deriko. And no, they don't look just like the Singheko. Almost, but not exactly. When he gets closer, you'll see the differences."

Marta gave in, put her rifle on safe, and stood up, gazing down the mountain at the distant figure slowly making its way up the trail toward them.

"Well, then, we'd better send someone down to escort him, or someone else is going to blow him away."

"Agreed," said Baysig. "Norali and I will do it. Try to keep your trigger-happy friends from shooting us."

Marta nodded. She spoke into her comm as Baysig and Norali passed her on the trail, headed down the mountain toward the figure below.

The three of them had scouted ahead. The main body of Tatiana's army was several klicks behind them. Yesterday, they had crested the divide and started down the other side, into an area of broken foothills. The cordillera behind them stretched for hundreds of kilometers to the north and south, snow-capped, granite-hard mountains unforgiving of man or beast or Bagrami or Taegu. But they had made it across, down into the foothills and into a thick forested area.

According to Baysig and Woderas, the next concentration camp was another fifteen klicks in front of them, just outside the edge of the forest.

Marta sat down on the big rock and waited. Below, she saw Baysig and Norali come up to the...

Not Singheko, she reminded herself. *Ampato*.

"Looks like a fucking Singheko to me," Marta muttered.

Shortly, the three figures made their way back up to Marta's level. As they arrived, Marta heard someone coming from behind. Looking, she saw Tatiana and Woderas coming down the trail to join them.

Baysig found another big rock and sat. Norali and the Ampato sat beside him.

Tatiana and Woderas came up to them and stopped. Tatiana held her rifle suspiciously, ready for anything, despite Marta's previous communication.

"This is Misrak," said Baysig. "He is a speaker for the Ampato."

The figure looked like a Singheko. He walked like a Singheko and smelled like a Singheko. But upon closer inspection, it could be seen he had no fangs, no vestigial claws, and the color of his coat was a cream color rather than the yellow-gold of the Singheko.

"Ampato?" Tatiana was suspicious, on her guard.

"Not Singheko," said Baysig. "Not an enemy. They hate the Singheko more than we do if such is possible."

Tatiana was still suspicious, but she managed to force herself to lower her rifle, pointing it toward the ground.

"What do you mean?"

"The Singheko have enslaved the Ampato for more than a thousand years," said Baysig. "They attack them on a whim, rape their females, kill them indiscriminately. Trust me, there is no one who hates the Singheko more than the Ampato."

"And where did he come from?" she asked.

"They are native to this planet," said Baysig. "At least, now. In the early days of the Golden Empire - twenty-two thousand years ago - the Singheko colonized this planet. Over time, the Ampato diverged from the Singheko into a separate race. When the Golden Empire fell two thousand years ago, a war broke out between the Singheko and the Ampato. The Ampato lost. The Singheko bombed them back to the stone age. You can still see the craters of their old cities, out there..."

Baysig waved vaguely at the barely visible plains out beyond the foothills.

"After the fall of the Golden Empire, there was no longer an Imperial edict against slavery. So since that time, the Singheko have enslaved the Ampato."

Tatiana sat down on a rock and stared at the figure, who had yet to say a word.

"And what does he want?" she asked.

Baysig gave his muted, inscrutable smile.

"He can lead us into the next Singheko complex unseen."

***

<We're approaching Dekanna, Commander. We'll enter the system in a half-hour>

The AI voice of the corvette *Banjala* was male, a bit unusual for warships in the fleet. Most AI voices were female. Winnie had never understood exactly why. She suspected it was something related to the early days of technology when comm speakers were small and thus less able to push the lower frequencies of male voices.

But in any case, this one was male.

"Thank you, *Banjala*. Please notify Lieutenant Gonzalez to meet me by the airlock for transfer."

<Wilco>

Winnie looked around the tiny cabin she had been assigned on the corvette. It was sparse; she had not seen any reason to bring a lot of possessions for this trip. Everything she needed was already packed in her flight bag, or still loaded aboard her Merlin. She picked up her flight bag and went out the hatch, letting it click behind her.

Moving out, she walked down the center passageway toward the upper airlock. Lieutenant Roberto "Razor" Gonzalez was already there, waiting for her. Just as she approached, she heard the descending whine and the slight thump that told her they had exited six-space and were entering the outskirts of the Dekanna star system.

"Morning, Razor."

"Morning, Commander. Well, I guess we're off to see the Wizard."

"Yep. You ready?"

"Always ready, Commander."

Winnie smiled.

"I meant to launch."

Roberto grinned.

"Yep. Good to go."

With a smile, Winnie started putting on her pressure suit.

In fifteen minutes, both she and Roberto were dressed, out the airlock, and buckled into the two Merlins affixed to the outside hull.

"Ready to launch," called Winnie to the AI.

<Receiving clearance from *Banjala*. Clearance received. Launching>

With a couple of loud clicks, Winnie felt the Merlin release from the triangular support structure attaching it to the *Banjala*. In a few seconds, she was twenty-five meters from the corvette, drifting to the left. At two hundred meters, the AI automatically stopped her drift and put her into formation with the corvette.

On the other side of the ship, she could see Roberto, taking his escort position two hundred meters to the right.

"Shepherd One, comm check," she called.

"Shepherd Two, five by five."

"Roger. The *Banjala* should be broadcasting Rita's greeting message now. But we don't know how they'll react. Anything could happen. The light speed delay to their home planet is 15 hours. But they probably have pickets out here somewhere who'll receive it sooner. So stay frosty."

"Wilco."

The next three hours were excruciatingly boring for Winnie. They accelerated into the system at 250g. They got to 1% of light - 107 million kph - and stopped their accel.

But absolutely nothing happened.

<Message from *Banjala*. We'll stop accel now, coast in for a while. We don't want to come busting in on them too fast>

"Agree," called Winnie. "Keep us posted."

They coasted for another six hours. Winnie was just about to lose her mind from boredom. She had taken a meal and drank some water when her early warning system pinged.

<Target, 015.002, 2 AU, direct intercept vector, time to merge 3.8 hours>

Thank God. Even if they fight us, anything is better than boring holes in the Black.

"*Banjala*, I show a destroyer-class vessel, do you concur?"

<Banjala confirms. Destroyer-class vessel, direct intercept vector, time to merge 3.8 hours>

12 - FOUND

Orma bent over the console. The technician pointed to the tiny blip on the display.

"Right there, sir. 14.75 AU above the ecliptic, a little bit off center of us. They departed three days ago, a direct entry into six-space. We couldn't see them until they powered up to leave. Then here..."

The technician switched to another display.

"...they returned this morning, but 14 AU below the ecliptic, almost directly below Ridendo. We got just a tiny tic as they entered the system. They were clever - when they entered the system, they had just enough momentum to put them into a solar orbit right where they wanted to be. They never even had to fire their system engines. And as soon as they powered down their tDrive, we lost them."

The technician leaned back in his chair, waved at the display, and smiled at Orma.

"When their engines are at idle, we just can't see them. Their stealth is too good. But this time, we know where they are."

Orma clapped the technician on the shoulder.

"Good work, Chief. Excellent news. Keep a close eye on that location. Put a dozen drones around them, box them in. I don't want them to sneeze without us knowing about it. But carefully, man. Don't give us away."

"Aye, sir. We'll do it."

Heading out of the Recon section, Orma smiled. He went straight to Zukra's office. With a light knock, he entered.

"Sir! We've got them!" he burst out, a big smile on his face.

Zukra sat upright in his chair.

"Where?"

"14 AU below Ridendo. They left the system two days ago and returned this morning. We got lucky; we had a drone pick them up as they came back into the system. We know right where they are."

"Outstanding," said Zukra. His eyes gleamed at the thought of action.

"And sir - even more good news. We found the signature."

"Yes? Human?"

"Well, actually ancient Golden Empire. Two thousand years old, in fact. We only found it by sifting through the archives."

"What the hell? An ancient Empire ship?"

Orma smiled.

"It has to be the Humans. One of the ships Garatella gave them, a relic so old it's not even in our primary database."

This time, Zukra did spring to his feet.

"Then we can attack them! The cease-fire doesn't apply to them!"

Zukra began pacing.

"I want an assault plan ready within three hours, Orma. I'll be on the *Ambush* - get me a shuttle immediately. Notify Captain Wenru I'm coming aboard to supervise the kill. And form up a task force to box them in. I don't want them escaping out the back door."

"Sir, if I may suggest..." spoke Orma.

"What? Yes, yes, of course, speak your mind, Orma," Zukra spat impatiently.

"Sir, they are near the mass limit. If they detect a force of ships coming at them, they can run to the limit and sink out. May I suggest a more stealthy approach..."

Zukra stopped pacing, stared out the window for a bit at the spaceport stretching out before him, a huge area covered with shuttles and warships.

"Yes. Yes, of course you're right, Orma. If we go charging at them, they'll just sink out on a random vector and be gone.

That won't work."

Zukra sank back down at his desk and rubbed his muzzle.

"If we had some way to lure them farther into the mass limit..."

Orma shook his head.

"Everything we've seen so far indicates their commander is quite sharp, sir. I don't think that would work."

"OK, let's think of something else. Do we have any warship stealthy enough to slip up on them? Maybe one of the new corvettes?"

"I don't think so, sir. Based on what we've seen so far, they are quite a bit stealthier than anything we have. So we have to assume they'd pick up any ship we sent at them."

Zukra slammed his hand against the desk, leaving a scratch where his claws smacked into it.

"Then we send a weapon directly! What's our smallest, stealthiest weapon that could do damage to them, and possibly not be detected coming in on a ballistic course? The M04?"

"Yes, sir. The M04 is small, and we could launch it from a goodly distance with some accuracy. It might work."

"OK. Put together that plan, Orma. I want it ready to go by tomorrow morning latest. Got it?"

"Yes, sir. An M04 passive strike, launched from a distance. We'll get right on it."

"Oh - and I want to be there when we launch it. We'll stand off and watch; then we'll go in fast as soon as the M04 hits. If we get any damage at all, they may be distracted enough for us to catch them by surprise. I'll go up to the *Ambush* tonight. Make it so, Orma."

"Aye, sir. I'll notify Captain Wenru you're coming aboard."

As Orma departed, Zukra leaned back in his chair.

It was a good plan.

And he had another good plan coming together. In a matter of days now, Zukra's ambitions would come to fruition.

He would no longer have to worry about Ligar and the Admiralty. There would be no more waiting for an expeditionary fleet command. He would have more than enough firepower to destroy any fleet that opposed him.

And tomorrow, he would attack the Human ship and destroy it.

Tomorrow would be a good day.

***

Tatiana, Marta, Mikhail, Norali and Baysig followed the Ampato Misrak down the narrow tunnel. The tunnel was crude, hastily dug. Only a dim bulb every few dozen yards provided illumination.

According to Misrak, the Ampato had been planning an attack against the Singheko for some time. The appearance of Tatiana and her small army had convinced them the timing was right.

Baysig continued to vouch for the Ampato. But Tatiana was still nervous, suspicious.

This could be a trap. We could be walking right into a nest of Singheko.

Baysig turned and gave his faint bear-like smile to Tatiana, as if he could read her mind.

Maybe he can, thought Tatiana. *I've never asked him.*

She smiled at the thought.

That would be something. A semi-bear that can read minds.

Suddenly Misrak halted ahead of them. He made some kind of sign language with his hands to Baysig.

Baysig nodded, turned to Tatiana, and silently gave a thumbs-up - something he had learned from the Humans.

Then three of them - Baysig, Marta and Misrak - disappeared forward into the gloom. Their heavy backpacks carried fifty pounds of explosive each.

Tatiana squatted down with Norali and Mikhail. Now they waited.

The closeness of Mikhail's body began to affect her. There was something about him. He was older than her, but still…

Stay focused on task. Don't let your mind wander.

But her mind wandered anyway. The muskiness of Mikhail's

body was so close to her. And his mind was so good - so logical, so reasoned, yet human, warm and approachable.

Get it together, girl. This is no time for such...

***

Twenty-four hours later, Tatiana lay on top of a small rise, two kilometers from the Singheko concentration camp they had code-named Bravo Two. It was three in the morning, local time.

Behind her, an army of three thousand men and women, armed with their liberated Singheko weapons, waited impatiently for the signal to attack.

Far to her right, three klicks from her position, a scout company of five hundred waited, just outside a ventilation shaft leading into the underground complex near the slave cages.

And in the secret tunnel the Ampato had dug, another five hundred of Tatiana's force waited. In addition to their own rifles, each of them carried a second rifle to give to Ampato prisoners as they freed them from their cages. With them were two dozen Ampato acting as guides, their chance for revenge now at hand.

With a muted "thump", Tatiana heard the first of the explosions go off, deep underground, almost like distant thunder.

"There goes their communication complex," she grunted to Norali, lying next to her. "They won't be calling for help."

Another muted "thump" and this time the ground vibrated a little.

"There goes the corridor to the factory. Now the bastards are trapped in their barracks. It'll take them hours to dig out."

Norali nodded.

Then a final thump.

"And that was the tunnel to their armory," Tatiana said. "They can't get to their heavy weapons now."

Tatiana stood, hands on hips, looking down through the night at the distant ventilation shaft.

She couldn't see them; but she knew the five hundred troops there were swarming down the ventilation shaft, which put them behind the on-duty guards in charge of the prisoner cages.

Cages which contained 12,000 Ampato slaves thirsting for revenge.

Tatiana heard Norali's comm buzz. Norali bent to it, talking to someone inside the complex. Then she turned to Tatiana, smiling.

"On schedule," she said. "The Ampato and our force have taken the guards under fire from the north, and our scout company have them under fire from the south. They're in a crossfire. Time to go."

Tatiana nodded.

"Let's do this," she said, and started trotting down the trail, her three thousand troops following close behind.

***

By dawn, they had the entire complex.

There weren't many prisoners. From the Human side, there were a few.

From the Ampato side, there were none.

Tatiana sat in a large office in the complex, the one formerly occupied by the camp commander. It was hers now - at least for the moment.

"What's our status?"

Mikhail, Norali, Marta, Baysig, Woderas and Misrak sat around her, a council of war in progress. As they talked, the quiet mutter of Woderas translating for Misrak was an undertone to the conversation.

"We liberated another three thousand rifles, a thousand pistols, thirty heavy machine guns, twenty cases of hand grenades, enough explosive to blow this place to the moon, and - get this - we found a hanger with six assault shuttles," reported Norali.

"What? Assault shuttles?"

"You betcha. Six big-ass assault shuttles. Two missile tubes, two lasers and four conventional machine guns in the nose."

"Interesting," Tatiana mused, tapping something that looked vaguely like a pen on the desk. "Prisoners?"

"Six hundred," said Norali. "Approximately fourteen hundred dead Singheko. The survivors are locked in the cages. And by the way, the Ampato are asking for the prisoners. They want to take them for a walk in the forest."

"No," said Tatiana. "We're not going to sink to the level of the Singheko. Keep the prisoners safe for now."

"So...next steps?" asked Marta. "Where do we go from here?"

Tatiana thought, her brow furrowed.

"I'm going to be honest with you all," she said, gazing around. "I never thought we'd get this far. I thought we'd all be dead by now."

There was a heavy silence. Marta broke it first.

"Yeah. To be honest, so did I."

Norali nodded.

"So..." Tatiana shook her head in wonderment.

"So now we have an unexpected success. We have to decide what to do with it."

Misrak interrupted with a sudden string of words, indecipherable to the humans.

Woderas translated. "Misrak says we take the planet and hold it."

Tatiana looked at Misrak, then at Woderas.

"How is that feasible?"

Woderas spat a string of words to Misrak, who came back with a long discussion. Finally Woderas turned back to Tatiana.

"While we were taking this camp, the Ampato took advantage of the diversion to capture the Singheko central headquarters on the planet. They didn't want to tell you because they knew you would object."

Tatiana was taken aback.

"What?"

Woderas continued. “Misrak received word just before this meeting that their attack succeeded. They have liberated another five thousand weapons and enough explosive to blow every Singheko on this planet to hell. The Ampato say they will rise in rebellion now. This may be their last best chance to kick the Singheko off planet for good. With these weapons, and the lack of central coordination, we can take the rest of the camps. It won’t be easy, but it’s certainly possible.”

Tatiana looked at Marta, who shrugged. At Baysig, who smiled. At Norali, who grinned.

“I guess we take the planet, then,” said Tatiana.

***

In the Dekanna system, the Dariama destroyer matched vector with the *Banjala* and ran along beside her from two hundred kilometers.

It was close enough that Winnie could see every cannon on the destroyer in her VR; and every one of them was trained on the little corvette and her two escorting fighters.

To sit passively in her Merlin with so many guns and missiles pointed at her grated on Winnie’s nerves; but there was little else she could do. Until the Dariama made an overture to them, all she could do was coast through space alongside the *Banjala*, her weapons powered off to show peaceful intentions.

It was uncomfortable. It made her skin itch in places she couldn’t scratch. She found her thumb unconsciously moving to a position where she could flick the Master Arm switch on with the twitch of a muscle.

She forced herself to move her thumb away. It wouldn’t do to blow the mission by accidentally turning on her weapons.

The destroyer paced them for thirty minutes. All attempts to communicate were ignored. They even tried laser signals, but to no avail. The warship simply watched them, incommunicado.

They’re paranoid, alright.

Winnie had listened to the message sent by Rita as the

Banjala continued to beam it out periodically.

The Singheko have sent an invasion fleet in your direction. Holo attached for your review.

As Humans have not previously met you, an introduction to our species is also attached for your review.

We are sending an emissary to provide you with further information and any assistance we can offer you at this time.

It seemed clear and simple, at least to Winnie's way of thinking. Winnie thought it was perfect - the message of a warrior, giving a warning to another warrior.

If they are warriors. If they're not, they're gonna be toast when the Singheko get here.

Her comm beeped.

<Incoming message from the Dariama destroyer. *Follow us. Do not deviate from vector or we will fire on you. Transmitting vector now*. End message>

Thank the Lord. At least they're letting us come into the system.

<Vector received. Time to destination 12 hours>

"Roger, *Banjala*. We'll re-dock and come inside. I don't relish sitting in this damn fighter for another 12 hours."

***

Major General Arzem was a distant cousin of Admiral Zukra. Zukra had made it clear to him - the family name was at stake. The Humans had humiliated Zukra. The Human slaves on Deriko had risen in rebellion, causing great discomfort to the Admiralty, and delaying the production of weapons for their conquest of the Arm.

It would not be tolerated. No species could be allowed to upset the balance between the Singheko as masters of all, and the rest of the universe as slaves.

Now, from his orbital vantage point high overhead the planet, Arzem gazed out across the landscape of Deriko.

He would crush these Humans without mercy.

"Send the drop ships!" he ordered.

Two large troop carriers in orbit began disgorging drop ships. In spears of plasma and heat, the drop ships made re-entry to the planet.

As the drop ships approached the level plain outside the second complex the Humans had captured, they flared and came to a not-very-gentle landing in the sand. The back ramps came down and the troops mustered out, forming up into their companies and battalions.

There were 50 drop ships.

Each drop ship contained 400 well-armed Singheko shock troops.

Within a few hours, 20,000 Singheko troops had formed up into their companies and battalions.

Two full brigades of nasty, pissed-off Singheko started marching toward the complex, with thirty assault shuttles covering them from the air.

13 - CRIPPLED

The missile came out of nowhere.

The Singheko launched it 1/2 AU from the *Dragon*, from a point 120 million kilometers away. They let it coast in, making minimal course corrections with tiny motors.

The Singheko M04 was small, stealthy. It didn't carry a large payload. It wasn't a shipkiller.

It was meant to slow you down, harass you, distract you.

The Singheko couldn't have known how good their luck was.

If they had attacked on a different watch, the odds are the attack would have failed. The AI would have picked up the incoming object, warned the Tac Officer on duty, and the Tac would have told *Dragon* to get the hell out of the way.

But it was Third Watch. It was 0645 in the morning.

Commander Larissa was ill in sickbay. They were shorthanded.

Bonnie had taken a chance and let Ensign Goodwin stand OOD on his own.

It was a mistake.

Goodwin was tired. And he was distracted.

And he was in love.

All he could think about was Ensign Gibbs.

Every time he thought about her, his heart skipped a beat and he started to sweat.

She is so beautiful. I've never seen a woman so perfect. Her curves. Her face...

The sweat started up on him again as he thought about her.

I love her. And it violates the ship rules on fraternization.

What can I do?

What can I do to make her know I love her?

<Incoming, impact in fifteen seconds. Evasive required>

The AI voice was loud on the command channel. It scared the hell out of Goodwin. He jumped in his seat.

"What?" he yelled. "What did you say?"

<Incoming, impact in ten seconds. Evasive required>

"What are you talking about?" screamed Goodwin, at a loss.

Then it started to click in his sodden brain.

"Yes! Evasive!" he yelled.

It was too late.

The missile hit aft, opposite the engineering spaces.

It punched a neat hole through the outer hull, the warhead passing cleanly through a radiation protection barrier between the outer and inner hull, exploding just as it exited the inner hull into Engineering Space Three.

The energy - along with assorted shrapnel - continued through the engineering space and impacted squarely into the tDrive, driving a hole the size of a basketball through the silver pyramid and out the other side.

Red hot pieces of shrapnel bounced off the opposite wall and rattled around on the floor before coming to a stop, smoke rising from them as they cooled.

And one piece of shrapnel killed Commander Sarah North, who had been in the compartment checking on a faulty sensor.

In a way, it was a small blessing. If the shrapnel had not killed her instantly, the loss of pressure and the radiation from the breached tDrive pyramid would have killed her slowly and in great agony.

The damage to the silver pyramid was extensive. *Dragon* no longer had a stardrive. The ship could not escape the Singheko system now.

On the bridge, alarms were blaring, and the AI was talking continuously on the command channel as General Quarters sounded throughout the ship.

<Enemy detection. 15 mega-klicks and closing, ETA 58

minutes>

<tDrive Inop>

<Ansible inop>

<Gamma lance inop>

<tDrive HE-4 pressure loss>

<tDrive radiation alarm>

<Pressure loss Engineering Space Three>

The alarms continued to blare as Bonnie and Luke ran onto the bridge almost simultaneously. Bonnie was wearing only pants and a bra. Luke was wearing pants and a T-shirt, carrying his uniform shirt in his hand.

Seeing Bonnie without a top, he tossed her his uniform shirt and ran to the Tac Console as Ensign Goodwin, now crying, vacated it abruptly.

Scanning the holotank, Luke saw the enemy ships coming, a gaggle of them.

"Two battlecruisers, two cruisers, and four destroyers," he yelled at Bonnie. "ETA 57 minutes, coming hard."

"Bit of an overkill, don't you think?" Bonnie quipped to Luke as she pointed to the incoming fleet, appearing clearly in the holo as the enemy ships ramped up their engines to full boost.

"Yeah," grinned Luke. "A bit much for one destroyer."

Luke finished his quick scan of the console. He turned back to Bonnie, his mouth set.

"Well, we're in trouble," he said grimly. "They got the tDrive. We're not gonna be leaving the system for a while. And that means we also lost the ansible and the gamma lance. We can't communicate with Rita."

"OK," said Bonnie, scanning her own console. "Do we still have the system engine?"

"I think so. It shows green, I'm bringing power up now. We're getting the hell out of here."

Bonnie felt the deck vibrate as the system engine powered up and the *Dragon* started to move.

"OK. If we have a good system engine, we can still outrun them. As far as I know, they're still limited to 255g normal,

260g overboost."

"Let's hope," said Luke. "System engine checks good. I'm limiting us to 270g until we see what they're gonna do. No use giving away all our capabilities at once."

Luke leaned back and stared at Bonnie.

"We've got a problem, though. We're well inside the mass limit. And we have to stay inside it. If we get outside it, they can translate out, jump, and re-surface right in front of us."

Bonnie looked grim.

"Yeah. But inside the mass limit, all we can do is just keep running."

"Yeah. It's gonna be the greyhounds chasing the rabbit," Luke said, thinking. "We'll have to go around and around the system with them chasing us while we try to repair the tDrive."

Luke thought some more as *Dragon* began to accelerate back into the system toward the star.

"And we've got another problem. Our higher accel and top speed isn't going to help us much. By the time we get halfway across the system, we have to start decel to turn around. Let me see…"

Luke did some quick calculations on his tablet.

"…we'll only be able to get 34% light before we have to start decel for the turnaround on the other side of the system. So our max speed of 50% light doesn't help us much."

"It's worse than that," said Bonnie. "Think about it. We have to build up tremendous speed to stay ahead of them. That means we can't just decel and turn on a dime. That's going to make our path very predictable."

Luke thought about it, frowned, and then shook his head.

"We can sling around one of the planets or the star to change our trajectory, come out on a random path."

"Yeah. But we can only do that once, maybe twice. Then they'll put a picket force on all the planets and the star, and we won't be able to go near them again. That's when we're really in trouble."

A huge sigh escaped from Luke as he realized just how much

danger was facing *Dragon*.

Bonnie smiled at him.

"No worries, Commander. We'll figure something out. But for now, just keep us inside the mass limit, as far away from them as we can get, buy us some time to think. And some time to work on the tDrive."

Bonnie turned to her console.

"*Dragon*, get me a damage report from Engineering."

***

The radiation alarms blared in the tDrive compartment, but nobody could hear them.

There was no air.

A thin layer of ice covered the floor and walls. Dan Worley walked carefully to the side and inspected the ragged hole in the inner hull.

His pressure suit also protected him from the radiation; but it made it hard to work. He squinted his eyes, trying to see clearly through the helmet.

Dragon's AI could dispatch nanobots to the area to fix the hole; but it took time for *Dragon* to migrate the huge number of nanobots needed for such a large repair.

Worley could expedite the process.

Lifting a large five-gallon bucket of glop that looked a bit like black treacle, he poured it slowly over the hole, then stepped away.

Behind him, another suited crewman poured another bucket of glop over the hole.

And then another behind him.

Even as Dan watched, the glop formed into a patch, slowly merging into the shape of the wall. Slowly closing the hole.

Dan stepped out of the line of crew pouring nanobots over the hole. They had things under control there. *Dragon* would complete the job of forming the nanobots into a plug that would restore hull integrity.

Turning back to the engineering space, he couldn't prevent his eyes from straying to the large red stain in the ice by the front control panel.

Sarah North's blood. They had removed the body - but cleaning up the blood-soaked ice would have to wait a bit.

With a shudder, he forced himself to look away, back to the tDrive pyramid, at the hole punched all the way through and out the other side.

That was a bigger problem.

Four ratings in environmental suits were installing scaffolding around the pyramid so they could work.

"Dan, can you give me a report?" he heard over his comm.

"Yes, Captain. There's a twelve-inch hole punched all the way through the tDrive pyramid. We're getting the scaffolding up to work on it. *Dragon* estimates we'll have pressure back in another two hours. But we'll still have to work in radiation suits until we seal the holes in the pyramid. We're about to start pouring nano on the pyramid. Once the pyramid is sealed, we can start the repairs."

"What's your ETA on getting our tDrive back?"

Dan shook his head inside his helmet, even though nobody could see it.

"At least three days, I think. Maybe four."

***

"We can't catch her," said Orma.

"Don't tell me what's obvious, Orma. I've got eyes," growled Zukra, staring at the holo. "But how the hell are they able to get 270g out of that destroyer? The signature on it is ancient!"

Orma shrugged. "I don't know, sir. But they're doing it. 270g to 34% light, right across the system to the other side. Clearly, we disabled their tDrive. They can't translate out. So all they can do is run."

Zukra grinned.

"Yes. They can run. But they can't go anywhere. And sooner or later, they'll make a mistake, and we'll have them."

Zukra returned to his seat on the bridge and pointed to the holo.

"I want you to hound them from pillar to post. Give them

no rest. Chase them around this system until either something breaks on their ship, or something breaks in their minds."

Orma looked at the plot.

"You know, sir, it occurs to me..."

"Yes, yes, Orma, spit it out!"

"Well, we can't catch them in a straight line, but maybe we can herd them."

Zukra shook his head.

"And what good will that do? They'll just take off in a different direction."

"Yes, sir. But maybe we can put a minefield in front of them, and herd them into it."

Zukra thought about it.

"That's not a half-bad idea, Orma. I'm shocked you came up with it!"

"Yes, sir."

"Let me think about it."

"Yes, sir."

"Sir - you have a call from Admiral Ligar!" called the Comm Officer.

"I'll take it in my cabin," muttered Zukra. He rose and went through the hatch to his day cabin off the bridge. Sitting at his desk, he composed himself briefly, then activated the screen.

"Admiral Ligar! How are you today?"

"Never better, Zukra. But what's this I hear about you chasing a Nidarian ship around our system?"

"It's not Nidarian, sir. It's one of those Garatella gave the Humans. An old one - so old, we had to dredge records out of our inactive database to identify it."

"Ah. You're sure?"

"Yes, sir. Definitely not Nidarian. Plus if it had been, they would have contacted us as soon as they realized they were detected. But they didn't, they just ran. It's those stinking Humans."

"Alright. That's good news. This is not a time to antagonize the Nidarians. We've got long-term plans to get those little bastards out of our hair once and for all. But it's important you don't cause any problems with them right now, understand? We don't want to give them any early warning."

"Yes, sir."

"So, tend to your knitting here in the system. What's your next move?"

"Well, sir, it seems this ship has some kind of improved drive system. We knocked out their tDrive, so they can't leave the system. But they can pull 270g accel and go all the way up to 34% light. I don't know how they're doing that - some kind of new drive improvements from Garatella, I guess - but we can't catch them in a straight race."

Ligar sounded surprised.

"That's strange! How is it we didn't know the Nidarians had that capability?"

"It's something new, sir. Something we haven't seen before."

"Ah. Well. Then you'd better capture that ship so we can get that technology, Zukra."

"Understood, sir. They just finished a run to the other side of the system, did a slingshot around a gas giant, and now they've reversed around and they're on their way back. But we've blocked off all the planets now - they won't be able to do that again."

Ligar laughed.

"So they're leading you a merry chase, are they, Zukra?"

"I guess so, Admiral. But we'll get them."

"I don't see how, Zukra."

"No worries, sir. We'll come up with something."

"Alright. If you say so. Keep me informed."

"Aye, sir."

Ligar dropped the link, and Zukra leaned back in his chair.

This could get embarrassing if it goes on too long. I think Orma's plan is best. We'll mine the hell out of someplace and then drive them into it.

"Orma!"

***

The Dariama destroyer led *Banjala* to a moon near their fifth planet, a frozen iceball 2.6 AU from the star - and 360 million klicks from their home planet of Dekanna. The corvette was ordered to enter orbit and await a shuttle.

The moon was hardly better than the iceball planet below, but at least there was a facility built on it, covered by a dome, and showing some greenery inside.

"These assholes are really paranoid," said Roberto, standing beside Winnie. Well behind them, Captain Shimbiro of the *Banjala* stood with his XO, more than content to let Winnie and Roberto handle the aliens.

"Got that right," agreed Winnie. "And not only will they not let us near their home planet, they won't even let us use our own shuttle to go down to the moon. What the hell could a shuttle do?"

"Yep."

With a clunk, they heard the Dariama shuttle docking to the outside of the *Banjala*.

"Showtime," said Roberto.

Winnie nodded.

This has to be the strangest thing I've ever done. Joining the Navy, learning to fly, fifteen years in the fleet, two wars. Being seconded to the EDF, training on the Merlins, getting ready to fight aliens in space...

...And now meeting an alien species for the first time. An emissary. An ambassador. How the hell does a fighter pilot get in this situation?

The telltale light on the airlock switched from red to green. The ratings at the airlock swung the hatch inward and pulled it back.

Two figures stood in the airlock. At first glance, they looked completely human. Both were roughly Winnie's height, about five-eight. Both were proportioned like Humans.

Both were dark-skinned, as was Winnie.

Was that why Jim picked me? Because I'm Black?

No. He wouldn't do that. He told me he picked me because I was the best. And that's certainly true. I am the best.

With a smile, Winnie stepped forward. She was afraid to hold out her hand. She didn't know greeting customs for these people, and she knew how the Nidarians didn't like to have their hands shaken.

So she stood, smiling, waiting for some sign from them. Her briefing materials - received from *Merkkessa* as they were departing - told her they were oxygen breathers like humans and could manage Human or Nidarian atmospheres with no problem.

But nothing in the briefing had covered greeting customs.

The smaller of the two stepped forward onto the deck of the *Banjala* and made a slight bow. Winnie decided this one was female - mainly because her hair was longer than the other, and she was smaller.

I hope I'm not falling victim to stereotypes here. It could be ass-backwards from that. Maybe the small long-haired ones are males.

The figure spoke in Nidarian. Like all members of *Merkkessa*'s crew, Winnie had been studying Nidarian for six months. She wasn't fluent, but she could understand most of it. Nevertheless, she waited for the translation from the AI.

<Greetings to the Nidarian and Human travelers. We received your message. We will take you to the facility on the moon below for discussions. Please board our shuttle at your convenience>

Well, at least they're polite. Hopefully, that means they won't shoot us on arrival.

Speaking in somewhat halting Nidarian, Winnie replied.

"Thank you. We are ready."

The two figures turned and re-entered the airlock. Winnie and Roberto followed. The airlock hatch closed. The green light on the outside wall was still lit, indicating a good seal with the boarding tube outside. When the inner hatch was sealed, the outer hatch opened and the two Dariama stepped forward, entering the boarding tube.

With a glance at Roberto, Winnie entered the tube behind

them.

14 - THE LONG EDGE

The mass limit for the Singheko system was a sphere 14.5 AU in diameter, centered on the primary star.

4.34 billion kilometers.

2.66 billion miles.

It seemed like a lot, saying it out loud.

But when you were trapped inside that sphere, running for your life from a fleet of ships trying to kill you...

It didn't seem so large anymore.

In fact, *Dragon* was trapped inside a slightly smaller sphere. If she got too near the mass limit, the Singheko fleet could translate a warship into space in front of her, firing at her as she went by.

Dragon had to avoid the edge of the sphere completely.

A rat in a trap.

Luke turned over in his bunk for the tenth time since lying down.

Sleep wouldn't come. It was hard to sleep with fifty warships dogging your every move, waiting for the slightest mistake to blow you to hell.

He cursed under his breath, flopped over in the bunk again, trying to find a comfortable position.

There was a light knock on his door. Just a slight couple of taps.

He wasn't even sure he had heard it.

"Come!" he yelled, in case it was real.

The door opened and a figure entered.

Luke didn't have to turn on the lights to recognize his Captain.

Before he could get out of bed, Bonnie moved quickly to his bunk and sank down beside him.

Behind her, the hatch swung closed and clicked as it latched, throwing the room into darkness.

Luke felt Bonnie's hands on his shoulders. She leaned over him, so close her bobbed hair fell in his face.

"Luke..." she started.

She was crying. One of her tears fell on his lips.

"I know this is a mistake..."

The saltiness of her tears was the most wonderful thing he had ever tasted.

She leaned forward, placed her head on his chest.

"This night is so long. And it has a sharp edge to it... knowing we're probably going to die soon. It's cutting me to pieces..."

Finally he spoke. Because it was real. It wasn't a dream.

"It's alright, Bonnie. It'll be alright."

She lifted her head. She kissed him, slowly, taking her time.

The taste of her salty tears on his lips...

Luke responded, all his love for her coming out at last.

"I just didn't want to die without telling you I'm in love with you," she said, adding another kiss for emphasis.

Luke pulled her into the bunk on top of him.

"I'm in love with you too, Bonnie," he said.

"So either way, live or die, we're totally screwed," said Bonnie.

Luke smiled.

"We are indeed."

***

At 0700 Bonnie entered the bridge.

"How're we doing?" she asked as she took over the command chair from Rachel, who had been standing Third Watch OOD.

"Not so good, mum," responded Rachel. "They continue their strategy of pinching us in, herding us around. We had to give ground again early this morning. They're a clever bunch."

Bonnie nodded, staring at the holotank, and reviewing recent events on her console.

"Yep. Well, you did a good job of limiting how much they pushed us in, I see. Good work, Lieutenant."

"Thank you, mum."

Rachel stared at her captain. There was something about Bonnie this morning...

Her face was bright - and she seemed a completely different person from the day before.

Bonnie noticed Rachel's look and gave her a big smile.

"We'll get out of this, Lieutenant. I promise you. Now go get some rest."

"Aye, mum," Rachel responded and turned to go. As she approached the hatch, Commander Powell entered the bridge.

His face was glowing, and his smile was a mile wide.

Oh my God, thought Rachel as she snapped to the situation. *Oh, I can't believe this!*

Luke went to his console and caught himself up to date on the situation as the rest of First Watch filtered in.

Then he turned to Bonnie.

"Good morning, Skipper. How are you feeling?"

"Peachy," smiled Bonnie. "You?"

"Wonderful," smiled Luke.

They stared at each other for a while, then suddenly came back to reality.

"Uh, yeah," agreed Bonnie. She stared at the holo. "What's our status?"

"The usual. They keep trying to pinch us in closer to the star. They've got battlecruisers and cruisers out in front of us again, so we'll have to change vector shortly. There's a flotilla of destroyers riding herd on our inside lane, and a gaggle of cruisers outside of us. So I guess we either go up or down - then make a break to the other side of the system again."

Luke scratched his head, and then continued in a thoughtful voice.

"You know, we could just make a break for the mass limit,

and just keep going, right up to 50% light. Even though they'll be able to translate in front of us once we're outside the mass limit, by then we'll be moving so fast they'll be hard-pressed to hit us."

"But they'll have forever to try," said Bonnie. "So sooner or later they'll get lucky."

"Yeah," said Luke. "But all we need to do is buy enough time for Rita to get here. Or to fix the tDrive."

Bonnie bit her lower lip, thinking it through.

"No, we'll keep playing rabbit and greyhounds with them here in the system for as long as we can. Just keep bobbing and weaving and hope Rita gets here soon."

"Aye, mum."

Luke was grinning as he said it, a glint in his eye. Bonnie gave him a side-eye.

Settle down, big boy.

"OK. Plan for another dash across the system the next time they try to box us in. We'll take another tour across our beautiful Singheko tourist destination."

"You got it, Skipper," grinned Luke, turning to his console.

***

Two hours later, the Singheko made their move.

A flotilla of cruisers took a vector that would intercept *Dragon* within a few minutes.

Dragon was forced to turn inward, back toward the star, to avoid them.

But she couldn't go straight in. That path was blocked by the flotilla of destroyers.

So she could go up or down at an angle to get by the destroyers.

She chose to go down, taking a vector that would put her beneath the ecliptic, to bypass the destroyer flotilla and let her run across the system again.

The M21 mines that had been planted in that path were lying completely inert except for their passive sensors.

Until *Dragon* came into close range of one of them.

The time between the mine's activation, firing its motor, and making the dash to *Dragon* was less than 6 seconds.

Even *Dragon*'s AI couldn't move her mass aside in that amount of time. She made a mighty effort - after the fiasco with the first missile and Ensign Goodwin's confusion, Bonnie had modified *Dragon*'s AI programming to allow independent action for anti-missile defense.

And *Dragon* almost made it. The mine caught only the barest corner of the right engine as *Dragon* slewed away hard.

It was just enough to knock a small chunk off the engine. It didn't disable the engine completely; but it substantially reduced its efficiency.

Dragon's accel dropped to 253g. Instantly Bonnie knew they were in trouble.

She sounded the overboost klaxon, gave the crew sixty seconds to react and find a safe place, then ordered the helm to slam the throttles to max to see how much accel the *Dragon* could actually produce now. It was something she had to know, and quickly.

The answer was not good. 260g was all the ship could muster, even with the throttles maxed out. And the compensator crapped out at 253g. The intense pressure of seven times their normal body weight crushed her mixed Human/Nidarian crew into their seats, limiting their ability to move around or fight.

Their max emergency accel was now the same as the Singheko could routinely do with their bigger, tougher bodies.

Behind her, Zukra's fleet converged on her from every direction.

It was a whole new ball game.

***

At Dekanna, Winnie and Roberto were prisoners.

Not officially, of course. They were well-treated, provided with comfortable rooms. They could walk down the hallway to the central garden, which was covered in greenery and had beautiful, colorful flowers under the domed roof.

But they had been cut off from communications with the *Banjala*. Each time they asked to send a message, they were told the same thing.

Tomorrow.

They had been on the iceball moon for two days. In that time, they had met with the Dariama representatives four times, twice each day, for an hour.

Each meeting had been the same. It was always the same two, the male and the female who had brought them down on the shuttle.

Winnie had started to see the differences now between the Dariama and Humans. They were universally a dark chocolate brown. Their ears were larger than a human's. Their elbow joints worked differently somehow, as did their knee joints. Their eyes saw in a slightly different spectrum - they could see farther into the infrared, but not as well at lower visual frequencies. And internally, she suspected, there would be many more differences.

The meetings always went the same way. The Dariama began by presenting the holo Rita had sent them, showing the Singheko fleet on a vector toward Dekanna.

Then they asked why the Humans had forged the holo. Was it to create trouble between the Singheko and the Dariama? Were they trying to start a war? Why did they want to start a war? How had they accomplished the forgery?

Winnie and Roberto tried to keep calm throughout all this. Winnie realized the Dariama were trying to rattle them, cause them to make a mistake, get caught in a lie. So she simply and calmly denied their accusations and fired back at them at every opportunity.

If the holo is a forgery, then prove it.

If the Humans wanted to start a war between the Dariama and the Singheko, there are easier ways to do it.

And if they did, why would they try to convince the Dariama that the Singheko were coming here? Wouldn't they try to convince them to come to Singheko and fight with the Humans?

No matter what Winnie said, however, the result was always the same. The Dariama were completely, totally paranoid, and convinced the Humans were up to some scam.

Then they would ask about the *Banjala*. Even if the Human story were true, how could the *Banjala* arrive before the Singheko?

We have a new drive technology which the Singheko do not have.

We cannot tell you about the technology if you are not allied with us.

This would go on for two hours.

And then the Dariama would take them back to their rooms.

On the third morning, Winnie lay back in her bunk, head propped up on her pillows. Roberto sat at the desk, twirling his dogtags.

"We're getting nowhere," Roberto complained to Winnie. "This is a complete waste of time."

Winnie nodded glumly.

"And this Nidarian food they're giving us - ugh," said Roberto. "Tasteless. So bland. I don't see how the Nidarians stand it."

"Well, you're not Nidarian," Winnie answered. "Maybe to them it tastes like burritos."

"Cute," said Roberto.

There was a knock at the door. Roberto got up and opened it.

The female - they had learned her name was Kumara - stood waiting.

"Will you come with us for a meeting?" she asked in Nidarian.

Winnie looked at Roberto. It was always the same greeting every morning.

Here we go again.

She got up and followed him out the door as they headed to the conference room.

But this time, when they entered, something was different. The larger male was not present. In his place was another female. This one wore military dress uniform, dark blue, with ribbons on the chest, some unknown rank insignia on the collar, multiple stripes around the sleeves. As they entered the room, the officer rose and waited patiently for them. Kumara ushered them to their chairs and they sat.

And then Kumara left the room, leaving them alone with the strange officer, who sat down and stared.

"It's incredible," she said in Nidarian.

"What?" asked Winnie.

"You look so much like us." The officer turned her gaze to Roberto.

"Except for him. Do you have many who are improperly colored?"

Winnie suppressed a smile. She could sense Roberto trying not to laugh.

"We have several colors in our species," Winnie said. "His color is normal for his race. My color is normal for my race."

"Ah," said the officer. "Like the Singheko and the Ampato, then."

Winnie was puzzled. "I'm sorry, I don't know about that."

"No matter," said the officer. "I am Admiral Sobong. I am Chief of Intelligence for the Dekanna Union."

"Pleased to meet you, Admiral. I am..."

"I know who you are, Commander," interrupted the Admiral. Sobong leaned back in her chair and stared at Winnie for a long time. The silence started to become awkward, but Winnie moved not a muscle. She stared back at Sobong, never dropping her gaze for an instant.

This is the crux. This is the moment. Make or break.

Finally Sobong smiled. She waved a hand, and the hologram showing the war fleet departing from Singheko toward Dekanna played once again over the table. They watched it silently until the end. Sobong waved her hand again, and the holo disappeared.

"Our scientific teams have decided it's within the realm of possibility that your holo is real, Commander. So we are faced with a dilemma. If the holo is real, then possibly your story is real. Or not, who can say. But my job is to treat it as real and formulate a plan based around that assumption. Do not worry, there are other officers assigned to treat it as false and make plans for that case also. So either way, we will be prepared."

Winnie nodded. "Good. I'm glad you're starting to take this seriously."

"Which brings us to the problem. My problem. If this is real, how do we confirm it? How do we provide support for your story? Do you have any suggestions, Commander?"

Winnie had been thinking about this very scenario. For the two days they had been stuck on the moon incommunicado, she had been thinking. Now she sat up straight, excited.

"Admiral. Do you think it possible to drop a message buoy in front of the Singheko fleet and cause them to retrieve it?"

Sobong stared at Winnie. The ghost of a smile pulled up one corner of her mouth.

"Perhaps. If they are actually on the way here, as you say. But how would you get to a place to drop a buoy before they arrive?"

"As we have tried to tell you, our ship can travel in six-space ten times faster than the Singheko. That's how we got here in time to warn you. We can board the *Banjala* and intercept them at least two hundred lights from Dekanna. Drop a buoy right in front of them."

Sobong shook her head in disbelief. "It's not possible. No ship can travel that fast."

"Let us prove it," said Winnie.

Sobong stared at her. Then she slowly pushed back her chair and rose.

"Let's go, Commander."

15 - A STRANGE WAY OF DOIN' IT

Rita's EDF fleet had arrived outside the Singheko system yesterday. Jim's fourship of fighters worked their way into the system carefully, watching for surprises, maintaining stealth.

They had not heard from *Dragon* in two days. Her reports had simply stopped, without warning, as they approached the star system.

Now Jim knew why.

He stared at the VR in the Merlin's small cockpit in shock. He could see *Dragon*, 10 AU away, on the other side of the star.

"Crap!" he exclaimed, before he could stop himself.

Dragon was running for her life.

Her accel should have allowed her to outrun any of the Singheko warships in a straight race. But she wasn't making her normal accel. Except for brief periods when she boosted to 260g, she was only making 253g.

She's lost her tDrive, and her system drive is damaged. All she can do is run a race around the system, trying to buy time.

A cloud of enemy ships was behind her, above and below her, trying to box her in.

The pursuers had the advantage in this race. Bonnie had little choice in her path - she couldn't get too close to the 14.5 AU mass limit, or an enemy ship would jump in and ambush her.

She couldn't use her greater top speed because by the time she got near 34% of light, she was already at the point where she had to start deceleration to prevent bumping up against the edge of the system.

And each time she reversed course to set a new path, another group of enemy ships would appear in front of her, forcing her to a new vector.

A path closer in to the star.

They were herding her, Jim realized. Herding her into a position as close to the star as they could, limiting the space she had to accelerate.

And sooner or later, they'd have her.

Jim had watched for hours, slowly moving in closer to get a better view.

He had already dispatched two of his flight back to the *Merkkessa* with the layout of the system, positions of the enemy ships, and the *Dragon*'s situation.

Now he wanted to go to Bonnie's aid, distract some of the enemy ships, give her some relief.

But he couldn't.

Rita had given him explicit instructions to remain hidden. The element of surprise Rita needed was too valuable to give away.

"Red 2 to Red Lead, message relay from Command. RTB, RTB, RTB."

RTB. Return to Base.

"Crap! She's just going to leave her there!" Jim shouted at the universe in frustration.

***

"We have to help Bonnie! She's in trouble!"

Rita glared at Jim across the briefing table.

"Commander Carter," she spoke, and her voice was like ice. "Please get control of your emotions."

Jim stopped speaking abruptly. He looked around, realized what he had done.

This is not our bedroom. I'm not a husband here. I'm a CAG. Think like one.

Captains Bekerose and Dallitta looked down at the briefing

table, pretending to ignore Jim's outburst. Five additional Captains were also present, having shuttled over from their respective capital ships.

"Sorry, Admiral," Jim responded. "You're right. I let my emotions get ahead of me."

Rita glared at him. She was not happy.

"Bonnie's a big girl. She can take care of herself. Let's plan our attack properly, and the sooner we get that done, the sooner we help Bonnie."

"Quite right," Jim said. "Sorry."

The short uncomfortable silence was quickly broken by Captain Bekerose.

"I recommend we perform a system entry here..."

Bekerose indicated a point directly above the planet Ridendo.

"...and drive straight for Ridendo. That way, no matter where they are in the system, they have no choice but to turn and face us. They don't dare leave the home planet undefended."

Rita studied the holo.

"Captain Sato? What do you think?"

"I agree, milady. This last intel from Commander Carter shows them pushing *Dragon* nearly up to the star. At some point, she has to try to break out. That would be the perfect time for our system entry. As they chase *Dragon* back out into the system, we let them get to roughly the orbit of the fourth planet - Deriko, they call it - then attack from above Ridendo. They'll have no choice but to break off and turn to face us. That puts us in the inner position to them, which is where we want to be. And it might allow *Dragon* to make her escape."

Rita studied the holo a bit longer.

"Dallitta, when do you think Bonnie will be forced to make a break for it?"

"Based on the scans Jim brought back, she'll be forced to do that sometime tomorrow, our time."

"Then that's when we attack. Where do you want to deploy

the Merlins, Commander Carter?"

Jim pointed on the holo.

"We'll leave three squadrons with you for defense. We'll drop the remaining two squadrons right here before you transit across the system. We'll ghost those two squadrons into the system and position them near the Singheko fleet chasing Bonnie.

"When the Singheko detect you coming into the system and turn to face you, that'll put two squadrons behind them, in good position for a surprise attack from the rear."

"How soon can we be ready?"

"We can drop the two squadrons of Merlins right now," said Bekerose. "Then we can be in position across the system two hours after that. We give the Merlins twenty hours to get into position, then we attack."

Rita nodded.

"Make it so, folks. Get us ready and let's put some hurt on these bastards."

***

Winnie found the Singheko 345.104 light years from Dekanna, right where the AI predicted.

Banjala surfaced into three-space at the designated point and they sat quietly, listening intently for the slight gravity ripples that would tell them the Singheko fleet was passing.

Sobong kept shaking her head in disbelief at the speed of the *Banjala* through six-space.

"How? How is this possible?" she asked again and again.

Winnie had given her the entire history - how *Dragon*, an advanced destroyer of the ancient Golden Empire, had been abandoned in Earth's Solar System two thousand years earlier. How Bonnie Page had tracked her down and restored her to operating condition. How Garatella had lent the Humans a rag-tag fleet of warships. How Humans had used those warships to fight off the Singheko invasion at Earth, using a combination of desperate tactics and the new drives obtained from *Dragon*.

And how the Humans were preparing to counterattack the

Singheko to prevent another invasion.

"But you can't trust Garatella," Sobong said. "He is a devil. He will smile at you with one hand and put the knife in you with the other."

"Perhaps," agreed Winnie. "But so far he has helped us. Without him, we would be slaves of the Singheko now."

"But you cannot win," Sobong said. "Zukra will crush you."

Winnie grinned at her.

"We may surprise you, Admiral. We've certainly surprised the Singheko so far."

And then the callout from the Tac Officer. They had detected the incredibly tiny ripples of spacetime that showed the Singheko fleet was approaching. Winnie showed the display to Sobong as Captain Shimbiro computed the Singheko course and speed in six-space and moved the corvette down their track a light year.

And there dropped a message buoy, one provided by Sobong, which she claimed would be a perfect imitation of an actual Singheko message buoy. It would contain an innocuous message, she said, one that would not arouse suspicion but should cause them to stop and retrieve it.

And they stood off and watched as an entire fleet of Singheko warships transitioned back into three-space to retrieve the message buoy.

"Two battlecruisers, four cruisers, eight destroyers, four corvettes and two supply ships," breathed Sobong, staring at the holo as the Singheko fleet sank out again and continued on their way. She turned to Winnie.

"Just as you said. Just as on the holo."

Winnie nodded.

"I've done my part, Admiral. The next move is up to you."

But Sobong called her bluff.

"No, Commander. The next move is up to you. The ability to travel faster than the Singheko in six-space would have given you some advantage. But not sufficient advantage to defeat them in three-space. You are holding something back. What other advantage did you have to defeat them at Earth?"

Winnie closed her eyes. She had known this was coming. Sobong was too smart to fail to see it. And there was no way around it.

"Yes, Admiral. We have another advantage. This ship can boost up to 300g in normal space - and maintain protection up to 50% light."

There was a long silence as Sobong absorbed the information.

"Take us back to Dekanna. Then show me."

***

Jim Carter, Commander, Earth Defense Force, sat in his Merlin and waited for launch.

The argument with Rita had been hot and nasty. She had come within an inch of ordering him out of the fighter.

When she found out Jim was buckled into a Merlin for the attack, his comm lit up like a convention of robocallers.

"Commander Carter, get your ass out of that fighter and back to Flight Control where you belong," Rita yelled.

"Admiral. Please listen," Jim had started.

"Bullshit! You have no business in a Merlin! Get back to Flight Control!"

Jim spoke very quietly, a faint smile touching his lips.

"Admiral. I need to see things firsthand. I need to be there. If you want me to do my job, then let me do it."

There was a long and pregnant pause.

Jim was sure she was going to order him out of the fighter.

But in the end, she relented.

"You're the CAG. If you say you need to be there, then go do it. But if you get yourself killed, you're fired. Not only that, you're demoted to ensign, then fired."

Jim grinned.

That's my girl.

"Aye, aye, milady," he answered.

***

The g-force pushed Jim back hard and he was out of the

ship, accelerating away. Fifteen Merlins were beside him, an array of fighters spreading out in a fan shape as they were ejected out of the sortie deck.

Behind him in his VR, he could see another squadron of sixteen fighters launching - his second squadron.

Reaching the required minimum distance, Jim called over his comm.

"Raider One, form up."

His squadron moved into their standard loose combat spread; four flights arranged in a square. Each flight contained four fighters in a modified finger-four formation.

His AI automatically issued orders to the AI of the other squadron behind him. With a burst of accel, the sixteen fighters of Raider Two squadron caught up and fell into position.

"*Angel*, take us to point Alpha-Four," Jim spoke. Obediently, his AI synced up both squadrons - all thirty-two fighters - into a single combat group and they headed into the system.

As their velocity increased and the *Merkkessa* was left behind, Jim sent one last comm to the battlecruiser.

"Good hunting, *Merkkessa*."

"Good hunting to you, Raider Lead," came the response from Captain Bekerose.

In his VR, Jim saw the *Merkkessa* and the rest of the fleet translate out behind him and disappear.

They would move to the top of the system, over Ridendo, and make entry there. Jim and his two squadrons of Merlins would enter on this side of the system, trying their utmost to sneak in undetected and come up behind the Singheko fleet in a surprise attack.

There were a lot of variables.

How good were the Singheko sensors? Would they detect the Merlins? How far away? Would the new gamma lances on the Merlins be strong enough to take down a capital ship?

And more personally for Jim: where was Bonnie and the *Dragon* now? Was she still alive?

But first they had to accelerate into the system. When they entered the system, they would be traveling at 10% light speed. It would take them twenty hours to arrive at their rendezvous point before Rita's fleet came busting in above Ridendo.

Time to get moving.

16 - THAT ONE WITH THE FEATHERS

"Keep pushing them in, Orma," ordered Admiral Zukra. "They've got no place to go. Just keep pinching them in."

"Aye, sir," agreed Captain Orma.

"Just use our numbers to keep herding them closer to the center of the system. Get them boxed in close to the star. Then their greater top speed doesn't help them. Sooner or later, we'll have them."

"Aye, sir. I've issued the orders."

"Excellent. Excellent."

Zukra sat on the Flag Bridge of the Singheko battlecruiser *Ambush*, staring at the holotank.

He could see the *Dragon*, making her latest run away from them.

They had damaged her stardrive, that was clear. She couldn't escape the system. And now they had damaged her system drive as well.

All she could do was run.

It had been a long three days. So far, they had chased her around the system several times, never quite getting into missile range.

But Zukra had fifty ships chasing her now - every warship, every corvette, even some tugs and tenders he was using to try and push her closer to the star. Some of them he had taken right out of the repair yards and pressed into service to run down this interloper.

And sixty fighters launched from his battlecruisers.

The enemy couldn't leave the mass limit. If they did, Zukra could translate a cruiser in behind them and blow them to hell.

But they knew that. They were being careful not to get any closer than 1/2 AU to the mass limit.

Zukra sighed.

"This would be so easy if they would just give up. They have no chance. They can't go anywhere. They have to know we'll get them in the end."

"Sir, it occurs to me we're a bit thin on ships in the Home Fleet right now," said Orma.

"So?" responded Zukra irritably.

"Well, sir, I was thinking. What if the Humans brought their old Nidarian fleet in on us now? That could be a bit of a problem."

Zukra laughed.

"Those old tubs? Look at this one we're chasing. So ancient, we had to pull her signature out of an obsolete database. They're a joke. Besides..."

Zukra shifted in his chair, smiling at Orma.

"...we're already certain the Humans took their borrowed fleet to Earth. And our expedition there would have wiped them out already. You have nothing to worry about, Orma."

"As you say, sir," said the aide.

***

Eighteen hours later, Bonnie looked at the holo, then turned to Luke.

"I think I've had about enough of this crap, Luke."

Since the exploding mine had reduced their accel, the Singheko had pinched them in closer and closer to the star at the center of the system. Now *Dragon* was only 0.4 AU from the star - about the same distance as the orbit of Mercury in the Sol system.

Dragon could still reach a faster final speed than the Singheko, but she couldn't out accelerate them anymore. When she overboosted to 260g, the Singheko did the same.

It was a tie, except for one thing. The enemy's physically stronger bodies allowed them to tolerate the crushing weight for longer periods than Humans or Nidarians.

And though *Dragon*'s higher top speed allowed her to get ahead of the enemy for short periods, inevitably another flotilla of enemy warships appeared in front of them and forced them into a new path.

Always closer to the star, tightening the circle around them.

Thus Bonnie and her crew had spent most of the last eighteen hours alternately crushed into their seats at +7g, struggling to breathe as they escaped another ambush - or gasping for air in the moments of brief respite when they got a little bit of lead on their pursuers.

"I'm tired of these fuckers," continued Bonnie. "They'll have us up against the star in another few hours. Let's make a run for it."

Luke nodded.

"If you say so, Skipper. I'm getting pretty tired of this cat-and-mouse myself."

Bonnie sat down in her command chair.

"Sound General Quarters, *Dragon*," she called.

<GENERAL QUARTERS, GENERAL QUARTERS. THIS IS NOT A DRILL. ALL HANDS MAN YOUR BATTLE STATIONS. GENERAL QUARTERS, GENERAL QUARTERS. THIS IS NOT A DRILL. ALL HANDS MAN YOUR BATTLE STATIONS>

"*Dragon*, warn plus 7g for ten minutes," called Luke.

<STAND BY FOR HIGH G MANEUVERS. PLUS 7G FOR TEN MINUTES. STAND BY FOR HIGH G MANEUVERS. PLUS 7G FOR TEN MINUTES>

"*Dragon*, give us a mark when all divisions are ready."

<Mark. All divisions are reporting ready for high-g maneuvers>

Bonnie tightened up her straps. She looked at Luke.

"Let's go."

And just like that, *Dragon* made her break. The element of surprise helped some. The two Singheko destroyers almost directly in front of her took a bit of time to realize what was happening.

But as she passed between them, both of the enemy ships started shooting.

Dragon had been moving at 447,549 kph when she made her break for it.

At 260g, she was moving 2,084,118 kph three minutes later when she passed between the two destroyers, flicking by them in a few heartbeats.

It wasn't quite fast enough.

A spread of eight missiles from each destroyer fanned out as *Dragon* approached. Sixteen missiles vectored in toward her, accelerating at 2,000g.

Fifteen of the missiles were taken out by *Dragon*'s point defense or ran out of fuel before they could catch her.

The sixteenth and last one was a near-miss just off the already damaged right engine, knocking her acceleration down to 250g.

5g less than the Singheko ships were running at standard military acceleration.

Streaking away from the two destroyers, *Dragon* continued her headlong run, fifty Singheko warships in pursuit.

They didn't have to hurry now. They had her.

***

<Five minutes> called Jim's AI, *Angel*.

Five minutes.

Five minutes until the Singheko fleet in front of Jim's lurking fighter group would see the light propagated from high above their solar system as Rita's fleet entered directly above Ridendo.

Five minutes until the enemy commander would know that two battlecruisers, four cruisers, three destroyers and three corvettes were bearing down on his world.

Five minutes until the commander of that fleet would have to make a decision.

And five minutes until Jim would have to make his own

hard decision.

Because if he followed his orders and continued his stealthy approach behind the enemy, setting up for an attack run on them simultaneous with Rita's attack from the other side…

…he wouldn't be able to help Bonnie.

And in that case, Bonnie would die. He could see her on the holo. She had tried to break out of the box. But she had taken another hit. She had lost another increment of accel, and now the Singheko were all over her.

Jim had watched it play out on his plot during the long, grinding trip in from the mass limit. And he knew what would happen.

Sure, the enemy admiral would turn his fleet to meet Rita's advance - he would have no choice, if he wanted to defend his planet.

But he would leave a force behind to kill *Dragon*. Jim was sure of it.

It was obvious. Because that's what any competent commander would do.

A couple or three destroyers could easily knock off a damaged ship limping along, unable to outrun them.

Surely Rita will see this when she comes into the system.

Surely, she isn't jealous that Bonnie and I were once lovers. I made my choice. I'm hers now. She knows that.

And for that matter, she was once in love with Bonnie as well. Probably still is.

Surely, she'll let me go help Bonnie.

And if she doesn't…I'll go anyway.

***

"We won't be hiding our entry, Captain," Rita told Bekerose. "In fact, I want to make it as splashy as possible. If *Dragon* is still alive, maybe we can pull their ships off her and give her some breathing space."

"Aye, milady," Bekerose acknowledged from his Captain's console.

Below Rita's elevated Flag Bridge, Bekerose issued orders to his crew. And then with a loud whine and a bit of a bump, *Merkkessa* translated back into three-space, 14.5 AU from the star, on a course direct to the Singheko home world of Ridendo.

"That should get their attention," called Bekerose. "We came back in with a bang. They couldn't miss us if they were bat-blind and stupider than a *nedgan*."

"*Nedgan*?" asked Rita.

"Oh, sorry," grinned Bekerose. "It's a Nidarian monkey that makes a bag of rocks look smart."

"Gotcha," smiled Rita.

"Increasing acceleration to 300g," called Tac. "Course set to the Singheko home planet."

"It's called Ridendo, Lt. Carlson," Bekerose said dryly. "Any sign of *Dragon*?"

"Aye, Captain," called Carlson. "I have *Dragon* on the other side of the star accelerating at 245g. She's got at least fifty enemy ships converging on her plus a ton of fighters."

"Aw, shit," said Rita. "She's lost some more of her accel. They're on her like flies. And we can't help her from here - we're too far away."

Bekerose nodded assent. "All we can do is hope to pull away some of the enemy and buy her some time."

Rita chewed her lip momentarily.

I can't just leave her there. I still love that woman; in spite of the fact she pisses me off sometimes.

"Where's Jim's group right now?"

"Coming in behind the Singheko, milady," answered Dallitta.

"Send an order to Jim. Detach one squadron to support *Dragon*. Other squadron to continue with the attack on the Singheko rear."

"Aye, milady. Do you wish to designate which squadron goes to help *Dragon*?"

Rita grimaced.

"No, it wouldn't matter what I said. Jim will go himself."

"Aye, milady," smiled Dallitta, sending the order on her

console.

***

"Admiral!"

Zukra was half-asleep in his Flag Chair, at the back of the bridge. His flagship *Ambush* was speeding toward *Dragon*. They were now only a few million klicks behind the strange enemy ship and making ground fast.

With an overtake accel of 5g, they'd have her in another two hours.

"Admiral!"

Drowsily, Zukra lifted his head.

"What?"

Captain Orma pointed to the holo. The Tac officer had highlighted a large fleet of ships entering the system, high above the ecliptic.

Headed directly for their home world, Ridendo.

Zukra came fully awake.

"Signatures?" he snapped at the Tac officer.

"Nidarian, sir. One of the battlecruisers is the *Merkkessa*. So it's the Humans. But sir..."

Zukra glared at the Tac Officer.

"What is it?"

"...one of the other battlecruisers is the *BlackWind*, sir. Our flagship from the Earth expedition. Also one of the cruisers and several of the destroyers are from our Earth expedition."

Zukra shook his head in disbelief. He looked across the bridge at Orma.

"There must be some mistake," he growled.

"Perhaps our fleet captured the *Merkkessa* and converted it to our own use," said Orma.

Zukra stared at the plot.

"No. Look at their accel. 300g. They have those crazy new drives."

Orma looked over at the holo again, reading the vector projections, and realized Zukra was right. He had missed it at first glance; but the fleet coming into the system was at 300g accel.

A cold and icy chill ran down Orma's spine.

"Then..."

Orma stopped, the shock of the concept too much for him.

"They've captured our fleet," Zukra finished for him, "and converted them to some kind of new drive system. Those are the Humans for sure."

Orma shuddered involuntarily.

"Well," Zukra said briskly, standing up to get a better view of the holotank. "Now we fight them face to face, ship to ship. A much better outcome than killing one destroyer. Tac, what's our merge ETA?"

The Tac officer bent over his console, studying it. Adjusting his screen, he turned back to the Admiral.

"At mil standard accel, we can intercept in 9.7 hours, about two hours before they get to Ridendo," said the Tac officer. "It'll be cutting it close, but we can do it if we change course right now."

"Damn it all to hell!" screamed Zukra, as he realized the decision he had to make.

If he continued to pursue *Dragon*, the Humans would arrive at his home planet before he could get back to oppose them. And that was not acceptable, not in his eyes, and certainly not in the eyes of the Admiralty.

Across the bridge, he could see the Comm console already lit up with incoming messages and the look of panic on the face of the Comm officer.

Zukra took one final look at the *Dragon* in the holotank, still limping away at 245g. He glanced at the intercept clock again on the holo sidebar.

He could kill her, personally, just 1.9 hours from now if he continued on his course.

And the Humans would devastate his home planet, and the Admiralty would kill him.

Heaving a huge sigh, Zukra gazed at Orma.

"Leave three destroyers here to take out that cripple in front of us and put the rest of the fleet on an intercept vector to the merge point, Captain. Let's go kill some Humans."

17 - BAKER TWO

"Big problems, Tat," said Norali. "There's about 10,000 Singheko troops coming in from the southeast, and another 10,000 coming in from the north. They've got assault shuttles in the air, at least thirty. No way we can make a break for the mountains without getting cut to pieces. We're boxed in."

Tatiana gazed out the window of the office. She could see the thin black line of Singheko on the northern horizon. The thousands of troops moving slowly toward them looked like a line of ants.

A line of ants that would kill them all.

In the distance, dozens of assault shuttles hovered over the enemy line. Tatiana knew what would come next. The assault shuttles would come boring in, probably in a matter of minutes, and start softening up the complex for the battle.

"We'd better get underground," Tatiana said. "They'll be hitting us soon."

"Yep," agreed Marta, standing beside her with Baysig and Norali.

They turned and started for the underground spaces. But they knew that was only temporary protection. The Singheko would surround the surface complex to trap them all inside.

Then the ground troops would come in, going tunnel by tunnel to kill them.

As they walked, Tatiana turned to them.

"I'm sorry, folks. I thought we actually had a chance. But I led us right into this trap."

Baysig made his usual grunt and smile.

"Not your fault, Big X. We had a good run. We almost made

it."

Marta nodded.

"We'll take a lot of Singheko with us. It was worth it."

But Tatiana shook her head, a tear moving slowly down her cheek.

"That's OK for us. We knew what we were doing from the start. But what about the thousands who followed us, hoping for the best? I've betrayed all of them."

Norali reached forward, placed a hand on Tatiana's shoulder from behind.

"Tatiana. You did exactly what you should have done. You showed the damn Singheko we won't go gently. You put them on notice that Humans are not the pushovers they thought. And we killed one hell of a lot of those bastards."

"And we're going to kill a hell of a lot more of them before this is done," added Marta.

***

In his command assault shuttle high overhead the battlefield, General Arzem watched as his troops slowly advanced into the complex, ready to root out the rebels inch by inch if necessary.

They had strict orders.

No prisoners. No survivors. Even the non-combatants in the cages were to be executed. There would be no witnesses to this insurrection.

Arzem had placed a ring of troops around the complex. There would be no escapes.

But he was wrong. As his troops advanced into the underground complex, moving forward tunnel by tunnel, faced with a fierce firefight at every intersection, he was surprised to see a large force of Humans burst out of a hidden tunnel to the northwest and charge toward the ring of troops he had placed there. At the same time, a half-dozen assault shuttles appeared out of the mountains, screaming toward his troops.

"Block those slaves running to the west," he yelled into his comm. "Assault shuttles move to the west, take on the enemy flight coming at us there!"

But to his chagrin, before his orders could be executed, the rebels reached his troops and broke through, creating a hole in his line. Hundreds more poured out of the tunnel entrance, all making for the hole, heading for the mountains. Then it was thousands, a vast mass of rebels moving toward the break in his line.

Overhead, the rebel shuttles fought valiantly, if hopelessly, against his thirty assault shuttles. One by one, the rebel shuttles were knocked down, exploding or falling to the ground in flames.

Slowly his troops began to pinch back in, filling in the gap in their line.

No more than a few thousand of the rebels escaped. They made for the mountains, running for their lives. The rest who had come out of the tunnel - at least another two thousand - were now trapped between his ring of troops surrounding the complex and his troops down below in the tunnels.

They put up a good fight, thought Arzem. *For slaves.*

***

"Mum!" yelled Rachel at the Tac console, pointing to the holo tank with her laser designator.

Bonnie turned to see where she was pointing.

On the other side of the system, a fleet of ships had entered, accelerating at 300g directly toward Ridendo. They were lighting up the sky, making no attempt at stealth whatsoever.

"Rita," breathed Bonnie. "Thank God!"

Luke worked at his console, assessing.

"She's trying to pull them off us," he muttered. "She's lit up like a Christmas tree..."

"That's Rita," smiled Bonnie. "Never a shrinking violet."

"Enemy fleet is changing vector," called Rachel. "All except three destroyers. The rest are heading for Admiral Page."

"Three destroyers," mused Bonnie, staring at the plot on the holo. "That's still enough firepower to kill us."

Luke nodded. He bent his head, muttering, a sign he was speaking on a private channel to someone. Then he looked up at Bonnie.

"Engineering still reports five to six hours to restore full accel, Mum."

"We'll be plenty dead in five to six hours," said Bonnie. "Any ideas?"

There was silence on the bridge. Then...

"Mum?" said Ensign Goodwin.

Bonnie looked at the ensign. Goodwin was still in the doghouse since letting the missile hit *Dragon*. So he had been extraordinarily quiet since then, ignored by the rest of the crew - completely shunned.

The black sheep. The Jonah. Bonnie had moved him to First Watch to be better supervised.

Now she stared at him.

"Yes, Ensign?"

"Well...I have a crazy idea. It probably won't work..."

"Talk to me, Goodwin. I'll take any crazy idea I can find right now."

"Well, mum. That planet Deriko...where the slave ships land..."

"Yes?" said Bonnie impatiently. "Spit it out, Ensign!"

"Well, mum...it's nearly right in front of us. We could go there...use the terrain to our advantage...run through a canyon or something. It would make it hard for them to shoot down at us."

There was another long silence.

Bonnie almost grinned at the irony of it.

Now why the hell didn't I think of that? That's exactly what I did on Earth when the Corresse *was chasing* Jade*...*

But I only had two ships after me then. I've got three now. It's a long shot...

But it's the only shot we've got...

"XO, set a new course for Deriko, put us on a vector that will drop us into the atmosphere at max survivable speed, bring us around on a looping orbit, and try to catch that last destroyer from behind. Let's try to even the odds a little."

"Aye, mum," Luke cried. He grinned at Ensign Goodwin, then bent to his console.

The vector of the *Dragon* began to curve back toward Deriko. They'd have to decelerate now in order to make orbit around the planet. That would bring the destroyers chasing them into range a lot sooner.

Luke did some quick computations and flicked them over to Bonnie. She looked at them on her console. She looked back at Luke and shrugged.

They would be in range of the enemy destroyers for nearly two minutes as they slowed to enter orbit around Deriko.

Two minutes was a lifetime in a space battle.

But it was the only choice they had. And to make things worse, the gamma lance would not help them. It derived its power from the tDrive reactor.

Which was still in pieces in the Engineering space.

"Luke, when they come into range, I want two full missile spreads as fast as we can fire and reload. I want to make them nervous. If these guys are experienced, then it won't make any difference. But if they're green, they might duck their heads and screw up on their first couple of volleys. Every little bit helps."

"Aye, mum," Luke answered. He walked over to Rachel and they started putting together the defensive plan.

The *Dragon*, like most Nidarian destroyers, had four missile tubes in front and four in the rear, allowing her to fire up to eight missiles at a time.

Now Luke and Rachel programmed their attack. In a few minutes, they were satisfied.

"We're ready, mum," Luke said as he walked back to his console. As he passed Ensign Goodwin, Luke clapped him on the shoulder, a tiny but recognizable reward for his efforts to redeem himself from his grand screw-up of a few days before.

"Execute," said Bonnie.

Luke nodded and waved to Rachel at Tactical. She pressed keys on her console. A warning klaxon started sounding the Condition Red alert, letting the crew know they were about to maneuver, and anything could happen.

With a slight whine and a rather loud bang due to her damaged engine, *Dragon* stopped accelerating. A few seconds later, the engines resumed, now decelerating at 245g, placing *Dragon* on a vector that would end up in an orbit around the fourth planet of the system, Deriko.

Behind her, the three destroyers couldn't believe their luck. Their quarry had just sealed her doom. She had stopped running for the mass limit and was now slowing to enter orbit around the fourth planet.

They viewed it as suicide.

Onboard *Dragon*, the crew had a similar view. As the word spread throughout the ship via the invisible but highly effective rumor mill, many of the crew thought their captain had gone insane.

Chief Nash came around a corner on the Missile Deck and caught a gaggle of ratings standing in a circle, talking excitedly.

"She's gone nuts!" he heard as he approached. "She'll kill us all!"

"Candridge, is that you?" boomed Chief Nash as he came into view of the group. "I should have known. If there's trouble to be found, you'll be in the middle of it!"

Petty Officer Ross Candridge stepped back from the group, taken aback by the appearance of the Chief but not willing to back down.

"Chief, the Skipper's gone around the bend! Look what she's doing!"

Ross pointed to a backup console that plotted the vector of the *Dragon* and her pursuers.

"She's slowing down! Letting them catch us!"

"Candridge, you're an idiot. No, I'm sorry, you give idiots a bad name! The Skipper knows exactly what she's doing, you miserable excuse for a failed fart! Shut your pie hole, get your ass back to your missile station and do your job - or I'll call the Marines to escort you to the brig right now. What's it gonna be, you fucking moron?" yelled Nash.

Sullenly, PO Candridge stalked back to his station. The rest of the ratings likewise turned back to their work.

"Now," Nash yelled in a loud voice. "For all of you, listen up. The Skipper is on the bridge doing her job, trying to save your sorry asses. The Engineering team is down in their space doing their jobs, trying to get the engines back. The best chance of survival you have is to do your fucking job and stop sweating the small stuff. The next asshole that makes a crack about the people who are trying to keep a missile from coming up our butt is going straight to the brig - or out the airlock, depending on the mood I'm in at the time. Any questions?"

"No, Chief," came a chorus from the group.

"Then get your heads down and get your job done!" yelled Chief Nash one last time and stalked out and down the corridor.

***

"180 seconds to atmosphere," called Rachel at the Tac console. "60 seconds to enemy in-range."

Bonnie nodded.

She didn't really need the verbal warning. She could see the holo.

They were just on the cusp of entering the atmosphere of Deriko, and a hard, grinding aerobraking maneuver that would allow them to slingshot around the planet and enter a tight orbit.

But the three enemy destroyers would be in range in 60 seconds.

No, make that 50 seconds. The time was clicking by fast.

God, give us just one little break, Bonnie prayed. *Just one little break and we can survive this.*

She looked over at Luke. He sat quietly; his eyes almost closed.

He's saying a prayer too, thought Bonnie. *Good. We need all the prayers we can get.*

"150 seconds to atmosphere. 30 seconds to in-range," called Rachel.

Gazing back over at the young lieutenant, Bonnie couldn't help but smile.

What a rock-solid officer Rachel's become. I wish I had a dozen like her.

She looked at Ensign Goodwin, sitting quietly at the Operations console, his hands poised over his screen. Ready to act as backup to Rachel if the Tac console went down.

A young kid who screwed up big time but recovered from it, moving on. Another good officer.

I hate to kill all these people, God. So please don't let me do it.

Rachel started the countdown. She didn't really need to do it, because the AI was also counting down in the holotank sidebar and on every console.

But it was SOP for the Tac officer to do a verbal countdown. Just in case an electrical failure occurred, and every console went dark.

"Nine. Eight. Seven. Six. Five. Four. Three. Two. One. Fire, fire, fire," yelled Rachel, just in case anybody didn't get the memo.

Bonnie felt the vibration and lurch as eight missiles left the *Dragon*, four from the rear and four from the front. She watched on the holo as the missiles from their front tubes arced up, turned over, and headed for the enemy behind them.

And she watched as 24 missiles came out of the three destroyers behind them.

God, we don't have a chance, Bonnie said, watching the cloud of missiles coming at them. *I was stupid to think we did.*

They had 60 seconds to live.

In sorrow, she closed her eyes for a second.

I've killed us all.

Luke looked at Bonnie across the bridge.

It was hopeless. Everyone on the bridge knew it.

And everyone on the bridge knew what they had to do. *Dragon's* technology could not fall into enemy hands.

Bonnie gave the order with excruciating formality.

"Commander Powell, initiate self-destruct with a 20-second countdown. Now, please."

To his credit, Luke never hesitated. He had expected it. They couldn't take the chance that the enemy could capture a damaged *Dragon* unable to fight back.

"Self-destruct initiated, 20-second countdown," he called.

A sound passed across the bridge - a sigh exhaled in unison so loud it seemed like a chorus of sadness. Everybody leaned back in their chairs.

It was all over.

The AI began its countdown.

<19. 18. 17. 16...>

Bonnie closed her eyes, making one last prayer to the Creator. She wasn't sure which Creator she was praying to; but she thought any of them would do in this situation.

"What the bloody hell?" she heard from Luke.

Snapping her eyes open, she stared at the holotank.

16 Merlin fighters were coming directly toward them.

Before she could react - before she could even take another breath - all 16 fighters fired their gamma lances.

Directly at the *Dragon*.

But no...she realized...

Almost directly at the *Dragon*. But not quite. Just missing them...

At the missiles coming up behind them.

And the cloud of missiles behind them disintegrated into scrap metal and exploding gases as the directed bursts of gamma rays from 16 fighters took them out.

"Yes!" screamed Luke at the top of his lungs, jumping up from his seat, throwing his arms in the air.

Rachel was also jumping up and down at her console, as was Ensign Goodwin. All around the bridge, officers and ratings were standing, yelling, screaming, laughing, crying.

Bonnie was no exception. Although she didn't understand why, she found herself standing, arms raised, shouting at the top of her lungs.

"That's Jim! That's Jim!" she caught herself yelling. "He came!"

Suddenly Bonnie realized the AI was still counting.

<...Five. Four. Three. Two...>

"*Dragon*! Abort Destruct! Abort, abort, abort!" she yelled.

<Self Destruct Aborted>

Suddenly Luke was beside her and she couldn't restrain herself. She gave him a hug. And across the bridge, there were others, everybody hugging everybody.

Now Bonnie let go of Luke and stared at the holo. The Merlins streaked past them, firing again at the destroyers behind them, knocking great chunks out of two of the enemy ships.

"Gibson!" Bonnie yelled. "Second volley!"

"Aye, mum!" grinned Rachel, turning to her console. With a quick press, another eight missiles departed *Dragon*, heading for the enemy behind them.

In the holo, she saw the flight of Merlins now fire missiles at the enemy destroyers. 32 missiles came off the rails of the Merlins, running hot and true toward the enemy, with *Dragon*'s second volley of eight missiles coming in right behind them.

And out in front, *Dragon*'s initial volley of eight missiles were still boring in toward the enemy.

The three Singheko destroyers vectored away hard, back toward empty space, trying to make a run for it. But they never had a chance. 48 missiles closed the gap as the destroyers desperately tried to escape.

In sixty seconds, all Bonnie could see on the holo were the 16 Merlins, now slowing to come back to her, and three large clouds of expanding gases and debris that were once Singheko destroyers.

18 - NARROW ESCAPE

Onboard the *Merkkessa*, Admiral Rita Page stared at her holo.

The time to merge was prominently displayed there for all to see.

Three minutes.

"Captain Bekerose, all is good?" she asked.

"Aye, milady, we're ready," said Bekerose. "They know about the gamma lance now, though. Commander Carter had to use them at Deriko to save the *Dragon*, so they got a good view of them. There goes part of our element of surprise."

"Can't be helped," said Rita. "He couldn't let them take *Dragon*. Even though Bonnie probably had the self-destruct going, they might have been able to re-create the technology from the wreckage. So he did the right thing."

"Aye, milady, I agree."

Rita could hear the hum of the fans; the low murmur of voices on the bridge; the breathing of Captain Dallitta beside her. The holo showed the Singheko fleet now just a few hundred thousand klicks away, decelerating hard as they entered the combat zone.

Out in front of the EDF fleet, the three squadrons of the fighter wing had already engaged the enemy fighters, a flurry of gamma lance pulses and missiles filling the space between them.

Behind the Singheko fleet, the lone squadron detached from Jim's original "back-door" force suddenly began firing, causing surprise and consternation in the rear guard of Zukra's fleet.

No time for doubt.

Two minutes.

No time for re-thinking.

One minute.

Creator be with us.

"Open fire, Captain," Rita said calmly.

It was just ritual. Unless Rita, Bekerose or the Tac officer called "Hold Fire" the AI would open fire at the right time regardless.

And the AI did its job. Every ship in Rita's fleet fired their gamma lance, sending beams of pure energy at the enemy now only 4,500 klicks distant.

The spears of energy tore into the Singheko fleet, a weapon they had not seen before. Ship after ship took damage, holes punched through them, great rents torn in their hulls, explosions surrounding them and suddenly puffing out in the vacuum of space.

And a few seconds later, the *Merkkessa* shuddered as 20 missiles spit out of her tubes and started their accel to the enemy at 2,000g. The other ships of Rita's fleet fired simultaneously, adding another 104 missiles to the mix.

Seconds later, a rainstorm of Singheko point defense came at the EDF missiles, a mixture of anti-missiles, shrapnel, chaff, and laser pulses that tore into Rita's attacking weapons with a vengeance.

1.4 seconds after that, nine surviving EDF missiles impacted into the enemy ships.

"Damn, their point defense is good," said Bekerose calmly, as he watched 100-odd Singheko missiles coming at them.

The Singheko had fired a few seconds later than the Humans.

Bekerose wasn't sure if that was a good thing or not; the extra seconds he had to think about what was coming were not a pleasant experience.

The noise of the *Merkkessa*'s own point defense cannon and anti-missile launches reached a crescendo as the battlecruiser threw everything she had at the oncoming flood of missiles...

And the enemy missiles struck. The *Merkkessa* lurched like a drunk at a wedding. Rita was knocked half out of her chair.

Something exploded in the front of the bridge, and Rita heard a pattering like rain against the back wall behind her as fragments of shrapnel splattered everywhere. She saw her personal sentry, Raphael, go down as something caught him in the shoulder, knocking him to the deck.

As much as she cared for the rugged Nidarian Marine, she didn't have time to worry about him now. The medics would have to take care of him.

And then the Singheko fleet flashed past and was gone. Both fleets had boosted hard to get to each other, then gone into heavy decel to enter the combat zone. But they were still traveling at better than 500 k-klicks per hour relative to each other, even under hard decel. The engagement window had lasted only 13 seconds.

Beside her, Dallitta studied her console, assessing the damage to the enemy and their own fleet. She glanced up at the holo, then back to her console, then turned to Rita.

"We lost one destroyer and one corvette. The cruiser *Artemis* has lost 5% of her accel but she's otherwise still combat ready. The *Asiana* lost one missile port."

"On their side, they've got two destroyers down, one cruiser damaged and falling off course. Several impacts on their battlecruisers but I see no significant damage. Both of their battlecruisers are still under max decel, so their engines are good."

Crap, thought Rita.

Below her Bekerose spoke calmly, as if he were out for a Sunday stroll.

"Our damage report, please, Mr. Satterwhite," he said to the Ops officer, who was half out of his chair, hanging only by his harness.

"Aye, sir," grunted the lieutenant, pulling himself upright again and working his console.

Bekerose turned and looked at Rita.

"Still breathing, Admiral?" he asked with a smile.

"Still breathing, Captain," replied Rita, with a grin of her own.

That was bad, though, she thought. *Much worse than I expected. This is nothing like the Battle of Jupiter. There, we caught them off-guard. Here, they are not intimidated at all and they know how to fight.*

Lt. Satterwhite at the Ops console turned to Bekerose, speaking loudly so that Rita could also hear - something he was trained to do.

"One missile tube out of action, two point-defense cannon inop, three compartments open to space. Engines and all other weapons good to go. Life support nominal. Sixteen dead or missing, twenty injured."

Bekerose nodded, glancing at Rita with a lifted eyebrow. He seemed to be asking if she was good to go.

Rita gave him a slow nod.

"Press the attack, Captain," she said loudly, ensuring everyone on the bridge heard it.

Now both fleets turned end-over-end, putting their firepower toward each other again.

It wasn't necessary for their deceleration - the system engines used for normal three-space travel could boost in either direction without turning the ship.

But the weapons were another story. The *Merkkessa* could fire twenty missiles per salvo; but because of the massive reactors in her rear engineering spaces, only eight missile tubes could fit in the back of the ship; the remaining twelve were in the front and sides, facing forward. To get maximum effectiveness, it was better to face the enemy.

And there was another factor.

It felt better. There was some indefinable need to be looking at your enemy. Nobody could really explain it, but all understood it.

Face your enemy as you fight them.

As the two fleets turned over and continued their

deceleration, they stopped moving apart; then they started to come back together again.

This time, they would be moving slower as they passed.

This time, they would get two volleys off in the short time they had in range.

This time, a lot more people would die.

***

"Two minutes to merge," Lt. Carlson called in Nidarian.

The lieutenant had studied the Nidarian language diligently over the last several months; he was becoming quite good in the strange language that was full of sounds that sounded like a lisp to a human ear.

Rita couldn't help but smile. It somehow seemed so typical of humans that they constantly, even in the face of adversity, had the hunger to learn.

We like to learn. Maybe that's why we evolved so quickly.

"One minute," called Carlson.

Bekerose had been standing near Rita's elevated Flag Bridge, making it easier for them to converse. Now he turned to her.

"This one is going to be rough," he said. "Check your harness."

Then he walked back to his chair, sat down and buckled in.

"Thirty seconds," called Carlson.

The tension made his voice quiver. In the first pass, many of the bridge crew had never experienced combat before. But now they knew what it was like. The smell of smoldering electrical insulation permeated the ship, and in the far distance, they could still hear alarms sounding as damage control crews worked on the broken weapons and hull breaches. The casualty count had just been updated. There were more dead and injured than initially thought.

"Ten seconds."

Bekerose lifted a hand, waited a pulse, and dropped it.

"Fire, fire, fire," he said, the ritual repeated every time, regardless of the AI that was in control.

The gamma lance fired, a high-pitched sound that grated

on the nerves. A few seconds later, the missiles went. The *Merkkessa* seemed to shudder a bit harder this time, thought Rita. Maybe because they were moving slower, or maybe due to the previous damage. But she could feel the distinct pulse in the deck as the missiles departed their tubes. She could hear the sound of the loading conveyors as reloads started moving into the tubes for the second volley. She could hear the sound of Dallitta breathing hard beside her, and even the tense exhalations of Captain Bekerose across the bridge.

"Incoming, ten seconds," called Carlson.

Rita heard the rippling pulse of the tubes firing again, as they sent another flight of missiles toward the enemy in their second volley.

She heard the point defense cannon on the hull start up, a sound like paper being torn slowly, or a zipper being pulled up.

The pong-pong-pong of the laser anti-missile defenses started up.

"Incoming, five seconds," called Carlson. Rita saw he was gripping the arms of his chair tightly.

She did the same.

As if it will do any good...

This time, the sound was louder, longer; the ship did a double shake, first one side then the other, like a small animal in the jaws of a dog.

Rita was knocked hard against the side of her chair; she thought she might have broken a rib.

But she didn't have time to worry about that. She looked at Dallitta beside her, working her console to make the initial damage assessment.

Dallitta seemed ecstatic.

"No losses in our fleet! We got one good hit on one of their battlecruisers. It's losing decel! I think it lost an engine! Another destroyer down!"

Rita nodded. Grimacing, she held her damaged ribs and looked over at Carlson.

"Our second volley impacts in ten seconds," called the

Tac officer loudly. "Their second volley incoming in fifteen seconds."

Rita watched the countdown clock in the holo. The point defense started again, a whirring of life and death, the gamma lance switching to point defense mode in the last seconds.

Seconds to decide the first phase of this battle, she thought. *This second volley will decide. Either we hurt him worse than he hurts us and take the advantage - or it's the other way around, and we have to retreat.*

"Second volley has impacted the enemy," called Carlson. "Incoming in five seconds."

And the car wrecks started again. Rita rocked from side to side as the *Merkkessa* took a beating. But...

That didn't seem as bad as the previous volley. And we did take one battlecruiser out of the equation last time...

She could hear alarms outside the bridge, down the corridor, a lot closer this time. Beside her, Dallitta worked her console. Then the little Nidarian turned to her, the ghost of a smile on her face.

"We took down a cruiser!" she spoke loudly, almost yelling in her excitement. "Two more destroyers, two corvettes, and the damaged battlecruiser is pulling away, vectoring off!"

Rita wanted to heave a large sigh. But she resisted.

I'm an admiral now. I can't be a normal human. I must be the rock.

"Very good, Dallitta. Bekerose, how's our old girl doing?"

"Actually, milady, better than I expected. We lost two more point defense emplacements and two more compartments are holed to space, but it could have been a lot worse. I think we've got them now."

Rita nodded. "Let's turn around and end this, then, Captain."

Bekerose grinned.

"Aye, milady..."

"Contact!" yelled Carlson. "Enemy fleet directly ahead! Two battlecruisers, three cruisers, six destroyers, four corvettes!"

Rita leaned forward, staring at the holo. Sizing up the situation. There wasn't much to size up, though. They were now hopelessly outnumbered.

"Order to fleet. Execute R-14. Now, now, now!" she called.

The AI issued the order immediately to all ships in the fleet. Like a well-coordinated school of fish, the EDF fleet turned and went to max accel, leaving the system.

They had knocked a fairly good hole in the Singheko Home Fleet behind them. But there was no way they could survive being caught between two enemy fleets.

They had to retreat.

***

Zukra watched the Human fleet turn and run.

Despite the damage to his fleet, and the embarrassment that he knew was coming, he smiled.

Run, you slaves. But there's nowhere you can hide from us. I'll find you. I'll kill you. And your admiral's skin will hang on my wall as a trophy.

The smell of scorched insulation and burning flesh permeated the *Ambush*. The Humans had very nearly taken out his flagship. It had been close.

So close, he suspected he would not have survived another pass from the enemy.

"Message from Admiral Nokru, sir. He wishes a status report."

Nokru. The head of the Taegu expedition. That asshole. He would come back now.

"Put him on with me," said Zukra. "Voice only - no video. Don't show him the damage."

With a click, he heard his fellow admiral come on the line.

"Zukra! What the hell is going on? I come back into the system and I find you involved in a full-scale battle with the Nidarians!"

"Those aren't Nidarians, Admiral Nokru. Those are Humans. That's the fleet Garatella loaned them. They had the audacity to enter the system this morning. We were just disposing of them."

There was a short cough over the comm line; the sound of a Singheko laugh.

"If you call that disposing of them, I'd hate to see what you call getting your ass kicked," Nokru responded.

Zukra shuddered in humiliation but held his tongue. Admiral Nokru was senior to him; it wouldn't do to argue the point.

Besides, the debris and broken ships littering his fleet spoke for themselves.

"Are you going to pursue them, then?"

"Of course, sir. I'm dispatching two destroyers to shadow them."

"Fine, fine. And what's this other business I hear?" Nokru continued. "A massive slave uprising on Deriko? I return from reducing the Taegu system and while I'm gone, you let this happen?"

Zukra rolled his eyes but responded calmly.

"Now that the Humans are on the run, I can handle it, sir," he replied. "I've already sent a task force to wipe out the rebel slaves on Deriko."

"See that you do that, Zukra. We can't have slaves pulling stunts like that. It undermines the whole plan."

"Aye, sir. We'll have them all dead and buried within a week."

"Good enough, Zukra. I'll leave this in your hands for now, but if you can't get this handled within the week, I'm taking over. Nokru out."

"Zukra out."

Fuck. That asshole. If he takes over, my career is finished. I need to get those slaves on Deriko dead, and quickly.

And I need to get Operation Broadsword moving. If Ligar and Nokru get together and decide to push me out, it'll be too late.

By tomorrow night, Nokru should be at home on Ridendo.

Operation Broadsword goes tomorrow night.

***

The *Banjala* returned to the Dekanna system, entering at 15 AU and coasting forward at 360 k-klicks per hour, the optimal entry speed as computed by their AI.

Admiral Sobong met Winnie on the bridge, and they sat in observer's chairs behind Captain Shimbiro. Roberto and Kumara stood behind them in the small bridge.

"Now show me," said the Admiral.

Turning to Captain Shimbiro, Winnie nodded. Shimbiro gestured to the Nav yeoman, who had heard the conversation.

"Take us up to 300g, Ginsberg."

The whine of the *Banjala*'s engines increased in pitch. The ship began accelerating. Already moving at 100,000 meters per second, each second the Banjala gained another 2,952 meters per second of velocity. In six minutes, she was moving at 3,616,776 kph and still accelerating, on a direct course for the iceball planet.

Sobong looked at Winnie silently.

"Time to destination?" called Shimbiro.

"19.8 hours, sir."

Sobong stood up. She gave Winnie a strange look.

"With me, please, Commander."

Winnie followed as Sobong left the bridge and walked to the galley. Entering, she let Winnie come in behind her, but waved Roberto and Kumara away. She closed the hatch and gestured Winnie to the table.

Winnie sat, preparing herself.

I think I know what's coming. This is one smart cookie. She knows there's something else. And she has a damn good idea what it must be.

Sobong sat opposite Winnie and stared at her for a long moment.

"Yes, I see that you can accelerate at 300g. And I take your word for it that you can go to 50% light with full protection. So yes, that gives you a second advantage in battle with the Singheko. But still not enough to defeat a superior force, as you said you did at Earth."

"What do you mean, Admiral?"

"You're still holding something back, Commander. What is it?"

Winnie grimaced.

"Admiral, I'm only a fighter pilot, sent to assist you. That's above my pay grade."

Sobong smiled.

"A fighter pilot you may be, but you know what I'm talking about. You have a new weapon. Something not seen before. That's the only way you could have beat the Singheko at Earth. And the only way you'd have the guts to attack them on their home turf. What do you have, Commander?"

Winnie shook her head.

"I cannot discuss it, Admiral. Not without a firm peace treaty in place between Earth and the Dekanna Union. Or at least a firm mutual defense treaty. An alliance."

"And who is authorized to execute such an agreement with us?"

Winnie thought for a moment.

"I believe our Admiral Page could do so."

Sobong frowned.

"Ah, but she is back at Singheko. By the time we journey there, execute such a treaty, and get back to here, we will have little time to retrofit our ships to your new and secret weapon."

"Perhaps not, Admiral. What would you say if I could contact her immediately?"

If it was possible to look even more shocked, Admiral Sobong managed it.

19 - OLLIE GOES FORTH

Dragon hurtled into the atmosphere of Deriko, flaming plasma building around her.

With the destruction of the three pursuing destroyers, she didn't need to dip so deeply into the atmosphere to come around the planet. But it had been a bit late to alter her orbit completely. Luke did manage to increase their vector somewhat as they entered atmosphere. But that only changed it from a desperate, near-suicidal attempt to warp around the planet, to a shuddering carnival ride through the upper atmosphere.

Red and orange streamers blanked out the front screen until they skipped off the atmosphere and were back out into space again.

And coming up behind two troop ships in orbit.

"What they hell are those?" asked Bonnie, staring at the holo.

"Whatever they are, they're Singheko," replied Luke, working his console. "I think they're troop ships of some kind."

Rachel at the Tac console turned to Bonnie.

"Mum, there's a lot of activity on the planet directly below those ships. One of the large slave complexes. There's some kind of battle going on. There's Singheko assault shuttles in the air and thousands of troops on the ground, in a circle surrounding the complex. There's lots of firing going on to the west of the building."

Luke looked at Bonnie, agony on his face. He didn't have to say anything; she could read his thoughts.

My daughter could be in the middle of that.

"Tac, take out those two troop ships in front of us."

"They're running, Mum. They're boosting out of orbit, heading for space at full emergency thrust."

"I don't care. Take them out."

"Aye, Mum."

Bonnie heard the distant thumps as a full broadside of eight missiles departed *Dragon*'s front and rear tubes, the rear missiles turning up and over the ship to re-orient to the front and start their boost toward the enemy.

The two enemy troopships ran hard, boosting at 260g toward the black.

The missiles ran harder. At 2000g, they caught the troopships in a matter of seconds. Several huge explosions later, nothing was left of them but parts and pieces on a short trajectory to nowhere.

"Scratch two troop ships," called Rachel.

"Luke, can you see what's going on with Rita and the fleet?"

"Aye, mum, but you're not gonna like it. They made two passes at the enemy and it looked good. But after the second pass another fleet came in the system in front of them. They've started a retreat back to the mass limit. They're collecting up the rest of the Merlins as they go. They'll be out of the system soon."

"Crap," breathed Bonnie. "Crap, crap, crap. What's Mr. Worley's latest estimate to restore full power and have the tDrive back in operation?"

"Five hours, mum."

"And how much time do we have before the Singheko can get reinforcements here?"

Luke frowned, his fingers flying across his console. It took him a minute to process all the data and turn back to Bonnie.

"The soonest they could have warships back here is six hours, mum."

"Right. Then we've got a window of time here to help these people. Comm Jim. Tell him to come in and clear out the Singheko troops around the complex."

"Aye, mum." Luke spoke quietly into his comm for a bit, then nodded at Bonnie.

"Jim's got it. He said they'll attack in five minutes."

"Good. And get Ollie on the horn. Tell him to load his Marines for a surface drop. I'm sure that'll make his day."

Luke nodded. He bent to his comm, speaking quietly into it, issuing orders to Major Oliver Coston and his Marine contingent.

Bonnie had turned away, her attention elsewhere, by the time Luke finished discussing the surface drop with Ollie.

So she didn't see the strange look on his face.

***

In the cockpit of his Merlin, Jim's AI beeped, letting him know they were coming up to the Line of Departure - the point where his attack would officially begin. He had scanned the surface and had a good idea what he wanted to do.

<Line of Departure, Commander>

"Roger, Angel. Prep all systems, arm all weapons."

Jim focused back on his business. The Merlins had been ordered to go down to the surface to help a group of rebels fighting Singheko troops.

And they didn't have much time to do it. The Singheko Home Fleet had already reacted. Bonnie reported a force of one cruiser and three destroyers only six hours away, coming hard.

Bonnie had said they would depart Deriko in three hours, regardless of the situation on the surface. They couldn't afford to wait around any longer than that.

Jim had only three hours to help the rebels on Deriko before he and *Dragon* had to make a run for it.

<Entering atmosphere in thirty seconds>

"Roger." Jim realized he was a little fast. He kicked his decel up to 305g, enduring the extra force for a while to slow the Merlin a bit more. His squadron, their AI slaved to his, followed suit as they crashed into the atmosphere, passing beneath *Dragon* as she sat in orbit.

Then Jim was burning through the atmosphere of Deriko, plasma building around the Merlin. The Merlin had automatically turned its belly to the airflow, providing him with some protection from the streaming plasma. A hard shudder started, the fighter buffeting from the abnormally high-speed entry.

But they didn't have a lot of time.

The overheat alarm went off for a few seconds. Then it stopped. The Merlin slowed, buffeting, swaying a bit from side to side.

"Angel, make a note, the autopilot for atmospheric entry is a bit unstable and needs some tweaking."

<Maintenance note logged>

Now if I only survive long enough for that note to get back to the maintenance guys...

"Angel leader, complex at your twelve o'clock low, cleared to engage."

"Roger, *Dragon*. Engaging," Jim replied.

Below him, the battlefield was coming into view. There was a large building, six or eight football fields in size. It was surrounded by thousands of Singheko troops, encircling it completely.

Outside the ring of troops, a large group of slaves - Humans, Taegu and Bagrami - were running for the foothills, harassed by a dozen Singheko assault shuttles.

Inside the ring, another two thousand or so slaves were being pressed back toward a tunnel exit on the northwest side, under heavy fire from the encircling Singheko. Another dozen assault shuttles were hovering over them, decimating them with withering fire from above. Bodies littered the battlefield in all directions.

In the distance, several klicks away, a long column of troops approached. Jim couldn't tell what they were.

Quickly he issued orders.

"Yellow Flight, Green Flight, attack the assault shuttles to the west. Clear them out of there and protect that group running toward the mountains."

"Yellow Flight wilco."

"Green Flight wilco."

Two of his flights peeled off, headed to the west of the complex.

"Red Flight, Blue Flight, we'll take the assault shuttles over the complex. Clean 'em out!"

"Blue Flight roger."

With a grimace, Jim put the Merlin's nose down toward the assault shuttles in front of him.

"Angel, give me targeting for the assault shuttles. Make sure you avoid the friendly personnel on the ground."

<Targeting complete. You'll need to get a lot lower to shoot up at the shuttles>

Jim pushed the nose down even more, all the way down to the ground. He was now skimming the surface of the plain south of the complex, so close the occasional tree branch licked the bottom of the Merlin.

"How's that, Angel?"

<More than adequate, Commander. Ready to fire in three - two - one>

Jim pushed the fire button on his stick. The gamma lance sent its long stream of focused gamma rays. His targeted enemy shuttle disintegrated. A gamma lance that could punch a hole in a battlecruiser was overkill for an assault shuttle, but it got the job done.

Angel automatically switched to a new target, and he pressed the trigger again. Another shuttle disappeared from the battlefield.

Beside him, the rest of his own Red Flight, as well as Blue Flight, were having a turkey shoot. Enemy assault shuttles disintegrated in groups of two and three.

By the time they finished their first pass, there were no Singheko assault shuttles left to shoot anymore.

"Red and Blue Flights, come back around and take out the enemy troops on the west side of the complex, focus on the ones firing at the friendlies," Jim called.

The eight Merlins of Red and Blue Flights swung around, now pointing their noses back to the southwest, angling down toward the Singheko troops on the west side of the complex. All eight Merlins opened fire simultaneously.

The Singheko panicked. The entire western side of the encircling ring of troops broke and ran, many throwing down their weapons as the strange black fighters bore down in a screaming attack.

***

"Last chance to back out, Major," Bonnie said over the comm.

In the *Dragon*'s launch bay, Ollie smiled in his helmet. Six of his Marines sat with him in the AMAG - Armored Mobility Attack Ground - a wheeled ground assault vehicle with two laser pulse weapons mounted on the front and one on the back.

And one old-fashioned 25mm cannon mounted in the turret.

Behind Ollie another AMAG sat with the rest of *Dragon*'s small Marine contingent, both vehicles facing the rear ramp of the shuttle and ready for a quick exit.

"Good to go, Captain," Ollie called back. "I wouldn't miss this for the world."

"OK, Major. Good hunting," Bonnie said. "Establish communications with the leader of the rebels, get the lay of the land, and we'll pick you up in five days at the rendezvous point."

She turned her attention back to the bridge. Glancing over at the empty XO console beside her, she felt a twinge of premonition - a vague feeling that something wasn't right.

Luke had insisted on going to the shuttle bay to ensure Major Coston got dropped on the planet per plan.

Now that Bonnie had some time to think about it, that had been strange. That was not normally an XO's duty, she thought. Why was he so adamant he needed to do that?

Something to do with his daughter, I guess. I guess he felt he had to make sure Ollie's mission got sent off with no glitches.

But it felt strange, to be in a combat operation without Luke by her side, in his usual place at the XO console.

"Assault shuttle away," called Rachel from Tac.

Bonnie watched as the assault shuttle departed, soon glowing red and surrounded by a sheath of plasma as it fell into the atmosphere. In a few more minutes, it disappeared from visual view, although she could still track it on the holo. After another dozen minutes, it landed to the west of the complex, in the space between the building and the Singheko troops that had scattered, most of them still fleeing to the south now. Bonnie watched the two AMAGs roll out the back ramp of the shuttle and head toward the entrance of the complex.

Luke should be back by now.

"*Dragon*? Page Commander Powell for me, ask him to report to the bridge."

<Commander Powell is not on board, Captain>

***

What the hell?

Ollie was thunderstruck.

"Major, our XO has evidently stowed away on one of your AMAGs. Would you please have him call me ASAP?"

Ollie shook his head. He looked around the interior of the AMAG as it trundled across the sand toward the entrance to the complex.

He's not in here. He must be in the other one.

He switched channels to the other AMAG, which was commanded by his senior sergeant, SSgt. Brown.

"Sgt. Brown, do you have an extra passenger in there?"

"Yes, sir, Commander Powell joined us at the last minute. He said you knew about it."

Fuck. That fucking idiot.

"Roger, sergeant. Please ask him to call the Captain. Thank

you."

Nothing I can do about it now. First of all, he outranks me. Second, I'm not going to get involved in family squabbles.

Ollie switched back to the *Dragon*'s loop.

"Captain, you are correct. We have picked up an extra passenger. He is in the other AMAG. I passed along your message."

"Thank you, Major."

Bonnie stood from her chair. She had a bottle of water in her console. She took it, hefted it, pulled her arm back.

It would be so easy to throw it at the damn wall. So easy.

But she didn't. She realized every person on the bridge was watching out of the corner of their eyes, while pretending not to.

With a force of will, she put the water bottle back down into her armrest and turned away from the other personnel on the bridge, facing into the corner.

I need to scream.

But she couldn't do that either.

She was the Captain.

That fucking idiot. That insane, stupid, fucking idiot.

Bonnie sighed.

Nothing she could do about it now.

Returning to her seat, she called Major Coston again.

"Major Coston, Commander Powell is an unauthorized passenger on this mission. You are not to take orders from him. You are in charge. Understood?"

"Aye, aye, mum. Understood."

"Any questions?"

"No, mum. Got it."

Ollie shook his head.

Family squabbles. Just what I needed.

***

As the AMAGs approached the complex after the drop, roughly a thousand rebel troops joined them. They were mostly Human, but there was an admixture of smaller creatures - Taegu, according to his database - and a bunch of big, bearlike creatures called Bagrami. The Bagrami all carried heavy weapons mounted on tripods.

Ollie was surprised and impressed by the organization he saw in the rebel troops. When they came up to join the Marines, they were already organized into platoons and companies, ready for action.

Somebody in charge knows what they're doing, he thought.

That organization allowed Ollie to quickly plan his assault. He assigned a rebel platoon to each of his twelve Marines, who then acted as a platoon leader.

Then they entered the complex, catching the Singheko by surprise, coming in on their rear. Ollie's troops had already cleared the massive receiving hall and pushed down the ramp into the first tunnel. Bodies of Singheko lay everywhere.

But their advance had not been without cost. There were bodies of his force lying about as well. Taegu and Bagrami.

And Human.

Ollie grimaced.

The cost of stupidity is war, and the cost of war is death.

In the distance, Ollie could hear firing from the other rebel force in the tunnels to the east and north. The Singheko troops in the tunnels were now sandwiched between Ollie's force and another rebel force to the north. Now it was just a matter of time, rooting them out of the underground passages.

Standing at the bottom of the ramp, Ollie heard SSgt. Brown come up beside him, escorting Luke from the other AMAG. Turning to them, Ollie stared at Luke silently for a moment, gathering his thoughts.

"Sir, I realize you're senior to me on paper, but down here in this mess, you're just a liability. Stay behind the reserve force. If I see you anywhere near the front of our line, I'll have you placed under arrest. Are we clear?"

Luke nodded.

"Clear."

Ollie smiled. He took his assault rifle off his shoulder.

"Here. Take this. Just in case."

Luke nodded gratefully. Ollie gave him one last salute. Turning back to his troops, Ollie signaled the assault to continue.

The AMAGS barely fit into the tunnels, with only a couple of inches clearance on each side.

But fit they did, and now an AMAG drove by him, three platoons following close behind - using it for cover. They disappeared into the tunnel leading off to the north.

The other AMAG drove into a second tunnel, headed east, also followed by three platoons.

Soon he heard the sound of the auto-laser as one of the AMAGs opened up on Singheko troops down the tunnel. Almost immediately after, the second AMAG in the other tunnel also opened fire.

His reserve force of six additional platoons stood in position behind him, holding the ramp in case of any counterattack by the Singheko.

It was going to be a long day.

***

Beneath the complex in the tunnels, it was a madhouse. People were running everywhere. Some were running toward the battle that was behind Tatiana, where Norali was trying to hold the line against the Singheko troops in the tunnels.

Some were running toward the battle in front of her, where the Humans and their allies had re-grouped and pushed out of the northwest tunnel exit, mounting a counterattack against the Singheko troops encircling the complex.

And some were running in abject terror in any direction they thought might save them.

Tatiana was jogging through a long tunnel toward the northwest, where they had made the emergency exit to the surface and where a major battle was occurring now. Beside her, Alina was speaking quietly into her headset. She looked over at Tatiana as they jogged through the tunnel.

"We've managed to establish comms with the Human ship

in orbit - the *Dragon.* The Human space fighters have rejoined her. They can't stay any longer. Singheko warships are on the way. But they dropped two Marine ground assault vehicles to help us. The Marines are entering the surface complex now behind the Singheko. That'll help pull them away from our rear."

Tatiana nodded.

We needed that. We were getting pressed on two sides. If the Marines can distract the Singheko behind us, take some of the pressure off Norali, then we have a chance here.

Except for those damn starships coming in from Singheko. They'll bombard us from orbit. We can't fight that.

I didn't think this all the way through. Holding the ground is meaningless. We have to hold the orbitals as well, or we're toast.

"Did you tell Norali?"

"Yes, boss. She's up to speed. The minute the Marines start to put some pressure on the rear of the Singheko in the tunnels, she's going to counterattack."

"Good," mused Tatiana distractedly. She was pre-occupied with the problem of the orbitals.

How can I defend against starships dropping crap on us from orbit? How good would their accuracy be? Who would know that?

"Alina, get me Baysig, please," said Tatiana, jogging along the tunnel.

Alina spoke into her comm unit, and then handed the headphones to Tatiana.

"Baysig? The Singheko are sending ships to Deriko right now, they'll be here soon. How accurate are the Singheko dropping shit on us from orbit?"

"They are extremely accurate. They can put a missile or a kinetic round in a twenty-foot circle from orbit, Tat. Count on it," she heard over the comm.

Crap.

"OK, thank you Baysig. How's it going with you and Norali?"

"A bit better. The unit your Human companions left behind - Marines, I believe you call them - which is strange, there's no oceans in space - but anyway, they have attacked the Singheko in the rear, from the bottom of the ramp. That has pulled a lot of pressure off us here. We're just about to counterattack."

"OK. Good luck. Keep me posted."

Tatiana handed the headset back to Alina. They were just about up to the northwest command post. She spotted Marta standing back from the steps leading to the surface and joined her. Misrak - the Ampato they had met in the mountains - stood a few feet from her, talking on a comm unit.

"How's it going?"

"A lot better now," replied Marta. "Your space friends disrupted their encirclement completely, sent a couple thousand of them running to the south. Most of them are still running. We've moved another three thousand troops out to the surface now. So now we've got five thousand rolling up their encirclement; we've already worked our way around to the south - so at least a quarter of the circle. I sent another thousand into the complex to help the Marines push down the ramp into the tunnels for the underground battle."

Tatiana nodded understanding.

"So right now, they've only got a half-circle around us. We control the west and south, they control the east and north?"

"Yep. But we've got that column of Ampato troops coming in from the northeast. And they're coming fast. Misrak has got comms up with them now. They're going to assault into the Singheko rear in about..."

Marta glanced at the clock on her comm unit.

"...in about ten minutes. I think that should end it. There's no way the Singheko can hold. The ones on the surface will have the Ampato behind them and us rolling up their flanks. The ones down in the tunnels will have Norali on one side, and the Marines and another thousand of our troops on the other side coming at them. I think it's all over but the cryin..."

Tatiana nodded, but had to say it.

"Except for the orbitals..."

"Yeah. Except for the fucking missiles coming down on our

heads from above once the *Dragon* leaves."

20 - DRAGON AWAY

Zukra had never been this angry.

The Humans were making a mockery of him.

The fleet that had fought him near Ridendo had escaped from the system, disappearing into the Black.

The enemy destroyer they had chased across the system for four days had somehow escaped and had attacked and destroyed his troop ships at Deriko.

Then, to make matters worse, enemy fighters had swooped down on the slave planet and decimated his ground troops.

General Arzem was dead in the wreckage of his assault shuttle at Deriko, and his ground troops there were in general retreat. Or dead.

All caused by these Humans!

I will kill them all, each and every one, right down to the last. I will not leave even one of them alive.

And then I'll go back to their planet and kill all of them there. We don't need slaves who are going to be this much trouble. We'll just wipe their planet and be done with it.

And Admiral Ligar wasn't helping matters any. The senior admiral at the other end of the video was clearly baiting him.

"In over our head, are we, Zukra?" he smiled on the screen.

"Never, sir. I will crush these Humans to the last one. By the end of the week, there won't be a Human left alive in this system!" Zukra vowed.

"Well? What's your plan?" Ligar persisted.

"The key is the slave rebellion on Deriko," said Zukra. "Notice when the rebels on Deriko were in danger, the Humans immediately sent a force to drive off my troops. So it's clear to me they value those rebels highly."

"Yes, yes," grunted Ligar. "So?"

"So, Admiral. I've sent a slightly larger task force to Deriko to resume the attack on the rebels. A cruiser and three destroyers. It will be a task force large enough to make an attractive target for a hit and run, but not so large they'll be afraid of it. They won't be able to resist - they'll put up some kind of attack to drive it away again."

Ligar smiled.

"Yes, I quite see it. And you'll be waiting nearby with the Home Fleet, ready to pounce."

"Exactly, Admiral. They'll never know what hit them."

"Who did you send to command the detached force?"

"Orma, sir. He's itching to fight."

"Orma? Your Flag Aide? I thought he was more of a staff officer."

"He's fine for this role, sir. In fact, I much prefer an inexperienced command officer. If he makes a mistake, it'll draw the Humans in even quicker."

"Very good, Zukra. Send me the detail plans."

"Aye, sir."

As Ligar signed off, Zukra leaned back in his seat and thought about his detail plans.

He didn't need to send them to Ligar.

Admiral Ligar wouldn't live out the night.

***

The black ops team Zukra had assembled was quite efficient. They slipped into Fleet Admiral Ligar's mansion at 0240 hours, made their way to his bedroom, and quietly removed him from the universe.

Between then and dawn, several other admirals also vanished, including Admiral Nokru, recently returned from reducing the Taegu system. Along with much of the civilian leadership of the Singheko Empire.

By the time the sun came up on Ridendo, Admiral Zukra Akribi was the senior admiral left alive in the Singheko navy, answering only to the figurehead Emperor - who was locked in his palace, incommunicado.

He had gone back to Ridendo for the coup, establishing his command post aboard the battlecruiser *Ambush* orbiting over the planet.

Now he took a shuttle down to the port and went to the Admiralty, consolidating his power. He marched into Admiral Ligar's empty office, ripping the name off the door as he entered.

"Get my name on that door immediately, Damra," he shouted at his new aide.

"Aye, sir."

"Any resistance?"

"A bit, sir. Nothing significant. We had to kill a couple of dozen captains and commanders who objected. Things are quiet now."

"Excellent, excellent. Has the Nidarian corvette arrived?"

"It's on approach, sir. Captain Simmala is aboard."

"Outstanding! How's our progress on the new fast drives and the gamma lance?"

"We completed that one cruiser as you requested, sir. Everything checks out. We can get 300g acceleration out of the new drives and the range of the gamma lance is 4,500 klicks, exactly as Captain Pojjayan promised. We're bringing in the first battlecruiser now for conversion."

"Excellent, Damra. Bring Captain Simmala to my office immediately. We have a lot of planning to do."

***

The bitterness of retreat galled Rita's taste, fouled her mouth, soured her stomach.

But retreat it was, and there was no help for it. The sudden appearance of a Singheko expeditionary fleet returning from some foreign assault had left her vastly outnumbered.

Her ships had escaped the system, reached the mass limit, and translated out to R-14 - a designated point in the middle of nowhere, a nothing point, an emptiness in the middle of emptiness 6.2 light years from Singheko.

From there, they regrouped for eight hours, patching the most severe damage to the fleet to ensure that all ships had life support and engine power for the next step.

Then the fleet moved to another rendezvous point, 300 AU from Singheko. There the supply ships *EDF John Wayne* and *EDF Marco Polo* were waiting for them.

Hastily constructed from obsolete wet-navy barges, the old iron barge frames had been stripped of ocean-going equipment, broken into pieces, hoisted to orbit with heavy-lift tugs, and re-assembled in space to become interstellar supply barges, with system engines and tDrives welded crudely into place on their rear.

The vast space on their decks was unpressurized, cargo storage only. A tiny space at the back of each ship contained life support and controls, and a minimal crew.

The ships had been loaded and sent off to meet Rita's fleet at the designated resupply point. The *John Wayne* was crammed with spare missiles and weapons. The *Marco Polo* was crammed with food, oxygen, and other supplies.

It was human ingenuity at its crudest and most effective, a move of desperation that served its purpose.

As the fleet resupplied, Rita and her staff assembled in the briefing room of the *Merkkessa.*

They had left behind a half-dozen drones in the system as they departed. The drones were transmitting good data back to them via their newly discovered ansible. Rita pointed into the holo with her laser.

"Keep in mind, we're looking at a drone signal that's currently 2 AU from Deriko. So we have a light speed delay of 16 minutes.

"There's Bonnie," Rita said, pointing into the holo with her laser. They could clearly see *Dragon* at Deriko. "We were initially puzzled by her actions. Instead of immediately fleeing the system after Jim fought off the destroyers chasing her, she went into orbit at Deriko and is still there, or at least she was 16 minutes ago.

"But now we've determined a rebel uprising was in progress on Deriko - right below her orbit. Clearly Bonnie decided it was worthwhile to provide the rebels some temporary support. She sent Jim's squadron down to assist them. I expect that means she's close to restoring her engines, because I know she wouldn't stay there otherwise.

"However, there's Singheko reinforcements enroute to Deriko to push her away and continue to attack the rebels on the surface."

In the holo, they could see a force of one cruiser and three destroyers on a vector to Deriko. They could also see the tiny blips representing Jim's Merlins that had returned from the surface of the planet and were now in formation behind *Dragon*.

Rita leaned back.

"So we have several competing priorities.

"One - we need to inflict pain and pressure on the enemy without letup, giving him no time to regroup and think through his options.

"Two - we need to support *Dragon* and ensure she can escape from the system if her engines are not restored.

"Three - we need to recover Jim's Merlins. He's out of missiles and needs resupply badly - and those pilots have to be exhausted. Captain Sato, assuming they get underway shortly and head out-system, please take the *Asiana* to fetch the fighters as they come out of the mass limit.

"And last but not least - we need to support the rebels on Deriko, if possible.

"I think we can accomplish all four with one mission. While we resupply and wait for *Dragon* and Jim's Merlins to rejoin us, I'd like to plan a hit-and-run attack on that cruiser and those destroyers that are approaching Deriko. What does everyone think?"

Dallitta never hesitated.

"We do it," she said. "It's a chance to sow discord and

confusion among the enemy. You never pass up a chance like that."

Rita grinned, the ferocious grin of a predator. Because ultimately, that's what an Admiral had to be. You were either the predator or you were the prey.

"I was hoping you'd say that."

The hatch opened and Captain Tarraine came in, joining them at the table.

"Sorry I'm late, Admiral. What's up?"

"We've got a group of rebels on the fourth planet, Deriko. Somehow, they've managed to start a rebellion on the planet. But they're boxed up in one of those underground complexes now and surrounded by Singheko shock troops. They're in trouble."

Rita pointed to the holo.

"As luck would have it, Bonnie happened to be at the right place at the right time. She's taken out the troop ships over the planet and sent Jim's Merlins down to support the rebels on the surface.

"There's a cruiser and three destroyers enroute from Zukra's fleet to drive *Dragon* out of the area. We assume they'll take over the attack on the rebels.

"We're discussing a hit-and-run attack on the cruiser and destroyers. How long do we need to prepare, Dallitta?"

"If we come in from below the ecliptic, say from about 12 AU out, then we can be ready in eighty-four hours. Three days to finish re-supply, two hours to get into position, 8.5 hours to boost, and 1.3 hours of coast time to get to Deriko."

Rita shook her head.

"Too long. It gives the enemy too much time to think and plan. We'll translate out right now and position ourselves 300 AU below the strike point. Then we'll start boost while we resupply. And I want re-supply time cut to forty-eight hours."

Dallitta looked confused.

"Milady, if we start boost that far out, it'll take forever to get there."

Rita spoke grimly.

"Not if we translate to the mass limit after we reach 20% light."

There was a shocked hiss of surprise around the table. Bekerose held up his hands in dismay.

"Milady! At 20% light, there's too much risk of error when we translate! Even the slightest miscalculation would result in catastrophe!"

Rita understood his objection. The mass limit was not a perfectly defined line in space. It wandered a bit, back and forth, depending on what the star was doing - and on the velocity of the starship. The faster the starship was moving, the more imprecise the location of the mass limit.

For that reason, no starship translated into normal space at high velocity near the mass limit of a star.

Any miscalculation would instantaneously liberate every atom of the ship into pure energy.

"Then we won't miscalculate, will we, Captain Bekerose?"

The long look of concern Bekerose projected across the table was suddenly interrupted.

<Priority One message received from *Corresse* via ansible>

Rita jerked her head up. She stared in shock at her staff.

They were just as stunned. The corvette *Corresse* under Captain Arteveld had been dispatched to Nidaria more than six months ago to report to Garatella, the High Councilor of the Nidarian Empire. Since that time, she had gone dark. And she was four months overdue.

"*Merkkessa*, read message to command loop," said Rita.

<Message is eyes-only for Admiral Rita Page>

"*Merkkessa*, override, read message to command loop," Rita repeated.

<Message as follows: Escaped detention. Returning to join you at Singheko. Garatella has executed secret alliance with commander of the Singheko Home Fleet, Admiral Zukra. Pojjayan delivered plans for new drives and gamma lance to Zukra. Zukra is secretly converting ships to the new

technology. Also a retrofitted Nidarian fleet with new drives and gamma lance is being prepared to support Zukra. See Nidarian fleet configuration attached. Watch six. Signed-Arteveld>

The shock and surprise on the face of her staff matched Rita's own.

"I knew it. I knew Garatella was up to something!" Bekerose exclaimed. "But how on earth did Pojjayan manage to get the plans for the gamma lance?"

Rita almost shuddered in her anger and disappointment.

"It doesn't matter. Somehow, he got them, probably before he left Earth to meet *Dragon* for the intel exchange. But he got them. And now Garatella and Zukra have them."

Rita glanced down at her console, where the fleet configuration Arteveld had attached to his message was displayed.

"Three battlecruisers, four cruisers, two destroyers, two corvettes. All being prepared to come at us - and all with the new gamma lance."

"And we know from our intercepted ELINT that Zukra has taken over," said Bekerose. "That means he's got sole command of the Singheko ships in this system, as well as designs for the new drives and the gamma lance. And a Nidarian fleet building and on the way."

There was a grim silence around the table. Rita closed her eyes for a minute.

"This doesn't change much. We've always known we'd be outnumbered. And we've always known this would be a guerrilla war, picking away at their weak points. This just expands the battlefield for us. Remember why we're here, folks."

Rita opened her eyes and passed her gaze around the table at her staff.

"We're here to make sure the battle is fought in the Singheko system - not at Earth. We're here to protect Earth from these animals - by focusing their attention on us while the people back home gear up to defend our planet. Nothing about that part of our mission has changed."

"Look at it as more opportunity. More targets to attack. Adapt your thinking to that."

The grim silence lightened a bit.

"Thoughts?"

Dallitta nodded, taking up the challenge.

"Aye, milady, we understand. So we should go ahead with the hit-and-run attack. The sooner the better, before they have time to retrofit any more ships to the new technology."

"Bekerose?"

"I vote to proceed, milady. Let's hit them before they have time to practice using their new toys. We may find their training deficient right now. It's not likely to remain that way for long. So hit them hard right now."

"Tarraine?"

"I agree, milady. Take it to them before they have more time to prepare. But I have one modification to the plan I'd like to suggest..."

***

Onboard *Dragon*, Bonnie had moved beyond anger. It was strange. Now she felt only a great sadness to be leaving Luke behind.

But she couldn't wait for him.

She had moved Commander Lirrassa to the XO position. Now Lirrassa sat in the XO chair, adjusting to her new role, while Bonnie adjusted to the fact that Luke was no longer beside her when she needed him.

"Time to go," said Bonnie. "That cruiser and her escort will be here in two hours. I suggest we get the hell out of Dodge."

"Aye, mum," replied Lirrassa. "All divisions report ready for movement."

"Notify Jim to form up behind us as we depart."

"Aye, mum. Message sent. Message acknowledged. Ready to depart orbit."

"Take us out of here, Lirrassa."

With a slight lurch from her damaged system engine, *Dragon* departed orbit and headed for the mass limit.

The bridge was much quieter than normal. Everyone on the bridge could feel the pain of their captain. It was a palpable thing, an invisible weight that hung over the bridge.

But they also knew she would shake it off. She was their captain.

Bonnie watched for a half-hour as their boost stayed pegged at 240g, but the incoming cruiser made no attempt to pursue them. When they passed 25% light and it was clear no Singheko ship could catch them - or even come close - she reduced her accel back to 200g.

Behind her, Jim and his squadron of Merlins, dog-tired after more than forty-two hours in their fighters, stayed tucked in a close combat spread until they were safely away, then moved out to a looser long-distance travel formation and put their fighters on autopilot.

They were asleep in seconds.

***

Lieutenant Dan Worley had never known exhaustion like this.

He had been working non-stop for five days. In that entire time, he had not slept more than three hours per night.

They had poured nano glop over the holes punched through the hull, got the breaches sealed up, got pressure back in the engineering space, and got the scaffolding up around the tDrive pyramid.

Then they got the holes punched through the pyramid sealed up. Dan put one crew to work removing the damaged tDrive components from inside the pyramid.

Then the iridium had to be extracted from the damaged parts and decontaminated. The residue and radioactive remnants were ejected into space.

A second crew decontaminated the interior of the tDrive compartment. When the decon crew was finally finished, the workers could at last shed their environmental suits and work in shirtsleeves.

Then they spent another three days fabricating new components and installing them in the tDrive, working nonstop, night and day.

Crew became so exhausted they fell to the floor in place without bothering to go back to their cabins for sleep. Their fellow crew mates just dragged them to a corner and continued with work.

It was life or death for the *Dragon*. So the call to Bonnie carried indescribable relief.

"Captain, tDrive ready for testing," Worley called over the comm. His voice grated like he was eating gravel.

Bonnie, sitting at her console on the bridge, breathed a huge sigh of relief. She glanced at the holo to double check.

They were past the mass limit. It was safe to use the tDrive.

She nodded at Lirrassa.

"Give us a test, Commander. Don't forget to warn the Merlins first."

"Aye, mum," said Lirrassa. She talked into her comm briefly.

"Merlins are ready," Lirrassa said. "Helm, bring up the tDrive, please."

"Aye, sir," called Chief Blocker. "*Dragon*, energize the tDrive," he called, watching his console as a backup. One by one, lights on the console flicked from red to green. Finally he was satisfied.

"tDrive is idling and all sensors nominal," called Blocker.

Bonnie looked at Lirrassa.

"Take us about 5 AU forward, *Dragon*," said Bonnie. "Be sure to provide a plan to the Merlins - I don't want to lose them. Tell them to continue on this course. We'll be back shortly and continue to escort them until Rita can send a ship to pick them up."

<Syncing with Merlins. They are notified. They acknowledge. tDrive coming up to full power. Standby. Ready for transition>

"Execute!" spoke Bonnie with emphasis.

The whine of the tDrive sounded normal, a sound that gave them a shiver of hope and joy as the *Dragon* sank out of three-space and disappeared from the view of the Singheko enemy behind.

"Captain to Lt. Worley. Job well done, congratulations."

There was no reply. Then a voice came over the comm.

"Sorry, mum, Lt. Worley is asleep on the floor of the engineering space. Shall I wake him up?"

Bonnie grinned.

"No. Let him sleep."

***

Alone in her cabin, Rita contemplated the ansible message she had received earlier from Lt. Commander Winston at Dekanna.

Winnie's briefing was thorough. The Dariama were truly a paranoid race, as evidenced by their initial reaction to the appearance of the *Banjala* and their detention of Winnie and Roberto for several days. They had believed nothing that Winnie said until it was demonstrated to them.

They're from Missouri, thought Rita. *The 'Show Me" state. If I don't see it, I don't believe it.*

But they were also technically astute. Winnie's description of how quickly their Admiral Sobong had understood the situation - and how she had correctly guessed the existence of a new and potent weapon - was a testament to their technical competence and intelligence.

With a sigh, she tossed her tablet on the bed covers and began pacing her bedroom.

So. They could potentially be valuable allies in the fight against the Singheko. And Winnie's message had included a draft mutual defense treaty sent by Sobong. Winnie had recommended that Rita accept the treaty.

But it gave the gamma lance to the Dekanna Union.

Rita had initially decided to reject the treaty. She did not want to give up her last remaining technological advantage to an unknown and potentially untrustworthy race.

All that was moot now. Thanks to Pojjayan's treachery, the Nidarians - and Zukra - had the gamma lance. The cat was out of the bag.

Rita was a realist. The odds were now against her and her small fleet. Even if she could win another battle or two against Zukra, the Singheko had at least two expeditionary fleets out that she knew about - one to the Bagrami system and now one enroute to the Dekanna system.

Zukra could easily retrofit one of his corvettes to the new fast drives, send it to meet the distant expeditions, and give them the designs for both the gamma lance and the new drives. It would be only a matter of six to eight months until both foreign expeditions could be back and ready to fight - and to invade Earth for the second time, overwhelming her meager defenses.

Reaching a decision, Rita reached for her tablet.

I don't have the authority to do this. Only the UN can accept a treaty in the name of Earth.

But...

Without allies, I can't survive. And if I don't survive, Earth doesn't survive. At some point, we have to trust somebody.

"Treaty accepted," she typed, and entered her thumbprint on the screen.

21 - BOMBARDMENT

Orma stood on the bridge of the cruiser, staring at the holo as his task force slipped into orbit around Deriko.

He knew why he was here.

He was the goat, tied out in the field to catch the wolf.

Zukra didn't have to say it. Orma had worked with Zukra for too many years.

He'd never give me a command, even a small one like this, if it were a real campaign. I'm the bait...the sacrificial lamb.

"Entering orbit, Commodore," called his XO.

Commodore. What a joke. Because I have a cruiser and three destroyers, I'm now a commodore. Zukra's idea of humor.

"Right. All ships prepare to bombard the rebels."

"Aye, sir. Missiles and kinetics prepared. Ready to fire."

His XO leaned over to Orma and whispered.

"But sir, we'll hit our own troops."

Orma snorted.

I know what Zukra would say and do. So I have to say and do the same thing. Zukra knew this when he sent me. Part of turning the screw, making me sweat.

"That's the price of failure. They deserve to die for not taking the complex already. Open fire, Commander. Clean this planet of these damn Humans."

"Aye, sir," acknowledged the Commander, and waved to his Weapons officer.

The ship vibrated as the first volley of missiles and kinetics left their firing tubes. In seconds, vast explosions of dirt and rock began to billow up from the surface below as Orma's task force created a living hell for any creature still on the surface.

The bodies of rebel and Singheko alike flew into the air as the buildings of the complex disintegrated into rubble.

***

Deep underground, the ceiling shook again, dust and chips of stone falling all around them.

"That was close," said Marta.

"Yup," agreed Tatiana.

They had been huddling like rats as far underground as they could get for ten hours, while the Singheko dropped everything but the kitchen sink on them. They were established in a smaller tunnel, in the angle where it turned to go west, creating a natural corner that seemed to be a bit stronger.

The temporary respite offered by the *Dragon* coming in for its hit-and-run attack had helped. The Marines dropped by the *Dragon* allowed them to clear out the remainder of the Singheko in the tunnels and move all the rebels back underground, to get ready for the punishment that was coming.

And she had known it was coming. The Singheko were definitely pissed off now. So pissed off, their bombardment had killed all their own Singheko troops on the surface.

They didn't seem to care.

In the near darkness, Norali stumbled over to them, almost tripping over the debris on the floor from ten hours of near misses. She was carrying her comm in one hand.

"The Marines that came down from that destroyer want to talk to you," Norali said. She handed the comm to Tatiana.

"Yes?"

"Is this Big X?"

"Yes, this is Big X. Go ahead."

"This is Major Oliver Coston. We're about two tunnels north of you, I think. I'd like to come over for a council of war if that's alright."

"That would be fine, Major. And I haven't had a chance to thank you yet for what you did. Without you, I don't think we could have cleared the tunnels out. We'd be on the surface now, getting pounded to bits. So you saved a lot of lives today."

"Well, thanks, but it's kind of hard to tell that right now. We're getting the shit kicked out of us. I only hope the fleet comes back."

"The fleet?" Tatiana was surprised. "What fleet?"

"I'll explain when I get there. We're on our way."

"Roger, see you soon," Tatiana said, signing off. She handed the comm back to Norali and looked at Marta.

"A fleet? What is he talking about?" she said.

Marta shrugged. "Don't know. Maybe Earth sent a fleet?"

Tatiana's eyes went wide. "Wow, that would be something. If there was a fleet here that could help us..."

Marta looked askance at her, shaking her head.

"Don't get excited, Tat. You knew from the git-go we have no chance in the long run. All we ever hoped to do was cause them pain and disruption."

Marta waved her hand in the general direction of the dozens of Singheko bodies that were still visible from their position in the tunnel.

"Well, we've done that. They knew we were here."

She looked back at Tatiana.

"But don't start thinking we can win. We're on a planet, at the bottom of a gravity well, and the Singheko hold the rest of the system. We'll never get out of here alive, Tat. You know that. Don't start believing in shit that ain't gonna happen. Just focus on causing them as much damage as possible."

Tatiana sighed. "I know, Marta. Thanks. Keep me grounded."

Behind them, Baysig spoke in his deep voice.

"You are wrong," he said.

Tatiana and Marta swung around to look at him.

"What?"

"You are wrong," Baysig said again. "You can win. It is possible."

"And how would we do that?" Marta asked derisively. "The

Singheko have fleets and fleets of warships. Even if there is an Earth fleet out there, it would be a tiny force compared to what they can bring to bear. It doesn't matter how many of their orbital bombardment ships we knock down - they'll just send in more. Eventually they'll grind us into dust."

Baysig nodded. "Everything you say is correct. If you take into account only the Human fleet."

Tatiana looked puzzled.

"What do you mean?"

Baysig waved vaguely at the heavens.

"There is another fleet out there," he said. "The remnants of the Taegu and the Bagrami fleets. When the Singheko invaded our systems, our fleets fought well. But they were outnumbered and forced to retreat. The survivors escaped and went into hiding. Now they have joined forces. If the Humans also join with them, it is a fleet large enough to take this system, if well commanded. And lucky."

"Bullshit," said Marta. "I don't believe it. Where are they?"

"That I can't say," replied Baysig. "But I know they have scouts watching this system. So they are aware of what is happening here."

Marta turned back to Tatiana. "Like I said, Tat. Don't get your hopes up."

Tatiana nodded agreement. But she sank deep into thought, running the possibilities through her head.

***

Ollie and Luke marched along the tunnel, staring suspiciously at the ceiling. Large cracks showed in the concrete above them, and dust came off the roof periodically in waves, causing them to shy to one side or the other as they walked. Every time one of the Singheko weapons impacted the surface, the tunnel vibrated like a drumhead. They half-expected the ceiling to come down on top of them any moment.

Ollie looked over at Luke.

"This really sucks," he said.

Luke nodded. "It does indeed, Major."

"Up here," called their guide, one of Norali's intelligence team. The woman had met them halfway, leading them back to the location of their commander - Big X.

"That's certainly a strange name for their boss," said Ollie.

Luke grinned. "Don't you get it?"

Ollie shook his head. "No. What should I get?"

"Females have two X chromosomes. Men have only one."

Ollie continued to look puzzled. "Still don't get it."

"Never mind," said Luke, smiling.

Turning a corner, they entered a slightly smaller tunnel. This one seemed to have a more stable ceiling. They didn't see the large cracks in the roof, although the ceiling still shook, and the dust filtered down at every impact.

"Here we are," said their guide, leading them to a clump of creatures sitting in the tunnel where it made a sharp turn to the west. Ollie could see one of the big bear-like creatures, a couple of the small ones they called Taegu, and one of the near-Singheko creatures they called Ampato. A number of large women sat on either side of a thinner, taller one, with her back to them.

"Big X, here's Major Coston," their guide called out.

The slender woman facing away from them rose and turned around.

Beside him, Ollie heard Luke gasp like he'd been punched in the stomach.

***

<You have a visitor>

Lt. Worley was half-awake. After repairing the *Dragon*'s drives, he had slept the clock around once, got up and did one shift, then returned to his cabin for more rest.

But he hadn't managed to sleep yet. His biorhythm was severely disrupted. He had been lying still, staring at the ceiling, trying to calm his mind.

A visitor? That's strange...

"Who is it?" he asked, knowing the AI would understand the context.

<Lt. Gibson>

"Ah. Come!" Worley said, pulling his blanket up and over his body to make sure it was covered.

The door cracked open and Rachel Gibson stuck her head inside.

"Can I come in?" she asked.

"Sure, come on," said Dan.

Rachel entered and closed the door behind her.

"Lights," said Dan. The lights flicked on, the brightness almost blinding him.

"I'd rather you left them off," said Rachel, holding one hand up to shield her eyes.

Dan was puzzled. *What's going on here? What does she want?*

He ordered the lights off, leaving them in the dark.

Rachel came over and sat on the edge of his bed. She was so close to him. The weight of her pushing the mattress down sent his pulse racing.

"I don't know if we're going to live or die anymore. Every day in this system could be our last," she said. "I need something from you."

Dan grunted in the dark.

"What?"

Rachel put her hand on him, in a place that was stirring.

"That," she said.

Dan reached for her.

***

Two days later, Rita glanced at the holo repeater in her cabin.

Jim and his Merlins had come aboard two days ago, all of the pilots dog-tired and scruffy after so many hours in their fighters. Jim had showered and gone to bed - and had slept for most of the last two days.

This morning he got up and had breakfast. Now he was waiting in her briefing room with the rest of her staff for the final planning meeting before their next attack.

And *Dragon* was back. Rita could see the destroyer just off

Merkkessa's stern quarter, holding position. The scorch marks and scars of her recent ordeal were clearly visible.

And Bonnie was also waiting in her briefing room, just arrived by shuttle from the *Dragon*.

How do I feel about this woman? Do I still love her? Am I jealous of her feelings for Jim? For that matter, am I jealous of Jim's feelings for her?

Rita shook her head in exasperation. She had made up her mind a long time ago not to let petty emotions influence her thinking.

What Jim and Bonnie feel about each other is bullshit to me right now. I don't care about any of that. I only care about fighting the Singheko.

Rita opened the hatch into her briefing room and stepped through, smiling at her staff as they rose to attention.

"Stand easy, folks," she said, sitting at the head of the table.

As usual, Jim was at the other end of the table, as far from her as he could get.

That never failed to amuse Rita.

Does he think that makes any difference? That somehow, people will forget we're married because he's sitting down there?

Dallitta as usual sat on her left, Bekerose on her right. Tarraine and Sato were next. Bonnie was farther down, in the middle of the table.

"Good morning, folks. How are we doing, Dallitta?"

"We've completed the re-supply and repair of all ships. We've completed boost to 20% light while we re-supplied. We're ready."

Rita nodded.

"Then this is your final warning order. You will execute plan A-7 as previously briefed. TF1 will be under the command of Captain Bekerose. TF2 will be under the command of Captain Page. We go per the schedule published.

"Are there any final questions about the plan?"

Nobody spoke. The plan had been thoroughly discussed; all questions had been answered.

Rita looked at Bonnie.

"Any problems with *Dragon*?"

"No, milady," answered Bonnie. "We're good to go."

She glanced at Jim.

"Fighters ready?"

Jim nodded.

"Aye, milady. Ready to go."

Rita stood.

"Then good hunting, people, and let's be about it."

22 - GO WHERE THEY AIN'T

Rita had violated one of the most sacred tenets of warfare.

Never split your forces in the face of a superior enemy.

But Rita also knew the EDF could not win this war by following convention. She had to out-think Zukra.

And if she failed, the EDF would be ground into nothingness by the greater numbers of the enemy.

And Earth would fall.

So Rita had thought about Zukra - how he would react, what he would do next.

And because Admiral Rita Page could turn off her emotions and be one of the most coldly logical people in the universe, she knew exactly what Zukra would do next.

He would prepare an ambush for her. And it would be at Deriko. The lone cruiser and three destroyers in orbit there, pounding away at the rebels on the surface, were the bait.

Because in her heart, Rita knew something. Something she was so sure of, she was betting the survival of her entire fleet - and the survival of the rebels on Deriko - on it.

She was sure Zukra knew where she was and what she was planning.

And as they accelerated toward the Singheko system, he would be watching their every move, positioning his fleet for his own ambush.

She was counting on it.

"Milady, we're on course at 285 AU and ready for the

transition to 15 AU," called Bekerose from his command chair on the bridge.

"Very good, Captain. Good luck on the transition."

Now they were about to execute the most dangerous part of the entire mission.

First, they were going to translate into six-space while traveling at 20% light speed.

That part was easy.

Then they would translate back into three-space at only 15 AU from the primary star.

That part was not easy. The window of error was only 200 milliseconds - 0.2 seconds.

Any ship that missed the window would leave a large cloud of high energy atoms in the void. Atoms that had once been a starship full of people.

But the advantage of the plan was that upon entry back into normal space, they would already be moving at 20% light speed. They would not have to boost again. Like the namesake of their attack plan - Silent Arrow - they would be near invisible as they approached.

***

Onboard *Dragon*, Bonnie tightened her straps. It was time for their transition into six-space.

She had to inwardly smile, though.

If we don't make the transition window when we surface back at 15 AU, it's not going to matter how tight my straps are. I'll be a large cloud of atoms smeared out across a hundred thousand klicks of space.

With a slight bump, *Dragon* translated. They would be in six-space for exactly 12.1 seconds.

Twelve seconds to live if the AI doesn't hit the entry point precisely.

Twelve seconds to think about your life.

Twelve seconds to think about Luke.

A smile lit up Bonnie's lips as she realized what she had done.

I thought about Luke. Not Jim.

With another whine and bump, *Dragon* transitioned back into normal space.

And they were still alive.

"Status!" called Bonnie.

"All systems nominal," called Lirrassa. "All ships appear to have made the transition successfully."

Bonnie heaved a sigh of relief.

It had been a huge gamble on Rita's part. The slightest error on the part of any of the AI systems would have destroyed an entire ship.

But they had made it. And now they were at 20% light speed, headed directly toward their target. They would not need to give away their position by boosting again.

But Rita had explained the full plan to her staff. So Bonnie knew what Rita was thinking.

She thinks Zukra already knows where we are. And what we're doing. So he's right behind us, his own fleet performing a Silent Arrow on us. He started boosting as soon as he saw us finish our re-supply and form up for the mission.

I hope she's right. Because if she's wrong, my part of this mission is a waste of time.

And truly, it's a waste of time anyway. Even if we knock out the task force over Deriko, Zukra will just dispatch another one from the home fleet.

Most likely she'd only buy the rebels a few days of grace. Maybe a week if they were lucky.

But they were going to do it anyway. It was still a chance to harass the enemy. A chance to kill a cruiser and three destroyers. Part of Rita's guerrilla war on the enemy.

Kill them at every opportunity, give them no peace.

Her focus coming back to the job at hand, Bonnie looked at the holo. *Dragon* was coasting, silent, engines idled, all unnecessary systems off, fingers crossed.

"Lirrassa, call Second Watch to the bridge to take over. Rest First Watch until two hours before merge. I'll be in my cabin."

"Aye, mum."

Bonnie rose and went out the bridge hatch to her cabin.

There's no use going into battle tired.

Going to her bunk, she lay down and tried to rest. But as she drifted off, she couldn't help a smile as she remembered her thoughts during the grim moments of transition, when she didn't know if she would live or die.

I thought about Luke. Not Jim.

I'm finally over him.

***

"What?" shouted Zukra. "Impossible! No, no, their target is Deriko!"

"No, sir. When they transitioned into the system, they adjusted their vector. Their target is Ridendo."

Zukra stood from his command chair, enraged. The veins on his muzzle popped out in anger. Grabbing the nearest object - his electronic tablet - he threw it with all the force he could muster, shattering it against the bridge wall.

"No! That bitch! She can't do this to me!"

Zukra kicked his chair, spun around, focused his attention on his personal slave standing behind him, and struck him with his fist, knocking him to the deck unconscious.

"That bitch! She'll pay for this!" he yelled, kicking the unconscious slave.

Finally, his anger spent, he stopped and turned back to Damra.

"Can we intercept?"

"Not before she reaches Ridendo, sir. But assuming she slows for her attack run on the planet, we can catch her just after her first pass. So we can prevent her from coming back for a second one. If we change vector now and boost at emergency."

"Do it!" shouted Zukra. "We can't let her have two passes at the home planet! Emergency boost, now!"

Zukra slammed himself into his command chair and strapped in. The warning klaxon started. Zukra completed strapping in and yelled across the bridge at Damra.

"Boost now! Get us moving!"

"But sir, we have to give the crew at least sixty seconds warning. They have to get to a safe place for overboost!"

"Screw the crew! Get this fleet moving now!"

"Aye, sir," Damra reluctantly agreed. With a wave at the helm, he indicated to start overboost.

Zukra laid back in his contoured command chair as the g-force came on and started building to a perceived +7g.

That bitch knew. She knew. Somehow, she figured out Deriko was a trap.

I'll kill her. I'll capture her and put her in the arena. I'll cut off her head in front of the crowd.

No...that's too good for her. Too easy. I'll kill her more slowly. I'll find a way.

***

"Battle Stations," called Bekerose.

Rita heard the klaxon start and the announcement over the comm.

<GENERAL QUARTERS, GENERAL QUARTERS. THIS IS NOT A DRILL, THIS IS NOT A DRILL. GENERAL QUARTERS, GENERAL QUARTERS. THIS IS NOT A DRILL, THIS IS NOT A DRILL>

The main EDF fleet had been moving at 20% of light speed after their transition into the system. But that was too fast for an attack pass. That would have been a firing window of only 67 milliseconds - 0.067 seconds.

Too fast for an attack pass, at least if you wanted maximum accuracy.

And Rita wanted maximum accuracy. So for the last half of their entry into the system, they had decelerated at 300g.

She didn't care if Zukra saw them now. The die was cast. They were on a direct vector to the Singheko home planet, Ridendo.

Zukra's fleet was clearly visible now, blazing away behind them at 257g, on a course that would intercept them roughly

200 k-klicks beyond Ridendo as they decelerated for their second attack run.

But of course, they weren't going to decelerate for a second pass. That had never been Rita's intention. Zukra's mad dash toward them was futile.

"*Merkkessa*, how we doin'?" asked Rita. It didn't matter that the countdown clock on the holo was right in front of her. It was nervous tension.

It was being human.

<We are one minute from merge. The main refit dock of the Singheko fleet is directly ahead. There are two enemy destroyers coming out to meet us>

Rita nodded.

Good. Not only will we hit the refit dock, we'll take a couple of destroyers too. A good day.

And if Bonnie can take care of her part, an even better day.

***

On *Merkkessa*, Rita was focused on the space dock in front of them. It was an orbital facility about two kilometers in width, containing a half-dozen large docks for building and repairing starships.

In the center dock was one of the big Singheko battlecruisers, being retrofitted with the designs stolen by Pojjayan and passed to Zukra; the fast drives and the gamma lance.

This had been her target all along.

Zukra had wanted her to come to Deriko and attack the bait he had so carefully positioned there. He was so sure she would do it; he had his entire fleet positioned to ambush her there.

Rita had another plan in mind.

Taking out one battlecruiser is infinitely better than getting my ass kicked. Plus Zukra is now pulled away from Deriko. Bonnie should have a clear shot at that cruiser.

So a cruiser and a battlecruiser. And these two destroyers coming at them.

Not a bad day's work. If they could pull it off.

Rita came back to focus as she heard the callout from Lt. Carlson at Tac.

"*Daeddam* and *Qupporre* engaging."

On the holo, Rita saw the two destroyers rising to meet them disappear in a cloud of gamma lance fire and missiles as Captain Tarraine and Captain Sato blasted them to bits.

"Scratch two destroyers," called Lt. Carlson, a bit of glee in his voice.

Rita remained silent. She watched as they drew closer to the spacedock, the decel bringing their speed down to only 300,000 kph now, giving more than adequate time for her purpose.

The battlecruiser was in dock. There would be no reason for the crew to remain on board while the new drives and weapons were installed. They were probably down on the planet on leave.

It's like shooting ducks in a pond.

"...fire, fire, fire," she heard from Lt. Carlson. The grating whine of the gamma lance came and went, and the *Merkkessa* shuddered a bit as twenty missiles left the tubes.

Rita watched the battlecruiser pass by below, the enemy's hull slashed by the gamma lance, explosions starting to pock her skin as the missiles impacted unopposed. The rumble of the reloading conveyors told her the second volley was almost ready. Then the second volley went out, and as they pulled away, she saw the missiles striking all around the battlecruiser.

And then the battlecruiser disappeared in a gigantic explosion, taking out not only the ship itself but the entire orbital dock and the two smaller ships next to her.

The fleet went to 300g accel to escape the system. They had no intention of coming back for another pass, and there was no need.

As they pulled away, Rita couldn't resist one non-logical thought.

Kiss my ass, Zukra.

***

On *Dragon*, the sound of the klaxon for battle stations faded away.

Through the bridge hatch, Bonnie could hear running feet as crew scrambled to their stations. Around her, the bridge crew seemed to sit up straighter, focus with more intensity on their consoles and screens.

<Ninety seconds to merge>

Bonnie often wondered what other people thought about during these tense moments before battle.

Do they think about their family? Their children? Or do they think about themselves, their own safety?

Typically Bonnie did neither of those two things.

Bonnie thought about the enemy, and what the enemy might do. About the plan, and what she was supposed to do to make it a success. About the worst case. About what could go wrong.

In front of her on the main screen, Deriko approached rapidly. They were down to less than 600,000 kph as they approached, under a hard 303g deceleration.

That would give them a firing window of 14 seconds - enough time for two volleys.

The Singheko had detected them. The three enemy destroyers were boosting hard, trying to turn up and around to face her. The cruiser had reacted differently, trying to run for it, trying to put some distance between them, gain some time to get organized and turn around for the battle.

In front of *Dragon* by thirty seconds, her own escort of four destroyers vectored away to meet the enemy, leaving her alone for the moment.

The Singheko destroyers fired their first volley of missiles at Bonnie's screen of four destroyers out in front of *Dragon*. The EDF fired back, both gamma lances and missiles. On both sides, ships staggered as holes were punched through them and explosions filled the space between them in a maze of violence.

<Twenty seconds to merge>

Bonnie watched the enemy cruiser on the holo.

He started too late, thought Bonnie. *He was ready for an attack by the full fleet from the opposite direction. He didn't pick us up coming in behind him.*

He'll just barely be able to get turned around in time.

<*Ten seconds to merge*>

Rachel at Tac started her countdown as always, a backup for the AI.

"Ten. Nine. Eight. Seven..."

Bonnie glanced around her bridge one last time, ensuring that everything was as she expected.

I am so proud of this crew. They have come so far.

"...fire, fire, fire!" called Rachel.

The grating whine of the gamma lance firing was followed instants later by the rumble of missiles departing *Dragon*.

And the port side of *Dragon*'s bridge ripped apart, the sudden decompression exploding the atmosphere out into space.

As Bonnie's faceshield automatically slammed down over her face and her pressure suit inflated, she had time for one last thought before the blackness took her.

He had a gamma lance too.

23 - ORMA

Bonnie came to her senses in darkness and pain. Her chest hurt like the devil.

There were faint points of light in her darkness. In her dazed state, it took her many seconds to realize what they were.

They were stars.

The sharp, metallic tang of the air she was breathing told her she was on suit air.

Slowly, it came to her.

She was floating in space.

Where's Dragon?

The thought was fuzzy in her brain.

What happened to my ship?

A memory came back to her. A huge impact on her chest. The port side of the bridge tearing apart, a gigantic hole ripped all across it. The helmet visor snapping down.

Then waking up to this.

She took a half-dozen deep breaths. Her mind started to function a little better.

Follow your training. Check for suit penetrations or broken bones.

She checked the suit gages, just visible in the corner of her vision. They showed steady; no indication of a suit penetration leaking her oxygen to space.

She flexed her arms and legs. They worked. Her chest hurt like the devil, but nothing seemed to be broken.

Bruised but not broken. That's good.

She took another few deep breaths, trying to clear the

cobwebs from her mind.

Where's the planet?

She tried to turn her head to look behind her, but the realities of weightlessness in space didn't allow that. She remembered a trick one of the Nidarians had taught them. If she moved her arms and legs in a certain, specific way, inertia could be used to turn her around.

Trying it, she was gratified to see it worked. As she flailed her arms and legs in a pattern somewhat like swimming, the stars slowly rotated around her. But it was exhausting in the suit.

Bonnie gritted her teeth and continued the drill.

I want to know how close I am. Which way I'm moving...

Slowly the planet came into view, first in the corner of her vision, then moving directly in front of her as she continued to work her limbs. When she had a full view of the planet, she stopped, panting.

It was a lot smaller than she expected.

I'm still moving at nearly a half-million kph. It's at least 200 k-klicks away.

I'm headed into deep space.

***

The Singheko lifeboat was spacious. Too spacious. There should have been two dozen survivors in it.

There were only three.

Orma closed his eyes, willing the events of the last two hours to go away.

But they wouldn't. His first command...

...and my last, he thought wryly...

...had disintegrated around him after the attack by the Human destroyer. The cruiser had split into three fragments, then the rear section - the engineering spaces - had exploded violently as reactor containment failed.

It was a miracle he had made it to the lifeboat. Not many of his crew did.

Raising his head and opening his eyes, Orma looked at the

other two survivors of his crew.

One was his XO, Commander Retga. The other was the rating who had been manning the helm. He couldn't remember the name.

"Retga."

The battered XO lifted his head. One arm was clearly broken, Retga holding it gingerly with his other hand. One eye was blackened, and blood was dried on his muzzle.

"Do I look as bad as you?"

Retga managed a slight grin.

"Yes, sir."

"Do you think any of the other lifeboats got away?"

Retga shook his head.

"No, sir. I'm sorry. There's a display on the instrument panel behind you. It shows the status of all lifeboats within range. We're the only one with a green status."

Orma grunted and turned, looking behind him. There was a minimalist instrument panel in the lifeboat, right behind his seat. He scanned it, trying to find the display. The rating leaned over and pointed to the proper place.

The display showed a matrix of tiny indicators. There were 64 of them.

Only one showed green. All the others showed red.

Orma sighed. He did the quick computation in his head.

A crew of 720 on his cruiser. Three survivors.

717 dead.

Glancing at the display again, he noticed another light blinking. A yellow one. He pointed to it.

"What's that one?"

Retga leaned to one side to see past Orma. He shook his head.

"I don't know, sir."

The rating spoke up.

"That's a Nidarian suit beacon, sir. There's a Nidarian survivor out there somewhere, close by."

Orma looked at Retga.

"Not likely to be Nidarian. Not from a Human ship."

Retga nodded.

"A damn Human, I'll bet."

Orma looked at the rating.

"What's your name, son?"

"Yeoman Alede, sir."

"Can this lifeboat maneuver?"

"Yes, sir, within limits. We can't make it to the planet, though. Not enough fuel."

"Can we make it to that suit beacon?"

Alede studied the instrument panel.

"Yes, sir."

Orma looked at Retga, who shrugged.

"I'd just leave them there to die, if it were me."

Orma nodded.

"I know the feeling. But I'm curious. I've never seen one of these Humans. And maybe we can learn something."

Orma turned back to Yeoman Alede.

"How about I get out of your way, and you take us over to pick up that suit?"

***

One of the points of light was blinking.

That's not a star, thought Bonnie.

It was blinking, and it was drawing closer to her.

That's a ship. Or something.

Dragon!

They're coming back for me!

Then reality hit her brain.

It can't be Dragon. *Even if she survived, it would take her at least an hour and a half to come to me.*

That means it must be Singheko.

A momentary spike of panic hit her.

Singheko. I'll be a prisoner.

Maybe I should just let the air out of the suit. That might be better. There's no telling what those animals will do to me.

But I've never been a quitter. Not going to start now. I'll fight them if I have to. If I have to kill myself, I'll wait until I can take some of them with me.

The light grew closer. Bonnie began to see a shape forming against the background of the stars.

It was tiny.

It's a lifeboat. Just a lifeboat.

The tiny craft drew up next to her. A hatch opened on the side.

An airlock.

Slowly the lifeboat moved closer, until the open hatch was within the reach of her arm. A cleat on the outside of the hatch cover was tantalizingly close.

Bonnie came to a realization. They couldn't force her to board. All she had to do was refuse to enter the airlock. They would have no choice but to leave her.

But then she would die out here when her oxygen ran out.

And there was an element of curiosity. She had only seen one live Singheko in person, when she had been on Nidaria, in Garatella's office.

Bonnie grinned inside her helmet.

This should be interesting.

She reached out, grasped the cleat, and pulled herself into the airlock.

***

The inner airlock door opened, and Orma stared at the Human.

He had never seen one. He had seen holos of them, of course. They were small, hairless things to a Singheko way of thinking, with an ugly flat face - no muzzle at all. No claws, no fangs. Nothing to show them as worthy of battle.

And of course, this one was still in their spacesuit. He wondered how they would communicate.

Suddenly a voice came out of the suit speaker, a voice he understood.

"Thank you for rescuing me," the voice said in Nidarian.

Well, that helps. It speaks Nidarian, and I can understand enough of that language to communicate.

The small, space-suited figure sat in one of the empty seats by the airlock hatch, as far from the three Singheko as possible. It looked tiny in the huge seat - almost like a child, pretending to be an adult.

These weak creatures killed my cruiser? My stars, they're not much larger than a Nidarian. How could something so small and weak cause us so much trouble?

Orma smiled inwardly.

The Syope snake is small and weak. But deadly. I ought to think of them like that. Appearances can be deceiving.

"Our atmospheres are compatible, I've been told. So you should be able to remove your helmet with no danger."

Orma couldn't make out the face clearly, but it seemed the figure nodded. Then the arms reached up and unsnapped the helmet catch, twisted it, and lifted it off the head. The creature removed an inner cap and placed it inside the helmet, then lifted its head and stared at Orma.

Orma gazed at his first real live Human.

It didn't seem very threatening. The face was indeed flat, as in the holograms he had seen. No beautiful muzzle at all, no functional fangs inside the lips. The hair was longer than he expected from the holos. There was something about that...

With a shock, he realized what he was seeing.

"You...you're female!" he exclaimed, amazed.

"Yes. Female," it said. "My name is Bonnie. What's yours?"

***

Zukra was well past anger. He had long since passed enraged.

He was far to the south of madness.

But it was a cold kind of madness. One that allowed him to think carefully, logically.

I've continually underestimated these Humans. I've fallen for their bullshit traps over and again.

No more.

From now on, I treat them as equal to Singheko. However

galling and bitter that might be, I have to accept it.

That bitch female is dangerous.

And I'm not going to catch her. She played this perfectly. She knew I'd have no choice but to come back to try and intercept her. If I had not, she would have made a second pass at Ridendo, destroying even more infrastructure. Causing more havoc, undermining my position even more.

And yet I can't catch her now. Once she was sure I had diverted back to try to intercept her, she just kept going, heading for the mass limit at max boost. Without those new fast drives, I can't even get close to her.

And then she came in behind me and destroyed the force at Deriko. All of them. A cruiser and three destroyers. Gone.

Zukra waved a hand at Damra.

"Captain Damra. Cease the pursuit. We can't catch them. Take us back to Ridendo."

"Aye, sir."

As his fleet began to decelerate and come about, Zukra considered his options.

I'm not going to play her game anymore. I'll let her have Deriko for now. It's not worth the trouble. I'm going to focus on converting my remaining ships over to the new drives and the gamma lance - and wait for the Nidarian fleet to get here.

Then we'll take this Human bitch apart, piece by piece, until I have her neck in my hands.

And then I'll squeeze the life out of her. Slowly. Ever so slowly.

24 - RIGHT HAND HOLDS THE SKY

Dragon had survived. But not by much. There were slices cut through both sides of the ship where the gamma lance from the Singheko cruiser had gone through. The majority of the spaces were holed to vacuum, all the air lost, the decks covered with dead bodies. The few passageways still having pressure were filled with smoke and fumes.

Rachel Gibson found herself on her hands and knees, still on the blasted bridge of the destroyer. Her faceplate had snapped down automatically and her suit was pressurized. She was alive.

She lifted her head and took in the devastation around her.

Everyone was dead. At least everyone she could see.

The lower half of Commander Larissa's body was still strapped into the XO console.

The upper half was nowhere to be seen.

Ensign Goodwin had been at the Ops console. He was still there. A nice, neat hole went all the way through his chest, front to back. The blood from the wound had sublimated instantly in the vacuum, leaving a reddish stain that looked like dried paint.

Harry McMaster was mostly just a smear of debris on the side wall of the bridge.

Rachel shuddered, looking away. She couldn't bear to see them anymore.

There was still gravity. That was a blessing. At least she

wouldn't go flying out the great hole in the side of the bridge.

Slowly she rose to her knees. A realization came to her.

Bonnie's console was completely missing. Only the base of it remained, bent bolts showing where it had been stripped away.

The captain was gone.

My sweet Lord, thought Rachel. *I'm the only operational officer left.*

"*Dragon*..." she croaked. She licked her lips and tried again. "*Dragon*...are you there?"

<I am here>

<Where's the captain?"

<Captain Page is adrift in space 275 k-klicks in front of us>

"Is she alive?"

<Her vital signs show that she is alive>

"So we're still decelerating?"

<We are decelerating at 50g>

So the engines are damaged but working. Bonnie shot out in front of us when she departed the ship because we were decelerating.

"Stop decel, *Dragon*."

<Decel stopped>

"Set a vector to pick up Captain Page."

<Course set>

"Execute."

<Executing vector to rendezvous with Captain Page>

That's done. Now to get a damage assessment.

"*Dragon*. Enumerate damage of priority components."

<System engine damaged, maximum boost available 50g. Gamma lance inoperative. Missile tubes inoperative. TDrive inoperative. Ansible inoperative. 62% of ship open to space>

"Do we have comms with the rest of the squadron?"

<There are three survivors from the rest of the squadron. They have communicated with us, and I have informed them of our status. They are forming up around us as an escort>

Rachel rose to her feet, standing in the middle of the

devastated bridge.

I'm the senior operational officer now, she realized. *Until we recover Bonnie, I have to figure this out.*

"Where's Mr. Gibson?"

Please Lord, don't let him be dead. Don't let him be dead.

<Lt. Gibson is in the engineering space working on the engines>

Thank you, Lord. Thank you, thank you.

"Do you have comms with Captain Page?"

<No. A Singheko lifeboat has approached her. She has entered the lifeboat. I do not have comms with the lifeboat>

***

"How do I talk to her? What do I say?" wondered Orma, staring at the strange creature they had rescued.

The Human had shed her spacesuit. Now she sat quietly in the seat at the far end of the lifeboat, staring at the floor. She had one hand on her chest, rubbing it.

"Are you injured?" Orma asked.

"It's not too bad," she answered. "It'll be fine."

She was wearing a uniform, but he had no idea what the rank insignia meant.

"May I ask your rank?"

She looked up at him. A flicker of apprehension went across her face. Clearly, she didn't want to answer the question.

"Captain," she answered, after some hesitation.

Orma leaned back, stunned.

Could this be?

"You were the captain of that ancient destroyer? That Nidarian artifact?"

She nodded silently.

Orma couldn't think of anything to say. It was just too crazy. This...this tiny, barefaced Human female had shot his ship out from under him.

Of course, I shot her ship out from under her too, he thought. *I guess we're even.*

"We're lucky to be alive," he said at last. It was all he could think of to fit the situation.

For the first time since the Human came aboard, he saw a smile. She nodded again, silently.

"Captain!" called Yeoman Alede. "There's a ship approaching!"

Orma spun around to look at the instrument panel.

"Ours or theirs?" he asked.

Alede looked up, a pained expression on his face.

"Theirs, sir. It's that ancient Nidarian destroyer."

Orma turned back to the Human in the corner.

"Well, Captain, it seems the gods of war have spoken. We are to be your prisoners."

The Human gazed at him steadily.

"They can be quite finicky, you know. Those gods of war."

Orma nodded.

"So I've heard."

***

Rachel watched in some satisfaction as the Singheko lifeboat was wrestled into the shuttle bay. She had thought about having one of the other, less-damaged destroyers pick it up, but in the end changed her mind. Her captain was on that lifeboat and she wanted Bonnie back on board as soon as possible.

In the ninety minutes it had taken to rendezvous with the drifting lifeboat, they had restored some of the basics. She had moved bridge operations to the Ops Center, two compartments behind the blasted bridge. Dan Worley had gotten three compartments sealed and re-pressurized between the new bridge and the rear of the ship, allowing movement between the bow and stern again.

The number of injured overwhelmed Stephanie Warner and her medical team. The severely injured had been carried to sick bay and were being treated. The walking wounded had been transferred to the other destroyers.

And the dead had been collected and stacked in a storage space in the bow of the ship. There were a lot of them - more than Rachel could have imagined. The realities of warfare were coming home to roost in her mind, and it was not pleasant.

A dozen space suited figures finally got the lifeboat settled into place on the deck with a slight thud. They began securing it to the deck with cables. The outer door of the shuttle bay closed, followed immediately by the inner door.

<*Dragon* Actual arriving> she heard over her comm.

Rachel left the large window looking into the shuttle bay and moved to the hatch, watching the telltale. It was red, indicating no pressure on the other side of the hatch. She waited impatiently, until suddenly with a *chirp* it turned green. She undogged the hatch and went through, walking to the lifeboat.

All of *Dragon*'s Marines were still down on Deriko, but Rachel had assembled a team of two dozen ratings and armed them with rifles. They marched behind her as she approached the lifeboat. She wasn't sure what she would find inside, but she assumed there would be Singheko, and with no idea how many or what kind of mood they were in, she was taking no chances.

"Lock and load."

She heard the clatter of two dozen rifle bolts charging as she came up to the shuttle.

"Spread out, don't bunch up," she ordered. The men around her obeyed, moving apart so as not to present easy targets, and lifted their rifles half-way to their shoulders, ready for anything.

The hatch popped loose then slowly opened. Bonnie stuck her head out and smiled when she saw Rachel.

"Hello there," she said.

Rachel braced up and saluted. Bonnie returned her salute, then looked around at the armed team surrounding them.

"I don't think we'll need all the firepower," she said. "Stand them down, please."

Rachel nodded.

"Stand down, people," she called loudly. The team lowered

their weapons and put them on safe.

Bonnie clambered down from the hatch and stood, holding it open for the next creature.

A Singheko appeared in the hatch. He looked around uncertainly, then stepped down onto the deck. He glanced at Bonnie, then at Rachel, then lifted a hand in salute.

In near-perfect Nidarian, he spoke.

"Permission to come aboard?"

***

Bonnie entered the new and temporary bridge of *Dragon* and looked around sadly.

"What's the estimate to get the old bridge back up and running?"

"Ten days, mum," responded Rachel.

"And the engines?"

"Four days."

"Weapons?"

"Six days for the gamma lance, ten days for the missile tubes, fifteen days for the point defense cannon on the external hull."

"Crap. That asshole really shot us to hell, didn't he?"

"Aye, mum," answered Rachel. "We didn't expect him to have a gamma lance. It was a damn good ambush."

"Don't let Orma hear you say that. He's still in a funk because we shot his cruiser out from under him."

Rachel couldn't help but grin.

"That we did, mum."

"Where did you put them?"

"In the brig, mum."

"I want them treated well, Rachel. They saved my life, and they treated me well on the lifeboat. We'll return the favor."

"Aye, mum. I'll see to it."

Bonnie sat at a console hastily reconfigured to be her new command station and waved Rachel to the console beside her.

"Lt. Gibson, you are hereby officially designated as my XO. You did an excellent job. I'm more than pleased."

"Thank you, mum."

"Well, the first order of business is what to do next. We're still within the gravity well of Deriko, I assume."

"Aye, mum. We're slowly drifting back toward the planet."

"Any sign of the enemy coming out to us?"

"No, mum. For some reason, their entire fleet has returned to Ridendo. They seem to be concentrating on bringing their docks back online."

Bonnie gave a wry smile.

"They've decided to ignore us while they convert all their ships to the new drives and the gamma lance. They know we're not going anywhere."

"Aye, mum."

Bonnie made a decision.

"That being the case, let's go back to Deriko and pick up our Marines. Set a vector to put us in orbit over their location. And I think I'll go down to the surface and meet this General Tatiana I've been hearing about."

"Aye, mum," said Rachel, bending to her comm.

Forty minutes later, *Dragon* - what was left of her - was in orbit over Deriko. Bonnie stepped into the shuttle and turned to Rachel.

"Keep a close eye on the Singheko fleet. If there's any sign of a task force coming out for us, comm me and prep the ship for emergency departure. Keep pressure on the repair teams, watch the prisoners, and let me know of any other problems."

"Aye, mum."

Bonnie gave Rachel a grim smile.

"It's your ship again for a while, Rachel. Take good care of her."

Rachel saluted as Bonnie closed the hatch.

Thirty minutes later, the shuttle touched down outside the complex that the rebels called Bravo-Two. Bonnie exited the shuttle to find a large welcoming party. It seemed she was a celebrity to these people because she had rescued them not once, but twice.

But her eyes went straight to Luke. He was standing behind the first rank, behind a tall young woman that she assumed was his daughter, Tatiana.

The young woman extended her hand.

"Welcome, Captain. I'm Tatiana Powell. We're so happy to see you so we can thank you personally for all that you've done."

"I'm glad to be here," said Bonnie, finishing the handshake. "You folks have done a tremendous job. I can hardly believe what you've accomplished."

Tatiana nodded. "We have a lot more to do before this is over. Let me introduce you to my staff."

Bonnie went down the line, shaking hands with each of Tatiana's team as they were introduced to her. A big woman, Marta, with a bad scar down the side of her face. A smaller woman, Norali, in charge of Intelligence. A Taegu, Woderas, who just smiled. One of the big bear-like creatures, Baysig.

Then…

A Singheko?

Tatiana saw the confusion on Bonnie's face and clarified.

"Misrak is Ampato. They are not Singheko. They look a lot like them, but they are indigenous to this planet, and they're on our side."

Bonnie nodded.

Strange.

Ollie came forward and saluted. Bonnie returned the salute, and then shook his hand.

"Fantastic job, Major. Really great job. I'm so pleased."

Ollie nodded, smiling. "Thank you, mum. But a lot more to do."

And then finally Luke.

It was awkward between them. He was very formal. He saluted, and she returned the salute.

"Commander Powell. How are you?"

"I'm good, Captain. And how are you?"

Everyone around them was trying not to look. But everyone

knew the situation.

"I'm good, Commander."

Bonnie forced herself to turn away from him, to get on with things. She looked at Tatiana.

"Shall we proceed?"

25 - LEFT HAND HOLDS THE GROUND

In Tatiana's office, they held a council of war. Bonnie learned a lot - some of it good, some of it bad.

According to Misrak, there were twenty-five more concentration camps on the planet. They contained an estimated 12,000 creatures each. There were seven other camps containing mostly Humans, twelve containing mostly Taegu, and five containing mostly Bagrami.

That was 300,000 more slaves still in concentration camps, building weapons for the Singheko.

And guarded by an estimated 2,000 Singheko per camp. 50,000 heavily armed Singheko, all with heavy weapons and some with assault shuttles. And now fully on alert.

"But for the moment, we hold the orbitals," Bonnie pointed out. "I don't know how long we can hold them, but for as long as we can, you're free to operate on the surface."

"Exactly," agreed Tatiana. "And we intend to take advantage of that. The Ampato have already taken the planet's command center. So now each camp is disconnected, on their own. There's no central command anymore. Even as we speak, a force of 5,000 Ampato are marching on the next camp. They attack tonight, along with five thousand of my own troops, so ten thousand total. I don't think the Singheko will hold out long. In fact, to be honest, I think they'll abandon the complex as soon as they see ten thousand troops coming at them."

Bonnie smiled.

"I certainly would. Hopefully, they have enough common sense to just bail out and run."

"So. Once we take that complex, we'll have another 12,000 or so people to add to our army. Also, the 7,000 we left behind at the first complex have had a change of heart and joined us. They sent a messenger over the mountains yesterday. I sent a team back to get them organized and formed into a workable force."

Bonnie wrinkled her forehead, thinking it through.

"So - assuming you take this third complex tonight - that's 12,000 from three complexes, plus the 6,000 Ampato that have joined you. That gives you a total force of...what...42,000?"

"Less casualties, more like 39,000," Tatiana said sadly. "Of which, only about 25,000 are true effectives. Most of the rest are in no condition to fight, or we've put them into support roles. Feeding the army is our biggest problem right now. For the moment, we've got captured rations that will feed us for six weeks. But after that, we'll have to re-supply by capturing more complexes, or obtain food from the Ampato."

Misrak spoke for a few seconds, and Woderas turned back to the group to translate.

"The Ampato will commit to feed the army. They have enough foodstuffs hidden away to carry you through the rest of the year. After that it may get a little iffy."

Tatiana nodded at Misrak.

"Thank you, Misrak. That's a load off my mind."

Alina came into the room, holding a message slip. She handed it to Tatiana.

Bonnie continued speaking while Tatiana read the message.

"So. Holding the orbitals. That's our biggest problem."

Tatiana looked up.

"Maybe not as big a problem as you think, at least not for the short term."

"What do you mean?"

Tatiana smiled broadly.

"Your Admiral just sent us a message. It says it appears

Zukra is concentrating his efforts on rebuilding the docks at Singheko and retrofitting his fleet with the new drives and weapons. So in the absence of any reaction from the Singheko to defend Deriko, she is bringing the fleet in to anchorage here for some R&R."

Bonnie leaned back in her chair in total surprise.

"She's bringing the entire fleet?"

"Evidently so," replied Tatiana. "And she left a personal message for you at the end."

"What? What did she say?"

"I'm not sure what it means. I think it must be idiomatic, something from some regional dialect of English I've never heard."

"What?" asked Bonnie, impatient.

"It says, 'Move over Rover and let a big dog in'."

With that, and the laughter that followed, the council of war finally broke up. Bonnie bade goodnight to Tatiana and her staff, and Alina led her to a suite of rooms.

"I hope this will be satisfactory, Captain," Alina said as she opened the door for Bonnie.

"I'm sure it'll be fine," Bonnie answered. Alina held the door open and Bonnie entered.

As the door closed behind her, Bonnie noticed bloodstains on the floor. Someone had attempted to clean them up, but Bonnie knew what they were.

"I don't care," she thought. "I know what they had to go through to capture this complex. That's least of our problems right now."

But before she could think what to do next, there was a knock on the door. Opening it, she found Baysig.

"May we speak briefly, Captain?" he asked in his growly but soft voice.

"Of course. Please come in."

The big creature trundled into the room and managed to sit in one of the overstuffed chairs.

"I have a private message for your Admiral," he began.

"Of course."

"Months ago, when the Singheko invaded the Taegu system, about half the Taegu warships escaped after the battle. The survivors came to our system and warned us the Singheko were on the way. They told us they were retiring to a secret location to repair and refit - and decide their next steps."

"I see."

"Soon after, the Singheko invaded our system. We also tried to put up a defense, but we too were overwhelmed by the Singheko attack. But having had some forewarning from the Taegu, we managed to save about half our fleet also. That remnant of our navy also joined the Taegu survivors."

Bonnie nodded as Baysig continued.

"The combined fleet has completed their repairs and refits and are now deciding what their next step will be."

"Will you help us? Will you join forces with us?"

"It has not been decided. I am hopeful that such could occur, but that decision is in the hands of our civilian leadership with that fleet. And their decision will be based on an assessment of how effective you Humans can be in fighting the Singheko. But I felt it important that you know the situation."

"Can we send a message to your command?"

Baysig smiled his gentle smile.

"That is why I am here. I am the only person on this planet who knows the location. If your Admiral will prepare a message, and provide me with a corvette, I will take it to them. However, there is a condition. I cannot reveal the location of the fleet. So you'll have to give me the corvette, but I'll have to provide a crew of all Taegu and Bagrami. No Humans can be aboard."

"I think that's a fair deal. Subject to my Admiral's approval, we'll have a message ready for you tomorrow morning."

Baysig rose from his chair.

"It is an honor, Captain."

"The honor is mine, Baysig. May I ask, do you have a rank in your military system?"

"I do," Baysig said. "But if you don't mind, I'll keep that to myself for now. I serve as an impartial adviser to Tatiana and I don't want her to have any concerns regarding ranks or positions. So if you don't mind..."

"I understand. Thank you for coming."

Baysig departed, leaving Bonnie standing in the middle of the room. Quickly she prepared a message to Rita, outlining the conversation with Baysig. She sent the message and confirmed receipt.

Then she had one more thing on her mind for tonight before she slept. She pulled out her comm and called Luke.

"We need to talk."

***

The morning light woke Bonnie at 6 AM local time. Maybe it wasn't as bright as the Sun of Earth, being 50% farther away from the star; but it was bright enough, blasting through the window of her room like a searchlight.

She lay still for a moment, thinking, then reached out a hand.

Luke was still beside her. She felt him move at her touch, and knew he was awake.

It had been quite a reunion.

"How are you feeling, Commander Powell?" she asked. She always used his title when she wanted to tweak him, and he knew it.

"Sore in places I didn't know I could get sore in, Captain Page," he responded with a slight groan. "When you called and said we needed to talk, I thought we were just going to talk..."

Bonnie was still facing away from him in the bed.

"I guess things went a little beyond talking," she smiled. Turning over, she put a hand on his chest.

"But we better get up and get moving. Rita will be coming down on the shuttle today, and we have an appointment with her at noon."

Luke grunted and started getting out of bed. Reaching for his clothes, he started dressing, then paused and looked at

Bonnie.

"Rita was cloned with at least half of her consciousness from you, right? Your mind and feelings? So can you predict what she'll do?"

Bonnie gave a negative shake of her head.

"Rita's gone far beyond the initial consciousness she inherited from Jim and me. She's a completely unique person now. Sometimes I can get a little insight into her, but mostly I have no idea what she'll do."

Luke mused aloud.

"So maybe she'll throw the book at me. The brig, the whole nine yards."

"Or maybe not," said Bonnie. "I just don't know. But you would deserve the brig for what you did. You know that."

Luke nodded.

"I know."

"She may ship you back to Earth for a court-martial."

Luke stopped dressing, looked at Bonnie.

"So we may not see each other for a while after today."

A slow smile started building on Bonnie's face.

"True. Are you thinking what I'm thinking?"

Luke grinned.

"One more round before we go?"

***

The EDF fleet had arrived in the night, sliding into orbital positions around Deriko, shutting their engines down to minimal power, and settling in for long-overdue repairs. The *Merkkessa* took a position in front of *Dragon*, positioned in geosynchronous orbit over Tatiana's headquarters. Rita took a shuttle down early in the morning. By 9 AM she was in Tatiana's conference room.

Tatiana introduced her staff, as did Rita.

Then they all sat and stared at each other over the tabletop, Tatiana sitting directly across from Rita.

Rita liked what she saw. A strong woman sat facing her. Young, to be sure. So incredibly young. But strong. It showed in her face and carriage. She sat straight yet relaxed in her chair, meeting Rita's gaze steadily.

Rita's own staff - Captain Dallitta, Captain Bekerose, Captain Tarraine and Captain Sato - were also in the conference room, sitting beside her. And her ever-present bodyguards Gabriel and Raphael stood by the door, never far from her side.

"You have done an extraordinary job, Ms. Powell," Rita began. "It's incredible. Starting from a cage of naked slaves you've put together an army and captured two - no, I'm sorry, three - complexes now. You are to be commended on your leadership."

Tatiana shook her head slightly.

"It's all these folks, Admiral," Tatiana said, indicating the members of her staff sitting beside her. "They take care of business."

"That they do," agreed Rita.

"And please, call me Tatiana. Or Tat if you like. That's what my staff call me now. No respect at all, you know?" Tatiana gave a sideways look at her team, smiling hugely.

Rita laughed.

"I know the feeling. I'll go with Tatiana if that's OK."

There was a short, pregnant silence. Nobody wanted to dispel the good feeling between them.

But it had to be done, and so with an inward sigh, Rita took the plunge.

"We have to face some grim realities here. Admiral Zukra is hard at work rebuilding his spacedock at Ridendo. As soon as he's able, he'll start retrofitting his ships with the new drives and the new gamma lance. Shortly after, he'll be coming for us. And with reinforcements from Nidaria."

The faces around the table turned more somber. Tatiana gave a slow, deliberate nod.

"That's true. How long do you think we have?"

Rita glanced at Dallitta, who had done the analysis. Dallitta leaned forward to speak.

"Ten to twelve days to rebuild the spacedock, we think.

Then he should be able to retrofit one ship every four days. We think he'll retrofit a dozen ships before he attacks, so that would add another forty-eight days. Throw in a couple of days for re-supply and preparation and we're looking at him attacking us in sixty days - two months."

Tatiana looked back at Rita.

"I don't know much about naval operations, but I assume you'll be greatly outnumbered?"

Rita nodded. "Based on what we know right now, we'll be outnumbered by about three or four to one. That's based on what Zukra has now plus the Nidarian fleet we expect to arrive in a month or two."

There was a bit of a silence. Nobody looked at the Nidarian officers in the room. But everyone was thinking about them. Bekerose stepped into the silence.

"Have no worries about the loyalty of the Nidarian contingent assigned to the EDF. There's no love lost for Garatella and his unholy alliance with Zukra. I assure you that an alliance with the Singheko is not the desire of the Nidarian people. We have made our choice and we'll be here when the missiles start flying."

Rita nodded assent.

"And I second that, Tatiana. Have no worries on that point."

"So. What will you do, Admiral? Will you have to retreat out of the system again?"

Rita gave a grim smile that didn't look like a smile at all.

"I intend to kill as many of the bastards as I possibly can, Tatiana. Retreating doesn't help us at all. All that does is move the fight back to Earth. If I'm going to get my ass kicked, I'll get it kicked here in their own backyard doing as much damage to them as I can. We must buy time for Earth to get up to speed, prepare infrastructure, build ships, train crews - all of that. And that takes time. Lots of time. So we'll fight them here.

"So...let's not dress up the pig and tie a bow on it. We're gonna get our asses kicked. But we're not going to make it easy for them. Every ship we take out, every ship we damage, every

Singheko we kill buys Earth a bit more time to get ready. So that's what we'll do."

Tatiana looked across the table at Rita, steadily, one warrior queen to another.

"As will we, Admiral. You kill them in the sky, and we'll kill them on the ground. They'll know we were here."

***

At noon, there was a knock on Rita's door. Raphael stuck his head in to the temporary office Tatiana had provided for Rita.

"Captain Page and Commander Powell are here, milady," he announced.

"Send them in, Raphael, thank you," answered Rita.

Rita put her tablet down on the conference table as Bonnie and Luke entered. Both braced up and saluted as they got inside the door.

"Stand easy, folks," said Rita. Rita waved them to seats beside her, Bonnie to her left and Luke to her right.

Rita had just finished a long meeting with Bekerose, Dallitta and Tarraine and - to keep her skill level up - had spoken Nidarian for the entire time. Although she was fluent, the constant use of so many sibilants was wearing on her. It was a relief to speak English again.

Rita picked up her tablet again but stopped and looked first at Luke, then at Bonnie, then back to Luke.

"First of all, Commander Powell, this is not a court-martial nor is it a court of inquiry. This is an Admiral's Mast. Are you clear on that?"

"Aye, milady," answered Luke. Bonnie nodded.

"Your Captain has escalated this to me because her personal involvement with you prevents her from adjudicating the matter objectively. I will therefore decide if the matter proceeds to a full court-martial or if I can adjudicate it myself."

Luke nodded again. "Understood, milady."

"Very good," said Rita, looking back to her tablet and reading the charge sheet. "An accusation has been made that you went absent without leave in the face of the enemy, to wit that you stowed away on a Marine AMAG, went to the surface of Deriko, and accompanied the Marines in the battle for the complex, neglecting your duties as XO of the *Dragon* for that period of time."

Rita looked back at Luke.

"How do you answer that charge, Commander?"

"Guilty, milady," responded Luke.

"I see," Rita mused out loud. She looked back down at the tablet for a bit, reading, then looked over at Bonnie.

Bonnie knew Rita better than anybody in the world. Bonnie's own memories and feelings had contributed more than half of Rita's initial consciousness when Rita was cloned by the sentient starship *Jade*.

So despite all the changes Rita had undergone since - in spite of the uniqueness of Rita's personality now - Bonnie was able to read Rita's emotions in that moment, and what she saw was totally unexpected.

She's trying not to smile, thought Bonnie in surprise. *She finds it amusing that I got involved with my XO and he did this to me!*

A glimmer of hope began in Bonnie's breast.

She had walked into this meeting assuming that Luke would be severely punished - removed from his position as XO of the *Dragon*, confined to the brig, and sent back to Earth in disgrace.

But what she saw in Rita's face was something else.

Amusement.

Understanding.

"And you did this because your daughter was in danger and you were concerned about her?"

Luke agreed. "Yes, milady."

"With no thought for your ship or your crew..."

"With many thoughts for my ship and my crew, milady. But I also knew *Dragon* was in good hands. The crew was well-trained and under a superior Captain, and the *Dragon* was in no immediate danger."

Good, thought Bonnie. *I was afraid he would just roll over and quit. I'm glad he's standing up for himself.*

"I see," Rita voiced again, reading more on her tablet. Finally she finished and looked at Luke.

"Commander, by all rights I should bust you out of the EDF, confine you to the brig, and send you home on the next transport to Earth."

Rita laid down her tablet.

"I'm not going to do that. We're in a battle for our lives here. The EDF is still learning. We're trying to get our feet under us and deal with a threat to our existence. I can't afford to throw away a good officer because of one serious lapse in judgment. I conclude that losing your services at this point in time would be damaging to the EDF.

"Therefore, taking into account the facts as I understand them, including the fact that the crew of the *Dragon* is so well trained because of your effectiveness as XO, and the fact *Dragon* was not in active combat at the moment, I sentence you to continue to serve as XO of the *Dragon* until the Captain gets tired of you and kicks your ass off her ship.

"However - you are confined to quarters for three months, subject to the needs of your ship. You will be on half-pay for six months. And you will not, under any circumstances, leave the ship without the express consent of your Captain. Do you accept these conditions, Commander?"

A wave of relief washed over Luke.

I'll still be with Bonnie.

"Yes, milady, and thank you."

"Don't thank me, Commander. You'll be going back into combat soon enough, rather than home to Earth in a nice safe corvette."

"Aye, milady."

"Get out of here, Commander. I want to talk to your Captain."

Luke stood, braced up, saluted, then turned smartly and left the room.

Rita looked at Bonnie, now allowing a slight smile to touch

her lips.

"I can't believe you, of all people, got involved with your XO."

Bonnie shrugged.

"You got Jim," Bonnie said, but with a smile.

Rita laughed.

"I'm not sure I got the best end of that deal," she said. "All he ever does is climb in that Merlin and bug out. He can't stand being stuck on the ship."

"That's not anything to do with you, though. That's just Jim. He has to be out there doing something."

"Yes, I know," Rita sighed. "I ought to bust him down to Squadron Leader and replace him as CAG before he gets himself killed out there."

Bonnie grinned.

"But you won't."

"No. I won't. He's done a fantastic job preparing the fighter Wing. They're ready for anything. So I'll let him lead from the front because that's what he has to do. That's who he is. But I don't have to like it."

Rita shook her head and picked up her tablet again.

"So. To business. Our scouts shadowing the two Singheko expeditionary forces say they're still at least five months away. That gives us a bit of breathing room here to continue to attrit Zukra's fleet.

"He's been quiet for the last few days, staying close to home. Working on his spacedock. Not even a corvette sent out to scout us."

Rita brought up the tactical holo over the conference table. She pointed to Ridendo and the Nidarian corvette orbiting over the capital city, Mosalia.

"But this Nidarian corvette docked this morning, and I'm sure it's trouble. Based on what Arteveld sent in his message, they're undoubtedly a messenger from Garatella. I'm willing to bet more Nidarian warships can't be far behind."

Rita turned back to Bonnie.

"How long until *Dragon* is combat-ready?"

"She's pretty busted up, Rita. I think a month."

"Well, you've done yeoman work this entire campaign, Bonnie. I know your ship is hurt and your crew is tired. But if a Nidarian fleet enters the system, I need as much intel as I can get. And you're the one I trust to get it right. So put together a scouting plan for me. I want a corvette or destroyer watching the Nidarian entry point twenty-four seven. Start with the least-damaged ship, rotate them on a two-week basis, I think. And put yourself last on the schedule, so that if possible, you'll be the one on watch when the Nidarians arrive. I trust you the most to get it right when they come in."

"Aye, milady," replied Bonnie.

Rita rose. Bonnie followed. They stood looking at each other.

"Do you still love me?" asked Bonnie.

Rita gazed at her steadily.

"Always," Rita said.

Then Admiral Rita Page turned on her heel and left.

26 - ARTEVELD RETURNS

300g. And full protection to 50% light speed!

What a rush!

The Nidarian corvette *Buccaret* flew through the Black at 270,351,647 kph, one full light year from the Singheko system.

Zukra was ecstatic.

And now we have their gamma weapon. I can rake them from stem to stern.

With a sigh, he waved a hand at Captain Simmala.

"Bring us back down to standard velocity, Simmala. I've had my fun. We'll wait here for your fleet to join us."

"Aye, sir," called Simmala. The whine of the engines changed as the *Buccaret* started decelerating back to a more reasonable speed.

Sweat glistened off Zukra's muzzle; just because Simmala had said the corvette would provide protection against space rocks up to 50% light speed didn't fully convince Zukra.

Because at 50% light speed, the energy liberated if they hit anything larger than a grain of sand would be that of a hydrogen bomb - if not more. Zukra shuddered at the thought of it.

That little Nidarian bastard better be telling the truth, thought Zukra. *Or I'll show him what torture is.*

Then a wry smile touched his mouth, his fangs coming out over his lips.

Except if he's wrong, I'll never get to torture him. We'll both be reduced to atoms.

Zukra paced the bridge, growing ever more impatient as he watched the approach of the Nidarian fleet in the holo. When they were a couple of million klicks away, decelerating for rendezvous, he could wait no longer.

"Prepare the shuttle," he ordered. "I'll go over to the *Ekkarra*."

"Aye, sir." Simmala passed the order to his XO. Zukra continued his pacing until the XO returned to the bridge.

"Your shuttle is ready, sir," he said.

Zukra growled an acknowledgment and headed to the shuttle. Soon Simmala felt the slight thud and lurch as the shuttle disconnected from the corvette and headed for the oncoming Nidarian fleet.

Good riddance, thought Captain Simmala. *I hope I never have to deal with that asshole again.*

***

"Welcome to the *Ekkarra*, Admiral Zukra. I'm Admiral Tallatta."

The Nidarian saluted crisply as Zukra stepped off the shuttle. He had spoken in Singheko.

That's good, thought Zukra. *At least I don't have to speak Nidarian. I hate that language. It sounds like a bunch of snakes having a convention.*

Zukra gave a perfunctory salute in response.

Another officer stood next to Admiral Tallatta. A commander.

"And you are?" Zukra asked, staring at him.

"I'm your liaison, Commander Mosseta."

"Good enough. Let's go to the bridge," growled Zukra.

In the briefing room off the bridge, Zukra sat, waving Admiral Tallatta and Commander Mosseta to take a seat.

"Here's the situation. The damn Humans have gotten themselves embedded in our system like ticks on a *zeltid*. They've got a good-sized rebellion in progress on the fourth planet, Deriko. In the last two months, they've captured over half the planet. Their fleet is sitting in orbit around the planet like they own the place. All our large expeditionary fleets are at least three months away from returning. So your arrival is timely.

"With your help, we can push these animals out of our system. Then I'll take over the Singheko expeditionary fleets when they return. Then we'll have everything we need to finish taking the entire Arm. Garatella and I will make a grand alliance!"

"Excellent," said Tallatta. "That's what we're here for."

Tallatta brought up a large holotank over the conference table.

"Where do we start?"

Zukra handed Simmala a recorded holo of the Singheko system as it had been when he departed. Simmala loaded it and Zukra pointed to the fourth planet.

"There are the Humans, sitting at anchorage around Deriko. They've been there for the two months it took me to convert my capital ships and my destroyers to the new drives and weapons."

Tallatta studied the holo, expanding it until he could see the system clearly.

"And they only have two battlecruisers - four cruisers - seven destroyers, assorted corvettes? Doesn't seem that tough to me," said Raffara.

Zukra got angry.

"Try taking them on when they've got those damn gamma lances and you don't, Captain. You'll find it's no picnic."

Tallatta smiled.

"Well, we've got gamma lances now. What's your fleet disposition?"

"I've got one cruiser still damaged from the last battle. That leaves me with two battlecruisers, three cruisers and three destroyers left. With your fleet, I'll finally outnumber them and have equivalent weaponry. That'll be a welcome change."

"Good," said Tallatta. He studied the holo some more.

"I think these Humans will break and run as soon as they see our fleet come into the system, Admiral. This should be an easy battle."

Zukra growled.

"They may surprise you, Tallatta. They seem to be a bit tougher than expected."

"We'll see. We'll see what they do when our combined task force of four battlecruisers and six cruisers bears down on them."

***

There was a knock on Rita's hatch.

"Come!" she called.

And to her surprise, Captain Arteveld of the long-overdue corvette *Corresse* entered the room.

"Arteveld!" Rita exclaimed. "You're here!" Rita jumped up from her desk and reached for the little Nidarian, bringing him into a hug. Then she abruptly let go and stepped back, suddenly remembering how the Nidarians avoided close personal contact.

But Arteveld smiled, understanding.

"It's good to see you too, Admiral. It's been a long time."

Rita stepped forward again, did a formal hand touch with Arteveld, then waved him to a chair in front of her desk. Returning to her seat, she smiled.

"I'm so glad you're here, Captain Arteveld. I've missed you terribly."

"And I, Admiral. I'm sorry for the delay. There was a little matter of escaping from Garatella's prison first."

"Yes. Tell me about that, please."

"Not much to tell. We arrived at Nidaria, I reported to Garatella and told him you had pushed the Singheko out of Earth's solar system. I gave him your messages and the plans for the fast drives we copied from *Dragon*. He smiled, thanked me for my service, and had me arrested."

Rita shook her head.

"That asshole."

Arteveld nodded.

"Myself and my entire crew were held incommunicado in prison. There were a lot of rumors swirling around. One of them was that Garatella was forming an alliance with Zukra. I heard about an underground movement forming to oppose that - most Nidarians hate the Singheko with a passion and would never support such an alliance.

"After six months, I managed to make contact with this new underground movement. They arranged to break a dozen of us out of the prison, enough to form a skeleton crew for the *Corresse*. We captured her in orbit and I sent you the ansible message. Then we took off for Singheko as fast as we could fly, with a dozen destroyers on our heels. But we outran them, and here we are!"

Rita smiled.

"Thank the Creator you're here, Arteveld. I really need your support and advice right now. I guess you've heard what we're up against."

"Aye, milady. Zukra's Home Fleet, retrofitted with the fast drives and the gamma lance. And the Nidarian expedition sent by Garatella can't be far behind me."

"Yes, we expect them any day now." Rita leaned forward over her desk.

"Captain Arteveld, I believe you are well overdue for promotion, is that not true?"

Arteveld smiled.

"That's not for me to say, milady."

"Well, it's for me to say, and I'm saying it. I'm giving you the destroyer *Riadda*. Her captain and XO were injured in our last battle with Zukra and we've had to evacuate them back to Earth. Can you take command today?"

Arteveld smiled broadly.

"Not a problem, Admiral!"

"Good. And can you and Flo make dinner tonight?"

"Aye, milady."

"Excellent," smiled Rita. "I've missed you terribly, both of you. See you at six?"

"Aye, milady, we'll be here."

Rita rose.

"Then go check out your new ship, Captain," she smiled.

Arteveld rose and saluted, turned on his heel, and departed. As he left, Bekerose rushed into Rita's office, his face dark.

"That Nidarian corvette that was in orbit around Ridendo? It left early this morning, their time. Headed out toward the Nidarian entry point."

Rita looked at him, her face turning as solemn as his.

"Well, I assume that means Zukra's gone out to rendezvous with the Nidarian fleet somewhere close by. Making their final plans."

"That would be my thought, milady," answered Bekerose.

"Button up the fleet, then. Let's get ready for them. Recall all personnel, stop all maintenance, prepare for departure."

"Aye, milady."

Leaving the room, Bekerose winked at Raphael as he went out the hatch. Everyone knew that Dallitta was pregnant. The Nidarian Marine was the picture of the proud husband, all smiles whenever anyone mentioned his impending fatherhood.

Rita watched the mini drama as the hatch closed behind Bekerose. The thought that came into her mind couldn't be suppressed.

I hope they live long enough for that baby to be born.

***

The Nidarian fleet entered the system at 0215 ship time. Bonnie and Luke were sleeping soundly in Bonnie's cabin when the alarm went off on the command channel, sounding in their implanted comms automatically.

It was a rude awakening.

<Priority alert. Nidarian fleet entering the system, 15 AU from star, accel 280g>

Bonnie snapped awake, hitting her head in the cramped

confines of the bed. It was never meant to be shared between two persons.

"Ouch. Shit!" she cried, rubbing her head.

Luke automatically rolled out of bed, grabbed his clothes, and started dressing, talking as he went.

"15 AU. So about 1 AU in front of us, relative," he said.

Bonnie moved to the edge of the bed and sat, naked, still rubbing the back of her head. Luke grabbed her uniform trousers and pitched them to her.

Bonnie caught them and glared.

"You don't mind if I wear underwear, do you, Commander?" she growled.

"Not at all," grinned Luke.

He pulled clean underwear out of her wardrobe and tossed them to her.

"Thank you." Bonnie pulled the underwear on, slid her trousers over them, and stood up. She went to her wardrobe and started pulling on additional clothing, talking as she did so.

<*Dragon*, priority message to *Merkkessa* on ansible. Nidarian fleet enters system at 15 AU. Include coordinates, vectors, fleet makeup, preliminary ship configurations, etc. Any questions?"

<No questions. Information compiled. Information sent via ansible. Acknowledgment received from *Merkkessa*>

Luke gave Bonnie a final look as he completed dressing and headed for the hatch.

"See you on the bridge, Captain."

"Get us moving into position behind them to shadow them," said Bonnie as he departed.

"Aye, mum," responded Luke.

***

Ten minutes later Bonnie stood on the bridge, assessing the holo.

Luke had got *Dragon* moving already. They were accelerating at 300g toward the Nidarian fleet far in front of them.

"They're probably going to see us at this accel," Luke noted.

"Maybe they will, maybe they won't," said Bonnie. "Remember, these faster drives are new to them. They may not have worked out every nuance of how to use them and how to detect them from a distance. But even if they see us, I don't care. We have to shadow them and keep Rita informed."

"Aye, mum," said Luke.

Bonnie moved to her command chair and sat, marveling at Luke's capacity for juggling his two roles.

He's truly a wonder. He can go from lover in my bed to the perfect XO in seconds. He never gets upset on the bridge. He maintains a perfect decorum, always following protocol in front of the crew.

Bonnie smiled inwardly.

Although it's not like we're fooling anybody. I know better than that. Everyone on the ship knows we're an item.

And I don't care anymore.

"*Dragon*, what's our merge time?" asked Bonnie.

<Time to merge 21.7 hours>

"It'll take forever to catch them at this rate," said Luke.

"No problem," said Bonnie. "We don't know where they're going anyway. They may go to Ridendo or they may start a direct attack on Rita at Deriko. Once we get a read on their intentions, we'll boost up to catch them."

"Singheko Home Fleet is moving out from Ridendo, mum!" called Rachel at Tactical. "Vector for Deriko!"

Luke smiled at Bonnie.

"Well, that answers that question," he said. "They're going to meet Zukra at Deriko and attack Rita."

Bonnie heaved a long sigh.

"You know what that means."

Luke nodded.

"Back to overboost to catch them up," he said.

"Yeah. But as long as they don't change accel, we've got the entire distance from here to Deriko to catch them up. Roughly 17.5 AU. *Dragon*, what accel is required to catch them up about one-half AU before Deriko?"

<Assuming they maintain present accel to 50% light, coast for a half AU, and decel at 300g for combat, *Dragon* requires plus 2g for 2.8 hours>

"*Dragon*, send all intel to *Merkkessa* via ansible and let *Merkkessa* know we're going to overboost for a while."

<All available intel sent to *Merkkessa* via ansible. *Merkkessa* acknowledges>

"Very good," said Bonnie. "*Dragon*, issue high g warning to crew for 2g, 2.8 hours."

<<STAND BY FOR HIGH G MANEUVERS. 2G FOR TWO POINT EIGHT HOURS. STAND BY FOR HIGH G MANEUVERS. 2G FOR TWO POINT EIGHT HOURS>

The klaxon was deafening in the quiet bridge. Bonnie let it ring for a minute, then irritably issued a command.

"D*ragon*, shut off that damn klaxon."

<Klaxon off>

The quiet was a blessing. Bonnie leaned forward in her chair, talking to Luke.

"Anyone who didn't hear that is so sound asleep the high g won't bother them anyway. Let's catch up to these bastards."

"*Dragon*, take us to plus 2g for 2.8 hours," called Luke.

<302g for 2.8 hours>

"*Dragon*, what's our new merge time?"

<Time to merge is now 14.9 hours>

Bonnie felt the g forces start to come in as *Dragon* slowly accelerated past the limit of the compensator. She tightened her straps and looked at Luke. He looked back at her, the hint of a smile on his lips.

Somehow, they both knew it. In fact, every person in the crew knew it.

This would be the last battle with Zukra.

27 - A DAMN GOOD SCRAP

"Well, what do you think, folks? I know what I've said up to this point. I've said we're going to fight them. But staring down the face of a fleet with twice our firepower, I'm going to pose the question to you again. Do we run or do we fight?"

Rita pointed to the holo over the conference table. Zukra's fleet advanced toward them from Ridendo while the Nidarian fleet came in from outsystem. If they stayed at Deriko, they would be sandwiched between the two fleets. And they were outnumbered by more than two to one now.

Bekerose rubbed his chin. "It all depends on how good the Nidarians are with their new weapons. They haven't had much time to train."

"But if they are any good at all, they'll cut us to pieces," Tarraine pointed out.

Dallitta objected.

"But if we run now, everyone on Deriko is dead. They won't leave a single one alive to tell the story."

"We can't leave them," said Jim. "We have to fight."

Rita bowed her head for a moment, lost in thought. Then she slowly got up from the briefing table and walked to the back of the room.

Everyone was completely silent. Everyone knew what was at stake.

Their Admiral had to make a hard decision - one that could well determine if they lived or died today.

Standing alone at the back of the room, Admiral of the Black Rita Page ignored her command team, staring at the wall.

On the wall was a picture of a P-51 Mustang fighter from World War II. Jim had brought it aboard, one of his mementos.

Rita focused on it, trying to make a final decision.

She had faced many desperate situations since she took command of the fleet. But never had so much been at stake.

If they fought and lost, there was nothing standing between the Singheko and Earth.

If she retreated in the face of the task force coming at them, everyone on Deriko would die - every Human, every Taegu, every Bagrami. And to her knowledge, there were at least 96,000 humans on the planet below. Probably twice that many Taegu and Bagrami.

Death is my business, thought Rita. *I should be used to it by now. But you never get used to it. It never stops hurting.*

So do I retreat - and condemn 300,000 sentient creatures here on Deriko to death?

And if so, where do we make a stand against these bastards? At Earth?

They won't waste any time chasing us back there. They'll be back at Earth blasting away at us in a matter of weeks.

So all I accomplish by retreating is to move the battle from Deriko to Earth.

Better to make our stand here. Kill as many of these fuckers as we can right now. Buy a little bit more time. Maybe the UN can get their shit together, build enough ships to defend Earth - if we can hurt these bastards enough, make them think twice about going back there.

Rita swung round to the group, her eyes flashing.

"We will fight. However, we're going to try a ploy first. We'll pretend to run. Bekerose, I need a well-developed plan for how far we should run before we turn around and come back at them. I'd like to let them detach a couple of ships into orbit around Deriko here if they will. Even a slight decrease in their firepower would help us."

The grins around the table told Rita she had made the decision they wanted.

The glint in Bekerose' eye was evident.

"Aye, milady. We'll run, and make it look real. My prediction is they'll detach a bombardment force here at Deriko to start blasting the rebels on the planet again. The rest of them will pursue us. So we'll give them just enough time to split their force, then we'll turn on them. How does that sound?"

Rita smiled at him.

"You are a devious fellow, Bekerose, has anyone ever told you that?"

"Yes, Admiral, I believe you told me that some time ago."

Rita sat back down, relieved now that the final decision was made. She spoke to the air, making a call to Bonnie via an ansible connection.

"Bonnie - do you think they've detected you?"

"I don't think so, milady. At least they've given no sign of it."

"In that case, try to attack into the rear of the Nidarians right about the time we merge. You never know, you might get lucky."

"I'm lovin' it," responded Bonnie.

Rita looked down the table at Jim.

"Commander Carter, you'll launch your fighters at the last minute, because I want it to look like we're running for Earth. You won't have much time to get your squadrons out and formed up."

Jim took in a deep breath and let it out slowly.

"Yes, milady, we'll do it," he said.

Now it had all been set into motion.

"*Merkkessa*, status report on the enemy?" she asked the empty air.

<The enemy fleet is 3.2 hours from Deriko> reported *Merkkessa*.

"OK, people, let's be about it. We don't have much time!"

With a scrunching of chairs, the group rose and exited the briefing room.

As they left, Rita sat silently, lost in thought.

I have just sent everyone I love into a battle we can't survive.

***

Four hours later, Rita sat on her Flag Bridge, Dallitta beside her, and listened as *Merkkessa*'s AI gave them a running commentary on the progress of the enemy fleet and their countdown to turnaround.

Bekerose' prediction had come true. As Rita's fleet accelerated away from Deriko - pretending to flee - Zukra detached a cruiser and two destroyers to enter orbit around Deriko and start a new bombardment of Tatiana's rebels. The rest of his fleet continued after them, overboosting at a crushing 307g, making one last desperate attempt to catch Rita's fleet before it escaped the system.

Except the Humans had no intention of escaping the system. They would turn and engage Zukra in a matter of minutes now.

Bekerose and his team had calculated the parameters carefully. There was a "sweet spot" where they could turn and engage Zukra, and the cruiser and destroyers at Deriko would not be able to come out and join the battle in time.

<Two minutes from mark>

Rita gnawed at her lip.

It was going to be a close-run thing. She could feel it.

"*Merkkessa*, what's the time to merge?"

<Time to merge is 2 minutes after mark, 4 minutes total>

"Where's Bonnie?" she asked

<Captain Page and *Dragon* are 3.5 minutes from merge>

Rita thought about Bonnie, coming up behind the Nidarians to intercept them 30 seconds before Rita's merge.

At best, Bonnie would surprise them, distract them, maybe even damage a capital ship.

At worst, she'd die in the attempt.

<Sixty seconds to mark>

The klaxon started, warning the crew of an imminent overboost.

Rita tightened her straps.

<Mark>

Rita felt a bit of Coriolis force as the ship started turning end-over-end, to put the gamma lance and the larger array of missile tubes to the enemy.

The warning for violent maneuvers came, sent by the AI over every speaker and comm on the ship.

<WARNING - STRAP DOWN, LIE DOWN. VIOLENT MANEUVER IN SIXTY SECONDS. WARNING - STRAP DOWN, LIE DOWN. VIOLENT MANEUVER IN SIXTY SECONDS>

The klaxon started a special, rarely heard singsong that meant only one thing.

If you were not strapped down or lying down, you were about to die.

There was a nearly instantaneous change from 1g of force to zero g.

Then she felt the g-forces build up again as *Merkkessa* switched from accel to decel - and this time the g forces didn't stop at 1g. The fleet overboosted to +8g, pushing them down hard into their chairs with the force of eight times their body weight as the entire fleet decelerated to go back and face Zukra. The brutal acceleration was their best chance to get back to him before he could fully prepare for their attack.

Anyone who wasn't strapped down hard into their seats or lying flat somewhere is probably dead now.

Rita managed to turn her head - slowly - and look at Dallitta.

Nothing was said. Dallitta knew what she wanted.

What a fantastic aide, Rita thought. *Tarraine really knew what he was doing when he sent Dallitta my way.*

She missed Tarraine terribly. Having the calm, logical Nidarian at her side had been one of her greatest comforts.

But Tarraine was captain of the cruiser *Daeddam* now, running a hundred klicks to her left, part of the EDF front line.

Dallitta read numbers off her screen and managed to grunt them out to Rita.

"Casualty report, milady. Two dead, ten injured in the

turnaround."

Rita didn't bother to acknowledge. It was impossible under the g-force anyway.

But it wasn't as bad as she had expected.

Two dead. Ten injured. But nothing we can do about it now. We can't even move them to sickbay with this decel on. They'll have to lie where they are until we reduce back to standard.

Until it was time to go to work.

***

Tatiana and Marta had talked about it.

Their future was not bright. Rita and her fleet would be heavily outnumbered. As far as Tatiana was concerned, Rita's plan to fight the combined fleet of Zukra and the Nidarians was suicide.

And once Rita's fleet pulled out, the Singheko would waste no time resuming their bombardment of the planet.

Neither Tatiana nor Marta wanted to die huddled in the tunnels again, waiting for a lucky strike from the bombardment to collapse the walls around them and bury them in concrete.

So for the last months as Rita repaired her fleet and they waited for the Singheko to come out after them, they had continued to march east, attacking complex after complex, freeing thousands more slaves. Doing what they had vowed to do until they died.

Killing Singheko.

And thus when the Singheko cruiser and her escorting destroyers slid back into orbit around Deriko and started firing missiles and kinetics at the Bravo-Two complex once more, almost nobody was there.

They had left a small force behind to create the illusion of an active military installation, full of troops and equipment, with comms broadcasting a false narrative centered around a demoralized force lacking food and water, and enduring death and disease killing thousands.

None of which was true.

Tatiana and Marta, with the majority of the army, were three hundred kilometers farther east, fighting Singheko in the tunnels of the ninth complex they had attacked so far.

"Marta! I'm getting pushed back up the ramp!" Tatiana called over her comm.

Enemy fire was a continual clatter of bullets chipping pieces off the concrete ceiling overhead as Tatiana and her troops retreated back up the ramp.

They had gotten their assault plans down to a fine art; but evidently this bunch of Singheko hadn't read the memo. They were putting up a fine resistance. Tatiana's company was taking a lot of casualties.

"Coming up behind them now, Tat. Hang in there!" she heard from Marta.

As usual in their planning, Tatiana's rebels had engineered a secret entrance into the underground tunnels on the outskirts of the complex. From that concealed entrance, a demolition team had gone in at 3 AM to set charges that would block access to the armory and the exit from the barracks.

But this group of Singheko had figured it out. When the charges blew at 6 AM this morning, it bothered them not a bit. They had exited the barracks in the night and camped out at the bottom of the ramp into the tunnels, with their heavy weapons already removed from the armory and ready to go.

We got complacent, thought Tatiana. *I got complacent. I didn't think they had any comms left with the other complexes; but somehow they did. They found out how we were doing it.*

And so this morning when Marta and her force of a thousand Ampato had entered their newly completed "secret" entrance to the tunnels, a large force of Singheko had been waiting for them.

Both Marta and Tatiana had been stalemated, each blocked by a thousand Singheko with heavy weapons.

Tatiana had been forced to send in her reserves, another 500 soldiers, to break Marta out of her position and allow her to resume her advance into the tunnels.

But now things were looking a little better. If Marta had broken free and was coming up behind the force facing Tatiana, then it was just a matter of time. They would have the Singheko caught in a crossfire.

And even as she thought it, she heard a change in the firing. In the far distance, she heard yelling as the Singheko realized Marta had got behind them. The volume of fire coming up the ramp at Tatiana's forces diminished rapidly.

"Let's get them!" yelled Tatiana, rising to a crouch and charging forward. A thousand throats behind her let out a cry as they followed her, boiling down the ramp and into the tunnels, crushing the Singheko resistance in front of them.

It was bloody work. Soldiers dropped beside her, behind her, but Tatiana kept running at the enemy, firing until the barrel of her rifle was so hot smoke curled off it. And still she kept firing, changing magazines, charging ahead, leading her company deeper into the tunnels.

Until suddenly and unexpectedly, there were no more Singheko to fight.

In a kind of wonderment, Tatiana turned, taking in the scene. Hundreds of bodies littered the floor in every direction. The vast majority were Singheko; but there were plenty of her own troops mixed in.

Then Tatiana Powell sank to the floor, sitting stupefied in the aftermath of battle. She let the rifle sink to the floor beside her, the barrel now glowing from the heat. Beside her, she felt others come up and sit with her while a platoon forged ahead, making sure there were no dangers lurking in the darkened tunnels. She heard occasional rifle shots as some wounded Singheko decided to go out fighting rather than surrender, but the sound of them steadily receded. Finally, after some time, she turned to see who was sitting beside her.

Mikhail smiled back at her, as she expected. She knew he had not left her side for the entire battle. On his other side, Norali was speaking into her comm, a strange expression on her face. Then Norali put the comm down and lifted her head to look at Tatiana. Two tears rolled down her cheeks. She made no effort to wipe them away.

Tatiana felt a premonition. She willed it away, but it wouldn't go.

It can't be.

"Who?" she managed to whisper.

But she knew. She knew it like she knew her own name.

Norali just looked at her. She couldn't say it.

And so Tatiana knew. She got up, silent, and started walking, Mikhail and Norali behind her, Woderas following, a silent and grieving parade. They walked a good half-mile to where Marta's body lay neatly arranged on the floor of the tunnel, her hands crossed across her chest.

She looked peaceful, finally at rest. It was hard for Tatiana to see clearly through her tears, but it seemed that the scar on Marta's face was nearly gone at last. The scar that Tatiana had given her that first day they met, when their destinies had become intertwined forever.

Tatiana knelt beside her, leaned forward, put her hands on Marta's shoulders, and kissed her. Then she stayed, kneeling, her forehead pressed against Marta's, and cried.

***

<1 minute to merge>

Rita looked around the bridge of the *Merkkessa*. The overboost had ended a minute earlier, the pressure on their bodies back to a normal 1g as they prepared for battle. During the previous minute, Jim had launched his fighter wing from the port and starboard sortie decks, formed up, and boosted hard toward the enemy.

Bekerose was at his command chair, intently studying the ships coming at them, while beside her Dallitta was doing the same.

In the holo she saw Jim's attack wing tear into the Singheko fighters, a furball of fighters and missiles and gamma pulses that moved so fast it was hard to make out what exactly was occurring.

And behind the Nidarian fleet, boring in like an arrow, was *Dragon*.

"*Merkkessa*, what's *Dragon*'s status?"

<*Dragon* will merge in 18.5 seconds>

Bekerose looked over at her.

"They should see her about now," he said.

And even as he spoke, Rita saw the Nidarian flagship jerk hard to one side in an evasive maneuver.

In the front screen, enemy ships that had been invisible in the inky background of space were suddenly illuminated by the harsh glare of point defense lasers and anti-missiles launching as *Dragon* came into range.

A long spear from *Dragon*'s gamma lance burst into view.

A large explosion lit up the back of the Nidarian flagship as the gamma lance struck home.

Then *Dragon* was gone, her speed taking her away at just short of six million kph. It would take her 19 minutes to decelerate and come back to the battle.

"Damage assessment on the Nidarian flagship!" barked Rita.

Dallitta worked her sensor net.

"A good hit on her rear...but no change in her decel. If anything, we may have taken out a missile tube or two. But that's all."

"Well, I hope that Nidarian Admiral shit his pants," said Rita with a fierce grin.

"That partially answers one question," called Bekerose from his command chair. "His crew didn't manage to get off a gamma lance shot at *Dragon*. They reacted too slowly. If that had been our crew, they would definitely have got one on her before she was out of range."

Rita nodded.

"So not as well trained as we are. Let's hope all their crews are like that."

<Merge in fifteen seconds> called *Merkkessa*.

Rita tightened her shoulder straps again nervously. She stared at the holo as if she could bore a hole through it with her eyes.

At 4,500 kilometers, both sides fired every gamma lance they had. Space lit up with the fierce glow of holes punched in a half-dozen ships. Pieces of warships flew in all directions. Hundreds, possibly thousands of sentient creatures were killed on both sides as compartment after compartment was opened to space, resulting in instant loss of atmosphere.

Rita's fleet was lucky - as bad as the damage was, none of her ships lost power or weapons. But two Singheko destroyers did lose engine power, causing them to lose their deceleration instantly.

As in all space battles, this didn't cause them to fall behind their fleet - it caused them to shoot ahead, flashing through their own fleet and then through the Human fleet, targets not worth shooting at anymore.

<Five seconds to missile range> called the AI.

And now we'll see. How many more of my people do I kill today?

With a rumble that sounded like an old car driving over a washboard road, the *Merkkessa* flushed her first volley of missiles at the enemy.

<Missiles away. Enemy firing. Incoming missiles. Impact in ten seconds>

Rita heard the anti-missiles go out, a long, drawn out "whoosh" that told her *Merkkessa's* crew were firing everything they had to fend off the incoming barrage. The pulse cannon on the hull outside vibrated the entire ship as they targeted the incoming.

<Impact in five seconds> called the AI.

Rita heard the point defense shredders start up, the "whirring" sound clearly audible even through the layers of hull between her and the weapons. There was a "chuff, chuff" sound as the electronic warfare systems sent out clouds of decoys and chaff to confuse the enemy missiles.

<Two seconds>

She grabbed the arms of her chair tightly and stared at Bekerose, their eyes meeting across the bridge in silent understanding.

Death was coming at them, and the fates would decide who lived and who died.

28 - CORNERED

It felt to Rita like a car wreck. Something she had never experienced personally - but which was in the memories she inherited from Jim and Bonnie. Then there was a long, grinding, tearing sound, almost like a combination of grease frying on a hot stove coupled with someone feeding aluminum foil into an electric fan.

A wave of intense heat washed over her. She turned her face away and instinctively held her hand up for protection.

The pressure alarm went off, a loud ding-ding-ding that meant the compartment had been holed and was losing air.

Rita saw several of the crew rise from their consoles and run to the back side of the bridge. Turning, she saw a large tear in the back wall. Smoke and dust departed through it in a rush, telling her that's where the pressure loss was occurring.

Gabriel, her bodyguard, had been standing by the rear hatch. She saw him on the floor now, unconscious.

<Second volley away> called *Merkkessa* over the command channel. <Second enemy volley inbound>

Returning her gaze to the holo tank, Rita realized the *Merkkessa* had finished turning end over end, putting her nose back toward the enemy. And she saw the large array of missiles headed toward them.

She ignored them. It wasn't her job to manage the *Merkkessa*. That was up to Bekerose and his crew.

It was her job to manage the entire fleet.

Studying the plot, she noted three of her ships were losing way, falling out of formation. The corvette *Wesker* and two destroyers were out of the battle.

The damaged ships moved away from the battle, and fast, as they lost engine power and could no longer decelerate to stay with the fleet.

Then the impact of the second volley of Singheko missiles knocked the *Merkkessa* hard to one side. There was a smash of acceleration as the inertial compensator failed, putting the engines into emergency mode - automatically limiting them to 5g in microseconds, but a 5g that was fully felt. Rita was crushed back into her seat, her weight more than 500 pounds now.

The bridge went dark as all the lights went out. The emergency battle lamps flicked on, bathing the bridge in red light.

Rita's console was dark, and the holotank was gone.

They were blind.

There were two emergency backup consoles, battery powered, one on the left side of the bridge and one on the right.

She had to get to one of them.

Rita unbuckled and tried to stand, but it was impossible under the g-force still on the ship.

At least the compensator failsafe worked properly, thought Rita. *Otherwise we'd be jelly now.*

She slid off her chair and down to the floor. On her hands and knees, she crawled off the raised platform of the Flag bridge, across the deck of the main bridge, and over to the emergency console. She saw Bekerose also crawling on the floor, headed for the other emergency console. She noted Dallitta behind her, following her, and Lt. Carlson crawling toward the electrical panel at the back of the bridge.

It looks like a nursery full of crawling babies, Rita thought wryly.

Reaching her destination, Rita was barely able to pull herself into the chair and buckle up. She hit the emergency touchscreen and it came to life. By default, it came up in tactical view, showing a 2d representation of the space around her and the disposition of all ships known to the sensors.

Zukra's fleet was now out of weapons range, moving farther away. He had turned end over end to put his primary weapons facing the EDF fleet and was decelerating at 307g, to come back for a second pass.

Her own fleet was doing the same, continuing their decel at 304g, also having turned end over end.

But the *Merkkessa* was out of the fight. Her decel at only 5g compared to the rest of the fleet's 304g left her streaking away from them at more than 65,000 klicks per hour, a velocity that was increasing by 2,892 meters per second every second.

In ten minutes, she would be 885,000 klicks away from the rest of her fleet, zooming through space in the opposite direction.

"Dallitta, what's the enemy damage assessment?"

"They lost two destroyers, milady."

"And us?"

"We lost two cruisers, two destroyers, milady. And of course, the *Merkkessa* is out of action."

Rita grimaced.

We lost that exchange.

"Which cruisers did we lose?"

Dallitta hesitated. She looked up.

She knew this was going to hurt her admiral. But she had to say it.

"The *Qupporre*, milady. And the *Daeddam*."

The *Daeddam*.

Tarraine, breathed Rita silently. *Oh, no, not Tarraine. Not my rock of ages...*

"*Merkkessa*, do you have comms to the rest of the fleet?"

<Yes>

<Orders to Captain Sato on *Asiana*. Take command of the fleet, hammer away at them. Rita out."

<Orders sent. Acknowledged>

***

"Damra, do you see what I see?"

"I see their flagship careening away with damaged engines,

sir."

"Exactly! I want that ship, Damra! To hell with the rest of the fleet - let the Nidarians mop them up! Charge that ship, Damra!"

"Aye, sir."

With a whine, the *Ambush* changed vector, pulling out of formation and heading directly for the distant *Merkkessa.*

"Sir, we have an overheat on Engine #4 where that missile impacted," called Captain Agrod.

"I don't care!" screamed Zukra. "Keep it at 100 percent!"

"Sir, if we keep it at 100 percent, the engine may explode and destroy the ship!"

Zukra heaved a large sigh.

"Alright Captain, have it your way."

Captain Agrod waved at his engineer, who pulled the throttle back on engine #4 to 75 percent. The *Ambush* decreased acceleration.

It was still more than enough to catch the *Merkkessa.*

"Message from Admiral Tallatta, Admiral. He wishes to know your intentions, as you have pulled away from the formation."

"Tell him to continue on and smash the Humans," ordered Zukra. "I'm going to capture their flagship."

"Message sent, Admiral."

Zukra waved a hand in dismissal, studying the holo.

We should catch up to them in ten minutes. Then I will have this Human admiral at last.

A thought occurred to him. A delicious thought.

First I'll torture her and find out everything she knows. I'll do it slowly. I'll make sure it takes days. Weeks. Maybe months.

Then I'll put her in the arena for a game. I'll humiliate her in front of the crowd, then chop her head off.

That's exactly what I'll do.

***

The *Merkkessa*'s damaged engines had finally stopped completely, so they were at zero g now.

Somehow, Lt. Carlson had managed to get the holotank back in operation. The quality of the display was poor. The damage to the electronics had left the holotank fuzzy, out of focus.

What Rita saw there didn't cheer her up much. The Singheko flagship *Ambush* was bearing down on them, clearly intent on capturing them or putting them away once and for all.

Behind the *Ambush*, she could see the rest of her fleet heavily engaged with the enemy. The second pass had been completed, and the two fleets were battling it out at close range now. Another EDF cruiser - the *Artemis* - was out of action. It was little comfort to her that the *Artemis* had taken down a Singheko cruiser before she was punched out. The two inert cruisers drifted in space, sided by side, pockmarked with holes that went completely through their hulls.

It would be a slugfest until one side or the other left the battlefield.

Or until one side had no ships left.

"Dallitta. Can you see Jim's fighters anywhere on your screen?"

Dallitta leaned forward and peered at her own display.

"I think...I think that's them on the other side of the *Daeddam* wreck. Between the *Daeddam* fragments and the Singheko."

Rita stared at the holo anew. She could just barely make out a smudge in the out-of-focus holotank.

Good. He's still alive. Still fighting.

"Do you want to comm him, milady?"

"No, thank you, Dallitta."

I don't want to talk to him right now. I don't want to have to say goodbye.

<Message from Commander Sato. Coming to you, hang in there> called *Merkkessa* over the command channel.

"What?" Rita looked back at the holo.

In the distance, the EDF fleet had started moving back

toward the *Merkkessa*, fighting a rear-guard action as they came.

"No!" cried Rita. "I don't want this!"

She comm'd Sato.

"Captain Sato! What are you doing?"

"Coming to fetch you, Admiral. Can you get *Merkkessa* underway again?"

"No, Sato, no! You know better than this! Leave us!"

"Sorry, milady. You put me in charge of the fleet, remember? Try to get your engines up. See you soon."

Rita yelled at the comm, but Sato was gone.

Why? Why is he doing this?

After a moment, Rita realized the answer.

None of us are getting out of this system alive.

He just wants us to be together when we die.

29 - SILENT ARROW

Jim broke hard down and right as another enemy missile came at him. He hit the button to spray chaff behind him and prayed. Somehow - he wasn't sure how - the deadly missile failed to get a direct hit, exploding behind, knocking the Merlin to one side and spraying shrapnel all over the exterior like gravel on a tin roof.

But he survived. Somehow.

They had been fighting non-stop for fifteen minutes; Jim's gamma lance had failed, the system holed by a shell fragment. He had one missile left, a hang-fire that refused to leave the rails. And now he had expended the last of his chaff, dodging the vast array of missiles the Singheko fleet sent at them.

Jim took a quick look at the status indicators on the side of the cockpit. He groaned.

He had managed to scrape together 74 fighters for this battle. Now only 42 were left. The battlefield was littered with smoking hulks, most of them spinning aimlessly. Some pilots had managed to eject; but there was no way to rescue them.

And they would probably not be rescued at all. He didn't think the Singheko would bother to save Human pilots merely to put them in a prison.

OK. It is what it is. Let's kill some more of them before they take us out.

Jim spun the Merlin around, searching the battlefield for another target. It was then he noticed the *Merkkessa*, far off and moving away fast, trailing fluids and vapor from her engines.

She's down, he thought. *No engines, out of action.*

Without hesitation, Jim called over his comm.

"Raiders, make for the *Merkkessa*, give her some support!"

With a wrench on his sidestick, he jerked the Merlin around and took a vector toward the damaged flagship. He accelerated to +8g momentarily, trying to get the Merlin moving. The remnant of his Raiders fell in behind him.

Gritting his teeth, he held the overboost as long as possible.

I'm the oldest pilot in the Wing. If I can take it, so can they.

But finally the force of eight times his body weight was no longer tolerable. He felt the familiar black tunnel starting as his g-suit could no longer force blood to his brain. He backed off first to +6g, then when he felt the black curtain of unconsciousness starting to fold around him again, he knocked it back down to +4g. By then, it was time to decelerate if he wanted to rendezvous with the *Merkkessa*.

And the *Ambush*. He could see the Singheko flagship approaching the *Merkkessa*, close now. Zukra wasn't firing at the broken EDF flagship, though.

He wants to take her alive. He wants my Rita alive.

Jim slammed the sidestick to one side, causing the Merlin to go into a vicious rotation, spinning like a dart on its way to a dartboard.

I need to free up that jammed missile.

The status light on his Weapons board remained amber, showing the missile still hung on the rails. Jim ramped his acceleration down a bit and called on his comm.

"Raider Two, take over lead. I've got a jammed missile. Hit Zukra's flagship, try to drive him off the *Merkkessa*."

"Raider Two wilco," Jim heard over his comm. He pulled his throttle back to idle and cursed in frustration as the rest of his Wing swooped by him, his Number Two sliding into position as Lead, starting an attack run on the *Ambush*.

Jim pulled on the sidestick as hard as he could, trying to free the missile. The g-forces came in as he exceeded the ability of the compensator to offset them. First +6g, then +8g, as he shook the sidestick, jerking it back and forth, trying to free his last missile. But nothing worked.

In desperation, Jim tried one last ploy to free the stuck missile on his external rack.

"Angel, reset overcomp protection to +12g," he spoke to his AI.

<Confirmation required>

"Confirm. Reset overcomp protection to +12g," Jim repeated.

<Overcomp protection reset to +12g>

Taking a couple of deep breaths, Jim released the last one slowly, exhausting all the air from his lungs. Then he smashed the throttle, at the same time pulling the sidestick to the full aft position.

The g-forces came in quickly, crushing him into the seat, first +6g, then +8g, then in a second to +10g and then to +12g.

The tunnel of blackness came quickly, like the shutter of an old-style camera, closing from the outside and growing smaller and smaller until everything was gone.

***

Rita watched the *Ambush* creeping ever closer, preparing to board the *Merkkessa*.

And beyond, the battle raged, Sato and his ships fighting a rolling action, always trying to move closer to the *Merkkessa*, but not quite able to get to her.

A lone tear slid slowly down her cheek.

I always wondered what I would feel as I died. Would I scream, would I cry, would I shake in terror?

But I feel only a great sadness. For my ships. For my crew. For Jim. For Bekerose and Dallitta and Tarraine.

For all of them.

I led them into this. This is my fault.

Rita sighed and rose from her command chair.

She realized she couldn't be captured alive. She knew a bit too much about some of the last-ditch defensive measures discussed on Earth before she left.

She had the means to protect those secrets.

I'll go to my cabin, she thought. *Zukra can find my body there.*

It was noisy on the bridge now. Bekerose was passing out rifles and ammunition for a last stand. Gabriel, with a large lump on his head leaking blood, had regained consciousness and was moving around, helping crew get their magazines inserted and rifles charged for action. There was a cacophony of voices, breeches being slammed home, questions being asked about how to position themselves in the bridge for defense.

It was noisy. She almost missed the Tac Officer's excited callout.

"Silent Arrow, merge 19 seconds, 300k, 0-0-181, unknown, count one!"

But she did hear it, just barely.

She stopped, spun to the holo, stared.

Moving so fast it was almost a blur on the holo, the icon marking the incoming warship was coded yellow, indicating an unknown.

Not EDF, which was coded blue.

Not the enemy, which was coded red.

What the hell?

The noise on the bridge had slowly died out as people started to realize something was happening.

"Missile launch, 20 missiles inbound!" yelled Tac again.

Rifles clattered to the deck, forgotten, as the instincts of hundreds of hours of training took over. People slammed into their console chairs, working their screens to put up a defense against the missiles coming at them.

But the missiles weren't coming at them.

They were coming at the ships of the enemy.

Rita stood frozen as most of the missiles impacted into the distant Nidarian flagship *Ekkarra*, throwing stray bits of shrapnel and smashed-up battlecruiser in every direction.

Then a huge explosion took off the entire back third of the *Ekkarra*, breaking it into two pieces. The stern of the enemy battlecruiser spun away into space, belching flames for a few seconds before the air and chemicals inside were quenched by the vacuum.

Bekerose roared at the top of his lungs.

"Get back to your stations! Clear for action!"

Rita unfroze. She slammed herself back into her command chair, assessing on the holo.

The Tac Officer yelled again; his voice almost joyous.

"Silent Arrow! Merge 12 seconds, 340k, 0-0-182, unknown, count six!"

"Designate!" snapped Bekerose.

"Designate six cruiser-class, unknown origin!"

Bekerose had gotten back in his command chair now. He raised his backup wrist comm to his lips.

"Engineering! Get my ship moving!" he yelled, so loud that the walls of the bridge seemed to reverberate.

Gabriel was walking around, picking rifles up off the deck and ensuring they were safe.

"Missile launch, I have 72 missiles inbound!" yelled Tac again.

"Target?" snapped Bekerose.

"Not us," called Tac. "But I can't tell if they're shooting at Sato or the Singheko - they're too close together and all mixed up!"

Rita held her breath - along with everyone on the bridge - as the six unknown cruiser-class warships flashed past, so close they went between the *Merkkessa* and the ongoing battle, traveling at a goodly percent of the speed of light.

Behind them, the 72 missiles the unknown cruisers had fired decelerated madly, pulling a negative 2,000g to slow down and smash into the warships their tiny electronic brains had been told to target.

The entire event had caught everyone by surprise. Neither the Singheko nor the EDF fired a single defensive missile or point defense cannon at the inbounds.

And then the missiles slammed into the remaining Nidarian capital ships, one after the other, explosion after explosion, a violent concert of death and destruction. Three

Singheko cruisers disintegrated into a mess of disconnected parts and fragments, creating a mess of debris in the battlefield that would take years to clean up.

Suddenly the Tac Officer made another callout.

"Fleet entry, merge 1.7 hours, 0.5 AU, 0.0.187 high, unknown! Five battlecruisers, four cruisers, many small boys!"

"Who are they?" yelled Bekerose.

The Tac Officer was working his console like a man playing a slot machine, sweat pouring down his face.

"Uh…I don't know, sir!" he called back.

"Find out!" snapped Bekerose.

Sweating, the Tac Officer continued to search his database of ship signatures.

"Uh…sir…the closest matches I can find are old signatures, one called Bagrami and one called Taegu. That's those bear-like creatures from Deriko and the little ones that look like Nidarians."

Bekerose turned to Rita, grinning like the cat that swallowed the canary.

"Well, Admiral, it would appear our friend Baysig found the missing fleets of the Bagrami and the Taegu!"

Rita nodded. But she pointed to the holo. Just off their rear quarter, the huge battlecruiser *Ambush* continued to approach, now only a few minutes from boarding them.

"We still have a problem, Captain. 1.7 hours before the rest of the calvary arrives. It looks like Zukra's not giving up. He's determined to take us. Any ideas?"

***

It took *Dragon* 8.5 minutes to decelerate to zero relative to the fight and start her return trip. It seemed forever to Bonnie and her crew. They could see the battle behind them clearly on the holo. But there was nothing they could do about it in the short term, except overboost to the limit of their bodies, +8g crushing them back into their seats, making every breath a groaning effort of will.

They saw the *Merkkessa* go down, falling away from the

battle at high speed.

There was nothing they could do about it except hope.

They heard Rita pass command to Captain Sato on the comm, and Sato in the battlecruiser *Asiana* rally his ships into a tighter formation, working his way back toward the *Merkkessa*, trying to get to her and provide some protection.

And there was nothing they could do about it except hope.

And they saw the enemy flagship *Ambush* tearing toward the *Merkkessa*, hell-bent on capturing her or finishing her off.

This time Bonnie didn't even attempt to hide her frustration. She pounded the arm of her command chair, cursing.

"Luke! Vector toward the *Ambush*! Let's try to distract them!" she yelled.

Luke nodded acknowledgment, and gestured silently to Chief Blocker at the helm, who changed their vector slightly to charge directly at the *Ambush*.

But they were still at least eight minutes away from the huge ship. That was more than enough time for the *Ambush* to finish off the *Merkkessa*.

"*Dragon*! Plus 9g!" yelled Bonnie. The overboost klaxon had already gone off minutes ago, as they completed their turnaround and headed back toward the battlefield. Now the overboost gradually increased, from +8g to +9g. Bonnie knew some of her crew would be unable to tolerate the increase and would be injured. Maybe some would die.

It is what it is. I won't let Merkkessa *go down without giving everything this ship has.*

Off to her relative right in the holo, she saw the Merlins coming in on the attack, trying to do the same thing as she - support the *Merkkessa*.

There weren't very many of them left, she realized. Only about half the fighters that had started the battle.

She wondered if Jim was still alive.

"Merge in two minutes, mum!" came from Rachel at Tac, a groan more than speech under the heavy g-force.

Bonnie spoke.

"*Dragon*. Reduce overboost to normal."

The pressure on their bodies slowly began to ease, a bit faster than it had ramped up. In twenty seconds, it had reduced to a normal 1g. Bonnie gasped for breath, trying to suck air back into lungs that had been severely abused.

"Rachel! Continuous fire on the *Ambush* as soon as we're in range, and don't stop shooting until we're out of missiles!"

"Aye, mum," called Rachel.

Bonnie looked across the bridge at Luke. He smiled back at her and winked. His way of telling her two things.

We're going to survive this. And I love you.

Bonnie shook her head at him. But the ghost of smile quirked her lips, and she gave the tiniest nod.

I love you too, asshole.

"Ten seconds to in-range!" called Rachel.

Bonnie re-focused her entire being on the holotank and the huge enemy flagship now pulling alongside the *Merkkessa*.

"Fire, fire, fire!" yelled Rachel. Bonnie heard the high-pitched whine of the gamma lance firing, felt the bumps and thumps as eight missiles departed *Dragon*, heard and felt the reloads sliding into the tubes. They were moving quite slowly now compared to their first dash through the battlefield.

Ambush fired her gamma lance at them; through some miracle *Dragon* anticipated and jerked to one side, the lance glancing down the port side of the ship, ripping compartments open to space, but failing to take her out of action. Bonnie heard the second volley of *Dragon*'s missiles go out, just as *Ambush* fired a dozen missiles at them. Dragon's gamma lance completed recharge and she heard it fire again. *Dragon*'s point defense started up, the noise clearly heard through the hull as flak cannons and laser emplacements tried to fight off the missiles coming at them.

Then the enemy missiles that had survived *Dragon*'s flak barrage impacted, shaking *Dragon* from stem to stern, a concert of destruction that would have killed a lesser ship.

Bonnie, knocked about in her seat, wondered how any ship could have survived that onslaught. She felt the ship go suddenly to zero-g, all accel disappearing. She listened to the callouts as *Dragon*'s AI enumerated the damage.

<Port engine down>

<Starboard engine shut down to compensate>

<Compensator inop>

<Front missile tubes inop>

<Gamma lance inop>

<Upper point defense emplacements inop>

<Nine compartments holed to space>

Bonnie felt some unbalanced g-force as *Dragon* started to spin, a result of the engines shutting down unevenly. She glanced at the holo. They would miss the *Ambush*, but not by much. In effect, they would go right over the top of the big battlecruiser. A sitting duck for the enemy to shoot as they passed over.

"*Dragon*! Rotate to put the good engine below us, then give me maximum controllable thrust on that engine. Try to set us on a vector away from them!"

<Acknowledged>

With the compensator inoperative and in zero-g, Bonnie felt the forces clearly as *Dragon* rotated, putting their only working engine to the bottom side of the vector taking them over the *Ambush*. Then the engine fired, *Dragon* offsetting the thrust vector as much as possible to move them away from the *Ambush*.

Bonnie and Luke stared at the holo. Slowly the vector moved away from the *Ambush*, not by much but by a little, perhaps providing them a little more room to avoid the enemy's missiles.

"*Dragon*! How long until we are out of range of the enemy?"

<1.7 minutes>

Bonnie looked across the bridge at Luke.

That was not going to work. The *Ambush* would have enough time to rip them to pieces.

But the enemy didn't fire. They were still well within range of the gamma lance and missiles as well, but nothing happened.

"He wants us too," said Luke. "He intends to capture the *Merkkessa*, then come after us and take us too. He wants the *Dragon*."

Bonnie didn't speak. There was nothing to say. Clearly Luke had called it. There was no other reason for the enemy to hold their fire.

***

The universe came back slowly. First there was a small spot in the center of Jim's vision. The spot got larger, and he could see the instrument panel, or at least the center of it. A few seconds more, and the rest of his cockpit swam into view as the blood returned to his brain. He dropped his head and shook it from side to side, trying to clear his thinking.

The stuck missile…

Jim stared at the status indicator for his last remaining missile. It was still amber.

It hadn't worked. The gross overloading of the Merlin had not freed the missile. It wouldn't fire.

"Fuck!" he croaked, his voice not working quite right. He looked around, trying to orient himself.

The rest of his Wing was far in front of him, in the middle of their firing pass on the *Ambush*.

His body felt like he had been run over by a rock crusher.

"Angel, reset default overcomp protection," he called. Jim spun the Merlin and pushed up the throttle. The Merlin ramped up to +6g as he tried to rejoin his Wing before their attack was over.

It didn't look good. Their flock of missiles, fired at close range, were being knocked down by the point defense systems of the *Ambush*. He could see four more broken Merlins tumbling through space. The emergency beacons of two ejected pilots showed in the holo.

As the Merlins finished their attack pass and pulled away,

Jim saw two EDF missiles impact the big battlecruiser.

Neither appeared to do any serious damage. The *Ambush* continued to pull alongside the *Merkkessa.* He realized Zukra was hell-bent on capturing the EDF flagship.

Not gonna happen, asshole.

The *Ambush* got larger and larger in Jim's VR. Some point defense started up but seemed a bit lighter than he expected. Jim realized most of the enemy fire was still focused on the other Merlins, who were departing on the other side of the battlecruiser and drawing most of the fire.

"Angel, go for the engine."

<Engines targeted. You have no weapons to fire, Jim>

Now the enemy gunners realized their mistake. Dozens of point defense weapons turned back to face Jim and began firing. Jim's world became a dense thicket of exploding flak shells surrounding him and laser streaks flashing close by his canopy.

Jim realized he wasn't going to survive this pass. The flak was too heavy. He was one ship alone. Every gun on the *Ambush* could focus on him.

"Angel, protocol K."

<Confirmation required>

"Confirm. Protocol K," Jim muttered grimly.

<Protocol K in effect. Goodbye, Jim>

"Goodbye, Angel," said Jim sadly.

Something happened to time in the last few seconds of his mad attack. Time both stood still and also moved faster than he had ever experienced before. He watched like a detached observer as the battlecruiser got closer and closer, his accel still building as the enemy came into missile range. But he had nothing to do. Angel would take care of the rest of this attack. He was just along for the ride now.

At the accel he was holding, the last few hundred miles went in less than a heartbeat. One instant he was watching the *Ambush* get larger and larger in his VR, flak painting a constant rain of shrapnel on the external skin of the Merlin, the range counting down so fast he couldn't follow the numbers. Then the faceshield on his helmet slammed down. The explosive bolts on the canopy went and his seat kicked him in the ass so hard he thought his back was broken. There was a moment of complete disorientation as the stars spun around him crazily, then the ejection seat attitude rockets fired and he stabilized. The main rocket in the bottom of the seat fired and he was pushed hard at +4g, away from his original vector, the seat computer making a last-ditch attempt to miss the *Ambush* hulking in front of him, blotting out the stars.

He had just enough time to think it.

Goodbye, Angel.

And he watched his Merlin kamikaze into the *Ambush*, just in front of the port engine, the energy of the speeding fighter combining with the explosion of the hung missile to create a cataclysm approaching that of a nuclear weapon.

***

Rita watched the *Ambush* disintegrate beside them.

She had seen the Merlins attack, and it looked like their attack had failed. In the limited resolution of the damaged holo, she couldn't distinguish individual Merlins. So she had no way of knowing which one was Jim. Or if he had survived the attack.

They completed their firing run and shot over the top of the big Singheko battlecruiser and away, with no visible effect.

And then, just when she decided nothing could stop the behemoth, something happened on the other side of it, out of her view.

And the enemy battlecruiser came apart, breaking into two large pieces and hundreds of smaller ones, spinning away slowly from the *Merkkessa*, spewing chemicals and fluids in its wake.

"Milady!" called Bekerose. He pointed to the holo. "Sato's nearly here!"

Rita focused on the distant EDF fleet in the display. She could see the *Asiana* roughly two hundred thousand klicks away, decelerating to rendezvous with the *Merkkessa.* Sato's battlecruiser was surrounded by the survivors of the EDF fleet - all of them fighting off the remnants of the enemy. It was still a slugfest, albeit a smaller one now. The battlefield was littered with wrecks, lifeboats and emergency beacons stretching across a million klicks.

We've got one battlecruiser left. A few destroyers and a couple of corvettes. A pitiful force. By the time the Bagrami get here, there won't be anything left but pieces.

Suddenly, Rita felt a slight g-force come on the ship. Items floating in the air around the bridge slowly moved, settling gently down to the floor. She glanced across the bridge at Bekerose in the red light of the emergency battle lamps. He smiled back at her, talking in a low voice on his comm. Then he lifted his head, giving her a smile.

"Milady! We have two engines back at 10% power! Gravity and compensator coming online!"

Rita nodded. The normal bridge lights came on and the emergency battle lamps faded away.

Rita hit the quick release on her harness and stood as gravity slowly came back to normal. She walked across the deck to her Flag bridge and buckled in. Dallitta joined her, buckling into her own command chair as the bridge returned to some semblance of normality.

"Bekerose! Does this mean we have weapons again?"

Without turning around, Bekerose nodded, focused on his task.

"We have seven working tubes, milady. Not much, but every bit helps right now."

"How about the gamma lance?"

"Not yet, milady. Damage control is working on it."

Rita heaved a sigh.

Seven lousy missile tubes. Less than a destroyer. But you fight with what you have.

Bekerose rose from the emergency display station and walked back to his normal command chair. As he buckled in, he turned to her

"Milady, it occurs to me, if we continue to just lie here doggo, as if we are still out of action, and let Sato bring the enemy to us..."

Rita nodded.

"We'll do that, Bekerose. Have I ever told you, you're a devious kind of fellow?"

Bekerose smiled, both of them harking back to the memories of their old battles in the simulator.

She turned her attention back to the holotank. In the distance, she saw a strange sight. *Dragon* was far behind them, trying to get back to them, describing a corkscrew pattern through space.

"What the hell is she doing?" asked Rita, pointing to *Dragon* in the holo.

Dallitta looked and a slight smile came over her face.

"She's badly damaged. She's got only one engine, and there's something wrong with her thrust vectoring system. So she's trying to come back to us by firing her one engine at low boost and rotating around her axis to average out the thrust vector."

Rita shook her head, but a burst of pride filled her heart.

That's my Bonnie.

"The cripple escorting the cripple," Rita quipped. Another thought came to her.

"Are you able to pick up Jim's fighter?"

Dallitta bent to her display for a few moments. When she finally lifted her head, it was with some sadness evident on her face.

"I'm sorry, milady. Jim's fighter doesn't show up in the tactical display anymore."

Rita nodded. She had already resigned herself to the news. She had never expected Jim to survive the battle. But it still hurt.

Imogen.

The thought came to her suddenly.

She'll grow up without a father.

Then she couldn't help a smile as she realized the grim reality of their situation.

She'll grow up without a mother too, I think.

30 - LUCK OF THE DRAW

Bonnie had to stop looking at the holo periodically. *Dragon* continued to limp toward the *Merkkessa*, spinning on its axis like a barbecue rotisserie in order to make a roughly straight course. The twisting perspective made her dizzy if she watched too long.

"How many enemy ships left?" she asked Luke.

"Two cruisers, six destroyers, four corvettes, mum," called Luke.

Then he bent to his comm for a moment. Lifting his head, he spoke again.

"*Merkkessa* reports she has two engines back in operation and seven missile tubes, mum," called Luke. "She's going to lie doggo until the enemy is in range, though, and try to fox them."

"Excellent," spoke Bonnie. "That's good thinking. *Dragon*, when you have a vector that'll put us close to the *Merkkessa*, stop all engines. Let's make it look like we finally crapped out."

<Acknowledged>

"Luke, we have to get the gamma lance up. That's our best chance to take out a cruiser."

"We're working on it, mum. Engineering is giving it everything they've got."

"Thank you, XO."

Bonnie felt the engines stop. Looking at the holo, she saw they were on a vector that would bring them up and over the

Merkkessa, a few minutes before Sato arrived with the rest of the EDF survivors.

And with the enemy right behind him.

***

Zukra fought his way through the wreckage of his battlecruiser, trying to get to the shuttle deck. The *Ambush* was smashed, fire and smoke everywhere. It shuddered every few seconds as another explosion occurred somewhere in the ship, chemicals reaching critical mass or ordnance lighting off. The fragment of the ship he was in was spinning, making it difficult to walk.

He had to get out.

I won't let them win like this. These animals cannot defeat me like this.

Pushing a wrecked beam out of his way, he pulled himself forward in the zero g, ignoring the bodies floating around him. Finally he saw the entrance to the hanger deck in front of him. The hatch hung down, hinges broken. He pulled it aside and squeezed through.

Now if the shuttle is not destroyed...

In the corner of the hanger deck, he saw his private shuttle. It appeared to be intact. Trotting to it, clumsy in his pressure suit, he keyed the entrance code and watched joyfully as the hatch popped open. Climbing in, he ran to the cockpit and slammed into the pilot seat. In seconds, he had the shuttle energized.

There was no chance of operating the huge, heavy doors of the sortie deck to get out the normal way. But that wasn't necessary. There was a hole in the side of the ship twice the size of the shuttle, right in front of him. He could see stars through the hole, as well as distant explosions from the battle. Carefully, he lifted the shuttle off, managed to poke it through the hole, and was out of the ship.

In the limited display of the shuttle, he could see the remnants of the two fleets battling it out, neither side willing to give up. And in the far distance, the incoming fleet of the

Bagrami and the Taegu were apparent, now only an hour away.

We've lost this battle. But at least we'll take out the Humans before the rest of them get here. That's something. I'll be happy if we can just rid the system of these damn Humans. After that, the Bagrami and Taegu will fold up their tent and run for cover.

Zukra had not planned on losing the battle; but Zukra hadn't survived these many years in the cutthroat Singheko navy without being prepared for contingencies.

So he headed out, ignored in the confusion, streaking for a small moon near the seventh planet. There he had hidden a tiny one-man starship, just big enough for the trip to Nidaria. In a matter of hours, he would be out of the system and on his way.

Garatella would not be welcoming him with open arms, he suspected.

But he knew he could convince Garatella to return to Singheko, with an even larger fleet.

And Zukra intended to be with them.

He had an admiral to kill.

***

Jim floated in space, rotating slowly. The seat rocket had exhausted its fuel. But it had managed to fling him clear of the *Ambush* before it shut down.

Then he had watched the *Ambush* come apart, two large pieces along with hundreds of fragments. Some of them zinged by him only meters away. There were still dozens of pieces close by, occasionally making him duck instinctively as they came madly spinning by him.

He could hardly see the *Merkkessa* now, as he drifted away from her. And behind the battlecruiser he could barely make out the *Dragon*, corkscrewing through space, clearly damaged, but trying to make her way back to the *Merkkessa*.

In spite of his dire situation, Jim had to smile at the sight.

Bonnie. Coming like a drunken sailor. She just doesn't know the word 'quit'.

Jim realized that his vector was rapidly taking him away

from both ships. He estimated he was already a dozen miles from them and moving fast in the other direction.

He tried his radio, calling *Merkkessa* on the emergency band. But there was no response. He tried the *Dragon*, then the *Asiana*.

Nothing.

I guess my radio is dead.

Suddenly his attention was caught by movement to one side. A tiny shuttle burst out of the wreck of the *Ambush*, turned, and vectored away, accelerating quickly and out of sight in seconds.

Zukra.

He knew it had to be. He could feel it in his gut.

He called on the radio again, but no response. The frustration was overwhelming.

That rat bastard is getting away, and I can't tell anyone.

***

Rita glanced quickly at her holo. Sato and the rest of the fleet was coming into range. That meant the enemy would be in range also. It was a matter of seconds.

They had seven missile tubes left.

Dragon had passed over them and taken a position between the *Merkkessa* and the enemy, determined to act as a shield.

With no weapons.

Rita had yelled at Bonnie over the comm, but Bonnie had ignored her.

"Get your ass out of there, *Dragon*!" Rita yelled again. "Tuck in behind us, use us as a shield. Not the other way around!"

There was no response. *Dragon* stayed in her position, between the *Merkkessa* and the enemy.

Rita slammed her hand down on her console in anger and frustration.

"Doesn't anyone in this fleet listen to me anymore?" she yelled out loud, no longer caring what the crew on the bridge heard.

Bekerose glanced at her, smiling in spite of their dire straits.

"Milady, this fleet will protect you until the end. You have earned it and you need to let us do it."

Rita bowed her head in frustration.

"In range in ten seconds," called Carlson at Tac.

"Charge them now, Helm," called Bekerose. "No use sitting here like a duck on a pond. Take us right at that battlecruiser on the left - the *Terror*."

"Aye, sir."

Rita felt a push as the engines ramped up, the ship managing a low accel in spite of her damage. They started moving directly at the last enemy battlecruiser as it came into range.

"Fire, fire, fire," yelled Carlson.

Rita heard their seven missiles depart with a thump. In the holo, she saw Sato and the rest of the EDF fleet fire everything they had at the same battlecruiser. They had agreed beforehand to focus on that one ship, in hopes of evening the odds.

But the entire enemy fleet fired their gamma lances at the *Merkkessa*, ignoring the other EDF ships. Around her in the ship, Rita heard the sound of explosions as compartments were destroyed, the sound of fresh alarms as pressure was lost. On the side of the bridge, damage control panels lit up like Christmas trees.

Strangely, no missiles came from the enemy. Rita realized they were probably out of ammunition, as were many of her ships as well. But it made no difference. They could kill *Merkkessa* with the gamma lance.

The enemy battlecruiser continued to bore in on them, reducing the range. Sato's *Asiana* fired missile after missile at the Singheko warship, but the enemy point defense swatted most of them away. Occasionally a missile would leak through, exploding against the enemy - but nothing seemed to stop her. She just kept coming, followed closely by the remaining Singheko cruiser and a covey of destroyers and corvettes.

Suddenly the *Asiana* stopped firing.

<*Asiana* is out of missiles> called *Merkkessa*.

Rita looked grimly at Bekerose.

They were down to seven missile tubes against two enemy capital ships with intact gamma lances, ready to tear them to pieces.

***

When Engineering reported the gamma lance operational, Bonnie literally leaped out of her chair. But she quickly sat back down, staring at the holo.

The enemy was ignoring them, throwing everything they had at the *Merkkessa*, boring in for the kill. Because *Dragon* had not fired any weapons during this latest engagement, the Singheko thought them out of action.

Which they were.

Until now.

"People. Take no action. No movement, no weapons, nothing. Just be dead in the water. No matter what they do, ignore it."

"Aye, mum," called her bridge crew.

In the distance, the *Merkkessa* let go another volley of seven missiles at the approaching enemy battlecruiser. But it was clear the *Merkkessa* was taking a pounding. Bonnie could see great tears and holes in her sides where gamma lance fire had gone through and through. The fact the *Merkkessa* was still fighting was nothing short of a miracle.

But it clearly couldn't go on much longer. The future of the *Merkkessa* could now be measured in minutes, if not seconds.

The Singheko battlecruiser *Terror* was even with them now. *Dragon* was marked from end to end by ragged holes, bent and broken emplacements, wires hanging out of her, one engine half torn away. She spun ever so slightly in space, out of control.

Ignore us. We can't hurt you, thought Bonnie. *Pass us by*.

The battlecruiser swept by, still firing at the *Merkkessa*. The enemy fired their gamma lance again, punching another hole through the *Merkkessa* near her bow. Taking out another pair of missile tubes.

Bonnie stood up again, focusing her entire awareness on the holotank as the second enemy capital ship - the cruiser *Kitai* - came even with them. Also ignoring the *Dragon* as a wreck not worthy of attention, she too fired at the *Merkkessa.*

And passed by them.

And presented her rear to *Dragon*.

"Fire at will," Bonnie spoke quietly.

Luke nodded, and Rachel pushed her console.

Dragon's gamma lance fired, a direct shot into the rear of the *Kitai*'s lower port engine at point-blank range. There was no way to miss.

There was a moment of silence on the bridge as the cruiser continued to advance, as if nothing had happened. There was no change in her vector, nothing that would show the shot had even been taken. Rachel looked at Luke in puzzlement, shaking her head.

Then with an explosion rivaling that of a nuclear weapon, *Kitai* vanished from the universe, leaving nothing behind but a spray of fragments and chemicals, a cloud of destruction that encompassed *Dragon* in a hail of shrapnel. Pieces of destroyed cruiser pinged off *Dragon*'s hull. A large fragment struck *Dragon* so hard Bonnie was knocked off her feet to her knees.

Yet she never took her eyes off the holotank, so focused was she on the other enemy warship, the battlecruiser *Terror*. That one began to turn, coming about to protect its engines from the sudden danger of *Dragon* behind it.

But it was too late.

Bonnie had said "fire at will." That meant Rachel was cleared to fire when she felt the time was right, and as the bright red light on her console blinked into life indicating the gamma lance had recharged, she pressed her console button again.

And a second gamma lance from *Dragon* impacted the rear of *Terror*, into the upper port engine nacelle, from the meager distance of 100 klicks. Practically next door.

This time there was no delay. The targeted engine of the battlecruiser exploded, torn completely off its moorings, flying off into space end over end. The unbalanced force of the engine's sudden departure, coupled with the other engines still pushing the huge ship forward, started it into a rapid spin. In a few seconds, the battlecruiser's crew re-balanced the engines, and the big enemy warship began to stop its spin with its nose pointing back toward *Dragon*.

Just in time for *Merkkessa* to fire one last volley of five missiles directly at the rear of the *Terror*, all of them targeted at her lower starboard engine.

The range was incredibly short - the battlecruiser had expected to pull right up to the *Merkkessa* and blow her away.

That turned out to be *Terror's* last mistake. Another tremendous explosion broke her back. *Terror* spun in space, the front almost detached from the back, hanging together only by a few structural members. In a few more seconds, lifeboats began to eject from it, as the crew abandoned ship.

Bonnie looked at the holo, assessing. The remainder of the Singheko fleet now consisted only of a few destroyers and a gaggle of surviving corvettes. Most of them were as damaged as the EDF fleet.

Like some leviathan that refused to die, *Merkkessa* advanced on the surviving destroyers of the Singheko fleet. Another five missiles came from her front tubes focused on the nearest destroyer.

And the distant fleet of the Bagrami and the Taegu was only fifty minutes away. Once they came into weapons range, the life expectancy of the Singheko survivors would go down dramatically.

Apparently, the same thought occurred to the Singheko. First one destroyer turned and vectored away, heading for Ridendo. Then another. Then three more followed, escaping the battlefield and running for home.

And then, as if choreographed, all the remaining Singheko ships turned and ran for it, heading back to Ridendo.

***

Jim tried his radio again, but there was no response.

I wonder if my emergency beacon is working.

He ducked his head inside the helmet and looked below the faceplate for the tiny LED that would blink if his emergency beacon were transmitting.

It was dead.

I'm not transmitting.

Jim looked up at the stars around him. In the far distance, he could see a pinpoint of light.

Deriko.

At this distance there was no way to tell that it was full of life, thousands of creatures, all fighting to survive.

A tremendous explosion in the distance caught his eye.

That ship is dead, he thought. *Nothing could have survived that. I wonder if it was ours or theirs.*

He tried to see if he could find any other ships nearby, but there was nothing visible to him. He wasn't surprised; warships were black for a reason. Unless they were firing, they were practically invisible to the naked eye.

He caught a glimpse of a distant gamma lance firing. It was in the same general location where the big explosion had occurred. Then there was another, smaller explosion. He thought he saw the outline of a Singheko cruiser, but he couldn't be sure. It was just too far away.

Jim looked back down at his indicators. He had roughly three hours of oxygen left.

Gonna be a short, cold night.

***

The battle was over.

The *Merkkessa* had stopped dead in space, a rally point for the rest of the fleet to use. Slowly, the crippled and damaged ships of the EDF fleet re-assembled around their flagship, some of them barely able to limp the few hundred miles to get there.

Search and rescue operations had begun. The surviving ships had launched all their shuttles and were sweeping the area for survivors, picking up ejected pilots and EDF lifeboats.

Rita had sent a comm to the departing Singheko fleet, offering them safe passage to come back and rescue their survivors if they wished. Three Singheko corvettes had accepted the offer. They had reversed course and re-entered the battle area, and were now collecting up their own.

Stomping down the corridor, Rita wasn't listening to anything Bekerose or Dallitta said.

"Admiral!" Bekerose tried again. "We've got every available fighter and shuttle searching! Going out there yourself is not going to help matters!"

Rita ignored him, marching toward the shuttle bay. She had her flight suit on and her helmet in hand. Reaching the hatch to the shuttle bay, she turned to Bekerose and Dallitta.

"Captain Bekerose, you know I respect your opinion. And you too, Captain Dallitta. But this is something I must do. I hope you can understand."

And with that, she plunged through the hatch, making for her Admiral's gig. Stepping into the small craft, she hit the button by the hatch and cranked it closed, sealing the craft. Through the window, she could see Dallitta and Bekerose standing impotent on the deck. Bracing up, they threw her a salute. She returned their salute and moved to the cockpit.

"Get us out of here, Raphael."

In the pilot seat, her bodyguard Raphael nodded and punched the activate button on his sidestick. Beside him, Gabriel sat in the copilot seat, setting up instruments. She heard the AI warning as the cradle beneath them started moving them into the sortie deck.

There was a jumpseat behind the two pilots. Rita put on her flight helmet and sat down, buckling in. The huge doors closed behind them, the turbo pumps screamed, and the outer door opened. Suddenly they were shot out of the ship at 4G, knocking her back into her seat.

"Take us to the last known position of the *Ambush*, Raphael," Rita said.

"Aye, milady. But there are already a half-dozen ships searching that area."

"Then there'll be a half-dozen and one," said Rita crisply.

"Aye, milady," acknowledged Raphael.

"How's your head, Gabriel?" Rita asked.

Ruefully, Gabriel touched the bandage on his head.

"It's fine, milady. I guess I forgot to duck."

As hard as it was at the moment, Rita smiled. Then her smile disappeared as she stared out the windows of the gig, looking at the millions of square miles of space around them littered with still-smoldering wrecks, unexploded ordnance, and parts and pieces of what had once been proud warships.

And one of the millions of items floating in the vastness of the battlefield was Jim. Maybe. If he was still alive.

Be alive, my love. Just be alive. I'll find you.

***

Jim racked his brain for anything he could do to attract attention. But nothing came to mind. In the absence of his emergency beacon, he knew the odds of being found were a thousand to one. Maybe a million to one. Space was vast, and he was just one tiny human floating in that vastness.

For some reason, he thought back to his Marine aviation days. There was an instructor at Pensacola. Lt. Gregory. He had never forgotten something Gregory had told the class.

"When you have an emergency, the first thing to do is wind your watch."

Jim laughed at the memory. Of course, it was a parable. An allegory. It meant, when an emergency happens, the last thing you want to do is the wrong thing. So take a tiny bit of time to assess, understand, and make a plan before you react.

Wish I had a watch to wind.

That thought made Jim's brain start working again.

Take inventory. What do you have to work with?

He went over the contents of his suit. The pressure suit was not designed for long-term survival. It had only 3.5 hours of oxygen, and he had already used up most of that. He was afraid to look at the indicator again; but he was quite sure it was below twenty minutes now.

He went through the pockets of his pressure suit. In the right leg pocket was the old letter from Bonnie - the "Dear John" letter as he thought of it. He should have thrown it away a long time ago. But he hadn't been able to do that. So it was still there. He stuffed it back into the pocket.

In the other leg pocket were three empty candy wrappers, left over from nearly three months ago when the EDF fleet had initially entered the system and he had spent 42 hours in the Merlin, supporting *Dragon* at Deriko.

And that was it. A "Dear John" letter and three candy wrappers. He stuffed the candy wrappers back into his pocket.

No help there.

But something tickled the back of his mind. He pulled out the candy wrappers again and looked at them in the dim starlight.

Two of them were plain paper.

One of them had an inner backing of something that looked like aluminum foil. It was silver, and metallic.

Could it work?

Carefully, knowing the material would be stiff and brittle in the vacuum of space, Jim smoothed out the wrapper until it was as flat as he could make it with the clumsy gloves of the pressure suit.

Then he carefully pulled it up to his faceplate and looked it over.

It was a flat piece of paper, with a silvered backing of some kind.

Would it be reflective in the radio band?

Pressing the paper hard against his face plate, he impressed a curve on it, as smoothly as he could. Then he carefully pulled it down and looked at it again.

Now it was a slightly curved piece of silvered paper.

Could it work?

In the distance, maybe a hundred klicks away, he could see

the largest remaining fragment of the *Ambush*, still turning slowly in the starlight, spitting occasional electrical sparks into space.

He thought they would be orienting their search in that area, since that was the last attack run the Raiders had made.

Carefully he turned the paper and pointed it toward the fragment. Slowly he moved it back and forth, like he was aiming a searchlight.

***

"Hmm...," said Gabriel, reaching up to adjust his display.

They had been searching for two hours. But they had come up empty. Many of the other ships searching for survivors had found some. Dozens had been rescued. But none of them were Jim.

Rita tried to look over Gabriel's shoulder at his display. She couldn't quite see what he was pointing to, so she unbuckled and rose to get a better view.

One of the radar sensors was flickering weakly. It was intermittent, periodically fading away, then coming back.

"What is that?" Rita asked.

Gabriel shook his head.

"Could be anything, milady. There's no equipment in our fleet that can produce a signal like that. So most likely just a piece of radar-reflective metal, spinning in space."

Rita watched the signal flicker a bit longer. There was something familiar about the pattern. A distant memory fired in her brain. Something that had transferred from Bonnie's consciousness to Rita's when *Jade* had formed her.

A knowledge of Morse code.

Slowly, a smile lifted the corners of Rita's mouth.

"No, Gabriel, that's not a random piece of metal spinning in space," she said. "Not when it's spelling out letters in Morse code."

"What?" Gabriel asked, not understanding.

"A code used on Earth. Letters in our language."

Gabriel smiled, understanding at last. Raphael turned the

gig and headed toward the distant signal as Rita read out the letters, her smile turning into a huge grin as the signal got closer and stronger.

"R" "I" "T" "A" "I" "M" "C" "O" "L" "D"

31 - THE VALIANT

Arteveld had made the arrangements, for which Rita was grateful. He had located Tarraine's body floating in space, far from the wreck of the *Daeddam*. He had taken it back aboard the blasted fragment that was once the bridge of the *Daeddam* and strapped the body into the command chair.

They had found a message from Tarraine on their tablets, evidently recorded months before and stored on the *Merkkessa*, to be sent in the event of his death.

It was simple. It was a few words of love for his closest friends.

And burial instructions.

They stood silently on the bridge of the *Merkkessa*, like warriors do when they have to say goodbye to one of their own, knowing there are no words that can make it right, make it better.

Rita turned and faced the group.

It was hard for her to start, but finally she was able to speak. In typical Rita fashion, she drove straight to the point.

"Everybody dies. So it's not how you die that counts, is it?"

A lone tear started down her cheek. She wiped it away.

"It's how you live. And Captain Tarraine lived. He lived big, and strong, and solid like a mountain. In many ways, he was the bedrock of this fleet.

"When I was in trouble, Tarraine was there at my side. When this fleet was in trouble, Tarraine was there in the front line. Earth and Nidaria owe him a debt that can never be repaid.

"Now we give him back to the universe..."

All could see that Rita wanted to say more; but she couldn't. The words just wouldn't come. She turned away for a moment, then lifted her head. Turning back to Arteveld, she nodded.

Then Arteveld gave the command, and auxiliary rockets launched the wrecked fragment of the *Daeddam* into the star - a star that was already the grave of thousands as Rita's fleet worked to clear shattered fragments of so many wrecked starships from the battlefield.

Leaving the bridge and heading back to their quarters, Jim walked beside her, holding her hand, a display of affection that he did not normally show in public, nor did she normally allow.

But today was different.

This afternoon, they would hold a second memorial service. One for the thousands lost in the battle. The thousands from the fleet and from Jim's fighter wing. His squadrons had taken greater than 60% losses in the fight.

More than half my people, thought Jim bitterly. *So many lives lost. The price of survival ain't cheap.*

***

They held Marta's funeral in the mountains, on the trail they had used to escape from the original slave complex and make their way to freedom.

Tatiana stood over the grave, tears washing her face, as people spoke about Marta, about the things she had done to save them, make them free.

There was a goodly crowd. Luke was there, with Bonnie, and the Marine major Ollie Coston who had fought with Marta in the tunnels.

Around the grave many others, hundreds, had made the long hike up through the foothills to the place where Marta had almost shot Misrak, the first Ampato they met.

Even the strange admiral called Rita from the fleet orbiting Deriko had come down to pay her respects, the one with the same last name as Bonnie, and some kind of weird clone story told about her origins.

Mikhail stood beside Tatiana, holding her hand. On the other side stood Norali and Baysig, and dozens from Tatiana's inner circle who had learned to love and respect the big, rough Ukrainian.

Finally, everyone who wanted to speak had spoken.

Tatiana didn't speak. She couldn't. It would have been impossible. Her heart was too broken.

They put Marta in the ground then, at the base of the big flat rock she had once used as a platform to sight in on Misrak, just before Baysig called her off.

It was the place Tatiana considered the beginning of hope, the first place where they had started to believe - to believe that maybe they could actually survive.

The crowd started drifting back down the trail, headed back to their new city, the city they had just named.

Misto Marta. City of Marta.

Tatiana walked along with Mikhail and Luke. After a bit, she wiped her eyes one last time, then turned to her father.

"Dad, I have some news for you."

Luke waited, a question on his face.

Tatiana gripped Mikhail's hand tightly.

"I'm pregnant."

***

Rita had been given an office in Tatiana's headquarters complex on Deriko. The door opened and Gabriel put his head inside.

"Captain Orma, milady."

"Send him in, Gabriel, thank you."

Rita rose to her feet as the Singheko captain came in and moved in front of Rita's desk, braced up and saluted.

It was a good salute, Rita saw. No disrespect, no arrogance.

Bonnie had told her about her rescue - and the way she was treated in the lifeboat by the Singheko captain, Orma.

Rita had an idea in mind. It probably wouldn't work.

But what the hell. Nothing ventured, nothing gained.

She returned the salute and waved him to a chair. She had

found a large one, big enough to accommodate the seven-foot frame of the leonine alien without discomfort.

"Please make yourself comfortable, Captain Orma. Can I get you anything to drink?"

Orma shook his head.

"No, thank you, Admiral. Or should I say, milady? I understand that's the form of address used in your fleet?"

"Either is fine, Captain Orma. Are you being treated well?"

"I have no complaints, milady. Although I'm concerned about the other members of my crew. I haven't seen them since we were captured."

"I assure you, your crew is fine. They were moved here some time ago. We couldn't keep them on *Dragon* while repairs were in progress. You shot her up pretty badly, you know."

"We do our best," Orma replied. Rita saw a slight quirk of a smile touch the captain's face, but he managed to suppress it.

Rita herself couldn't resist a slight tinge of a smile.

Two warriors talking shop, she thought. *Opposite sides of the same business.*

"Moving on, then, Captain. We understand that when your Admiral Zukra staged his coup and took over the government, there was a group of officers who resisted that. Most of them were killed, but...perhaps there might be some who still live."

There was a slight, almost imperceptible freezing of Orma's face. The silence stretched on for a long time. Rita wasn't certain he was going to respond at all, but she waited.

If he speaks first, then there's a chance. A slight chance.

Finally, he replied.

"Admiral Zukra is my superior officer, milady. I am a good soldier. I follow my orders."

Rita sat. Her outward demeanor was like a stone, immobile, giving nothing away.

But inwardly, her mind raced.

He hates Zukra. And he hates what Zukra has done.

I don't even know if the Singheko have a religion, or a code of ethics, or a common morality. I know nothing about him, nothing about his background. How do I approach him?

"Captain Orma. In every society, there comes a time when the moral and honest are faced with evil and corruption."

Orma did not respond. But in his eyes, Rita saw a glint of something.

Something akin to understanding.

"I'll not insult you by asking you to do anything against your moral code, Captain. But I would ask you this simple question. What is best for Singheko? What is best for your people? This continued descent into the madness of war? Fighting every other species in the Arm for the next hundred years?"

Again, Orma sat silently.

Rita was not an expert on Singheko facial expressions or body language. But there was something there. She was sure of it.

"Captain Orma, I'm going to take a huge chance. This may be a tremendous mistake, but it won't be the first one I've made and certainly not the last.

"I'm releasing you and the two who were with you in the lifeboat. I'll provide you with comms to your Admiralty and you can make arrangements to be picked up at a neutral location between here and Singheko. We'll deliver you there and send you on your way."

Rita rose from her seat and straightened her tunic. Orma, realizing the meeting was over, also rose.

"Captain Orma, I'm not asking you to do anything your conscience won't support. But someday - if you find yourself in a position to stop this madness - please try. Good luck to you, sir."

Orma braced up and saluted. Rita nodded once and returned his salute. Turning on his heel, he left the room.

As the hatch closed behind him, Rita saw his Marine escort fall into place to take him on his way.

Think about it, Orma. Think long and hard, please.

EPILOGUE

The Singheko had slunk back to their anchorage at Ridendo, the remnants of the Nidarian fleet with them. For the first time in a year, Rita had given herself a day off. She arranged for a shuttle to take them into the mountains - Jim, Bonnie, Luke, Tatiana, Mikhail, and her bodyguards Gabriel and Raphael.

The day was exquisitely wonderful. The air was crisp, cool on their skin without being cold. Living aboard a starship had many limitations, and lack of exercise was one of the worst. So getting out into the world was a treat.

After hiking in the afternoon, they settled in for the evening. Jim, with his vast experience at wilderness camping, set up a marvelous campsite. Raphael and Gabriel volunteered to cook, and Rita let them.

The rest sat on a large rock, watching the sunset. As the star sank toward the horizon, the sky came alive. Red, orange, yellow, purple - every color of the rainbow was visible, great streaks of light that covered the horizon. The fire in front of them crackled and spit. The breeze on their skin was cool. The night was perfect.

They sat in companionable silence for a while, letting peace settle around like a warm blanket.

"How about that Baysig?" Bonnie finally said.

They all smiled together. Baysig had finally revealed his true identity to them.

Fleet Admiral Baysig - in command of the combined fleet of the Taegu and Bagrami. He had led the charge that broke up the Singheko fleet and turned the tide of the battle. He was now on his way to Dekanna, taking his fleet to support Admiral

Sobong. Bonnie would leave tomorrow to join him, with a detachment from Rita's fleet. When the Singheko invasion fleet arrived at Dekanna in six weeks, they were going to have quite a surprise.

Rita knew it was far from over. They had a long, hard slog of a war ahead of them. Zukra had escaped to Nidaria. He was there now, plotting with Garatella for another attack on the Humans.

But they had won a respite. News from Earth had come in - the UN had finally got their act together on the manufacturing side. They had completed a new battlecruiser and two new destroyers. The three ships were on their way to Singheko and would arrive in two weeks. Earth-side manufacturing was ramping up. The schedule called for a new cruiser every two months and a new battlecruiser every six months.

And beside me are the people I need to fight this war, thought Rita. *There is no one else in the universe I would want standing with me.*

"Tatiana, seems like you've got the planet pacified now. Will you be going back to Earth?" asked Jim.

Tatiana shook her head, glancing at Mikhail.

"No. We'll see to sending home all those who want to return, but Mikhail and I are staying here. This isn't over yet. We have more work to do."

Rita grinned. She liked this young, smart commander who had formed up a handful of slaves and taken an entire planet. She noticed that Tatiana had Mikhail's hand gripped tightly, holding on to the man she loved.

She turned her face back toward the sunset, watching the star sink into the horizon. She didn't have to look to know that Bonnie and Luke were holding hands too.

Without looking, she reached out a hand. Somehow Jim's hand was there automatically.

Funny how things work out, Rita thought. *There's a lot of hate in the universe right now. But there's love in the universe too.*

Enough for everybody to have some if they want it.

###

AUTHOR NOTES

Thanks so much for reading this book. I have a confession to make: Jim, Rita, and Bonnie are becoming my favorite characters. Every time I decide to end the series, a little voice says, "But no – you're having so much fun with them. One more book!"

So below, you'll find a sneak preview of the next book in the series, The Short End, available on Amazon. Always free if you have Kindle Unlimited!

Finally, don't hesitate to contact me with thoughts / ideas at the locations below!

Sci-Fi, New Books, Hard Science, and General Mayhem
www.facebook.com/PhilHuddlestonAuthor

Author Page on Amazon:
www.amazon.com/author/philhuddleston

Special bonus - if you have not already signed up for my newsletter, sign up now and get one of my books for free!
www.philhuddleston.com/newsletter

All the best,
Phil

PREVIEW OF NEXT BOOK

The Short End - Broken Galaxy Book 4

Sol System - Earth
United Nations Building - Beijing, China

"Right now she's stalemated. She sits in the Singheko system, facing off with them like a gunfighter in some Old West movie! But she doesn't have the forces to take them out. And she knows that! And still she won't give up, bring the fleet back to Earth! She's leaving us utterly exposed! We have to take action!"

Ken Elliott, newly appointed Fleet Admiral of the UNSF - the United Nations Space Force - practically yelled his last statement. His tirade had gone on for several minutes. And the subject of his ire was one person - Rita Page, Fleet Admiral of the Earth Defense Force – the EDF.

And the fact that drove Elliott over the edge was simple. Admiral Rita Page considered herself independent of the U.N. To defend Earth, she did exactly as she wished. He had no control over her.

That was why he hated her so much.

Across from him, Ingrid Stoltenberg, Secretary-General of the United Nations, glanced briefly to her left. There sat Zhao Zemin, Premier of the State Council of China - the real power behind the throne in the modern U.N. But Zemin held his peace, waiting for someone else to respond.

On Ingrid's right, Viktoria Chernenko, Prime Minister of the Russian Federation, nodded in slow agreement.

"We don't disagree with you," said Viktoria cautiously. "She's sitting there at Deriko like a bug on a leaf. God knows what she's thinking."

Taking Viktoria's cautious statement for more than it actually was, Elliott spoke excitedly. "We have to force her to bring every ship back to Earth! We have to put a ring of warships around our planet and prepare for the Singheko! Staying there in their own system, facing them down eyeball to eyeball - that's insane!"

Zemin finally spoke. "I think you should do whatever is required to bring that fleet back to defend Earth. We cannot trust her to do what is right. That is the whole point of creating the U.N. Space Force - to centralize the command of all space forces from every country into one and create a unified defense for Earth. And therefore, it makes sense for us to force the EDF under the umbrella of the UNSF."

"Then I have your support? To take whatever action is necessary?" asked Elliott.

Zemin hesitated. "Within reason, Admiral. I'm sure you understand, China cannot be overtly involved. Admiral Page has tremendous public support. She has saved Earth from the Singheko not once, but twice. She is incredibly popular among the masses. They think she walks on water. Whatever you do, you must do it quietly - no negative publicity. Put her out to pasture or promote her to a desk job. Something like that. But nothing obvious."

Elliott, his emotions settling down as he realized he had won the decision, grunted in frustration. "I would prefer to just kill her, actually. We all know she's some kind of misbegotten clone. A creature of the devil, they say."

Ingrid Stoltenberg looked at Elliott, trying to hide the horror in her mind. Elliott's predilection toward overt religious zealotry was well known. He claimed to be a

Christian. He went to church, contributed to charity, and made great display of his faith. But anyone who knew him quickly realized he was a CINO - a Christian in name only. It was amazing to Ingrid that he had achieved his high position. She would never have let him into the role of Admiral of the new U.N. Space Force if she had been able to control the appointment. But it had been out of her hands.

The Chinese control the U.N. now, thought Ingrid. *With the change of headquarters location to Beijing and the creation of a UN Space Force, they're sitting in the catbird seat. They got everything they wanted. Including an Admiral they could control. And non-thinking religious zealots like Elliott are easy to control - you don't have to delude them, they delude themselves.*

And the Chinese are masters at pretending to give him what he wants. They keep him twisted right round their little finger.

Lord, why did President Hager allow this to happen? What a tremendous mistake - just for an agreement to let Taiwan have her freedom, and to help rein in Iran? Foolish, foolish. What was Hager thinking?

Now they'll use the U.N. as a club to batter the rest of the world forever...and by creating the U.N. Space Force, they will effectively control every military asset in space.

Except Rita and the EDF. So far. I have to go along with this for now. But I have to find some way to checkmate Elliott and the Chinese, without being too obvious about it.

"No, Admiral. No bloodshed. This must be done smoothly, carefully," Viktoria said.

Ingrid came back to the present, glanced at Zemin to see if he would offer any further comment. But he stayed silent, looking down at his briefing papers.

So, if this all goes south, he can claim he wasn't involved in the actual details. Typical.

Across from Ingrid, Elliott closed his eyes and shuddered, as if he was undergoing some kind of religious fit. But then he opened his eyes and nodded understanding.

"Yes, I understand. No bloodshed. Just find a way to get her back here to Earth, take the fleet away from her, and tuck her away where she can do no more harm."

Zemin nodded at last. He knew that he had to give the final blessing, or the deal was not done - at least, not in Elliott's mind.

"I perceive you have understanding, Admiral. China will provide you with any personnel or materials that you need. Quietly, of course. Just inform my aide Li Xiulian and it will be done."

Elliott, now happily excited, made a slight bow of the head to Zemin. "Thank you, Premier. Your understanding and support is greatly appreciated."

Zemin stood, signifying the top-secret meeting was over. The other three stood as well. Ingrid watched in disgust as Elliott made a full-on Oriental-type bow to Zemin.

The way Elliott fawns over him, you'd think he's some kind of royalty!

Viktoria stepped forward and shook hands with Zemin. Ingrid knew she should follow suit, but she was just too disgusted at the moment to do it. Instead, she pretended to be busy collecting her tablet and other things from the table. Finally, Viktoria and Ingrid followed Zemin out of the room, their handlers picking them up in the hallway. While Zemin disappeared to the right, Ingrid and Viktoria turned left. Reaching the landing that led to the rooftop heliport, Ingrid stopped to say goodbye to Viktoria.

"Have a safe trip, Prime Minister."

Viktoria offered her hand and Ingrid shook it. Then she waited patiently as Viktoria was led up the stairs to the heliport by her minders. There, a plain-wrapper Chinese executive helicopter waited to take her to the airport.

In an hour, she would be wheels-up, heading back to Moscow. Except for Ingrid and Zhao, no one outside the Chinese minders, the crew of her planes, and her President would know Viktoria had traveled to Beijing.

Returning to her top-floor office, Ingrid thought about what had just occurred.

Against my will, I was just forced to gave the green light to a half-crazy religious zealot to perform a coup on the Admiral of the EDF - and force the EDF fleet to return to Earth and put itself under the command of the U.N.

God help us. I have to find some way to keep this under control. Without the Chinese killing me.

Continue the story with The Short End on Amazon!

WORKS

Imprint Series
Artemis War (prequel novella)
Imprint of Blood
Imprint of War
Imprint of Honor
Imprint of Defiance

Broken Galaxy Series
Broken Galaxy
Star Tango
The Long Edge of Night
The Short End
Remnants
Goblin Eternal

Now available – the entire box set of the epic space saga Birth of the Rim in <u>one</u> collection. 629 pages of true military sci-fi!

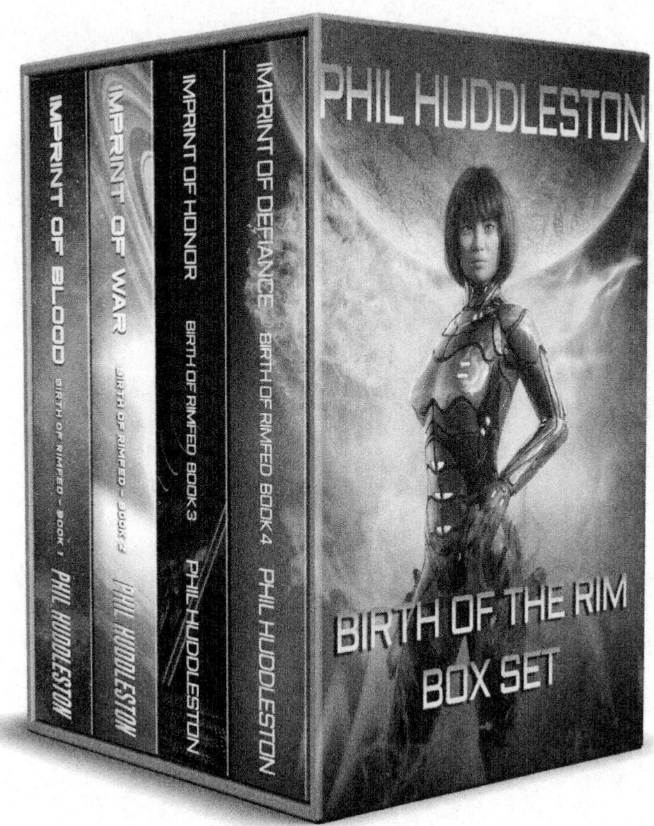

Available on Amazon!

ABOUT THE AUTHOR

Like Huckleberry Finn, Phil Huddleston grew up barefoot and outdoors, catching mudbugs by the creek, chasing rabbits through the fields, and forgetting to come home for dinner. Then he discovered books. Thereafter, he read everything he could get his hands on, including reading the Encyclopedia Britannica and Funk & Wagnalls from A-to-Z multiple times. He served in the U. S. Marines for four years, returned to college and completed his degree on the GI Bill. Since that time, he built computer systems, worked in cybersecurity, played in a band, flew a bush plane from Alaska to Texas, rode a motorcycle around a good bit of America, and watched in amazement as his wife raised two wonderful daughters in spite of him. And would sure like to do it all again. Except maybe without the screams of terror.

Printed in Great Britain
by Amazon

62575558R00198